REST HARROW

A COMEDY OF RESOLUTION

Wrote deliberately to each of her sisters.

REST HARROW

A COMEDY OF RESOLUTION

BY

MAURICE HEWLETT

" Rest Harrow grows in any soil. . . . The seeds may be sown as soon as ripe in warm, sheltered spots out of doors. . . . It is a British plant."

—WEATHERS

WITH ILLUSTRATIONS BY FRANK CRAIG

CHARLES SCRIBNER'S SONS
NEW YORK : : : : 1910

ΤΗΙ ΚΑΛΛΙCΤΗΙ

CONTENTS

BOOK I

PAGE

OF THE NATURE OF A PROLOGUE, DEALING WITH
A BRUISED PHILOSOPHER IN RETIREMENT . I

BOOK II

SANCHIA AT WANLESS HALL 45

BOOK III

INTERLUDE OF THE RECLUSE PHILOSOPHER . 193

BOOK IV

SANCHIA IN LONDON 235

BOOK V

OF THE NATURE OF AN EPILOGUE, DEALING WITH
DESPOINA 363

ILLUSTRATIONS

Wrote deliberately to each of her sisters . . . . . *Frontispiece*

FACING PAGE

The hum of cities, and buzz of dinner tables . . sound in
    his ears not at all 42

The housekeeper! This—person! 72

He had eloquence, he thought, as he watched her, he had
    won. But he was anxious She was such a deep one . 116

Ploughman in the vales would sometimes see his gaunt
    figure on the sky-line 196

"Well, Sanchia," he said, "here I am" 318

The great music went sobbing and chiding through her
    frame, like wounded nightingales 354

Senhouse came back to her bedside and put a little flower
    into her hand 398

BOOK I

OF THE NATURE OF A PROLOGUE, DEALING
WITH A BRUISED PHILOSOPHER IN RETIRE-
MENT

I

An observant traveller, homing to England by the Ostend-Dover packet in the April of some five years ago, relished the vagaries of a curious couple who arrived by a later train, and proved to be both of his acquaintance. He had happened to be early abroad, and saw them come on. They were a lady of some personal attraction, comfortably furred, who, descending from a first-class carriage, was met by a man from a third-class, bare-headed, free in the neck, loosely clad in grey flannel trousers which flapped about his thin legs in the sea-breeze, a white sweater with a rolling collar, and a pair of sandals upon brown and sinewy feet uncovered by socks: these two. The man's garniture was extraordinary, but himself no less so. He had a lean and deeply bronzed face, hatchet-shaped like a Hindoo's. You looked instinctively for rings in his ears. His moustache was black and sinuous, outlining his mouth rather than hiding it. His hair, densely black, was longish and perfectly straight. His eyes were far-sighted and un-blinking; he smiled always, but furtively, as if the world at large amused him, but must never

3

know it. He seemed to observe everything, except the fact that everybody observed himself.

To have once seen such a man must have provided for his recollection; and yet our traveller, who was young and *debonnaire*, though not so young as he seemed, first recognised the lady. "Mrs Germain, by George!" This to himself, but aloud, "Now, where's she been all this time?" The frown which began to settle about his discerning eyes speedily dissolved in wonder as they encountered the strange creature in the lady's company. He stared, he gaped, then slapped his thigh. "Jack Senhouse! That's the man. God of battles, what a start! Now, what on earth is Jack Senhouse doing, playing courier to Mrs. Germain?"

That was precisely the employment. His man had handed the lady out of her compartment, entered it when she left it, and was possessing himself of her littered vestiges while these speculations were afloat. Dressing-case, tea-basket, umbrellas, rugs, and what not, he filled his arms with them, handed them over to expectant porters, then smilingly showed their proprietress the carraige ridded. He led the way to the steamer, deposited his burdens and saw to the bestowal of others, fetched a chair, wrapped her in rugs, found her book, indicated her whereabouts to a mariner in case of need. All this leisurely done, in the way of a man who has privilege and duty for his warrants. Enquiring then, with an engaging lift of the eyebrows, whether she was perfectly comfortable, and receiving with a pleasant nod her answering nod of thanks, he left her and returned to the train. Tracked through the crowd, and easily by his height, bare head, and leisurely motions, he was next seen shouldering a canvas bag on his way back to the boat. Jack's belongings, his bag of tricks; Jack all over, the same inexhaustible Jack! It was delightful to our traveller to find Jack Senhouse thus verifying himself at every turn. He was for the steerage, it appears—and of course he was!—where depressed foreigners share with bicycles, motor cars, and newly boiled pigs the amenities of economical travel. In this malodorous and slippery well his interested friend saw him sit down upon his bundle, roll a cigarette, and fall into easy conversation with an Italian voyager who, having shaved, was now putting on a clean collar and a tartan necktie.

The traveller, Mr. William Chevenix, who had watched him so long, a well-dressed and cheerful Englishman of some five-and-thirty summers, with round eyes in a round and rosy face, now assuring himself that he would be damned if he didn't have it out with the chap, descended the companion, picked his way through the steerage, and approached the seated philosopher. He saw that he was known, and immediately. Nothing escaped Senhouse.

"How d'ye do, how d'ye do?" He held out his hand. Senhouse rose and grasped it. The Italian took off his hat, and strolled away.

"I'm very well, thanks," he said. "Have you no-

ticed those shores beyond the canal? Samphire there
just as we have it at home. Leagues of samphire."

The younger man looked in the direction indicated cheerfully and blankly. "'The samphire by
the ocean's brim,'" he said lightly. "I attach no
importance to it whatever, but it's very like you to
lift one into your privacy at a moment's notice.
I'm all for the formalities myself, so I observe that
I haven't seen you for years. Years! Not since—
why, it must be eighteen."

"It's precisely eight," said Senhouse, "and I've
been abroad for four of them."

His friend inspected him with candid interest.
"At your old games, I take it. You've filled England with hardy perennials and now you're starting on Europe. Great field for you. You'll want
a pretty big trowel, though. A wheelbarrow might
be handy, I should have said."

Senhouse fired. "I've been planting the Black
Forest, you see. Great games. They gave me a
free hand, and ten thousand marks a year to spend.
I've done some rather showy things. Now I want
to go to Tibet."

The other's attention had wandered. "I saw
you come on board," he said. "I watched you
play the Squire of Dames to a rather pretty woman
whom I happen to know. She was a Mrs. Germain
in those days."

"She still calls herself so," Senhouse said. He
was staring straight before him out to sea. The
steamer was under way.

"Married a queer old file in Berkshire, who died worth a plum. Goodish time ago. They called him Fowls, or Fowls of the Air. So she's still a widow, eh?"

Senhouse nodded. "She's his widow." Then he asked, "You know her? You might go and amuse her. I can't, because of these bonds." He exhibited his sockless feet with a cheerful grin.

"Oh, I shall, you know," he was assured. "You're not dressy enough for Mrs. Germain. She'd never stand it."

"She doesn't," said Senhouse. "She dislikes a fuss, and thinks me rather remarkable."

"Well," said the other, "I think she's right. You always were a conspicuous beggar. Now look at me. Think I'll do?"

Senhouse peered at him. "I think you are exactly what she wants just now," he said. "Go in and approve yourself, Chevenix."

Mr. Chevenix, the spick and span, had something on his mind, however, which he did not know how to put. He continued to reflect upon Mrs. Germain, but only by way of marking time. "She used to be very good fun in my young days. And she made things spin in Berkshire, they tell me. I know she did in London—while it lasted. What's she doing? There was a chap called Duplessis, I remember."

"There still is," Senhouse said, but in such a manner as to chalk No Thoroughfare across the field. Chevenix perceived this rather late in the day, and ended his ruminations in a whistle. "She kept him dangling—" he had begun. Instead of pursuing, he said abruptly, "I say, you remember Sancie Percival, of course."

A change came over Senhouse's aspect which a close observer might have noticed. He was very quiet, hardly moved; but he seemed to be listening with all his senses, listening with every pore of his skin. "Yes," he said, slowly. "Yes, I do; I'm not likely to forget her. She was my dearest friend, and is so still, I hope."

The solemnity of his intended message clouded Mr. Chevenix's candid brow. "She's still at Wanless, you know."

Senhouse set a watch upon himself. "No doubt she is," he said. "She's well?"

The other probed him. "She's never made it up with her people. I think she feels it nowadays."

Senhouse asked sharply, "Where's Ingram?"

"Ingram," said Chevenix, "is just off for a trip. He's to be abroad for a year. India."

Senhouse shivered. "Alone?"

"Well, without her, anyhow. He always was a casual beggar, was Nevile." He could see now that he was making a hit. "Got old Senhouse where he lives," he told himself, and then continued. "Fact is, I've been out with him as far as Brindisi. He asked me to. I had nothing to do. But I want to see Sancie Percival again. I was awfully fond of her—of the whole lot of them." He reflected, as a man might deliberate upon familiar things, and discover them to be wonders. "What a family they were, by Jove! Five—of—the—loveliest girls a man could meet with. Melusine, what a girl she was! Married Tubby Scales—fat chap with a cigar. Vicky, now. How about Vicky? She was my chum, you know. She's married, too. Chap called Sinclair—in the Guides. But Sancie beat them all in her quiet way. A still water—what?"

Senhouse, his chin clasped in his bony hands, contemplated the sea. His face was drawn and stern. There was a queer twitching of the cheek-bones. "Got him, by Jove!" said Mr. Chevenix to himself, and pushed on. "I say, I wish you'd go and see her," he said.

Senhouse got up and leaned over the bulwarks. He was plainly disturbed. Chevenix waited for him nervously, but got nothing.

Then he said, "The fact is, Senhouse, I think that you should go. You were the best friend she ever had." Senhouse turned him then a tragic face.

"No, I wasn't," he said. "I think I was the worst."

Chevenix blinked. "I know what you mean. If it hadn't been for you and your confounded theories, you imply that she——"

"I don't know——" Senhouse began. "God only knows what she might have done. She was not of our sort, you know. I always said that she was unhuman."

"That's the last thing she was," said Chevenix, neatly. Senhouse scorned him.

"You don't know anything about it," he said. "What are the doings of this silly world, of our makeshift appearances, to the essentials? Antics—filling up time! You speak as if she gave Ingram everything, and lost it. She did, but he never knew it—so never had it. Ingram had what he was fitted to receive. Her impulse, her impulsion were divine. She has lost nothing—and he has gained nothing."

"If you talk philosophy I'm done," cried Mr. Chevenix. "Well, I say to you, my boy, Go and see her. She's so far human that she's got a tongue, and likes to wag it, I suppose. I don't say that there's trouble, and I don't say there's not. But there are the makings of it. She's alone, and may be moped. I don't know. You'd better judge for yourself."

Senhouse, trembling from his recent fire, turned away his face. "I don't know that I dare. If she's unhappy, I shall be in the worst place I ever was in my life. I don't know what I shall do."

"That's the first time you ever said that, I'll go bail," Chevenix interrupted him. But Senhouse did not hear him.

"I did everything I could at the time. I nearly made her quarrel with me—I dared do that. I went up to Wanless and saw Ingram. I hated the fellow, I disapproved of him, feared him. He was the last man in the world I could have tackled with a view to redemption. He was almost hopelessly bad, according to my view of things. Fed by slaves from the cradle, hag-ridden by his vices; a purple young bully, a product of filthy sloth, scabbed with privilege. I saw just how things were. She pitied him, and thought it was her business to save him. She did nobly. She gave herself for pity; and if she mistook that for love, the splendid generosity of her is enough to take the breath away. The world ought to have gone down on its knees to her—but it picked up its skirts for fear she might touch them. What a country! What a race! Well, feeling towards her as I did, and loathing him, I urged him to marry her—to make her his property for life. Dead against my conviction, mind you, but what else could I do? God help me, I played the renegade to what I sincerely believed. I couldn't see her done to death by a world of satyrs."

"Of course you couldn't, my dear man," cried Chevenix. "Girls of her sort must be married, you know."

"I don't know anything of the kind," replied Senhouse, fiercely; "but I loved her. You may put it that I funked. I did—and to no purpose."

"If you were to see her now," Chevenix put in, "you could do some good. She'll be pretty lonely up there." Senhouse got up.

"I'll see her," he said. "Whatever happens."

"Right," said Chevenix. "That's a good man. That's what I wanted of you. I'll tell her that you're coming. Now I'm going to do the civil to Mrs. Germain."

Senhouse had turned away, and was leaning over

the bulwarks, lost in his thoughts. He remained there until the passage was over.

Mr. Chevenix, having approached the lady with all forms observed, made himself happy in her company, as, indeed, he did in all. "Now this is very jolly, Mrs. Germain, I must say. I'm a companionable beggar, I believe; and here I was in a ship where I didn't know a living soul until I met you and Senhouse. Didn't even know that you knew Senhouse. Queer fish, eh? Oh, the queerest fish in the sea! But you know all that, of course."

Mrs. Germain, a brunette with the power of glowing, coloured becomingly, and veiled her fine eyes with somewhat heavy and heavily-fringed eyelids. "Oh, yes," she said, "I have known him for a long time."

"Met him abroad, I suppose—tinkering round, as he does. The everlasting loafer, artist, tinker, poet, gardener. 'Pon my soul, he's like the game we used to do with cherry-stones round the pudding plate. Don't you know? Soldier, sailor, tinker, tailor, and all the rest. He's all those things, and has two pair of bags to his name, and lives in a cart, and's a gentleman. Not a doubt about that, mind you, Mrs. Germain."

She smiled upon him kindly. "None at all," she said. "I like him extremely."

"You would, you know," said Chevenix, his tones rich in sympathy. "All women do. You couldn't help it. You've got such a kind heart.

All women have. Now, I've known Senhouse himself five or six years, but I've known about him for at least eight. I used to hear about him from morn to dewy eve, once upon a time, from one—of—the—loveliest and most charming girls you ever met in your life. Did you know her? A Miss Percival—Sanchia Percival. We used to call her Sancie. Thought you might have met her, perhaps. No? Well, this chap Senhouse would have gone through the fire for her. He would have said his prayers to her. Did you ever see his poems about her? My word! He published 'em after the row, you know. He as good as identified her with—well, we won't mention names, Mrs. Germain, but he identified her with a certain holy lady not a hundred miles from the Kingdom of Heaven. Blasphemous old chap —he did, though."

Mrs. Germain, toying with her scent-bottle, was interested. "I never heard him speak about a Miss Percival," she said. She used a careless tone, but her flickering eyelids betrayed her.

"You wouldn't, you know," he told her with the same sympathetic earnestness. "There was too much of a row. He was cut all to pieces. I thought he'd go under; but he's not that sort. Who called somebody—some political johnny— the Sea-green Incorruptible? Oh, ask me another! You might call old Senhouse the Green-tea Irrepressible; for that was his drink (to keep himself awake all night, writin' poems), and there never was a cork that would hold him down—not even Sancie Percival. No, no, out he must come— fizzling."

"I see," said Mrs. Germain, still looking at her fingers in her lap. "I'm very much interested. You mean that he was very much—that he paid her a great deal of attention?"

Chevenix stared roundly about him. "Attention! Oh, heavens! Why, three of his letters to her would fill *The Times* for a week—and he kept it up for years! She used to get three a week —budgets! blue-books! For simple years! Attentions!" He shook his head. "The word's no good. He paid nobody anything at all when she was in the same county. He used to sit listening to her thrilling the waves of air. He used to hear her voice in the wind—and when it changed, he used to fire off his answers!"

Mrs. Germain laughed—whether at Chevenix or his preposterous hero is not to be known. "You are rather absurd," she said. "Mr. Senhouse never gave me the idea of that sort of person. Why did they never——?"

Chevenix narrowed his eyes to the merest slats. "*Marry?*" he said, in an awed whisper. "Is that what you mean?"

Mrs. Germain showed him her soft brown orbs, which for two seasons had been said to be the finest pair of dark eyes in London. "Yes," she said, "I do mean that. How clever of you to guess!"

Chevenix bowed to her. "Not at all," he said. "I'm quite good at that kind of thing. You have to be, if you knock about. Besides, that's the whole point. Bless you! He would just as soon have married Diana of the Ephesians. He said so. I heard him. He would have thought it an insult to hint at it. Didn't I tell you that he was a poet?"

"Yes," the lady said quickly. "You did. But I suppose poets occasionally marry."

"Not that sort," Chevenix pronounced, with a shake of the head. "At least, they don't marry the right person. They never do. Or there are two or three persons. Look at Shelley. Look at Dante. I happen to know all about both of 'em. Senhouse drank 'em up—and gave 'em out like steam. He thought no end of Dante and Shelley. As a matter of fact, he didn't believe in marriage, as a game—as a kind of institution, you know. He thought it devilish wrong—and said so—and that's where the trouble was. Marry Sancie! I wish to heaven he had. There'd have been no trouble at all. They were made for each other. She loved his fun—and was easy with him, you see. She was queerish, too—a shy young bird; but she was quite at home with him. No, no. The trouble really began with him putting her out of conceit with marriage. And then she didn't care for him in that sort of way, then. And then —well, the less said the better."

"Oh," said Mrs. Germain, absorbed by the devolutions of the tale. "Oh!"

"'Oh' 's the sort of expression one used at the time," said Chevenix. "There wasn't much else to be said. It was a holy row." He mused, he brooded, and said no more. Luckily for him, he discovered Dover at hand, and escaped. Mrs. Germain was put into a first-class carriage by two attendant squires, provided with tea and a foot-warmer; and then Chevenix bowed himself away and Senhouse disappeared. She had a novel on her knees, but read little. She looked out of window, frowning and biting her red lip. When she reached Victoria she tightened both lips, and you saw that, so compressed, they made a thin red line straight above a square chin. Her charm and favour both lay, you then discovered, in expression.

Senhouse, hatless and loose-limbed, stood at the door to help her out. She accepted his services, and was put into a cab.

"Where's he to take you?" he asked her pleasantly.

She said at once, "To Brown's Hotel." Then, before she got in, with a hand, unperceived by the general, just touching his arm, "Jack, I want to speak to you, but not to-night. Will you come in the morning, please? I am rather tired, and shall dine early and go to bed. Is my maid here?" She looked about. "Oh, I suppose she's seeing to the luggage. You might find her, and tell her where to come to."

Senhouse smiled and nodded. "Certainly. All

these things shall be done. Anything else before you go off?"

She hesitated for a minute, then said, "Yes, there *is* one more thing. You mustn't come to Brown's like that. You must put on ordinary things."

He raised his eyebrows, then laughed—throwing his head up. "Wonderful lady! Wherewithal shall I be clothed? Do you really think these things matter?"

She was firm. "I really do. I hope you will be kind enough to—to—please me."

He looked very kindly at her. "My dear," he said, "of course I shall. Be quite easy about it." He held out his hand. "Good night, Mary."

She took it, but didn't meet his look. "Good night," she said, and drove away without another signal.

Senhouse, shouldering his bundle, found the lady's maid, and gave her her sailing orders. His manner to her was exactly that which he had shown to the mistress, easy, simple, and good-humoured. Leaving her, he went a leisurely way through the press, and took a tram-car from the corner of Vauxhall Bridge Road in the direction of Battersea.

II

SENHOUSE, after a night of solitary musing upon certain waste places known best to outlanders, walked up Saint James's Street at six o'clock in the morning, talking lightly and fiercely to himself. A long life of loneliness had given him that habit incurably. Discovering the hour by a clock in Piccadilly, he realised that it was too early to wait upon Mrs. Germain in Albemarle Street, so continued his way up the empty hill, entered the Park, and flung himself upon the turf under the elms. Other guests were harboured by that hospitable sward, shambling, downcast lice of the town. These, having shuffled thither, dropped, huddled and slept. His way was not theirs: to him the open space was his domain. He ranged the streets, one saw, as if they had been the South Downs, with the long stride and sensitive tread of a man who reckons with inequalities of footing. The country and the town were earth alike, though now of springing grass and now again of flagstones.

His face, after a night of fierce self-searching, looked its age, that of a man past forty; his aspect upon affairs was no more a detached observer's; his eyes were hard, his smile was bleak. Sodden misery, stupor, and despair lay all about him, and would have drawn his pitying comments if it had not been so with him that all his concern must be for himself.

"She wants me, and I must go to her," was the burden of his thought; but, like a recurring line in a poem, it concluded very diverse matter.

"I played the traitor to her; I could not wait —and yet I must have known. I said to myself, It is enough to have known and loved her; watch her happy, and thank God. That should have been enough for any man who had ever seen the blue beam of her eyes shed in kindliness upon him; but I grew blind and could not see. I lost my lamp and went astray. I ran about asking one after another to stop the bleeding of my wound. God is good. After eight years, *she wants me, and I must go to her*.

"I love her, as I have always loved; for she is always there, and I have come back. She can never change, though her beauty grow graver, and all knowledge of the vile usage of the world have passed before her young eyes. Artemis no more, for she has stooped to the lot of women; but still invincibly pure, incapable of sin, though she know it all. It can never touch her; she goes her way. She wears a blue gown now, not a white one. Demeter, the sad, bountiful Mother she will be—yet the same woman, the sweet and grave, the inflexible, the eternal. And, standing as she has always stood, *she wants me, and I must go to her*.

"I remember the wonder, I remember the morning glory of her first appearing. The spell of the woods was upon her. Bare-headed, gowned in white, she girt up her vesture and dipped her white limbs in the pool. I went to her, all my worship in my face; I worked with her at her task. Together we pulled the weed, we set the lilies free. High-minded as a goddess, she revealed herself to me. I was the postulant, dumb before the mysteries; I adored without a thought. I was nothing, could be nothing, to her but her lover—and now *she wants me, and I must go to her.*

"For two years I was close to her side—either I or my words never left her. She became humble, suffered me to lead her, opened to me her mind, shared with me her secret thoughts. I told her the truth; I hid nothing from the first. From the first day she knew that I loved her. There was no presumption in this—I asked nothing, expected nothing. I told her often that I looked forward to her wedded state—and then it came, and I was not ready for it as it came. Horrible thing, her nobility was her punishment. She has suffered, she suffers; *she wants me, and I must go to her.*

"How am I to go, tied and bound as I am? What can I do? I have been false to my vows. I belong in duty to another world, to another woman, who can command me as she will. I don't know, I don't see. I know only one thing, and see only her, calling me with her inflexibly grave eyes. *She wants me, and I must go to her.*"

He got up and left the Park. It was ten o'clock of an April morning. Crocuses—her flowers—were blowing sideways under a south-west wind. Blue sky, white clouds, shining on the just and the unjust, covered her in Yorkshire and him, her grim knight, in Mayfair. He stalked, gaunt and haggard-eyed, down the hill, threading his way through the growing traffic of the day, and faced his business with the lady in the case.

Mrs. Germain was serious when he entered her sitting-room. She was in a loose morning gown of lace and pink ribbon. Pink was her colour. Her dark eyes looked heavy. She should have been adorable, and she was—but not to him just now. He stood before her, looked at her where she sat with her eyes cast down at her hands in her lap. She had let them rest upon him for the moment of his entry, but had not greeted him.

Now, as he stood watching her, she had no greeting.

"Good morning, Mary," he said presently, and she murmured a reply. He saw at once that she was prepared for him, and began in the middle.

"A friend of mine," he said, "is alone and unhappy. I heard of it yesterday from Chevenix. I must go and see her. I shan't be away long, and shall then be at your disposition."

Her strength lay in her silence. She sat perfectly still, looking at her white hands. Her heavy eyelids, weighted with all the knowledge she had, seemed beyond her power of lifting. He was driven to speak again, and, against his will, to defend himself.

"I am in a hatefully false position. I ought to

have told you long ago all about it. It seemed impossible at the time, and so from time to time, to open the shut book. I closed it deliberately, and from the time of doing it until this moment I have never spoken of it even to myself. Chevenix, who knew her well, broke it open unawares yester-day, and now we must read in it, you and I."

He stopped, took breath, and began again. "I don't see how you can forgive me, or how I can, so to speak, look myself in the face again. I have played the knave so long with you that it is per-haps the greatest knavery I can commit to be honest at last. But I am going to do it, Mary. I want to tell you the whole story. You have told me yours."

Her eyes flickered at that, but she said nothing. Passive as she sat, heavy in judgment, she was yet keenly interested. All her wits were at work, commenting, comparing, judging, and weighing every word that he said.

He told her a strange, incoherent story of poet's love. This mysterious, shrouded Sanchia figured in it as the goddess of a shrine—omnipresent, a felt influence, yet never a woman. He spoke her name with a drop of the voice; every act of hers, as he related it, was coloured by sanction to seem the dealing of a divine person with creeping man-kind. To Mrs. Germain it was all preposterous; if she had owned the humorous sense it would have been tragically absurd. For what did it amount to, pray, but this, that Jack Senhouse had been in love with a girl who had loved somebody else, had married her choice, and was now repenting it? Jack, then, in a pique, had trifled with her, Mary Germain, and made love to her. Now he found that this Sanchia was to be seen he was for jumping back. Was he to jump, or not to jump? Did it lie with her? Jack seemed to think that it did.

If it did, what did she want? As to one thing she had long been clear. Jack Senhouse was a good lover, but would be an impossible mate. She had found his gypsy tent and hedgerow practice in the highest degree romantic. With gypsy practice he had the wheedling gypsy ways. An adventure of hers in the North, for instance—when, panic-struck, she had fled to him by a midnight train, had sought him through the dales and over limestone mountains through a day and night, and cried herself to sleep, and been found by him in the dewy dawn and soothed by his masterful cool sense—wasn't this romantic? It had drawn her to him as she had never before been drawn to a man. She felt that here at last was a man indeed to be trusted. For she had been there with him, and not a living soul within miles, entirely at his discretion, and he had not so much as kissed her fingers. No, not even that, though he had wanted to. That she knew, as women do know such things. Romantic, indeed, trustworthy! Why, a Bayard, a Galahad of a gypsy! After this adventure, after he had driven her back to her duty, she had owned allegiance to nobody else in the world. And when her

husband died she had renounced her widow-right,
embraced hardship, kept herself by teaching; and
when, finally, he came to her and offered her her
choice, she had chosen Poverty for her lord as single-
heartedly as ever did Francis find his lady in a
beggar's garb.

And that being done, it did not "do." That
was how she put it now; but the process had been
slow, and never defined. He had carried her off
to Baden for his work of naturalising plants. He
had a great name for that, a European name. In
three weeks his work absorbed him; within that
time she knew that she was no mate for him. You
can't be picturesque for ever, she thought. She
had never reckoned with his incredible simplicity,
and never for a moment connected his talk with his
acts. Perhaps this Jack was the only really logical
man in the world. Now she found that in talking
of Poverty as the only happiness, he literally and
really believed it so. He would own nothing but
the barest necessities—neither pictures, nor furniture, neither clothes nor books. Pictures, furniture?
Why, he had no roof to shelter them! Clothes?
Where was he to carry them, if not on his back?
Books? He had half-dozen, which contained all
the wisdom of the world. So he used to cry. Now,
this might be as it was; but when he seemed to
expect her to be of the same mind and behaviour,
you will see that he must needs be mad.

Yet so it was. He had lived in a tent for twenty
years, so took his tent to Germany, and went on

living in it. In that, with complete gravity, he received the Grand Duke of Baden, and several uniformed high officials, who wore plumed head-gear and incredibly high collars, and glittering boots of patent leather. Folded superbly in cloaks of milky blue, they looked to Mary like gods; to Senhouse they were amusing fellow-creatures, inter-ested in his plants and plans. He spread maps on the ground and followed his racing finger with racing speech. His German was faulty, but exceedingly graphic. His words shook the tent curtains. With-in half-an-hour, such was the infection of his elo-quence, he had most of his company on their knees beside him, and the Grand Duke, accommodated with a camp-stool, buried his hand in his beard and followed every line without a breath. Of all in that tent, she, Mary Germain, had been the only person to feel the indescribable squalor in the situation—and she the only one who might have been born to it; for her upbringing had been humble, and her rise in the world sudden and short of durance. But she knew now that she had hardly been able to live it out for very shame.

Directly the visitors had departed there had been a scene—she in tears of vexation which scalded, and he concerned at her trouble, but unable for the life of him to see what it was all about. He had been kindness itself. He always was the kindest and gentlest creature. If she wanted a house, hotel or what not, she should have it. In fact, he got her one, installed her, and undertook to keep her there. She bit her lip now to remember that she had agreed—and the ensuing difficulties. He had no money, and would have none of his own, and he refused to live under a roof on any terms whatsoever. Of ten thousand marks a year, which he was to receive from his Grand Duke, half was to be hers; he would see her when she would, and she might follow him about as she would—or not, if she would not. He could not see that there was anything extraordinary in these propositions. To him it was the simplest thing in the world that two people should do as they pleased. Society? What in the name of God had society to do with it? She remembered her tears, and his blank dismay when he saw them. He thought that she was unhappy, and so she was; but she was grievously angry also, that she could not make him see what things would "do" and what things "never do."

His work had inflamed him; he had marched from place to place, unencumbered and without a thought or care in the world—inspired with his scheme, in which plants stood for the words in a poem. He slept out many nights on the Felsenberg, on the ground, wrapped in a cloak. He disappeared for weeks at a time in impenetrable forests, sharing the fires of charcoal-burners, mapping, planning, giving orders to a secretary from the Botanical Department, as wild as a disciple should be. There was nothing for her, poor lady, but to sit about in hotel saloons—as the widow of an English gentleman, occasionally visited by an eccentric friend. So she put it for the benefit of society; but this had not been her idea of things when she had tumbled into Senhouse's arms—nor had it been his.

Her ruling idea in these days of disenchantment and discomfort—and it was her ruling idea still—was to preserve appearances. The great, invincible, fundamental instinct of the class from which she had sprung—to keep oneself unspotted by the world. The variation upon the text is Senhouse's own, done in a moment of exasperation over her untiring effort to appear what she was not and did not want to be. She loved the man sincerely; if she had been married to him she would have kept faithfully to his side. But she had no lines; her wedding ring was not of his giving. Without these assurances she simply could not love him. It came to that.

He had, when they had approached the matter of alliance, put aside marriage, literal marriage, as out of the question. He took it airily for granted that she agreed with him. The servitude of the woman which it implied was to him unspeakably wicked. He could not have treated the vilest woman in such a manner. But he had reckoned without the woman in her case. To her, freedom to love, without sanction or obligation, destroyed love. When he found that out, which he did after a year of her German vexations, he offered himself and his convictions to her. He humbled himself before her—but by that time she would not. By that time she had recovered her widow's portion (which had been dependent upon her remaining sole), and was entitled to some thousands a year and a good dower-house in Berks. She declined to marry him, and acted as such. She had been his wife in fact for a quarter of a year; she was his friend—as he was hers—for the rest of their time abroad. He had respected her wish, but had kept himself at her free disposal, until now of late, when this disturbing Sanchia Percival arose out of the nothingless and was shown to her as a goddess newly from the shades. And so now here sat Mrs. Germain, with her eccentric friend pale and gaunt before her, unlike himself as she had always known him, about to take her at her word, and to behave as a friend might. What should she say?

He would come back if she chose; he had said so—and he was incapable of lies. If he came back, and if she chose, he would marry her, and be the imperturbable, delightful, incalculable, impossible companion she had always known him. He would marry her—and decline to come under her roof. He would, perhaps, pitch his tent in her paddock; he would sit at her table in sweater and flannels, sandals on his feet, while she and her guests were in the ordinary garb of—gentlefolks. Gentlefolks! Yes. But the maddening and baffling thought was a conviction that he would be the greatest gentleman there. She knew that. Lord of his mind, lord of his acts, easy in his will, and refusing to bow to any necessity but that, he would be the superior of them all. Could this be borne? Or could she bear to surrender so rare a friend to a Miss Percival?

Who could Miss Percival be? It was a good name—better than Middleham, which had been her own, as good as Germain, which had been her husband's. Sanchia, an extraordinary name, an unusual name. It sounded Spanish and aristocratic. The Honourable Hertha de Speyne: she had known the daughter of a noble house so styled in her governess days, her days of drudgery, and even now it had a glamour for her, who had since hobnobbed with many honourables, flirted with many young lords, and been kissed by a duchess. Miss Sanchia Percival: the Honourable Sanchia Percival. No doubt this was a high lady. And she must be beautiful, or Jack wouldn't speak of her as he had. He hushed his voice down, he spoke as if she were a goddess, as if to disobey her call was out of the question. A dull heat stirred deeply within her, and she found herself setting her teeth together. No! Jack had brought her to this pass—and she would not be left there.

These were the thoughts of Mrs. Germain as she sat very still, with heavy-lidded eyes, listening to Senhouse's story. He ended it in these words: "You charmed me, Mary, and you still charm me. You are very sweet, and I shall never want a dearer mate than you might be, if you would. I vow to you that you are the only woman with whom I have wished to live, as we might live if you would.

I can't make you see, I'm conscious, what I feel about Sanchia—but it's certainly not that. My little dear, can't you trust me?" He looked down, and saw her tears slowly dropping; he was very much moved, knelt by her side. She turned her face away, dangerously moved also. She struggled with her tears, her face contorted, her bosom heaving in riot. Senhouse took her hands, but she wrenched them away and covered her face with them. Passion grew upon her, passion of regret, of loss, of rage, of desire—"Oh, leave me, leave me! Oh, cruel, cruel! No man in the world could be so cruel—" and then she sprang up, and faced him, flushed and fierce as a woman whom love has made mad.

"I believed in you, I gave you everything I had. You have had it, and you leave me. I made no pretences—I told you all my secrets. You said that you loved me—and now you leave me. Go, please. I hope I shall never see you again."

Her great eyes loomed in her hot face like beacons. Her colour was high, her lips vivid. She looked as beautiful as an Indian flower. She was fighting for her own like a cat. An absent, shadowy, icily-pure Sanchia could never contend with this quivering reality of scarlet and burning brown; and the man stood disarmed before her, watching her every movement and sensible of every call of her body. Her wild words provoked him, her beauty melted him; pity for her, shame, memories of what he had believed her, impossible visions of what she might be; he was tossed this way and that, was whirled, engulfed, overwhelmed. There is only one end to such strifes. With a short cry, he threw up his arms. "God help us, I stay," he said.

III

HEAR now of the immediate end. This gentleman, a philosopher and poet, rich in theory, having reached a middle point in his career, had found that he had, without knowing it, encountered a Fact which had gripped him in a vital part, squeezed the very fibres of him, sucked him apparently dry of human juices, even of the zest to live, and presently departed, leaving him faint by the wayside. Not until he was clean gone did he have the least suspicion that it had been there, and (if he could have known it) the first glimmering of reawakening pulse in him was the considering of its nature. Brooding upon it, while he grieved over his languor, he discovered that it had not been hard and scaly, like your ordinary vampire, but soft-lipped, brown-eyed, warm-fleshed, cloudy-haired; in fact, a pretty woman. Now, in all his previous relations with that sex, while he had given much of himself, he had never met before with a woman whose need was the measure of her allure. If she had not wanted him so much, he would never have thought of her twice. But this was precisely what had happened. She had acted upon him as a vacuum upon air. Her helplessness, her ignorance, her appealing belief in him, her clinging power, heightening her physical

32

charm, had sucked him in a stream; and when she was full of him, he was empty. She had been the first to find it out. Having trailed him in her wake for a season, against his instincts, against his conscience, she presently coaxed him to let her go. Let her go! He asked nothing better than to see her happy, and saw no other way of being so himself. When she had gone, and was safely married to an old admirer, our expended friend lay, like a gaffed salmon, faintly flapping on the bank. For a year or more he lay, and dated his recovery of tone from the moment of finding out the nature of his disaster. "She was hungry, and I fed her. She was thirsty, and I gave her drink. The Lord gave, and the Lord hath taken away. Blessed, by all means, be the name of the Lord."

He proposed now to resume his former life of sojourn in tents and desultory practice of the arts, a life which, as it was at once highly practical and entirely dependent upon enjoyment, we may call one of contemplative activity. For twenty years he had not lived in a house, slept in a bed, or owned anything beyond the barest necessities. (The only thing he had, indeed, found himself owning, had at last removed itself.) He had been by turns poet, painter-in-water-colours, tinker, botaniser, antinomian, and anarchist; and attributed his success in all these busy walks to the fact that he was as strongly averse to the possession of property as he was incapable of getting any. Here, then, was his capital, with which to commence the world again.

With this at his back, you would have said, he had
but to pack his knapsack, stow his tent, and take
to the road. But that was not so.

He had, with the purest intentions, broken all
the laws of Society. Entitled to a competence,
he had had neither house nor gear, earned just
so much as would keep him in food. He knew
what it was to go without a dinner, and what to
sleep under the stars. Yet he had been extraordinarily happy. He had held up his head, and kept
it, alike with the learned—for he had learning—
and with the simple, whose simplicity he shared.
He had had the knack, in fact, of getting himself
accepted on his own terms, exorbitant as they
were; and of both rich and poor alike he had demanded entire equality. "Barefoot I stand," had
been his proposition, "of level inches with your
lordship, or with you, my hedgerow acquaintance.
Take me for a man, decently furnished within,
or take me not at all. Take me never, at least,
for a clothes-horse." In all these things, which
he had proclaimed far and wide, in divers tongues,
all of them eloquent, he had violated the unwritten
laws of our country as great and small know them
to be. Chiefest he broke them in being happy.
That was outrageous. But he was now, it seemed,
confronted with a Law of Nature when he found
that, having broken with a way of life, you cannot
resume it, not because it isn't there (for there it
is), but rather because you are not there yourself.
You are elsewhere, and the road is hard to find.

At forty-two you are not the mountaineer of thirty-five. Worse than that, worst sign of all, you don't want to be.

Here was a shock for the poet in him, which it was the philosopher's task to allay. In heated debate the two contended for his reasonable soul.

Poet. I am young.

Philosopher. You put it so. You are forty-two, and as old as you feel.

Poet. Away with you. I am young, I tell you. There are worlds to see.

Philosopher. Europe, Asia, Africa——

Poet. Alas! I have never been to Tibet.

Philosopher. My friend, if you wished to see Tibet you would be half-way there by now. I know you so well. Believe me you have seen more than enough. The world is so much larger than you, that five-and-twenty acres in Sussex will yield you more wonders than you can use. Take them, make them yours, and from them build up your Tibet. I understood that you were a poet.

Poet. My heart fails me. I have loved and lost. I have seen the dawn, and it has blinded me.

Philosopher. Mary is happy. You could never have made her so.

Poet. A sweet, good girl, but—I was not speaking of Mary.

Philosopher. So I supposed. Let me remind you——

Poet. Remind me of nothing. I remember everything. She was like the dayspring from on high. When I think of Greece, I think not of Plato and Sophocles, but of things more delicate and shy; of the tender hedge-flowers of the Anthology, of Tanagra and its maidens in reedy gowns, of all of this in a sweet clean light, as she was, and is, and must be. Ah, and I think of her, as I saw her first in the woodland, in her white gown, with the sun upon her hair. She was like the fluting of a bird; she was clear melody. She girt herself high and set her foot in the black water. She dipped her pure body in above the knees; she, the noblest, the wholesomest, the youngest of the gods. Remind me of nothing, I beg you.

Philosopher. I must really remind you of this. You renounced her of your own deliberation, and promised to dance at her wedding.

Poet (with a sob). So I would, God bless her!

Philosopher. That is a charitable sentiment. I have done you good.

Poet. You are an ass.

I have summarised an argument which was really prolonged and very acrimonious. The philosopher prevailed, and the poet, beaten at every point, forswore what ambitions remained to him, built himself a shepherd's hut in a valley of the Wiltshire Downs, and planned out his memoirs in three stout volumes. He believed that he had reached that stage in life where retrospect is all.

Volume I., *Open Country ;* Volume II., *Halfway House ;* Volume III., *Shepherd's Crown*—are titles which indicate the scope and spirit of the projected work. They were characteristically chosen before a line was written; nor, indeed, was a single other word put to paper, not so much as an Advice to the Reader, for two years. The building of his house with his own hands, and the disposition of the land about it occupied him for the better part of one; the next, with its progressive seasons of fruition, was spent in meditative ecstasy; by the beginning of the third his cure was complete. The poet in him was now the philosopher's humble servant, as should surely always be the case. Resolved that the world should be sweetened yet, he attacked his book.

He began with the third volume, in which, under the heading of *Shepherd's Crown*, he proposed to discharge himself of the conclusions of his ripened manhood upon the world, as he now saw it from his grassy outlook. Not yet could he trust himself with *Open Country*. That was for Thoughts. That was to be filled with spheral music which lay under lock and bolt deep within his nature. Before he could set that free to throb and beat in his brain, he must be quite sure that it could not win a way back into his heart. For she of whom it must consist, whose very name was music, whose presence, as he said, was like the fluting of a bird, was the renounced, impossible She; that She whom for reason clear and good he had loved (upon his knees, with covered eyes), and suffered go her ways. The philosopher was clear upon the point that Volume I. must be withheld for a season, and that Volume II., if it was to deal with the enchantment of the flitted Mary, must wait also. Mary must be charitably handled; give her time. In Volume the third, now, we were to have neither music on the one hand, nor the sharp fragrance of loose hair and warm breath on the other; but green thoughts, rather, "calm of mind, all passion spent," as surely at forty-two it must be. Let the wise book deal with life, not the living; with love, not of woman; with death, but not of the body.

Early in the third year this wanderer, come to anchor, began his book, and at his desk I propose to leave him until near the end of mine. But, that he shall know the man again when the tale hath need of him, the reader will be pleased to accompany me into his neighbourhood for a moment.

Into the great ridge of chalk which is the backbone of South Wilts, and runs east and west from Sarum to Shaftesbury, there cuts up from the south a deep, winding, and narrow valley. The hills, between whose breasts it runs a turfy way, fold one into the other; a man coming up from Blandford, and minded to strike across country to Marlborough, might well pass within two hundred yards of our recluse and never see a sign of him. It was at the head of this glen, sheltered by hills from north, east, and west, but open full to the south, he had built his one-storied, deep-eaved house of larch and shingles. Here, under the sky, he watched and laboured and slept, and saw nobody, living principally on vegetables of his own growing, and cheese, which he made from the milk of a flock of goats. Bread he had once a week from a peasant's cottage at the valley's foot; gypsy folk brought him occasionally tea and tobacco. For the most part he drank water, and was too good a traveller to be rooted to his pipe.

The group behind him sloped sharply up to the ridge, which we call the Race-Plain in those parts, and had nourished, when he first took up his rest below it, little but nettles, mulleins, and scrub of elder. A few fair trees—ash, thorn, spindle, service—struggled with the undergrowth which should live. He was for the trees, needing their shade; cleared the ground, terraced it with infinite pains, and utilised the water of a mist pool which he had made on the high land by a system of canals of remarkable neatness and ingenuity. Tree-trunks, split and hollowed out, conveyed what water he wanted as and whither he would.

To the west of his dwelling the slope was gentler, and there woods and brake-fern grew peacefully together and made a fine refuge from the heats. Behind this shelter, hidden from sight of the house, he had a broad lynch for his vegetables, and grew and protected them to be the envy and despair of rabbits. In the woods, and below, in the valley bottom, where wind-sown thorns made a natural park, his goats found eatage. He reserved

the terraces about the house for the flowers which
he loved and understood.

He was an expert gardener, who in his day had
been famous for his skill in naturalisation. His
feats in this work have made a stir beyond our
shores. Alpine plants grow wild upon English
rock-faces at his whim, irises from the glaring
crags of the Caucasus spread out their filmy wings,
when he bids them, on Devonshire tors. These
wonders he chose not to repeat—for reasons. Pence,
to begin with, failed him. The work itself was as-
sociated with the happiest and the saddest moments
of his life; he had not the heart to begin it. Moreover, in the course of his year's work of house-
building and settling in, he had kept an eye for
Nature's way in his valley, and when it came to
making a flower-garden he found that she had one
there to his hand.

He said, "Nothing is lovelier in flowers than
true colour. Form is nothing to Nature; it is
one of Art's tricks. Here I may have a succession
of pure washes by mere concentration of what I
find. The downs give me everything; all I have
to do is to group them.

"Here is my design. For early spring, cowslips
in a cloud. Scattered broadcast, they are happy
accidents which you come upon walking; but if you
mass them their scent tells, and you find they are
nearer the colour of oranges than of limes.

"For mid-April and early May I have the orchids
—a blood-spatter on the bottom; higher the flecked

white, the pink, and the yellow with brown. Then for a shelf among rocks the milk-worts, the sky-blue, the white and the pink; with these I float out May like Fra Angelico. For June there are Ragged Robins like filaments of rosy cloud, and Forget-me-not to drift like wood-smoke over the chalk rubble. In July I have a pageant. Fox-glove and Eglantine make melodious my woods; Ladies' Slipper gives a golden cope to the hillside, with purple campanula to wind about it like a scarf. After this—August, September, October— our uplands faint out in semitones: grey scabious, grey harebell, pale bed-straw, white meadowsweet, like the lace of an old lady's cap. But even so, if I must have a sunset glow of brown-pink, herb-willow gives it me. Pinch out the leader of each slim spike, and you make a different plant of it." Thus the poet embroidered the philosopher's text, and kept away from his memories, and husbanded his pence.

These things, at any rate, he did, collecting with diligence the plants to his hand, separating them from the grasses and bents in which they hid, massing them and marshalling to his purposes. The thing was done with extreme art and infinite patience; the result, a rainbow stream of colour through the working year.

He added a few foreign growths: cyclamen for the woods, because he did not see how one could do without them who had once seen them in Calabria; wild gladiolus, because it loved the corn, and there

was land in tillage within a mile of him; a few
primulas for his conduit's edges; wild crocus, because She whom he had loved best had loved them;
colchicums for the bottoms in Autumn, because
once She, straying with him in meadows, had
picked some for her bosom and at parting given
him one. He had it still, though he never cared
to look at it. She and it belonged to his first volume,
and neither crocus nor colchicum had been added at
the date of which I write. He planted them when
he reopened that book, and they are thriving now.

Here was work enough for a man somewhat
mauled by the world to forget his hard knocks
withal; and he forgot them. Looking about him,
the length and breadth of his silent and lonely
valley, he could see nothing but amenity in the
earth which owed man so little. It was so with
him at this time that the more he saw to love in
Nature the less he could find admirable in man,
who denied her at every turn. It was men, not
She, who had given him his bruises; it was She,
not men, who had taught him how to forget them.
When outraged Society cried him down for a breaker
of laws, he had replied that, so far as he knew,
he had broken none of Nature's; and had it been
argued that we live otherwise than as the beasts
that perish, he would have retorted, "Whether
the beasts perish or not, it is very clear that they
live to the full in this world, and that we don't.
Suppose they perish, at least they have lived. If
we are to live hereafter, as to which no one is cer-

The hum of cities, and buzz of dinner-tables . . . sound in
his ears not at all.

tain, we are faced at our temporal death with the fact that, born into this world with certain faculties, instincts, appetites, and senses, we have let most of them atrophy, and the rest rot, by many contributory causes, of which the chief is over-eating. If I die, to live again, I have it behind me that I have lived well already. I am that much to the good. And, that others may have the same fortune, I shall devote what time remains to me to teaching the truth, *The less you have the more you are.* This was his intention when he sat down to pen his *Shepherd's Crown ;* before he dared look back upon *Open Country*, or to plant the sacred crocus, or to look upon the dry colchicum flower which had been granted the grace of a fair breast.

We meet him again, but not yet. We have him fast in his moorings, and are to see him rather as a fixed point about which other wandering lights stray in narrowing circles, to which they converge. We are to conceive of him, if you please, as writing his Book, while the hum of cities, and buzz of dinner-tables, noisy enough to us and full of excitement, sound in his ears not at all. And when I have done, you will discover, if you care, why he changed the title of his third volume from *Shepherd's Crown*, and chose it to be called *Rest Harrow*.

The way thither is long, and many things are to happen to many people; but little happens to him except the wheeling of the years.

BOOK II

SANCHIA AT WANLESS HALL

I

A TELEGRAM was handed to her as she came in
from the garden, her broad-brimmed straw hat in
her hand, and a bunch of fritillaries nodding in
her blouse. That dates and places her at once:
the time was April, and she was fond of curious
flowers. She stood in the doorway to get the
sunset glow upon the missive, and was herself
ensanguined and enhanced, a sunny-haired, low-
breasted young woman of middle height, rather
faintly coloured, wholesome to see, with a bowed
upper lip, and clear, grey-blue eyes of extreme
directness and candour. A trick of looking you
full, of considering you and her answer together,
she had—a mild, steady beam, a radiance within
the orb which told of a hidden glory. Her brows
were level, eyebrows arched; her bust, though set
like Aphrodite's of Melos, was full. The curving
corners of the bow of her lips assured her the possession, even when she was most serious, of a lurk-
ing smile. Taking off her gardening gloves that
she might break the red envelope, she disclosed a
pair of fine, white, nervous hands, and pointed
fingers which wore no rings.

The address, which she was careful to read before she tore the envelope, was—

Miss Percival, Wanless, Felsboro'.

Opening then, she read as follows:—

Home to-morrow seven people Ingram.

If she frowned slightly, it was a mere approach of the fine eyebrows to each other. She certainly smiled—wisely and meditatively, without showing her teeth. She touched her chin—a rounded, full chin—with the telegram, as she looked up at the maid who brought it.

"I must see Mrs. Benson about this. It's from Mr. Ingram."

"Yes, Miss Percival."

A friendly desire to share the puzzle was now manifest in the clear eyes.

"You see, Minnie, it might mean one of two things, and I am not quite sure which of them it does mean." She looked again at the message with amused interest; but one could not have said whether she was amused at her interest, or interested in her amusement. That was part of Miss Percival's charm, that she was always baffling you.

But Minnie, the maid, was demure and monotonous under the attack of friendly desires. "No, Miss Percival," she said, and added, "I am sure I couldn't say." She stood aside from the doorway as the young lady entered the billiard-room, saying, as she went, "Ask Mrs. Benson to come to my room, Minnie, please; and tell Frodsham I should like to see him directly he comes to-morrow morning."

She heard Minnie's "Very well, Miss Percival," as she disappeared, smiling still, and with a slight heightening of colour. When her colour rose, it rose evenly, flooding her face and neck with the dawn-hue. There were no patches or streaks of flame; she showed, as it were, incandescent.

She crossed the hall in the deepening dusk, a fine, littered room, where a great log-fire revealed the tall portraits of ladies and gentleman of long ago—sportsmen with spaniels at their feet, general officers in scarlet, pointing through smoke the direction of the enemy, a judge in ermine and full bottomed wig, a lady in white satin leaning against a broken column in a park, and backed by a brewing thunderstorm; and as she went her way gave a couple of glances to right and left, picked up a *Bradshaw* from a side-table, stooped to put a tiger-skin straight. She continued down a long corridor, swinging her hat, and entered an open doorway at the extreme end. By the way she tossed the hat on to a chair and stirred the crackling logs with the point of her shoe, it was to be supposed that she was in her demesne. Standing with a foot on the fender she presently fell into a reverie, and presently reopened and re-read her telegram. Certainly she was smiling, and certainly her colour was enhanced.

The room, though business-like, was feminine. It had a Chippendale bureau between the windows, its pigeon-holes stuffed with papers; but there were flowers upon it, and elsewhere many photographs, and pictures evidently chosen by the tenant. The *Dante* from the Bargello was one, the three headless *Fates* of the Parthenon another; the *Hermes* and the *Sophocles*, all in autogravure. It had a piano and a small bookcase containing the poets in green morocco, a uniform set. Elsewhere, in a larger bookcase, were miscellaneous volumes, by no means all novels, though novels there were. One shelf was filled with household books: cookery, bee-keeping, poultry, the *Dog in Health and Disease*, the horse, the flower-garden, *Botany*, *British Edible Fungi*, the *World of Vegetables*, were some of the subjects treated of. Below the bookcase was a row of japanned tin boxes, carefully lettered in white paint. House Accounts, Garden Accounts, Stable Accounts, one read. A fourth bore the words "Wood Sales and Miscellaneous."

If you were alone, waiting in the room, you would glance at the photographs perched about, like alighting butterflies, upon piano and mantel-shelf and occasional table. You would pass over, I believe, the children on ponies and in sailor suits, that elderly, ample lady, brooched and in black, beaming under the status of Grandmamma, that gaitered gentleman with a square-topped felt hat upon his head and grizzled whiskers below his ears, in favour of a group of five girls in black muslin and lace, sisters evidently, prosperously together, an uncommonly happy five. They look on good terms with themselves and with each other. They look frankly at you out of the frame—and how they must have dazzled the photographer with their five pair of bright, uncompromising eyes! Hands rest easily upon familiar shoulders, elbows on knees. One of them smiles outright, two are very ready to smile; one is more serious, as becomes the eldest of five; and one is round-cheeked and solemn—the baby.

Miss Percival and her sisters, it's clear. One can't mistake the rounded chin, the level brows, the promise of womanhood. Women should always be photographed in evening dress if, like the Misses Percival, they have nothing to hide. But now to pick out our Miss Percival. You will observe that the young ladies' names are neatly printed beneath their persons.

Even if I were sure of dates, I should not insist upon the serious one. So far as I can judge, the photograph is some eight or ten years old. I go by the style of hair-dressing which it shows, and by the name of the photographer, who signs from Wigmore Street. He is out of date; fashion has deserted him. Then that grave, watchful young goddess, who sits enthroned with her nymphs about her, must be a great deal older than our lady of this room, of the doubtful smile and friendly desires. She has the sedate air of eight-and-twenty, and by this time must be thirty-six or even more. She is Philippa, anyhow, we read. Who comes next? Here is Hawise, standing behind her of the throne and the centre, with a hand on her bare shoulder. She is laughing, sleepily; she is distinctly pretty, but distinctly, also, fat. She cannot be the owner of this room.

There's a taste for names in the Percival family: we have Philippa, Hawise. Now for the seated pair, one on either side of Philippa: they are Melusine, who has a long neck and a very demure look, and a great deal of hair, and Victoria, who, having just tossed back her head, lifts her chin and glimmers at you through half-shut eyes. Her lips laugh snugly at some mischief meditating. Neither of these can be our lady, who must therefore be the last and youngest, this child of eighteen or so, round-cheeked, round-eyed and serious, with critical lids, like those of the Farnese Hera, and a beautiful mouth: Sanchia-Josepha, crouched on the floor at the feet of Philippa. A charming bevy of maidens—Philippa, Hawise, Melusine, Victoria, Sanchia-Josepha; ten years ago happily sisters and rich in promise, looking out boldly at the veiled years ahead of them. Ten years ago? Call it eight, and you make our Miss Percival, say, six-and-twenty by this time.

There are many other photographs—girls and women, most of them; but here is a man, dignified by a place apart upon the bureau. He occupies one side of it by himself, balanced by the sisters

at the other. A youngish man in yeomanry uniform, he appears only in torso. He has the smooth
head of a soldier, and rather a low, but very square,
forehead. His eyes are smallish, and set deep.
They look to be grey, light grey, but may be light
blue. He has a good nose, high-bridged, large,
thin, and practically straight. Such noses are seldom perfectly straight, and his is not. I observe
that he has curled his moustache with the tongs,
so that it is well away from his upper lip. If I had
been he I should not have done that. It is too
much trouble—and if a man takes pains about his
toilette, those pains ought not to be evident. Moreover, the mouth is by no means this young man's
best feature. There is a twist, the hint of a snarl
in the upper lip. The lower protrudes. The gentleman is the least in life underhung. Consider his
chin. It has the jut of the Hapsburgs', of Charles
the Fifth's, not pronounced by any means, but
undoubtedly there. Firmness, or perhaps obsti-
nacy, hard judgment, an uneven temper, a leaning
to autocracy, I read in this portrait. There is no
signature, nothing to tell you who he is. Certainly,
no Percival.

I call your attention to one more photograph,
in marked distinction to others of your notice.
Those were, in every sense, full-dress affairs; this
one, in all senses, undress. It is the work of an
amateur, you can see at once—small, rather blurred
to begin with, not perfectly focussed, and fading
now towards the end of all such gear. It repre-

sents a bareheaded young lady in a white gown
pinned very high. She is standing in a pond, with
the water well over her knees. One hand keeps
her balance with a pole, the other grasps a streamer
of water-weed. Floating beyond her upon some
kind of raft is a man, bareheaded also, in a white
sweater with a rolling collar. His face is shadowed
—you can see that his hair, black and straight,
falls over his eyes. He is raking up the weed with
his hand, his arm bare to the shoulder. Below is
written, in a round, sprawling hand, "To Sanchia
from Percy." Both the workers are intent upon
their task, with no idea that they are posing. The
girl has a Greek face, and a very fine pair of legs
heedlessly displayed. The man is as thin as a
gypsy. Out of the dark in which his face is hidden
gleam his white teeth. A classical, rather than
romantic scene. The absence of draperies suggest
it; but the absence of self-consciousness is con-
clusive.

But I keep Miss Percival too long at the fender.
She had been standing there for some minutes after
her entry, first re-reading her telegram, next strok-
ing her chin with it. She was thoughtful still, and
still smiling. Once she looked over her shoulder
through the window to the dying day, and lightly
sighed. The time was April's end, and had been
squally, with violent storms; but the last onslaughts
of the north-wester had routed the rain-clouds.
The day was dying under a clear saffron sky, and
a thrush piped its mellow elegy. Miss Percival

heard him, and listened, smiling with her lips, and with her eyes also which the serene light soothed. Her lips barely moved, just relaxed their firm embrace, but no more. She held the light gratefully with her eyes, seemed unwilling to lose a moment of it, wistful to be still out of doors. Again she lightly sighed, and presently resumed her downward gazing at the fire.

Knuckles quavered at the door. She straightened herself, turned, and called out definitely, "Come in." Mrs. Benson stood before her, vast, massive, black-gowned, cloudy for trouble, a cook.

There was instantly to be observed in Miss Percival's lifted head and eyes the same frank appeal for interchange of sentiments as had been manifested to Minnie the maid. Her brows were smoothed out, her smile became less dubious; her intention to be friendly was deliberately expressed. But truth will have it that, just as before, Mrs. Benson's guard turned out at the same moment, as at a signal. To vary the figure, her vedettes, in touch with the advancers, fell back upon the main body.

If the young lady perceived this she did not cease to be amiably disposed. "Oh, Mrs. Benson," she said, "I've had a telegram."

Mrs. Benson, with strict non-committal, lifted her eyebrows to "Well, well!" It was as if she implied that such things were to be expected in a world full of trouble. "So I hear, Miss Percival," she grimly said.

"It's from Mr. Ingram, you know."

"Ah, well—" Mrs. Benson could have been heard to sigh; but among the many things which Miss Percival chose to ignore, this sort of thing was one. Trouble to her, always, was a signal which braced the nerves and sinews.

"It's to say—but I think you had better read it." It was held out unfalteringly, while Mrs. Benson dived for, opened, wiped, tested, and fixed her spectacles. These operations concluded, it was received as might have been a dangerous explosive.

Punctuating as she went, Mrs. Benson read, "*Home to-morrow—seven people—Ingram.*" Then she looked, confirmed in her omens, over the rim of her spectacles. "Seven people, Miss Percival! A house-party! And, as you may say, at a moment's notice. Dear, dear, dear!"

Miss Percival remained cheerful. "Oh, I don't read it like that," she said, went behind Mrs. Benson, and read over her shoulder, pointing the words with a pencil still wet from her mouth. "'Home to-morrow, seven—with people—Ingram.' That's what it must mean, of course." She spoke wooingly, but Mrs, Benson was not to be won.

"Then, why does he say 'Seven people,' Miss Percival? Why does he say that?"

"But he doesn't, according to me." She laughed. "He is telling us the time of his train. How could we meet him and his people if he didn't?"

"Ah," said Mrs. Benson, heavily prepared for

the worst, "how could we? That's where it is, you see. But of course he wouldn't think of *us*."

"But he does, you know. He has. He says that he will have people with him. That is to prepare us." Mrs. Benson's fist crashed into the paper.

"How many people, Miss Percival? How many people? Why, seven, of course? What else could it be? And where's the fish to come from for seven people? And what about maids and valets? Does he count up the likes of them? He's not Mr. Ingram if he does. Not he! Nor his father before him. And what's Frodsham going to do about carriage-room for seven—and the servants as well—and the luggage, and all? Dogs, very likely, dogs and cats, and parrots. Who knows? I've seen 'em bring scritch-owls and hawks on their wrists before now. Oh, they'll do anything, some of 'em—anything to be looked at. That's what it is; they want looking at. And I'd look at 'em if I had my way!"

Mrs. Benson, shining with indignant heat, had to be pacified. She required much tact, the exercise of a low and musical voice. It cooed upon her like a dove's. Miss Percival used her hands, too, and in the end had one of them on Mrs. Benson's shoulder. The charm worked. Dinner should be cooked for five or six; Frodsham should meet the seven-four from London with the omnibus and luggage-cart. There would be no dogs at this time of year. Parrots were urged upon her again, but tentatively. She chuckled them away, musically, with real relish for the picture. She was sure there would be no parrots. Now she must see about the bedrooms—but Mrs. Benson peered round into her glowing face.

"And what about your supper, Miss Percival? It's just upon ready. And there's a sweet-bread."

Miss Percival almost caressed the ridiculous good soul. Her arm remained about her shoulder, her hand touched it. "How nice of you! I'll go and get ready at once. Then I'll see what rooms we had better have. Wasn't it lucky we did the drawing-rooms last week?"

Gloom gathered again. Mrs. Benson thought that some people didn't deserve their luck. It was clear to whom she referred; certainly not to Miss Percival, for instance. But the young lady, with really extraordinary simplicity, replied that surely Mr. Ingram deserved credit for having well-chosen his ministers. "Yourself," she said, "for the kitchen, and me for the hall." She exploded this little bomb with some heightening of colour.

Mrs. Benson, glancing at her sideways, observed the blush, and was scared. She blinked. Miss Percival's blush deepened.

In the awkward pause that ensued the friendly hand was about to be removed, when Mrs. Benson, with an effort which did honour to her resources, said, "We all have our troubles, Miss Percival, else we shouldn't be here, as the Bible says. The good Book! Well for them as read therein. Now, only this afternoon Mr. Menzies was talking to me about things at large, and he says, 'Mrs. Benson, what's to be done with Struan Glyde?' quite sudden. So I says, 'And what should be done with such a one, Mr. Menzies, but wallop him?' and he shakes his head and says, 'He's on the catarampus, ma'am—in one of his black fits. Tells me to go my way and let him alone; then turns his back.' Now, what about such troubles as that, Miss Percival?"

Miss Percival looked serious, but not especially interested. Her eyes looked before her, but seemed not to see anything. She asked, "What did Mr. Menzies say to him next?" but if she was interested it was not in that matter.

Mrs. Benson brandished her voice. "Ha, you may well ask me. 'No, my man,' he says, 'but 'tis you that must go mine while I'm head-gardener at Wanless,' he says. That's what Mr. Menzies told him, the elderly man that he is—and now look at this. Young Glyde turns his back upon him, with no more notice taken than you or I would have of a flea on the arm. Insolence, that is. Downright insolence of an elderly man. Ah," said Mrs. Benson with tightening lips, "if you come to troubles!"

Miss Percival's tone was sympathetic, if her eyes were still sightless. "Really! I'm very sorry. I'll see Mr. Menzies about it to-morrow, and of course I'll talk to Struan. He *is* difficult—it's very tiresome of him. I saw him this afternoon but had no

notion of all this. I can't think how it is. Nerves,
I suppose. He's a human creature, you see, as well
as a gardener."

Mrs. Benson was incapable of seeing such a possible combination: her explanation was simpler.
Human! She scorned him. "Bad blood," she
said with energy; "bad, black, gypsy blood. He'll
be murdering one of us in her bed in a day or two.
You see if he don't."

Miss Percival did not deny the suggestion. She
considered it rather—its effect, its effectiveness.
"Struan is tiresome, of course," she said, "but I do
think he has tried to restrain himself lately. He
promised me he would." She turned her full gaze
suddenly upon Mrs. Benson, and almost disarmed
that lady. "I like him, you know. He's very nice
to me."

Mrs. Benson gasped, but recovered just in time
to resume the dark oracles in her keeping. "Ah,"
she said, "he *would* be. If you can call it nice——"

"He's wonderful in the garden," Miss Percival
calmly continued. "Even Menzies admits it. He'll
work all day. He's never tired."

"Nor's a tiger," the cook snapped. "Nor's a
tom-cat."

Miss Percival looked pitifully at her and smiled.
"Poor Struan—you don't like him. I'll see him
to-night. I have an influence, I think."

Mrs. Benson touched the hand that lay within
her reach, which had lately been upon her shoulder.
"Don't, my dear, don't," she said.

"Why not?" asked the lady with her lifted brows. "Why shouldn't I?"

"Influence! The likes of him!—Gypsy blood at midnight—soft-voiced, murderous——"

She gave no coherent answer, but smiled always, then leaned forward and stroked Mrs. Benson upon her personable cheek. "Dear old thing, let me do as I like. It's much better for everybody," she presently said.

II

It had clouded over after sunset: there was no moon visible, but an irradiance was omnipresent, and showed the muffled yew-tree walks, and the greater trees colossal, mountains overshadowing the land. Here and there, as you went, glimmered daffodils, like the Pleiades half-veiled, and long files of crocuses burned like waning fires.

Miss Percival, at about nine o'clock, came gently down one of these alleys, with a scarf over her head and shoulders. She looked like a nymph in Tanagra. And as if she knew where she was going, exactly, she walked gently but unfalteringly between the linked crocus-beacons to where the alley broadened into a bay of cut yews, to where ghostly white seats and a dim sun-dial seemed disposed as for a scene in a comedy. The leaden statue of a skipping faun would have been made out in a recess if you had known it was there. And as she entered the place a figure seated there, with elbows on knees and chin between his palms, looked up, listening, watching intently, then rose and waited.

"Struan," said Miss Percival comfortably, "are you there?"

"I'm here," she was answered.

Thereupon she came easily forward and stood near him. She was in white from top to toe; he could see the clean outline of her head and neck, defined by the hooding scarf. He had not as yet taken off his hat, but now, as she stood there silent, he slowly removed it. Still there was nothing said. Miss Percival was very deliberate.

Presently she spoke. "You didn't tell me this afternoon that you'd had a bother with Mr. Menzies. Why didn't you tell me?"

"Why should I tell you?" The words seemed wrung from him. "Why should you care?"

"Of course I care," she said. "You know that I care. Why didn't you tell me? . . . But I know why you didn't."

"You do not." He denied her hotly.

"Oh, but I do. Because you were ashamed."

"It was not. I'm not ashamed. He's an old fool. He thinks he can teach me my business. Melons! Plants! Why, I'm one of them. What can he teach me?"

"He's a very good gardener," Miss Percival began, but the rest was drowned.

"Gardener—he! He's a botcher. He measures his melons by the pound. It's money he wants, money-value. So much dung—so much meat. He says, 'Be careful, you, of the water-pot; go steady with your syringe. You'll damp off those plants it you're not handy,' he tells me. To me, this! Don't I know what the life of a plant must have, and how, and where it must be fed? He's an old fool, and you know it. And I'll not be told things I have got by heart before a lad new to his breeches. Besides," he added darkly, "he'd vexed me before that, and bitterly."

"How did he vex you?" Miss Percival's voice came cool and clear, but commanding.

"That I cannot tell you," said he.

"But I want to know." This seemed to her sufficing reason.

But he was dogged. "Then I can't help you. You cannot be told."

"But perhaps I ought to be told. Do you think I ought?"

"Indeed, I don't know."

"Well, will you tell me?"

"I will not, indeed. That is, I cannot."

"It's very extraordinary."

He made no answer.

"Struan," said Miss Percival, after a while, "you are angry."

He turned quickly. "With you? Never."

"I didn't say that. I said you were angry."

He said, "Ah—and so I am."

"I am included, I suppose."

"You are not. It could not be."

She laughed. "I don't know——"

He was vehement. "But you do know. You know it very well."

She had no answer; but she smiled to herself; and I have no doubt she knew.

For two minutes or more there was silence, a

time of suspense. Then Miss Percival said, "I've had a telegram. Mr. Ingram is coming to-morrow."

To this he said nothing. She went on.

"He is bringing people with him. Mrs. Benson was very funny about it. He is coming at seven with some people, and she would read it that he was coming with seven people. When I asked her, how could we meet him if he had not told us the time? she made a grievance of it, and said that was so like him. So it is, of course."

Struan remained speechless, and had turned away his face. Miss Percival continued her reflections aloud.

"How long has he been away? More than a year. He wrote once from Singapore—then from Rawal-pindi—and that was all, until I got this telegram. He's very casual, I must say." Here she paused.

Struan said suddenly, "Miss Percival, I'm going."

She turned with interest, and asked, with not too much interest, "Oh! Why?"

He said, "You know why."

She lowered her voice by a tone, but no more. "I hope you won't. It would be a pity. There's no real reason for it. I'll speak to Menzies to-morrow. He doesn't mean any harm to you. He's only old and grumpy."

"He's a fool," said Struan. "Certainly, he's a fool. But that's neither here nor there."

Miss Percival, ignoring what she chose to ignore, said again, "I hope you won't go."

The young man shifted his ground, and dug his heel into the turf. "I must—indeed, I must."

"Where shall you go?"

"God knows."

"Why must you go?"

"You know why."

"Is it because of Menzies?"

He threw his head up. "Menzies, forsooth!" He scorned Menzies.

"Then I don't see why you should go. I shouldn't like it. I hope you will stay."

He looked at her now across the dusk, intensely. "You hope I will stay?"

"Yes, certainly I do."

"You hope I will stay? You ask me to stay?"

She considered. Then she said, "Yes, I think so. Yes, I do."

"Then," said Struan, "God help us all. I stay."

Miss Percival said cheerfully, "I'm so glad. I'll speak to Menzies to-morrow, and get him to leave you alone. He knows how well you do the melons, but of course he would never admit it." She broke off the interview shortly afterwards.

"I'm going to bed," she told him. "I've got lots to do to-morrow. Heaps of things. You must get me some of your flowers for the rooms."

He was not appeased, "Menzies will do it," he said. She laughed.

"You know what Menzies will say—'Pelargoniums for the hall, Miss Percival, and some nice maidenhair.' He's not inventive, poor Menzies."

"He's an old fool," said Struan. "He takes flowers for spangles in a circus."

Miss Percival again laughed softly, and held out her hand. "Good-night," she said. "I'm going."

He touched her hand, and then put his own behind his back.

"Aren't you going to bed?" she asked him.

"Presently," he said. "I'm going to walk round for a while."

She hovered for a moment, seemed to hesitate, to weigh the attractions of walking round. It had a charm. Then she decided.

"Good-night," she bade him for the third time.

He grumbled his good-night, and watched her fade into the dark. Not until she was completely hidden up did he put on his hat again. Then he prowled noiselessly about among the breathing flowers.

III

WANLESS, as they call it there,—Wanless Hall,
Felsboro', as it is politically,—stands squarely and
deeply in the hills of a northern county, plentifully
embowered in trees, with a river washing its south-
ern side. To reach house from river you ascend
a gentle slope of lawns and groves for some hundreds of feet, then find a broad stepway. That
takes you to a terraced, parapeted garden very
well tended, as one should be which has four men
at its disposition. There stands the house of Wanless, stone-built in the days of Charles the Second
—a gleaming, grey front, covered to the first-floor
windows with a magnolia of unknown age. The
main entrance faces north, from which point the
true shape of the place is revealed as a long body
with wings, an E-shaped house. Here are the
carriage-drive and carriage-sweep; then there's a
belt of trees, and beyond that, shaped by the valley,
which gradually narrows to the incline of the hills,
kitchen-gardens, glass-houses, a pond (fed by a
beck), water meadows, and hanging woods. Above
those again heather-clad slopes climb to piled rocks
and a ragged sky-line. It is a fine property with
5,000 acres of shooting, a good many farms, and a

hill village to its account. The lodge at the gate
was half a mile away, at the end of a good avenue
of beech and sycamore.

Mr. Nevile Ingram who, at thirty, had still the
air of a brisk young man and was owner by inheri-
tance of this place, arrived with his guests by the
7.4 train from London. The omnibus brought
the four of them, with a maid sitting on the box
beside Frodsham, and a bank of luggage behind
her head. No parrots, no dogs; but a Mr. Chevenix
brought his fishing-rods. Besides this Mr. Chevenix,
who had been here before, there was an elderly Mrs.
Devereux, white-haired and short-sighted, who used,
whenever she could find them, a pair of long-handled
glasses, and a young Mrs. Wilmot, pretty, very fair,
rather helpless. It was her maid who shared the
box-seat with Frodsham.

The absence of a footman at the station had
been noted by Mrs. Devereux, the absence of any
man-servant at the house struck her as remarkable.
There was none, and had been none since Miss
Percival assumed command; but at this time
Mrs. Devereux knew nothing of Miss Percival.
Nevile Ingram, banging the door open with his
knee, jumped out first, and stood to help the ladies;
the next to emerge was Mr. Chevenix who, the moment he touched earth, said "Right!" and looked
as if he had sparkled. It was clear that he had
abundant health and was satisfied with all the
arrangements of Providence. He surveyed the
house, the awaiting virgins at the door, wished

them both good evening, nosed the upper air, snuffed the gale, said "Good old Wanless—my precious rods!" and dived for them before the ladies could descend. Thereafter a timidly poising foot and some robust breadth of stocking revealed the anxieties of Mrs. Devereux. On alighting she shook herself like a hen, and her draperies rustled to their length. She found her lorgnettes and surveyed (so to speak) the absent men-servants with blank misgivings. A maid advanced for her jewel-case, but Mrs. Devereux, shutting her eyes, said "Thanks, I carry it," and pressed it to her bosom. A butler would have had it. Meantime, Mrs. Wilmot, a hand to each cavalier, was descending from the omnibus. She was a pretty, bedraped lady, with wide blue Greuze eyes, and soft lips, always wet and mostly apart. She murmured, "How kind you are to me," and liked it from Ingram to Chevenix. Ingram said nothing, but Chevenix dropped down his brisk "By Jove, Mrs. Wilmot, that's nothing to what I *could* do for you —nothing at all." And then they turned to the house.

When Miss Percival, looking frailer than she really was because of her black gown, fairer, that is, and paler, entered the hall, she found the party at a loose end. Mr. Chevenix was in a deep chair, turning over *Bradshaw*, and whistling softly to himself. Ingram, hands in pockets, was deprecating the portraits of his ancestors to the two ladies, who were not at all interested in them. He appeared to be considerably bored by his guests, and they to be aware of it. Miss Percival's arrival was timely, if only because she effectively chased out *ennui*. Chevenix, as if he had been waiting for her, jumped up and went to meet her. He shook hands. "Hulloa, Sancie!" he was heard distinctly to say. "By Jove, I'm glad to see you again." The latter sentence was not quite audible, but sufficiently so to send Mrs. Devereux' lorgnettes up to her nose. Sanchia herself, receiving civilities as if born to them, impelled her to keep them there. She had appeared silently and suddenly out of the blue. And now she hovered, smiling, fair, and unconcerned, like a goddess out of a chariot come to deal judgment, and listened charitably to Mr. Chevenix. How odd! How more than odd! Mrs. Wilmot looked as if her eyes were full of tears, but let nothing escape her. As for Ingram, he greeted the apparition with a smile and a nod sideways. But Mrs. Devereux could have sworn to a scare in the eye. "How are you, Sanchia?" he said, and then to his guests, "Miss Percival will show you where you all are, if you'll— Dinner's at half-past eight, I believe. At least, it always used to be; but I've been away for a year, and they may have changed all that. Have you, by the way?" he asked, with a sudden turn to Miss Percival.

She looked calmly at him. "No. It's still at half-past eight," she said. He lit his cigarette.

"Will you show these ladies their rooms?" he

required of her, adding as an afterthought, "Mrs. Devereux, Mrs. Wilmot. Mrs. Wilmot has a maid somewhere."

It was a quasi-introduction, awkwardly done. Sanchia gravely bowed, and all might have been well had not her gentle smile persisted. The baffling quality of this, the archaic enigma of it, made Mrs. Wilmot stare at her helpless with brimming blue eyes. It made Mrs. Devereux shiver. It was she, however, who accepted the inclination of the head. "Good evening to you," she said. The housekeeper! This—person! The pair of them followed her upstairs, Mrs. Devereux marching before, like one of the old *régime* to the guillotine, Mrs. Wilmot trailing in her wake.

Young Chevenix, when they had disappeared, returned with a grin to his *Bradshaw*. "No change from Sanchia," he said; and "Let's see: *Birmingham depart* 4.45. By Gad, that's a good train. No," he resumed; "no change out of Sancie. How long is it since you were here, Nevile?"

Ingram was staring blankly out of window. "I think a year. I don't know. You went out with me to Brindisi, I believe, and that was April, and so's this—just. So you can work it out. D'you want me to fix you up? You're in the east wing, you know—I expect you are, anyhow. Where you were before."

"Right," said Chevenix; "right. Only we're none of us where we were before, my boy. Don't flatter yourself." He shut *Bradshaw* with a bang,

The housekeeper! This—person!

and went off, singing softly, to a tune of his own, "No change, no change from Sanchia," which he turned into "Who is Sanchia? What is she, that all our swains . . . ?"

Miss Percival, having played the exact and perfect housekeeper above—with no apparent interest in life but submergence in her duties—returned to the ground floor and sought Minnie in the dining-room. She made her survey calmly, and gave such orders as pertained in smooth tones which could not jar. She seemed to consult where she really directed. "Shall we have the *épergne*? I think we will, don't you? Yes. It's a grand occasion. I don't think we have ever had ladies at Wanless before." An admission which staggered Minnie. Her "Oh, yes, Miss Percival," and "Oh, no, Miss Percival," were appreciative and good to hear.

She was butler, we find, as well as housekeeper, for as she stood there, meditating the table, Ingram came in, in a hurry, with ideas about wine. He gave them out in jerks, without looking at her. Sherry, of course, a hock, Lafite. No champagne: it's beastly unless you are tired. Oh, and old brandy—the very old. Nothing of the sort to be had in India. The climate kills it. He stood very close to her as he spoke. When he remembered the brandy he put his hand on her shoulder, and finding it there, kept it so. Minnie presently went out of the room upon affairs; and then he looked into her face and said in a new tone, "How are you, Sancie?" He let his hand slide down,

encircled her waist lightly with his arm. She gave
him her grey eyes and a slow, patient smile. "I
am quite well," she said. "Are you?" Ingram,
watching her still, seemed disconcerted, as if he
wanted to say or do more, but couldn't, for some
reason. What he did was to remove his hand
quickly and thrust it into his trouser pocket. It
might have been suddenly stung, judging from his
way of whipping it away. "Oh, I'm all right, of
course. I must go and dress, I suppose." A year
is a long time for an absence. In the doorway he
stopped and looked back, a last look. "Supper in
my room, you know. We'll talk." She held to
her mysteries, and he went.

Dinner passed gaily, Miss Percival away. Ingram was loquacious, though rather caustic; Chevenix a good foil, easy-tempered, always at a run, a
very fair marksman for all his random shooting.
His was that happy disposition which finds Nature at large, including men, as precisely there for
his amusement. He relished, never failed to relish,
the works of God. But then he had perfect health.
Mrs. Devereux was something of a grandee, though
not quite so much of one as she suspected. Her
white hair towered; she wore black velvet and
diamonds. Mrs. Wilmot was very much of a pretty
woman, and knew to the turn of a hair how much.
She had the air of a spoiled child, which became her;
was golden and rosy; could pout; had dark blue
eyes, which she could cloud at will, and fill, as we
know, with tears. She excelled in pathetic silences,

to which her parted lips gave an air of being breath-less. She was beautifully dressed in cloudy, filmy things, and had a soft, slight, drooping figure. Innocence was her *forte :* her rings were superb.

One odd thing was noticeable, and noticed in-tensely by Chevenix, that Ingram hardly ate any-thing, though he pretended to a hearty meal. It came, Chevenix saw, to dry toast and three glasses of wine, practically. But he made great play with knife and fork, and talked incessantly. He re-vealed himself at every turn of his monologue—for it came to be a monologue—as one of those men whose motives are so transparently reasonable to themselves that they need never be at the trouble to explain or defend any act of theirs. He was witty, though occasionally brutal, as when he spoke of a dragoman he had had in Egypt, whose defence of his *harem* had cost him his place. This man, a cultivated Persian, had proposed hospitality to his patron in Alexandria, where he lived. Accepted, he had made a great supper for Ingram, invited his friends and acquaintances, procured musicians and dancing-girls. It was magnificent, Ingram allowed. The trouble came afterwards, when the native guests had gone their ways and patron and host were together. Ingram proposed a visit to the ladies—"the civil thing, it appeared to me. But no, if you please! Mirza turned very glum, pronounced it not the custom: I must excuse him, he says. But I say, Will they excuse *me*, my good man? He makes a sour face, so of course I know that they won't,

and that he knows they won't. Then he marches
away upon some errand or another, and when he
comes back finds me tapping at a door. You never
saw such a change in a chap; upon my soul, it was
worth it. He went white, he went grey, he went
livid. His eyes were like stars. No, I'm wrong.
They were not. They were like the flaming swords
which kept Adam and Eve out of the garden. Magnificent police arrangements in Eden, they had.
I heard his breath whistle through his nose like
the wind at a keyhole. He says 'You mistake, sir.
You forget. Or do I deserve to be insulted?" I
told him that I was the insulted person in the party,
and the ladies came next. I swear I heard a chuckle
behind the door. That I swear to."

Chevenix, round-eyed and staring, was heard
to mutter, "Good old Nevile! Well, I'll be shot
. . . ." Ingram cut short his tale.

"I can't go into what followed. Much of it
was irrelevant, all of it was preposterous. It ended
by Mirza directing me to the nearest hotel, in perfect English. The crosser he got, the better his
English. That's odd, you know. Of course, I
chucked the chap. He lost a soft billet."

There were no comments from the auditory,
save such as Mrs. Wilmot's eyes may have afforded.
She sighed, and laid her hand for one moment,
caressingly, upon her neck. Her rings were certainly superb.

The dessert being on the table, Minnie served
the old brandy and retired. Ingram drank of it

freely, and began his cigarette the moment that the coffee and spirit-flame appeared. The ladies withdrew to the drawing-room, and Mrs. Wilmot sought the piano. But two chords had not been touched before her eyes found those of Mrs. Devereux, who stood by the fire. Eyebrows exchanged signals.

Then Mrs. Devereux said, "I am most uncomfortable," and Mrs. Wilmot sighed, "I know."

IV

THE quiet cause of discomfort, slippered and loose-robed, sat meanwhile in an easy-chair, with her feet in the fender. Her hair floated free about her shoulders, silky from the brush. She had a book on her knees, but did not read it. Instead she looked into the fire, frowning.

Faint lines now printed themselves upon her face; two between her brows, one defining the round of each fair cheek. Her eyes showed fathomless sapphire: whatever her thoughts were of they held the secret close. Their gaze was one of fascination, as if she saw things in the fire terrible and strange, figures of the past or of the future, from which she could not turn her face. The curve of her upper lip, where it lay along its fellow and made a dimpled end, sharpened and grew bleak. Poring and smiling into the fire, she looked like a Sibyl envisaging the fate of men, not concerned in it, yet absorbed, interested in the play, not at all in the persons. This friend of Mrs. Benson, this midnight mate of young gardeners, disturber of high ladies' comfort, serene controller of Wanless, she was, it would seem, all things to all men, as men could take her. But now she had the fell look of a cat, the long, sleek, cruel smile, the staring and avid eyes. A cat she might be, playing with her own beating heart, patting it, watching its throbs.

These moments of witchcraft gazing were not many. They had been deliberately begun, and were deliberately done with. Within their span her cares were faced and co-ordinated; and the business over, she sighed and sank more snugly into her chair. She leaned back; her hands crossed themselves in her lap; she shut her eyes. All the lines upon her face softened, melted away. She looked now like an Oread aswoon in the midday heats, pure of thought or dread or memory. Her bosom below her laces rose and fell gently. She slept.

Outside, in the dusky dark, was one who padded up and down the grass on noiseless feet, passing and repassing the window, with an eye for the narrow chink of light.

She slept for a very short time. Towards ten o'clock she awoke. Collecting herself luxuriously, she was seen to face her facts again. Evidently they held her eyes waking; they were dreadfully there, still unresolved or still unpalatable. Before them now she plainly quailed. The flush of her sleep gave delicacy to her carven beauty; she looked fragile and tremulous; it would seem that a little more pity of herself would bring her to tears. As if she knew it, she took her measures, rose abruptly, and after two turns about the room went to a safe, opened it, and plunged herself into the ledger-book, which she took from it. Upon that and a cash-box—with certain involuntary pauses, in which her eyes concentrated and stared—she remained closely engaged until half-past eleven.

At that hour, having ascertained it, she put by her work, went into her bedroom, and began a deliberate and careful toilet. She was pale, serious, and evidently rather scared at herself; she lifted her eyebrows and opened wide her eyes. But she did what she had to do as daintily as ever Amina, in the Arab tale, figured her rice. A person of great simplicity, who did extraordinary things in an ordinary way, at the hour when all Wanless was going to bed, she brushed and banded her shining hair, and dressed herself in silk and lace as for a dinner party. To herself in the glass she gave and received again a face of pure pity and sorrow. She saw herself lovely and love-worthy, sleek under the caress of her own beauty. Yet she knew exactly what she was about to do, and how she would do it, and did not falter at all.

At a quarter past twelve her summons came—a knock at the door, the turning of the handle, the push to open, and Ingram's voice. "Come along, Sancie," he said, and went away without any more ceremony. She got up from her chair, put her book down, having marked her place, and followed him after a few minutes' meditation. Ingram's quarters were on the ground floor of the house, as hers were, but in the opposite wing. She had two rooms in the western arm of the **E** ; the whole of the eastern was his.

He was at table when she came in and shut the door behind her, at a table fairly naped, with fine glass, silver, and flowers upon it. There was hothouse fruit, too, a melon, a little pyramid of strawberries in fig-leaves. He was eating smoked salmon and bread and butter with appetite. By his side, half empty, was a champagne glass. A pint bottle stood at his elbow.

He hailed her gaily, with a jerk of his head, a "Come along," and a lifted glass. Leaning back as she came on, watching and waiting for her, he stretched out his left arm. She smiled rather conventionally, did not meet his eyes, but came within reach. His arm encircled her, and drew her in. "Well, my girl, well!" he said, glancing up, laughing, tempting her to laugh. She looked down gently, blushing a little, and condescended to him, stooped and brushed his forehead with her lips. Condescension expresses her act. It was exactly done as one would humour an importunate child, excuse its childishness, and grant it its desire of the moment.

So it must have been felt by him, for there was a sharp, short tussle of wills. She would have had him contented, but he was not so to be contented. There was a little struggle, much silent entreaty from him, much consideration from her above him—her doubting, judging, discriminating eyes, her smile, half-tender and half-scornful; but in the end he kissed her lips, the more ardently for their withholding. Then he allowed her to sit by the table, not far off, and resumed his smoked salmon and his zest. She declined to share the meal; was neither hungry nor thirsty, she said. "Have your own way, my dear," he concluded the match; "you'll feel all the better for it, I know." She cupped her chin in her hand, and watched the play of knife and fork, her thoughts elsewhere.

"Now, Sancie," he said presently, in his usual direct manner, "how long is it since I've seen you?"

She answered at once, without looking up, "A year and ten days."

He shook his head. "That's too long. That's absurd. I don't like that kind of thing, as a man domestically inclined. But I've been a devil of a way. I wrote to you—from where?"

"From Singapore," she told him.

"So I did. I remember. But I went to Egypt before that. First-rate place, Egypt. I know it well, but am always glad to be there. Fine river of its own. We went to Khartoum, and two marches beyond; then Singapore and the Straits, Burmah, Ceylon; then India. Didn't I write to you from India?"

"Yes," she told him. She was balancing a salt-spoon idly on a wine-glass, and seemed scarcely to listen. He rattled on.

"Had great days in India. Shooting, fishing, pig-spearing; polo, dances, rajahs, pretty women, pow-wows of sorts, and a chance of a fight. All in a year, my friend—I beg your pardon—and ten days. Quick work, eh? One crowded year of glorious life. A cycle of Cathay."

She was looking at her saltspoon, stretched beyond her the length of her arm. "I'm sure you were very happy."

He looked at her directly. "Oh, I was, you know. Otherwise, I guess I should have written. I was idiotically happy. And you?"

"I was busy," she told him, "idiotically busy." He laughed gaily.

"That's one for me—and a shrewd one. Oh, you deep-eyed scamp! Sancie, you never give yourself away. I've noticed that many and many a time. And not I only, I can assure you. Bill Chevenix, now——"

Her thoughts, her regard, were far away from a world of Ingrams and Chevenixes. She may have heard, but she gave no sign. He rattled on.

"Oh, you're splendid, of course you're splendid. The comfort of you! I go off to the ends of the world—without a care left behind me—or taken with me, by Jove! No bothers, no worry—letters opened, the right ones, answered and done with. Letters forwarded, the right ones, unopened. How you can guess, it beats me! No worry. You don't ask me to write to you—or expect it. You don't write to me—and *I* don't expect it. You know me just as I know you. There's a confidence, a certainty about you. That's what's so splendid. There can't be a girl in the world like you." He clasped her in triumph. "My Sancie! Back I come at the end of my time, and everything's in apple-pie order. And to crown all, there's you at the door, to welcome me—and wait your turn—and wait your turn. Always the same—my wise, fine Sanchia!" He leaned forward, picked up and held her hand. "My dear, I love you," he said, and jumped up and kissed her. Then, as he stood above her, the triumphant young man, with the hand of possession on her shoulder, "Upon my word," he declared to the assembled universe, "this is a very satisfactory world, so far as I am concerned."

When he was seated again, and invited her to talk domestic affairs, she returned from her reverie, and gathered in all her self-possession. The estate, the household, the parish, the county: there was no mistaking his interest in these matters. He was interested in the smallest particulars: her broods of young chicks, her pigeons, the tabby cat's kittens, the Rector's baby. He asked searching questions. How many cows were in milk just now; when would Menzies have asparagus fit to eat? The servants— was all well there? Their young men? Nothing escaped him. She was quite ready for him, took a dry tone, showed a slight sense of the humour of the situation, descended to trifles, had statistics at her fingers' ends. She met him, in a word, as he wished to be met, as jointly concerned in these minute affairs.

He lit a cigar, and drew her to the fire. He would have had her on his knee, but she would not. She sat on a straight chair beside his easy one, and allowed him to play with her hand.

He talked now in jerks, between puffs, of his

adventures; his first shot at a tiger, some trouble with hillmen at Peshawur, a row at a mess-table, in which two chaps lost their heads, and one his papers. He had been present as a guest, but had kept well in the background. There had been a lot of drinking done—luckily he was all right. He had a good head, you see; could carry a lot of stuff.

He had, by the way, "picked up" that little Mrs. Wilmot on board ship. She was coming home in the convoy of Mrs. Devereux. Of course he had known Mrs. Devereux for years; she was an institution. The little Wilmot person was a widow, it seemed. Niceish sort of young woman; knew the Trenchards up here, was a kind of cousin of Lady Trenchard's. In fact, she was going on to them from here; but not due for a week or so. She had, you might say, asked to be asked, or spelled for it out of those eyes of hers. You get awfully friendly on board ship, you must know. You can say anything—and do most things—oh, all sorts of things! He had no objection—to her coming, he meant; indeed, he rather liked the young party. He thought Chevenix did, too. But Chevenix was very much at Sanchia's disposal; "he talked a lot about seeing you again, my girl." To meet him again might carry her mind back—how long? Eight stricken years. Was it possible that she— he and she—had been here together eight years? Yes, he could see that she remembered. Dear, sweet Sancie!

There was bravado here on his part, and nervousness to be discerned beneath it; for it is most certain that her reverie was not exactly as he would have it. Her chin was in her hand, her caught other hand lay idle in his own; her eyes were far-gazing and sombre; her smile was bleak. Whatever she heard, whatever she thought of, she betrayed nothing.

Her brooding calm spurred him in that sensitive spot whose throb or ache tells a man whether he is centre of a woman's mind or not. He must know whether she was glad to have him back; the wanderer returned, eh? She had not told him so yet, he must observe; no, nor looked it. She was mysterious, it seemed to him. "And you can speak with your eyes, my dear; none better. Your tongue was never very loose; but your eyes! Now, you know what you can do with them, Sancie; you know very well. Speak to me, then, my dear, speak to me. Speak to me only with thine . . . no, not *only!* You can speak in a thousand ways—with your hands, with the tips of your fingers placed here or there, with a bend of the head on that lovely neck you have, with your faint colour, with your quick breath." . . .

Fired by his own words, he worked himself into enthusiasm, was enamoured of what himself proclaimed. "My beautiful—my goddess!" he called her, and drew her to his heart.

And she allowed him, allowed herself to be pressed there, while within her the dull fire smouldered, and the deep, slow resentment gathered like clouds about the sun. But he held her face now between his two hands and forced to meet his own her unresponsive eyes; and when with ardour he had kissed her grave lips, the flippancy of a fool ruined him, and his triumph was flattened into dust, as when one crushes a puff-ball.

He suddenly held her at arms' length as he was struck by an idea. "Oh, by the way, I forgot," he said, and looked vaguely across the room. "Claire is dead."

Sanchia's eyes concentrated and paled. The pupils of them were specks. She paled to the lips, then slowly flooded as with a tide of sanguine. She withdrew herself from him; simply dropped him off her. She said nothing; but she watched him steadily, while within her the masked fire gleamed and fitfully leapt.

Bravado made him hold on to his airy tone. "She died, I'm told, at Messina, some time in March. I heard it at Marseilles. Met a man who told me. Yes! She's dead—and buried."

Sanchia had nothing to say. She looked, however, towards the door—and he detected that. Her silence spread about the room, caught him and enveloped him. That she was calculating how long it would be before she could escape by that door was absolutely clear, and the frost of her silence struck down upon him so that he could not gainsay her purpose. He paused irresolute, glancing askance at her directed eyes. Then he gave in, left her, opened the door for her. She went out, folded in her own mystery, but as she went by him he caught up her hand, and kissed the fingers. They were very cold, and made him shiver.

"Good-night, my dear," he said, all his dash gone out of him.

She said good-night very simply and went away. He looked after her until she had turned the corridor, then went to the table and poured himself brandy and soda-water, drank deeply, and set down the tumbler with a crash. "By God! I am a fool," he told himself.

From the garden that narrow chink of light which shone through Ingram's shutter was seen to collapse by one who watched it. Shortly afterwards, that same haunter of the dark saw a shining slit part the shutters of a window in the west wing, and sighed, short and quick. He returned, to prowl among the secret flowers.

V

WHEN, after dinner, Mrs. Devereux had told her
young friend that she was uncomfortable, there
had been no need of the words; but the slow answering "I know" with which Mrs. Wilmot expressed sympathy was not intended to imply that
she shared the feeling. She herself was not at all
uncomfortable, because, while she saw the whole
state of affairs, she was not unhopeful of coping
with it. Touching the place where the tender point
of her breast lay nestling, she assured herself that
she could hope. But Mrs. Devereux, moving about
in worlds not realised, was incensed. Nothing that
followed during the next few days served to clear
the surcharged air. It is hard to say what vexed her
most, where all was as it should not be. Ingram,
bluntly unconscious of her sufferings, gloomed over
his own; Chevenix spied about for what he could
not find, spy as he would, and made the cause of
woe more conspicuous than ever. As for her, the
disastrous fair, the deliberation with which she went
about her duties, and ease with which she did or
caused them to be done; her self-possession, gentle-
ness, suavity, yes! and benevolence, were sights
to make angels weep. Tears of blood! If Mrs.

Devereux, by any means, could have compressed tears of blood, they had been shed. Nothing less vivid would have met the case: to exhibit her scarlet handkerchief to Ingram with a "There, see, I weep. Tears of blood!" Day by day in that mild spring weather, under pale blue skies, fanned by zephyrs, she could but pace the terrace walks, and stiffen herself, and stare about her—with dull disapproval for the very flowers, lest theirs, too, should be frail beauty, and repeat for her only comfort that she was most uncomfortable. So she was. But it was because she did not understand, not because she did. Curiosity ravaged her.

On one of these days, breakfast over at half-past ten, young Mr. Chevenix declared his intention with cheerfulness and point. "Twentieth of April— Dizzy's birthday, or Shakespeare's. Nevile, I'm going to fish your river. They are leaping like the boys in *Eugene Aram*, and I'm going to give them something to leap at. Now, what are all you people going to do? Because, I'll be free with you, I don't want you to come and look on. Mrs. Devereux, I let you off. You needn't gillie me. Nevile, you run away and play. Amuse Mrs. Wilmot. Do now: she likes it. I'm all right."

The elder lady fixed him keenly with a look which saw through his saucy assurance; Ingram's eyes sought those of Mrs. Wilmot across the table. She lent him their wonder for a moment, then looked down at her bosom. He was satisfied. There were still women in the world.

"What shall we do?" he asked her. "Will you be driven? Will you drive? Will you ride?" Another shaft rewarded him, which said, "Do with me as you will."

Ingram rang the bell. Minnie appeared. "Tell Frodsham, the horses at a quarter past eleven. I ride Sea-King, Mrs. Wilmot Lorna Doone. He had better come—or Butters will do. That's all."

Mrs. Devereux had been ignored, but was not displeased. It showed, at least, that Ingram knew she was not to be disposed of like a white rabbit. It was, however, necessary to say something, to declare one's presence, as it were; so she collected her papers. "I have letters to write. You will excuse me, I know."

Chevenix sprang to the door. "By George, I should think so," he said, which was well intended, but too brisk. He bowed her out, shut her out, and stood with his eyes on the others.

Ingram remained before the fire looking out of window. "She's in a wax. I don't know why."

"Oh, don't you, my boy?" said Chevenix to himself.

Mrs. Wilmot trifled with her tea-spoon. "And I don't care—much," he added. Mrs. Wilmot smiled.

Mr. Chevenix, going a-fishing, saw, as he had intended to see, Sanchia in the rose-garden, talking to Struan Glyde, who was tying ramblers. "Morning, Sanchia — morning, Glyde!" Each greeted him, but the youth grimly.

He talked at large. "I'm for murder. I must flesh my steel. It's too good a day to lose. Clouds scurry, sun is shy; air's balmy: a trout must die. That is very nearly poetry, Sancie. It is as near poetry as I can hope to get this side the harps and quires. Now, what on earth is Glyde doing to his roses at this time of year?"

The dark-skinned, sharp-chinned young man, aproned and shirt-sleeved, turned a shade darker. His black eyes glowed. He was quietly arrogant, even to her. "It doesn't matter," he had once told her, "what you say or do. I love you, and that's the sum and end of it." Now he allowed her to answer for him.

"There was a wind in the night which tore them about. I asked him to make them safe. I hate to think of their bruised ribs."

Chevenix whistled his satisfaction with this and all things else. "I see. Works of mercy. There's a blessing on that, somewhere and somewhen. All to the good, you know, Glyde. You never know your luck, they tell me." He left Glyde and his roses, and turned to the young lady. "Well now, look here, Sancie—if works of mercy are toward, what d'you say to one on your own account? Here I stand, an orphan boy, upon my honour. The master's gone riding with the widow." He stopped his rattle, as a thought struck him serious for a moment. "By George, and he's a widower—so he is!" Discharged of that, he resumed—"Yes, and Mrs. Devereux has got the hump, as they say—and here

I am at your mercy, to be made much of. Who's going to admire me? Who's going to hold my net? Who's going to say, 'Oh, what a beauty!'" He had now got her thoroughly at her old ease with him. Her eyes gleamed, and there was no doubting her smile. "Now, I'll tell you what. Your roses are all right. Glyde will see to that. You leave that to Glyde and his strong right arm. His strength is as the strength of ten, because . . . you follow me, I think? Now, Sancie, I put it to you—I'm an old friend of the family, and haven't seen you for—how many years? Aren't you going to give me half-an-hour of your morning?"

He pleaded by looks. He was quizzical, but in earnest. Her brow was clear.

"Yes," she said. "I'll come—for half-an-hour."

"Right! Right, goddess of the silver brake. Come, hold the pass with me." He turned to go, and she caught him up. "I mix my poets like salad, but that's because I'm in such high spirits. By Jove, Sancie, it *is* good to see you again." She met his laughing eyes with hers. She swam by his side—took his net, and was happy. Her face glowed. She had the power of casting troubles behind, recuperative power, resiliency. Glyde, the olive-faced, watched them down the walk, and owned to a heart of lead. "As well shut down the west wind as a spirit like hers!" He turned to his affair.

Below the steps, in the nut-walk which led to the bridge, Chevenix altered his tone. "It's good

of you to come with me, Sancie, my dear. I'm a
very friendly beggar, and Nevile, you know—I
say!" and he turned her a sober face—"You know,
I suppose? His wife—eh? Dead, you know. Oh,
but of course you did!"

She met him unfalteringly. "Yes, he told me."

Chevenix shrugged. "I must say, you know—
what? Oh, of course, it was a ghastly affair all
along. But *you* know all that, as well as I do.
Why, her temper! Oh, awful! I've seen her myself dead-white in one of her rages—she had hold
of a wine-glass so hard that it snapped, and cut
her hand. She looked at the blood—she didn't
know how it happened. And he—well, *you* ought
to know—was as bad, in his way. 'Pon my soul,
Sancie, Vesuvius might just as well have married
Etna—every bit. But there! What's the good of
talking! Everybody knew how it would be." Words
failing him, he stared about him.

"But still—oh, damn it all! To hear of your
wife's death—casually—on a platform—from a chap
you happen to know—happen to have met somewhere—oh, well, I call it casual. That's the word,
I believe—casual. Well, it *is* pretty casual—what?
Now, just tell me what you think—between friends,
of course."

She stopped him: she was short in the breath.
"I think not. If you don't mind."

He became as serious, immediately, as he was
capable of being. "I'll do as you like, my dear—
but you'll let me say this, that if I could see you

with all your belongings about you again, I should sing a hymn. That's all, Sancie; but it means a lot. When you went out of Great Cumberland Place, it became, somehow, another kind of place. I hardly ever go there now, you know. And now they're all married but you, and—I say, you heard that Vicky had a son and heir? Did you hear that?"

She had averted her face, but she listened intensely, nodding her head. "Yes, yes, I knew that. Papa told me. He always writes to me, you know; from the office, poor darling!"

She appealed to him urgently. "Please don't talk about them just yet. Please don't."

He saw the mist in her eyes, and was afraid. "All right, Sancie, all right. I'm frightfully sorry. Beastly painful all this, you know." He was much disturbed. To his simple soul a fine day, a fine-fettled river demanded, as of right, a happy mood in man, for whom all things were made. And a fine girl by his side, a good, a brave, a splendid girl —down on her luck—on such a day! What could one do? If, when you began, she choked you off! Wouldn't meet you half-way—bottled it up! And here he was, geared for fishing, and without the heart to wet a line, because of all this misery. Sanchia, sharply in profile to him, from cheek to chin, from shoulder to low breast, all one sinuous, lax, beautiful line, broke in on his rueful meditations. "There's a rise," she said. "Look, look."

His eye swept the river. "You're right. By Gad, that's a whacker. That's a fish. Now, you stop just where you are, net in hand. Don't move, and you shall see something."

He left her, and ran stooping down the bank, all his little soul concentrated in his cast. The dimpled water ran and swirled, the line flashed in the sun. Three casts, four; a splash, a taut line, and his shout, "Come on, quick; I've got him." Sanchia glided swiftly down the bank, her eyes alight, the lines of neck and shoulder finely alert. Her eyes shone, her lips parted; she looked the Divine Huntress to whom Senhouse had once likened her. She stooped, the net jerked; she watched, waited, tense to the act. Within the swirling water the great fish plunged: she watched, strung to the pounce; the net dipped and darted; she lifted it to land.

Chevenix admired. "By George, you are a one-er, I must say! Born to it. You strike like an osprey. That's a fish—what?" They peered together into the net, where, coiled and massy, beaming rose and pale gold, the trout writhed.

"Splendid!" breathed Sanchia, glowing and alight.

Chevenix gloried in her beauty. "If Nevile don't know what his chances are—if he ain't on his knees —my heavens, what a mate for a chap!"

A shadow falling upon him caused him to look up. Mrs. Devereux, grey and tall, boa'd, gloved, umbrella'd, stood regarding him and his companion from the bank. Instinct prompted him immediately to screen Sanchia by dragging her into the party. He held up the net and plunged. "First prize," he cried out, as heartfully as he could, "to me and Miss Percival."

"So I see," said Mrs. Devereux. "Ah, good morning."

This was to Sanchia's bland greeting, which, as always, made the lady shiver. It is difficult to say what a shock it was to her to be greeted cheerfully by Sanchia. To see one in so painful a situation occupied by anything less painful, interested in anything at all, was truly shocking. Mrs. Devereux's idea of irregularity was that it absorbed the devoted victim, kept her aghast. If it did not, surely, there was no reward left to the virtuous. But here we had a highly irregular young woman behaving with extreme regularity. Was the world turning upside down? Was black, then, really white? She shivered, she blinked her eyes; but she descended the bank and stood beside the pair, yet rigidly apart.

Chevenix, having got her there, knew not what to do with her. It seemed to him that he had better, on the whole, go on, so turned the lady a knowing face.

"This is not the first time by any means that Miss Percival and I have gone fishing, you must know. We began by tickling 'em—we were urchins together, you see."

"Really!" said Mrs. Devereux, who still saw nothing but depravity.

"I remember," he went on, "the first time we went fishing. I was at Alnmouth with a governess;

awful lonely little beggar I was. I used to moon about on the sands, while she read the *Morning Post*, with spectacles and a red parasol. And I used to hanker about all the other young 'uns, and wish I was one of 'em. *Her* party was there, you know—five of 'em, all girls and all pretty girls —eh, Sancie? I would have given my hopes of heaven—if I'd had any, you know—to go and paddle with 'em. Jolly party you were, my dear—jolly old plump papa, rosy mamma—and Philippa like a young tree, and Melusine and Hawise bright as apples; and then Vicky and you—little dears, you were. I was like a spent salmon, I believe, lantern jawed, hollow-eyed little devil, as solitary as sin." He turned, flushed, to Sanchia, and put his hand on her arm; she turned away her face, and Mrs. Devereux believed she saw tears. "It was *you* who took me in, you know."

"No," said Sanchia, turning him her shining eyes. "It was Vicky. She asked you to come fishing." He accepting her ruling.

"Bless me, it *was* Vicky. Always a frisky one. But after that it was always you and Vicky and me. And we had the time of our lives—at least, I did." Even Mrs. Devereux felt an emotion from the beam with which Sanchia rewarded him—a tender, compassionate look, as if she understood and excused him.

"You are old friends, I see," she said; and her smile was not unfriendly.

Chevenix shook his head wisely. "Frightfully

old—I've ' all—all my life." Mrs. Dever-
 made a distinct advance.

 it must be very nice for you," she said to Sanchia.

Sanchia's eyes were now clear, and her smile
absolutely general. "To see Mr. Chevenix? Yes,
indeed." She collected herself. "But I'm afraid
I must go now. I've a great deal to do." She admonished the young man. "Now you had better
catch some more," she told him. "I must go."

His face fell—without any regard for Mrs. Devereux—to "Oh, I say!" but it was then revealed to
him that there might be a part for him to play.
"Right, Sancie—you're mistress here. See you
later." He met her eyes gallantly, and lifted his
hat. Sanchia bent her head to Mrs. Devereux, and
went staidly away, her duties gathering in her brows.
The elder lady and the young man stood face to
face without speaking. Then Mrs. Devereux sat
deliberately down, and Chevenix braced himself.

"You said just now," the lady began, "to Miss
Percival, that she was mistress here. What did you
mean by that, exactly?"

Chevenix sprang sideways to this flank attack.
"Oh, you know, Mrs. Devereux! you can't take a
chap—literally—what?"

He wanted time; but she gave him none. "You
must forgive an old woman of the world—of a
certain world. I come here—to a house which belonged to Nevile's father, an old, old friend, and I
find—installed—a young lady—who does not dine

—who is extremely capable. I am bewildered, naturally."

Chevenix's "I know, I know," and his friendly nods ran on as an accompaniment.

"And then," said she, raising her voice, "I find that this young lady—and you—are old friends. You speak of her—people—as if they were really —of the sort which—as if she were—of the kind —whom—" It was impossible. "Really," she said, "it's most unusual. I don't frankly know what I ought to do."

Chevenix listened carefully to her truncated phrases, where what she did not say was the most eloquent part of her discourse. He nodded freely and sagely; he was conciliatory, but clear in opinion. "I know, I know," he said. "It's very rum —you must naturally find it so. I know exactly how you feel about it. Oh, rum's the only word for it. Or rummy. Yes, you might call it rummy —or a go, you know—or anything like that." Then he grew plausible. "But I'm sure it's all right. It's a long story, but I'm quite sure. You've no idea what a fine girl that is. Ah, but I know it." He tapped his forehead. "I saw the whole thing through—from beginning to end. She's a perfect beauty, to begin with."

That was a bad note. Mrs. Devereux asked him at once if he thought that a good reason. "Well," he said, "I do, you know—in a way. I can't explain it—but I think you see it in her face, you know—and manner. Yes, in her manner. She's uncommon, you see, most uncommon. And as cool as—well, it would be hard to say how cool a hand I thought her." He paused, having got off this effective estimate, round-eyed and triumphant.

"It seems to me, Mr. Chevenix," said the dry lady, "that the less you say the better."

"Not at all, Mrs. Devereux, not at all." He was eager to explain. "I don't think you quite follow me. What I meant to say was, that when a young woman can be as cool as she can be; can run a big place like this, and manage a staff of servants,—outdoors, mind you, and in; no steward, only a bailiff; keep all the accounts; and hold her head up—for she does that, you know, uncommonly well; why, then I say that she must be allowed the benefit of the doubt, you know. You must say, 'Well, it's rum, it's rummy,' or how you like to put it—'but she's got a head on her shoulders, and I suppose she knows what she's doing. I suppose she's seen her way.' For she's all right, you know, Mrs. Devereux; she's as right as rain. It's irregular, dashed irregular—but, by George, I'll tell you this, Nevile was in a bad way when he first met her; and she's pulled him through. He's steady enough now, is Nevile. Don't drink —nor do other things. He threatened to be a waster in his day; but he's no waster now. She did that, you know; she pulled him through. Why, bless your heart, Mrs. Devereux, he used to rave about her—rave, and chuck himself about on sofas, and cry like anything, and bite his nails down. There never was such a girl under heaven, he used to say. He called her a goddess. Love! Oh, Lord! And I assure you, on my solemn oath, that he never did a better day's work in his life, nor any girl a finer, than when he put in his word for himself, poor devil, and she said, 'Yes, I'll do it.'"

"Did she—" Mrs. Devereux asked, or began to ask, and he shrugged, and exclaimed,

"Ah! There you have me. Now you've done it. I don't know. That's the fact—I don't know. Everybody thought so. She went on as if she did; but now,—no, I don't know. You see, she's such a cool hand, she's such a deep one—you can't tell. There's no telling with that sort. All I can say is, it looked uncommonly like the real thing. We all thought so at the time. The symptoms were right enough—or wrong enough, you'll say—and then, look at her since! She's stuck to him through everything—good report, bad report, everything. She's chucked her people—or been chucked. Had four beautiful sisters—glowing, upstanding, fine girls, all of them; and chucked. Old father, in the City: chucked. Mother, big, handsome, hot-tempered: chucked. And all for Nevile, who (between ourselves) ain't worth it. He's not a bad one, but he's not a good one, either. He's got a cruel temper, Nevile has—like that ghastly wife of his. But—" he cried, opening his arms—"there you are. They're like that, her sort. Mighty quiet about it, you know; was turned into the streets, you may say; father, mother, sisters, all showed their backs. What does she do? Sets her teeth together, looks straight ahead, and takes old Nevile. And here she is now oh, as—right as rain. What a girl, eh?"

Mrs. Devereux was certainly moved. She was almost prepared to admit a genuinely exceptional case. But she had a question to ask. Did Ingram intend to marry her—now?

At this Chevenix stepped back, as if to avoid a blow. "Ah!" he said. "Ah! That's it. Ask me another."

"Do you mean to say of your friend, and mine," she pursued him, "that he would dare—after all that you tell me—to——"

"No," said Chevenix, in a desperate stew; "no, I don't mean that. I think he would have her this moment—if he could get her. But—the fact is— Well, you know—" and he glanced anxiously at the lady, "I've nothing to go upon, absolutely nothing as yet; but the fact is, I'm not sure whether she would take him, you know—now."

"Is that possible?" was all the lady could find to say, with a throw-up of the hands. "Is that possible?"

"Quite—with Sanchia," said Chevenix. "Through with him, you know—got to the bottom of him— sick of him. I believe he bores her, you know." Mrs. Devereux looked at him, more in sorrow than in anger, and then walked slowly away. Most eloquent comment.

VI

WHATEVER may have been the net result upon
Mrs. Devereux's mind of the explanatory revela-
tions made upon the river bank, two things became clear as day succeeded day. One was that
Miss Percival avoided her, the other that she sought
out Miss Percival. Being entirely unable to suc-
ceed, she did not renounce her now benevolent attitude towards the young lady, but she decided to
leave Wanless.

All that she could do, she did. No wheedling
of Mrs. Wilmot's could draw any further comment
from her, and she said nothing to Ingram either
for or against what she supposed now to be the
desire, the honourable desire of his heart. Oddly
enough, though it was against all her upbringing,
Chevenix had so far succeeded in impressing her
that she rather respected Sanchia the more for
being cool now that rehabilitation was in full sight,
and practically within touch of her hand. Chevenix, in fact, had made her see that Sanchia was a
personality, not merely a pretty woman. You can't
label a girl "unfortunate" if, with the chance of
being most fortunate, she puts her hand to her
chin, and reflects, and says, Hum, shall I? or shall
I not? Short of deliberately knocking at the girl's

door, she would have done anything to exchange views. That she could not do. She found herself waiting about in corridors and halls for Sanchia's possible passage. Once she had marked her down in the garden, flower-basket on arm, scissors in hand. She had been fluttered, positively felt her heart-beats, as she sailed down in pursuit; but then Sanchia, under the brim of her garden hat, must have divined her, for, with a few clear words of direction over her shoulder to the young gardener who was helping her, she had steered smoothly away, and, without running, could not have been caught. The thing was marked, not uncivilly, but quite clearly. What could one do?

Two more days of fine weather and perplexity, and she announced her departure as imminent. We were at Thursday. She must positively leave on Monday. "No more letters to write about my shortcomings," was Ingram's comment upon this intelligence to Mrs. Wilmot apart. "It's a mistake to have people to stay with you who've known you all their lives. They are for ever at their contrasts: why isn't one still a chubby-faced boy, for instance? They see you in an Eton jacket once, and you're printed in it for ever. So you glare by contrast, you hurt, you wound. In other words, you have character, you see, which is dashed inconvenient to a woman who remembers you with none. You upset her calculations—and sometimes she upsets yours. No offence to Mrs. Devereux; but I rather wish she hadn't come."

Mrs. Wilmot, who had no general conversation, thought that they ought to be "nice" to Mrs. Devereux; to which Ingram replied, snarling, that he was always "nice" to her, but that if a woman will spend her time writing letters or disapproving of her host, she can't expect to be happy in such a world as ours. But the worst of Mrs. Devereux, he went on to say, was that she couldn't be happy unless she did disapprove of somebody. Mrs. Wilmot, aware of whom the lady did disapprove, dug holes in the turf, and wondered what she herself ought to do. Supposing Mrs. Devereux went on Monday, ought not she—? Now, she didn't at all want to go just now.

At luncheon Ingram proposed a visit—to certain Sowerbys of Sowerby, and pointedly asked Mrs. Devereux to come. "You like her, you know. It's beyond dispute. So I do hope you'll come. I'll drive you over in the phaeton."

Mrs. Devereux agreed to go. Chevenix said that he should fish. He hated calling—except on Mrs. Devereux, of course. He braved the discerning eyes of the lady, who had already caught him at his fishing.

The phaeton safely away, he found Sanchia, as he had hoped, in the garden. Her gauntlets were on, an apron covered her; she was flushed with the exercise of the hoe. Struan Glyde, silent and intent, worked abreast of her. He had just muttered something or another which had given her

pause. She had her chin on her hands, her hands
on her hoe, while she considered her reply. Then
Chevenix heard her slow, "Yes, I suppose so.
I don't like it at all, but I'm afraid you're right.
We are poor creatures, made to be underneath."

The cheerful youth rubbed his head. "Candid
—what? Where *have* we got to now?"

Glyde had stopped in the act to hoe: he was
stopping still, his blade in the ground, but he turned
his face sideways to answer her. "Not so," he
said, "unless you will have it so. She is queen of
the world who is queen of herself." Then Sanchia
saw Chevenix, and waited for him.

"Philosophy—what?" the cheerful youth hailed
them. "Plain living, hard thinking, what? Upon
my soul, you are a pair! Now, Miss Sancie, I can
expect the truth from you. What's Glyde preach-
ing? Heresy? Schism? Sudden death?"

"He was talking about women," Sanchia told
him.

"Ah," the youth mused aloud. "He was, was
he? Glyde on Woman. He ought to wait for his
beard to grow; then you might listen to him."

Glyde, who was dumb in company, was hacking
into the clods, while Chevenix, to whom he was
negligible, pursued his own affair.

"I say, Sancie, I'm going to ask a favour of
you—not the first, by any means; but I always
was a sturdy beggar. The Lord loveth a sturdy
beggar, eh? Well, look here, I'm at a loose end
again. Nevile's taken 'em out driving—to a tea-

party—to the Sowerbys. I jibbed, though I was asked. I lied, because they drove me into a corner. I couldn't face old Sowerby's chin—and all those gels with their embroidered curates—what? You know what I mean. I mean their churchwork, and the curates they do it for. So I said I was going fishing—which was a lie—and Mrs. Devereux as good as said it was a lie. Now, suppose you invite me to tea; how would that be?"

"Then you *do* go fishing," said Sanchia, and smiled. "Very well. I do invite you."

"Bravo! You're a true friend. O woman, in our hours of ease . . . ! Trust me for an apposite quotation . . . and new, what? I believe I'm pretty good at quotations. My people used to play a game. You write down a name on a bit of paper; then you fold it down; then a quotation; then another name. That's my vein of gold. Now you have it—the secret's out. I'm coming, you know. I accept. Many thanks. What's your hour?"

"Half-past four," she told him. He bowed, and left her with Glyde. He turned to look at them as he left the walled garden, and saw them near together,—Glyde vehement in his still way of undertones, she listening as she worked.

At half-past four she received him in her room. Though her blouse was of lace and her skirt of green cloth, she looked like a virgin of the Athenian procession. Her clothes flowed about her, clung to her like weed as she swam. As he met her friendly, silent welcome, he expressed her to himself—"By the gods above, you are—without exception—the healthiest—finest—bravest—young woman—that ever made the sun shine in grey weather." Aloud, he made things easy.

"Here's your tea-party, Sancie, dressed in its best, eager for the fray. When I think of old Sowerby taking whisky-pegs while his family has tea and curates, I bless my happy stars that I've got a friend at court—to save me, don't you know, from the wicked man. When the wicked man—what? You know the quotation, I expect. Not one of my best—but give me time."

While she made tea he pried about her room, looking at photographs. He paused here and there as one struck him, and commented aloud. "Old Nevile, with his sour mouth. Looks as if the tongs had nipped him in the act. Why *will* he roll his moustache like that? It's not pretty—shows him like a boar, with his tusks out, don't you think? But he's a good-looking beggar, and knows it. Ah! and there you all are—or, rather, were—all five of you! Philippa, Hawise, Melusine, Vicky, you. What a bevy! I say—" He turned to her. "I met old Vicky, for a minute, the other day. Met her in Bond Street. Sinclair'd got the pip, or something, down at Aldershot. Expensive complaint, seemingly. So she'd come up to see a palmist, or some kind of an expert about him. She spoke of you, of her own accord. I said I was coming down here."

Sanchia's hand at the kettle was steady, but her eyes flickered before they took the veil. "Tell me about Vicky. What did she say—of me?"

Chevenix came to the tea-table and stood by her. "I think Vicky's all right. I do indeed. It seems to me she'd give her ears to see you—simple ears. Sinclair, you'll find, is the trouble. He's the usual airy kind of ass. Makes laws for his womankind, and has 'em kept. Vicky likes it, too."

"I suppose he is like that," Sanchia said, as if it was a curious case. "I have never spoken to him. He was about, of course—but Vicky took him up after—my time." For a moment emotion, like a wet cloud, drifted across her eyes. "I should like to see Vicky again. It's eight years."

Chevenix was anxious. "I do think it could be managed, you know—with tact. I'd do any mortal thing, Sancie—you know I would, but—" He despaired. "Tact! Tact! That's what you want."

Her soft mood chased away. She looked at him full. "I can't use what you call tact with Vicky. That means that I am to grovel." She drove him back to his photographs. He peered into the little print on the wall.

"What have we here? A domestic scene, my hat! You appear to be bathing—well over the knee, anyhow. High-girt Diana, when no man is by. Awfully jolly you look. But he *is* by. Who on earth's this chap?" He peered. Sanchia from her tea-table watched him, in happy muse. He shouted his discovery. "I remember the chap! Now, what on earth was he called? Your casual friend, who lived in a cart and only had three pair of bags. Nohouse—Senhouse! That was the man." He looked with interest at the pair, then at Sanchia. "Mixed bathing—what?"

She laughed. "Yes—we both got wet to the skin. Percy Charnock took it ages ago—oh, ages! Before I was out, or knew Nevile, or anybody except you. It was ten years ago. I must have been eighteen. It was when I was at Gorston with Grace Mauleverer—trying to save water-lilies from drowning in green scum. He—Mr. Senhouse—came along in his cart, and saw me, and lent me his bed for a raft—and worked it himself. That was the first time I ever saw him—" she ended softly in a sigh: "before anything happened."

Chevenix listened, nodding at the photograph. "Wish to heaven, my dear, nothing had ever happened. The less that happens to girls the better for them, I believe. Not but what *this* chap would have been all right. If *he* had happened, now! He was as mad as a hatter, but a real good sort. Did I tell you?" He grew suddenly reminiscent. "I saw him a little more than a year ago—with a pretty woman. Had a talk with him—asked him to come up and have a look at you. It was when Nevile went off on this trip. No, no, I liked old Senhouse. He was a nice-minded chap. Not the kind to eat you up—and take everything you've got as if he had a right to it. No. That's Nevile's line, that is. You wouldn't see Nevile lending you his bed, or risking his life after water-lilies."

Sanchia's eyes were narrow and critical. She peered as if she were trying to find good somewhere in Nevile Ingram. "He'd risk anything to get what he thought were his rights. But not upon a bed for a raft. He'd write to London for the latest thing in coracles. He's very conventional."

"You have to be," said Chevenix with sudden energy. He wheeled round upon her as he spoke. "We all have to be. We go by clockwork. You get the striking all wrong if you play tricks." He resumed the photograph. "By Jove, but that suits you. Child of Nature, what? I suppose you're happiest when you're larking?"

"Mud-larking?" she asked him, laughing and blushing.

"Well, we'll say rampageing; going as you please."

"Yes." She owned to it without hesitation. "I can't be happy, I think, unless I can do just what I like everywhere. It was one of the first things Jack Senhouse ever taught me. He was an anarchist, you know—and I suppose I'm one, too."

"Your gypsy friend?" He jerked his head backwards to the photograph. "By Jove, my dear," he added, "you must have knocked him sideways—even him—when you carried out his little ideas—as you did."

She opened her eyes to a stare. She stared,

rather ruefully. "Yes," she said, "I believe I did. I know I did. He was dreadfully unhappy. He and I were never quite the same after that. But I couldn't help myself. It was before me—it had to be done."

"No, no, no!" cried he vehemently, but checked himself. "Pardon, Sancie. We won't go over all that, but surely you see, now, that it won't do. Now that escapade in the pond, you know. That was all right—with only old Senhouse in the way. You must admit that you were rather *décolletée*, to say the least of it. Now, would you say that you can do those sort of things—go as you please, you know, anywhere?"

"Why not?" Her eyes were straightly at him.

"What! Whether you're seen or not?"

She frowned. "I don't want to know whether I'm seen or not."

"And mostly you don't care?"

"And sometimes I don't care."

"Ah," said Chevenix, "there you are. Your 'sometimes' gives you away."

She changed the subject. "Do have some tea It will be quite cold."

He had been staring again at the photograph— Sanchia's gleaming limbs, the gypsy's intent face shadowed over the water. He now relinquished it with an effort. "Thanks," he said. "I like it cold." He sat beside her, and they talked casually, like old, fast friends, of mutual acquaintance. But for him the air was charged; she was on his conscience. Reminiscences paled and talk died down; he found himself staring at the wall.

He resumed the great affair. "Nevile's rather jumpy, don't you think?"

Her serenity was proof. "Is he? Why should he be?"

"Ah, my dear!" cried the poor young man. "Let's say it's the old Devereux. *Salmo deverox*, eh? Sounds fierce."

Not a flicker. "Mrs. Devereux? What has she been doing to him?"

"Nothing," he said; "and that's just it. She won't have anything to say to him."

Then she went a little too far. A man charged with friendly impulse, charged also with knowledge, must be handled tenderly. You must not be fool-hardy. But here was bravado, nothing less. For she arched her brows, and showed her eyes inno-cently wide. "Oh!" she said, "why? Why won't Mrs. Devereux speak to Nevile?"

"Oh, come, you know." He looked at her keenly. He didn't wink, but he blinked. Then he crossed the room. "Look here, Sancie. Will you let me talk to you—really—as an old friend?"

She looked up into his face, nodded and smiled. "Of course you may say what you like."

He sat by her, collecting himself. "Well, then, what I shall say is just this. The whole thing is in your hands—now. You can put it square. There's absolutely nothing in your way—now— well, now that Claire's gone, you know." He watched her anxiously for a sign, but got none. So still she sat, glooming, watching herself—as on a scene.

"Mind," he said in a new tone. "You know all about me. I jibbed at first when you broke away. I'll own to that. I couldn't do otherwise. Why, old Senhouse himself went half off his head about it. Anything in the world to get you out of it, I'd have done. Any mortal thing, my dear. But there! There was no holding you—off you went! But when once the thing was started—the extraordinary thing was that I was on your side directly. And so I always have been. Ask Vicky —ask your mother. I've done, in my quiet way, what you would never have asked of me. You must forgive me—I've defended you everywhere. I won't mention names, but I've explained your case, only lately, in a rocky quarter—and I know I've made an impression. I'm not much good at talking, as a rule, but I do believe that I put the thing rather well. You make your own laws— eh? Like Napoleon Buonaparte—eh? And some-how—the way you do it—it's all right, eh, Sancie?"

He got nothing from her. She sat on rigid, with unwinking eyes, staring at herself, as she saw her-self on the scene. Chevenix leaned to her.

"And Nevile knows it. He believes it. He would say it anywhere. He's difficult, is Nevile; a wayward beggar. He's been his own master since he was sixteen; asked, and had. It's hard to make him understand that he can't go on. But

he can't, the old sweep, when you put in your say.
You know his way—he puts his desires in the
shape of truisms. He states them—that's all he
has to do—they become immutable laws. Very
imposing, his desires, put like that. They've imposed upon me; they've imposed upon *you* in their
day. Well, with a man like that, you know, you
can't take him up too short. Go slow, go slow.
What was it I heard Glyde saying to you just now?
Who's queen of herself is queen of the world—
what? Now, that's quite true. One for Glyde.
Apply that to old Nevile. Queen of herself! Why,
what else are you? And what's Nevile but the
blundering world in a man's skin? Well, queen it,
queen it—and there's your kingdom under your
feet. Marry the old chap, Sancie. You put everything right; you take your proper place. The
county! But what are counties to you? You
smile—and you may well smile. Let the county
go hang; but there's Vicky. She's more than
county to you. There's Melusine, there's Philippa,
there's Hawise; there's your good old dad, there's
your lady mother. You get 'em all. And Nevile's
biting his nails for it. And a free man. Come
now."

She had listened, that's certain; she hadn't been
displeased. He had seen her eyes grow dreamy,
he had marked her rising breast. Rising and falling,
rising and falling, like lilies swayed by flowing water.
That betokened no storm, nor flood; that meant the
stirring of the still deeps, not by violent access, but by

He had eloquence, he thought, as he watched her, he had won.
But he was anxious. She was such a deep one.

slow-moving, slow-gathered, inborn forces. Had he had eloquence, he thought, as he watched her, he had won. But he was anxious. She was such a deep one.

When she spoke there sounded to be a tinge of weariness in her voice; she dragged her sentences, as if she foresaw her own acts, and was tired in advance. She seemed almost to be pitying her fate. At first she looked down at her hands in her lap, at her fingers idly interweaving; but midway of her drawn-out soliloquy—for she seemed to be talking to herself—she turned him her eyes, and he plumbed their depths in vain.

"It's very nice of you to be interested in me. You are much more interested than I am—and it's a compliment, a great compliment. I think you are very loyal—if I can call it loyalty—if you'll let me call it that. I like my work here; I'm perfectly happy doing it. It was hard at first. I knew absolutely nothing of housekeeping and managing things when I came here. I had to work —to learn book-keeping and accounts—cooking— building — carpentering — stock-raising—oh, everything. I had to feel that I knew very nearly as much about everything as the people who were to do what I told them. And of course that was quite true; but it wasn't at all easy. It has taken me eight years to get as far as I am now. And I could go on for years more. There's nobody on the place whom I can't manage: they all like me. I'm quite comfortable—if I can be let alone."

. . . Speaking so, she believed it. But, thinking it over she was driven to explain herself.

"People seem to think that girls—that women —care for nothing but one thing—being married, I mean. I'm sure that's a mistake. One gets interested, one may get absorbed—and then there's a difficulty. For it's very true, I think, that unless we care for the one thing, and that thing only, we don't care for it at all. At least, that is how I feel about it. I have got lots of interests in life—all these things here—management of things. I don't want Nevile—or to be married. I don't want anything of the sort; I can't be bothered. I cared once—frightfully; but now I don't care. All that was long ago; at the beginning—eight years ago. Now it's done with, I only want to be let alone— to do my work here. It doesn't seem to me much to ask; but——" . . .

It was then that she looked at him, and was beyond the power of his sounding. She grew vehement, full of still, passionless rage. She was like a goddess pronouncing a decree; she was final.

"I don't want to marry Nevile. It bores me. And he doesn't want me, really. He thinks he does, because he thinks that he can't have me any other way. But he would be miserable, and so should I. It seems to me impossible. You can't put life into dead things. When he came back here the other day he had been away a year: a year and ten days. He had written to me twice——"

Chevenix interrupted. "Excuse me," he said. "How many times had you written to him?" He had guessed at pique; but he was wrong.

She replied slowly. "I forwarded his letters. I hadn't written at all." Her simplicity! Chevenix allowed her to go on.

"The thing—all that it began with—was over. I felt that. I showed him that the first evening he was here. He has never spoken to me again— of that sort of thing, and I don't think he ever will. He doesn't understand being refused any- thing. I suppose he never has been before in his life."

"Weren't you, perhaps, a little bit short?" he hazarded; and she considered the possibility.

"No, I don't think so. I wasn't more abrupt than he was—after a year." She paused. "He threw out her death—Mrs. Ingram's death—" she forced herself to the name—"quite casually, as if he had been saying, 'By-the-by, the Rector's coming to dine.' If he had wanted me, do you think he would have put it like that?"

"Nevile," said Chevenix, "would put anything —like anything. He's that sort, you know. He'd take for granted that you understood lots of things which he couldn't express. But I will say this for Nevile. He's not petty. He's fairly large- minded. For instance, I'll bet you what you like he didn't mind your not writing to him—or reproach you with it."

She opened her eyes. "Of course he didn't.

He was perfectly happy. He told me he had been idiotically happy. He knew I was here, because I forwarded his letters—and that was all he cared about. I was here for—when he chose. I assure you he didn't want me at all until I showed him that he couldn't have me."

"But he did, you know," said Chevenix; "he does. He was sure of you all through, from the beginning, as you say. That's why he didn't write or expect letters from you. He flattered himself that he was secure. Poor old Nevile!" He felt sorry now for Ingram. She was really adamantine.

She arose, with matches in her hand, knelt before the fire and kindled it. She blew into it with her mouth, and watched the climbing flames. "I don't think you need pity Nevile, really," she said. "He will always be happy. But I am going to be made unhappy." She proclaimed her fate as a fact in which she had no concern at all. Chevenix rose and paced the room.

"Well, you know—I must be allowed to say— your happiness is so entirely in your own hands. It's difficult—I've no right to suggest—to interfere in any way. I'm nothing at all, of course——"

"You are my friend, I hope," she said, watching the young fire—still on her knees before it, worshipping it, as it seemed. Chevenix expanded his chest.

"You make me very proud. I thank you for that. Yes, I am your friend. That's why I risk your friendship by asking you something. You won't answer me unless you choose, of course. But—come now, Sancie, is there, might there be— somebody else?"

She looked round at him from where she knelt. Her hands were opened to the fire; her face was warmed by its glow; it was the pure face of a seraph. "No. There's nobody at all—now."

He was again standing before the little photograph of the nymph thigh-deep in water. That seemed to attract him; but he heard her "now," and started. "I take your word for it, absolutely. But, seeing what you felt for Nevile in the beginning, I should have thought—in any ordinary case —there must have been a tender spot—unless, of course, you had changed your mind—for reasons——"

She got up from her knees, and stood, leaning by the mantelpiece. Her low voice stirred him strangely.

"There are reasons. The spot, as you call it, is so tender that it's raw."

"Good Lord," said Chevenix. "What do you mean?"

She was full of her reasons, evidently. Rumours of them, so to say, drove over her eyes, showed cloudily and angrily there. Her beautiful mouth looked cruel—as if she saw death and took joy in it. "I think he is horrible," she said. "I think he is like a beast. He doesn't love me at all until he comes here—and then he expects me—Oh, don't ask me to talk about it." She stopped her tongue,

but not her thought. That thronged the gates of
her lips. She hesitated, fighting the entry; but the
words came, shocked and dreadful. "He wants
me, to ravage me—like a beast."

Chevenix began to stammer. "Oh, I say, you
mustn't—Oh, don't talk like that——"

The door opened, and Ingram came in.

He looked from one to the other, sharply. "Hulloa," he said. "What are you two about in
here?"

Sanchia looked at the fire, and put her foot close
to it, to be warmed. "Tea-party," said Chevenix.
"That's it, Nevile." He nodded sagely at his
host, and saw his brow clear. Ingram shut the
door and came into the room, to a chair. "That's
all right," he said. "I hope it was a livelier one
than mine. That old Devereux was on her high-
stepper. I'm sick of being trampled. I thought,
though, that you had been having words. You
looked like it."

Sanchia said, smiling in her queer way, "Oh,
dear no. Mr. Chevenix is much too kind for that.
He's been talking very nicely to me. He's been
charming."

"Oh, come, Sancie—" cried the brisk young man,
quite recovered.

Ingram, in a stare, said, "Yes, Sancie, you may
trust him. He's a friend of ours."

"I do trust him," she said.

Chevenix said, "I shall go out on that. I declare
my innings. Good-bye, you two. I'll go and pacify

the Devereux." He hoped against hope that he might have warmed her.

Ingram, when they were alone, threw himself back in his chair, crossed one leg, and clasped the thin ankle of it. He had finely-made, narrow feet, and was proud of his ankles. Sanchia was now again kneeling before the fire.

"Quite right to have a fire," he said. "It's falling in cold. There'll be a frost. What was Chevenix saying about me?"

She had been prepared. "Nothing but good. He's your friend, as you said."

"I said 'our friend,' my dear."

She looked at him. "Yes, certainly. He's my friend, too."

"I hope he'll prove so. Upon my soul, I do." He remained silent for a time. Then he leaned forward suddenly, and held out his arms.

"Oh, Sancie," he said, his voice trembling. "Love me."

She looked at him with wide, searching, earnest eyes. They seemed to search, not him, but her own soul. They explored the void, seeking for a sign, a vestige, a wreck; but found nothing.

"I can't," she said. Her voice was frayed. "The thing is quite dead."

Ingram flushed deeply, but sat on, biting his lip, frowning, staring at the young, mounting fire, which she, stooping over it, cherished with her breath and quick hands.

VII

Ingram, at supper in his private room, had his elbows on the table, and spoke between his fists to Chevenix, let into these mysteries for the first time.

"I ought not to complain, you'll say, and in my heart of hearts I don't, because I'm a reasonable man, and know that you don't make a row about sunstroke or lightning-shocks. We call 'em the Act of God, and rule 'em out in insurance offices. No, no, I see what I've let myself in for. I've been away too much; she's got sick of it. I shall have to work at it—to bring her round. By God, and she's worth it. She's a wonder."

"Pity," said Chevenix, "you've only just found it out."

Ingram frowned, and waxing in rage, stared at his friend as if he had never known him. "You don't know what you're talking about. Why, she adored me. I was never more in love with a woman in my life than I was with Sancie."

Chevenix tilted back his chair. "Oh, you had it pretty badly—at the time. The trouble with you is that you are such a chap for accepting things. You're like a hall-porter in a Swiss hotel. You take things for granted. Do nothing—hold out your hand—and get your perks. Perks! Why, they ain't perks at all. They're bounty—what you get from a girl like Sancie."

All this Ingram took as his due—as due, that is, to a man of passion and reasonable desires. He fell into a reverie. "Yes, yes, I know. She was devilish fond of me."

Chevenix gritted his teeth, but Ingram went on. "It was a false position, I know, and I never ought to have looked at her twice. But she was awfully queer or awfully deep—one never knew which. Why, when we got thick together—always meeting out, always reading poetry and philosophy —Shelley, Dante, Keats (I forget half their names now)—I take my oath I hadn't a suspicion that she was getting to like me, in that sort of way, as we call it. She made all the difference in the world to me, I can tell you. You know what I was doing after Claire bolted with that swine: killing time and killing myself—that's what I was doing. It was like going into church out of the sun to hear her at her poetry, and see her. Oh, a lovely girl she was!"

"She's a lovelier woman than you and I are fit to look at," said Chevenix, "if you ask me."

"Damn you, I know all about that. D'you think I want telling, now that I can't get her? Well, then I found out what was the matter with me—and then we cleared the air."

"Who had stuffed it up to begin with?" Chevenix murmured; but Ingram ignored him.

"I told her the whole thing——"

"After she had found it out!" cried Chevenix with energy. "Let's have cards on the table. I told Vicky all about it at a dance—and Vicky told her."

"I told her," Ingram said, "that I was in love with her, and promised to behave—and so I should have, only——"

"Only you didn't, old chap."

"She loved me—there was no stopping it then. The thing was done. Mind you, her people knew it all, too."

"The mother always was a fool," Chevenix agreed. "And she liked you."

"I know she did. I took care of that."

"Not a bit of it, my boy," the other objected. "That's just what you didn't do. She liked you because she thought you didn't care a curse whether she liked you or not."

Ingram raised his eyebrows at such *naïveté*. "That's what I mean, of course. So it went on all that summer. We used to shake when we met each other, and be speechless. By heavens, what a time that was! Do you remember the tea-party?"

Chevenix blinked. "I wasn't there; but I remember what happened afterwards. The poor child —as white as a sheet—and every hand lifted against her. By God, Nevile, what girls—mere chits—will go through!"

"I know," said Ingram dreamily. "Isn't it awful?" Chevenix looked at him. He was quite serious. What can you do with such a man as this?

"They left us alone in the room, you know," Ingram continued. "Vicky went out last and left us in there—and the whole place was charged with electricity. You could feel it, smell it, hear it crackling all about. My heart going like a drum; my ears buzzing with it all. I hadn't been able to speak when they spoke to me. I don't know what the devil they must have thought of me—and I didn't care a damn. And over across the tea-table, on a low chair—there she sat—my girl! Her eyes downcast, her mouth adroop." He shut his eyes for a moment. "And Vicky went out, and left us there!"

"You had it badly, old chap," Chevenix said. "Go slow. Take your time. Or chuck it, if you'd rather."

Ingram appeared not to hear him; he was staring at the tablecloth, at his two hands locked in front of him, and at his knuckles white under the strain.

"I don't know how long I stood gaping at the window, I don't indeed. I could feel her sitting shaking in her chair; but neither of us said anything. Somebody came to take the tea out—and then I turned and looked at her; and she turned and looked at me. Something drew me—set me on the move. It was all over with me then. I went straight across the room to her; I stood above her, I stooped and took her hands. I don't know what I said: she looked at me all the time in a strange, clear way. She got up—I was beside her, and took her. Not a word said. I had her lips. Honey of flowers! Her soul came forth from them: new wine. Oh, God! I thought so, anyhow. And so did she. Chevenix, she meant giving."

Chevenix nodded shortly. He believed that. Ingram had covered his eyes.

He drained a glass before he went on with his account. "I suppose you know the rest as well as I do. I never had the details out of her. One of them—that Mrs. King—Philippa, it was—came slam into the room; and what was there to do? I stuck it as long as I could—until I was practically kicked out. The mother came back and turned me out. I had to leave her to brave them all—and I never saw her again until I found out where she was in London."

"Don't you trouble to tell me all that part," said Chevenix frowning at him. "I know more about that than you do. I was in it. My head, how they treated her! What I never did understand, you know, was how you found out where she was."

Ingram smiled. His memories now amused him. He looked straight at his friend. "I'll tell you that. It was rather neat. You remember that chap Senhouse—loafing kind of artist? Anarchist, gypsy-looking chap, who wore no hat?"

Chevenix opened his eyes. "By George, I do!"

Ingram nodded. "She thought no end of him. He took her affair with me very much to heart."

"As well he might," said Chevenix. "I fancy that you were the only person who took it easy."

"Sancie used to tell him everything," Ingram went on, "and she told him all the trouble. She'd been turned adrift with fifty pounds to her name."

"Not quite so bad as that," Chevenix put in. "They locked her up with an aunt, and she bolted."

"Same thing," said Ingram. "Well, this chap Senhouse comes here one day in a mighty hurry— turns up at breakfast, and makes a row. Wants me to swear I'll divorce and marry Sancie. Says he thinks I'm a blackguard and all that, but that, on the whole, I'd better marry her. Refuses to give me her address, all the same. We had a row, I remember, because he began to tell me what he thought about her. The man was a bore, you know."

Chevenix screwed up one leg. "All men are, if they're sweet on your sweetheart, I suppose. He was worth fifty of you, all the same—but go on."

Ingram laughed. "I set my wits against his," he said, "and found out that he'd come straight from seeing her—in London. That was good enough for me. I got rid of Master Senhouse, and went off to town. He had no promises out of *me*, you may believe."

Chevenix felt very sick, and looked it. "The less you say about your promises, my good chap, the better I'll take it." But Ingram by now had got back to his holier reminiscences:—

"I hunted for her high and low for three months—advertised, turned on detectives, I had even dared her friends' eyes and their cold shoulders—couldn't hear anything. . . . I was walking in hell for three months. . . .

"Then, one day, I met her—in Chancery Lane. Of all squalid places on earth—there. . . .

"I'd been to my lawyer's, in Lincoln's Inn. I'd settled money on her—in case anything happened to me while I was abroad. I was going to travel, because I'd given it up. And then I met her. Chancery Lane!

"I was passing some school or another—Commercial Academy—book-keeping, shorthand, type-writing—that sort of place; a lot of ogling, giggling girls, and boys after 'em, came tumbling down the steps—all sun-bonnets and fluffy hair; and down the steps she came, too—Sanchia came—like a princess. She was in white, my dear man—as fresh and dainty as a rose, I remember. Daisies round a broad-brimmed straw: some books under her arm. The sun was on her, lit the gold in her hair. She looked neither right nor left, spoke to no one, had no one with her, or after her. She was never showy. You had to know her well to see how lovely she was. She never showed off well, and was always silent in company. Oh, but what a girl!

"When she saw me she flushed all over, and stood. She stood on the last step, and looked at me. Looked at me straight, as if she waited. I went directly to her, and took her hand. She let me. I couldn't speak sense. I said, 'You!' and she said, 'I knew I should see you like this.' It sounded all right. I never questioned it." . . . He stared, then broke out. "Good God, Bill! To think of her then—and to see her now! She won't look at me! I don't exist." He plunged his face between his hands, and rocked himself about. Chevenix watched him without a word. Suddenly he lifted his pinched face, and complained bitterly.

"I can't understand it—I don't know what's changed her. Why, it's awful to make a chap suffer like this!" He stared about him. "Why, Bill," he said, hushing down his voice, "is she going to drop me, d'you think—let me go to the devil?"

Chevenix rose and stood with his back to the fire. "I'll trouble you not to whine, Nevile; I've got something to say to all this tale of yours. I've got to ask you a thing or two. When you found her, now; and when you knew all that she'd gone through—a child like that! You brought her up here—hey?"

Without shifting his head to face his cross-examination, Ingram answered between his hands—"No, I didn't. She wouldn't budge from her school till she'd finished her course. I courted her for a month. It took me all that to make her listen to reason."

"Reason!" Chevenix rated him. "You call it reason!"

"It was what *she* called it—not I," said Ingram from between his fists. Then he looked up. "She refused the idea of going abroad. Said she wasn't at all afraid of people talking. Said she wanted to work for me. Must be doing something, she said. I tell you, it was her idea from the beginning. And I do say, myself, that it was reasonable." He searched for agreement in his friend's face, but got none. "It suited better," he said presently, with indifference. "It suited better—in every way. I had to be here."

"Why had you to be here, man?" Chevenix raised his voice. "What the devil did it matter to you, having her, where you were?"

"It mattered a lot. I like this place. It's mine. I've got duties up here. I'm a magistrate and all that."

Chevenix was now very hot. "Magistrate be damned. Do you mean to tell me that you profess to love a woman, and turn her into a servant because you want to try poachers? And you talk about the sun in her hair! And then—upon my soul, Ingram, you sicken me."

"You fool," said Ingram. "I tell you it was her own idea. She loves the place. She loves it a lot more than she does me. It's been a continual joy to her. Why, where would she have been while I was in India—all that year—if she hadn't had all this in her hands? You don't know what you're talking about."

His voice rang down his scorn. Chevenix began to stammer.

"You're hopeless, Nevile, utterly hopeless. Every

word you say gives up your case. What's it to
do with you whether she likes it or not? I'm
not talking of her, but of you. You silly ass, don't
you see where you are? You fall in love with a
woman and make her your head housemaid. Then
you say, Oh, but she likes it. It's not what she
likes we're talking about; it's what you can bring
yourself to do with her. Wait a bit now. There's
more to it. You play about here, there, and all
over the shop. Off you go for three months at a
time, sky-larking, shooting antelope, pigeon-shooting,
polo, and whatever. She sits here and minds the
gardeners—she whom you saw with the sun in her
hair! Year in, year out it goes on. Now here you
are back from India. Good. You leave her for
a year, and write to her twice—then you say, Why,
where would she have been if she hadn't had something to do? The sun in her hair, hey? Love, my
good chap! You don't know how to spell the word.
You ought not to touch her shoe-string. You're not
fit. By Gad, sir, and now I remember something!
And it's the truth, it's the bitter, naked, grinning
truth." He did remember something. He saw her
curled-back lip—he saw her fierce resentful eyes.
He heard her say it: "I think he is like a beast.
He wants to ravage me—like a beast." "You've
been judged, Nevile," he said. "You've done for
yourself. And now I'll go to bed."

Ingram's face was very cloudy. He looked for
a moment like quarrelling. "Do you mean to leave
me like this?" he asked.

"Yes," said Chevenix, "I do. I don't want to stop and hear you protest that you intend to marry her. Marry her! Why, man, if you'd meant to marry her, you'd have posted home express from Marseilles the moment you heard that you could do it. But no! You've got her there—in cap and apron—she'll keep. You know she's here— you have your fling. And you stop three days in Paris, and drop it to her casually, when you please, that you're a free man. Yes, by George, I do mean to leave you like this. You're best alone, by George. Good-night to you."

He went smartly away; but he had worked himself into a shaking fit, could not have slept to save his life. A cigar at the open window was inevitable.

He leaned far into the night. It was densely dark, and had been raining. Soft scud drifted over his face; clouds in loose solution drenched the earth. He smoked fiercely, inhaling great draughts and driving them out into the fog. Being no thinker, his sensations took no body, but he broke out now and again with pishes and pshaws, or scornfully—"Old Nevile—hungry devil, what? Stalking about like a beast. Oh, she was right, she was right. Pish! And there's an end of it."

He was aware of softly moving feet below—a measured tread. He listened and heard them beyond dispute. "Nevile!" he said, "like a beast, padding about his place." He listened on, grimly amused. Let him pad and rage.

But he was to be startled. A voice hailed him, not Ingram's. "Beg your pardon, sir."

"Hulloa!" he cried. "Who are you, my man?"

"Glyde, sir. Is all well?"

"What do you mean, Glyde? What are you doing?"

"I was passing, sir, to my houses. I heard voices, and I wondered——"

"Oh!" he laughed. "You thought there was a scrap, did you? It's all right, Glyde. I and the master were having a talk. Nothing for you to worry about. I shared his lonely meal. Don't you be disturbed."

"No, no, sir. Thank you, sir."

Chevenix called to him when he was at some distance. "I say, Glyde."

"Yes, sir?"

"You can go to bed. It's all right."

"Thank you, sir. Good-night."

He chuckled as he undressed. "Rum fish, Glyde. Watch and ward, what? Watching his shield. Bless her, she's got friends, then." He considered for a while, flicking the glowing end of his cigar. "That chap—Senhouse—Jack Senhouse. I wonder what's become of him."

VIII

THE discrepancies of an unfortunate party caused
no disturbance to the staff of Wanless Hall. Sanchia,
whatever her private cares—and they seemed less
than those of other people on her account—suffered
nothing to interfere with her housekeeping. Ingram
might rage for her in vain, Chevenix agonise, or
quarrel with his host and friend, Mrs. Devereux disapprove to the point of keeping her room; but Sanchia, with front serene, moved from office-table to
kitchen, to the garden, to the home-farm, inter-
viewed Mrs. Benson, consulted with the stockman,
pored—her head close to Glyde's—over seed-pans
and melon borders, was keenly interested, judicial,
reflective, pleading, coaxing by turns—seemed, in
fact, not to have a perplexity in her fair head. Her
health was superb, she never had an ache nor failed
of an appetite. To see her sitting in the stable-yard
on a sunny morning, her lap full of nozzling fox-
hound pups, was to have a vision of Artemis Eile-
ithyia. So, it seemed, the grave mother-hound, erect
on haunches, with wise ears, and sidelong eyes
showing the white, knew her certainly to be. Beside
and over her stood Frodsham of the stables, and his
underlings, firmly her friends.

She looked up, beaming. "Oh, Frodsham; aren't they sweet? One of them tries to suck my finger. What are you going to call them? I do hope you mean to keep them all."

"I doubt they're too many for the old bitch, Miss Percival. She'll not feed the lot of them. We'll be wise to duck the latest cast."

"Oh, no,—please. I'll feed it—I will, really. I couldn't let you drown it. Now, what are their names to be?"

"There's Melpomeen, Miss Percival, and Melody, and Melchior, and Melchizedek. That's for the bitches."

She quizzed him. "No, Frodsham, really that won't do. I'm not quite sure about Melchizedek; but Melchior was a man—he was a king—a king of the East. And I believe Melchizedek was an angel."

Frodsham rubbed his chin. "May be you are right, Miss Percival. An angel, was he now? Wings to him? 'Tis a name for a bird, then. If we kept the hawks the old Squire used to love— there's a name for a peregrine! Melchizedek—a fair mouthful."

"A Priest for ever," mused Jacobs, a wizened elder, the kennel man, who yet bowed to the coachman in his own yard. "We may put him among the dogs, I believe. We've Proteus, and Prophet; but no Priest."

Frodsham looked to Sanchia for direction, ignoring Jacobs. She flashed him a name. "Melisande, Frodsham. Call her Melisande, and save

her life; and she shall be mine. I'll look after her.
Please do." He owned to the spell of her eyes, of
the sun upon her hair. "Melisande she shall be,
Miss Percival, and your own," he said. "The
Missus shall rear her if the old bitch won't. She's
had six of her own, and knows what it is."

Regretfully, one by one, she put the striving
blind things down; then rose and went her way
into the gardens about the house. Slowly through
the kitchen gardens she passed. Glyde, thinning
walled peach-trees, saw her, felt her go. She shed
her benediction upon him—"Good morning, Struan,"
—and went on. He watched her for a while, then
turned fiercely to his affair. Through dense shrubberies, over drenched lawns her way was; it led
her to the lily-pond, which lay hidden within rhodo-
dendron walls, with a narrow cincture of grass path
all about it. Dark-brown, still and translucent like
an onyx it lay before her. It was her haunt of
election when she was troubled, as now she was,
when she gave herself time to remember it.

She stood, her hands clasped before her, close
to the water's brim, and looked over the shining
surface. She had never yet squarely faced her
difficulties. Her sceptre was slipping from her;
her realm, usurped at first, hers by sufferance
first, but then by love of them she ruled, could
hold her but a little while more. The shadow of
coming eclipse made her eyes grow sombre. Doubt
of the unknown made lax her lips.

If Nevile's wife, with all her sins clotted on her,

was dead, what was she herself going to do, or allow
to be done? She had yielded to love—her first love
and her last; but that had been long ago. Love,
the fire, the trembling and the music in her heart;
pride, the trust, the loyalty, the bliss of service;
the wonder, the swooning, the glory like a sun
upon her—all gone, burned out, or worked out.
Why, how long had it lasted her? Her lips stretched
to a bleak smile to think of it. Three months joy
in herself, three months joy of him; then work,
incessant and absorbing; and then the growth of
a new pride, the pride of mind (for she found that
she had a brain), and of a new love—for she found
that she loved the creatures more than man. Education indeed! To draw from a child caught unawares the force and the brooding love of an Earth-
Goddess.

In the beginning, she could have told herself
(but never did), she was to be pitied, not blamed.
Reticent among her free-speaking sisters, shy, what
the maids call "a deep one," rarely a talker, keeping
always her own counsel, she had first been moved
to utter herself by the extreme carelessness of
Ingram whether she did so or not. The blame—
if it is to be laid—must be upon her mother when
she, knowing Ingram's story of miserable marriage
and separation, allowed the man to continue a
friend of the house, be much with her girl, and
unfold himself under her clear young eyes. What
she was about—that masterful, self-absorbed woman

—there's no saying. It was always supposed that, with five beautiful daughters to market, she had pushed Welbore Percival—Thomas Welbore Percival, East India merchant of The Poultry—into lavish entertainment of his friends and acquaintance. Ingram, a squire and son of squires, was perhaps a shade above her degree; she may have required him to give a tone. This, considering that wretched marriage of his—a month's engagement in defiance of head-shaking, a blazing Hanover Square wedding, a year's bickering, one month's acrimony (done by letter) and Ingram's unquenchable hatred of the woman—this, I say, you may well doubt. But I can give no other explanation. He came, he talked in his high-voiced, querulous, bitter-humoured way, he saw and sought the grave young Sanchia, and he won her pitying heart directly he had engrossed her watching eyes.

She was a girl intensely interested in a hundred dawning things, to whom love had come late. Until she was near twenty you would have thought her sexless. Senhouse, her poetical friend and teacher —her only friend, her only confidant—had dubbed her Artemis; and it may well have been his adoring service of her pure flame which first turned it inwards, to scorch her heart. All that she had learned of this scholar gypsy she poured out as balm over the stricken Ingram, who swallowed it and her together. Then the truth about him was blared upon her suddenly, and she found that he was to be pitied. Guileless victim of a hateful woman as she believed him then, she found that she held a store of balm. She pitied him deeply, she opened, she poured out her treasure. Enthusiasm for the saving work captained her thereafter; nothing would turn her from her purpose. Ingram was to be saved by love: she gave him all.

To do him justice, a young man born to possess and command, he did his best to repair what was beyond repair. He told her the truth unasked by her; he confessed that he loved her, and owned that he had no business to do it. Nearness, circumstance, brooding on that which was true of both of them and must not be uttered by either, did the rest. Upon that evening in the drawing-room when they found themselves alone, each trembling under the god, they simply drifted together, and without effort to resist, mingled their natures through the lips. Discovery, earthquake and eclipse, her mother's chill rage, her father's tears, her sisters' dismay; all this and more she endured. She passioned like a young martyr. She admitted the facts without comment, and accepted the consequences without a falter. They might have whelmed a greater heart than hers; turned on to the town as she was to all intent, at two-and-twenty, a girl with the face and figure of a goddess, with fifty pounds between her and the devil. They might have sent her, at the least, weeping and trembling into Ingram's arms. But they did not. She was of finer clay. She took a lodging in Pimlico, and, to fit herself for employment, went to school. The commercial course which she chose was the shortest possible, but all that she felt she could afford. "My dear young lady, we can only promise you a smattering—really no more for the money." "It must start me," said Sanchia, and began. There was a month more to run when Ingram found her, and, glad as she was of him, doting and doted upon, in the first flood of youth and love, she persisted in it, finished it out, and got her diploma for what it was worth, before, as he put it, she would listen to reason.

It sounded extremely reasonable to him what he then proposed; and also to her, though Chevenix scorned its propounder. As Ingram put it to her, it attracted her newborn pride of knowledge. She was to flesh her steel, so to speak, in reality: in plainer words, she, with her smattering of accounts, was to manage a great house, an army of servants, possibly an estate. Excessively in love as she was, with all the music of it in her untried ears, she knew already in herself that her mind must have other food than her heart's rapture. I think, indeed, that she would have declined him altogether if he had proposed nothing more tangible to her than perpetual honeymoon. That was what Senhouse would certainly have proposed to her—she saw that in every look of his, and read it in every line he sent her; but that had never attracted her. She had given Senhouse her confidence, but not her heart. Ingram's proposals, therefore, pleased her. She had not a sweet enough tooth, nor the taste for flattery which the other involved. She was entirely without vanity. Therefore, however little honourable and however much a lover of his ease Ingram may have shown himself in making them, his reasonable proposals were gratefully received. It was he who suggested, but she who took the lead. She began immediately to plan her new career—was perfectly business-like. Ingram was to leave London at once, and go to Wanless—to his duties of the bench, his delights of the field, cares of the farm. He was to announce to his household his intention of "settling down"; and he was to announce the advent of a housekeeper. In this very outset of his bliss he must needs do as she bade him. He went, and made her ways as smooth as they could be made. Her rooms were assigned to her; her duties mapped out, the exact range of her authority. Her wages were fixed, to be paid quarterly. She would take nothing else from him—no jewellery (she wore nothing but simple things, which had been given her by her parents or sisters—amber, a string of cowries, an agate heart, a bangle or two), no frocks. She was to have two hundred a year, and throughout her time to this present she had no more, and kept herself exquisitely upon it, with a sense of what was due to him, to herself, and to her position, which was admirable, unhesitating, and never at fault. In due time she arrived and entered upon her career. That which was unlawful seemed now justified; the secret intimacy, the wedded amity, the giving, which was the dearest gain she had. Discretion, on her side unsleeping, on his the more effective because he never seemed to have any, secured them. There was no open scandal among the neighbours; whatever the household may have suspected, very little was said. Within a year her servants were her slaves. The Rector, it is true, reproached her for not going to church. She deprecated his indignation, but didn't go.

Up to the day when we first met with her, her garden-hat in her hand, reading her telegram by the garden window, she had been eight years governor of Wanless—and for nearly two of those years alone. For the first two or three of them Ingram, revelling in his snug ease, with little to do but devise things—alterations, extensions, ventures into farming, and the like, which it was her delight to execute— never left the county, hardly cared to leave the estate. He entertained very sparingly: Chevenix came once or twice, his own brother, Maxwell Ingram; there were some other dinner-parties to the countryside, hunt-breakfasts, once a hunt-ball, at none of which ceremonies did she appear. He endured these wearinesses, shrugging them away as soon as he could, to hasten from a dinner of dry toast and knives and forks to his room—the Master's room—where supper, Sanchia, sweet intimacy awaited him. He spent thus by far the cleanliest and most sane years of his wayward life. She soothed, amused, stimulated him at once. He taught her all he knew of country-lore, gave her, as they say, "the hang" of landed estate; he learned by teaching, and might have become a wholesome gentleman.

But domestic business called him to London presently. He went, and was away three months, with lawyers, fierce threatenings from Claire, intermediaries, friends of both parties, and the rest of them. He was worried, flurried, put into a rage; exploded, put himself a thousand times in the wrong; finally, he came back to Wanless embittered and restless. He came back to find himself welcome, but not excessively so. At least he thought not. His extensions, suggested in that first wonderful time—a range of glass-houses, new heating apparatus, acetylene gas installations, were well advanced. Sanchia's brows were often knit over estimates, specifications, and bills. He had to pay for novelties from which the salt had evaporated; he he was never very fond of paying, and now, it seemed, he wasn't very fond of what he had to pay for. Sanchia was kind to him, but there was a difference. She was as happy as the day was long, always at work, outdoors or in, had not a moment for him (business apart) until the very end of the day, when (at eleven or so) she dressed with care and went to him at his supper. Sanchia was perfectly happy; but he was not.

He stayed six months that year—from April to September; but then went to Scotland, deerstalking, shooting pheasants. He was back for Christmas and brought a houseful of guests—all men. Again she welcomed him, again she was kind. He was now a little blunted to the fine shades of love, took his happiness as it happened to come, and could rub his hands over the household blessing she was. By-and-by, at the end of her fourth year, she took over the gardens as well as the house, was accepted by Mr. Menzies as his liege-lady and by young Glyde as much more than that. The estate-management, home-farm, woods, tenancies, were given up to her at the end of the fifth year, just before Ingram sailed for West Africa on a shooting expedition. By that time he had grown to depend upon her entirely for everything. She was become the faithful well-tried wife of standing, which in a man of Ingram's bone means that nothing remained of love but entire confidence and occasional gratification. After this, he left her for long periods together; for the whole of the eighth year he was abroad, "idiotically happy," as he had told her.

During all this time no intercourse with her family—except those furtive letters from her adoring old father, which were pitiful to her, because they could not be answered as he would have had them; and nothing from her friend of the Open, who had at last got himself a mate. It seemed that she had made a clean break, and that nothing of what had made her dawning life sweet and sane was to mingle with the sweetness and sanity which she had brought into Wanless. And then—after eight years—she caught herself looking back. And now —here was an end of the dream.

If you are to ask me what had changed her regard for Ingram during that solitary year, so that

she received him at the end of it as she did, I don't
know that I can tell you. Slowly discovery—of
herself, of him—came to her, slowly combustible
stuff was heaped within her; it slowly kindled, and
smouldered long. No doubt he himself blew it
into clear flame by his let-drop news of Claire's
death. She had not known that: she never read
the newspaper, having neither time for the world's
affairs nor interest in them. Suddenly, by that,
she was offended; suddenly saw him as he really
was, always had been, and always must be. Suddenly, also, she saw herself, as brimming with life,
energy to live and to make live, at the end of her
music-time. The folds fell from her eyes, she could
see Ingram as a man, squalid. Nay, more: she
could now see him as a beast, ravening. Thereupon
he gave her horror, so that she dared not look back
upon her hours of blindness.

Perhaps he had offended her by his silence—
his two letters, which she had neither invited nor
answered. That can hardly account for it, since
she had not written to him of her own initiative.
Their parting certainly had been discrepant: the
clinging and wistfulness had been hers, though
she had uttered nothing of complaint or misgiving.
But perhaps he had been too gay and nonchalant,
a little too much the husband secure. For a week
she had shivered at her loneliness; then she had
plunged anew into the flood of affairs, and had
come out, as from a cold bath, braced and tingling.
Round went the wheels of Wanless. The house

was new-papered, painted, carpeted; every month brought new wonders to the garden. Under Glyde's tuition, seeing with his eyes, watching with his tensity of vision, she had come closely into Nature's arms. Perhaps she was unwise with the young man: the fact is she never stopped to consider him. She liked him and his queer, secret, passionate ways. She took a royal line of her own. She required much of him, and if he made much of it, she didn't know it. She dreamed no harm to him or to herself. Her absorption in the business of the moment, or the needs, was so manifest that not even the maids, who saw her frequently with the youth, could have thought harm for a second. It was just Miss Percival all over—as "keen as mustard." Perhaps it was as much under Glyde's fostering as any other nurture that she came, during that year alone, to love the earth so well that she could appraise the worth of human love. I don't know. It was a critical year for her.

As she was anything but a fool, there's no doubt that she came, before the end of that year, to know what was the matter with Glyde. She had had experience—of herself and another—and he was utterly incapable of concealing his feelings. Of course she knew what was the matter with him, and was tenderly and quietly amused. She approached him gradually, let herself play elder sister, and let him play what he chose, within severe limits, never overstepped by him, never unwatched by herself. He was a passionate, sensitive, inarticulate creature, narrow-faced, sharp-eyed, scowling and thin. He always looked cold, mostly angry, and never seemed contented, even when his plants flowered themselves to death to please him.

A woman, any woman, knowing that a man covets her possession, stores her knowledge, exults in it in secret. It is a fund, a store against lean years or wry ones. You can see it throned sedately in her eyes, when she is with him, however much she may feel his absurdity or presumption. So it was with Sanchia. She was fully conscious of Struan's preposterous state, strictly the elder sister, never the patroness, for were they not bond-slaves both? She patronised nobody at Wanless, yet, with a steady eye for distances, kept a perfect length, varying with each oncomer. With Mr. Menzies, lord of the gardens, so far on she came; with Frodsham, master of horse and hound, so far; with the engineer so far; with Minnie nearer; nearest of all with Mrs. Benson: her attitude to the stout woman was that of favourite pupil to a family governess of immemorial service. She could wheedle Mrs. Benson, and often did. The elder sister attitude was kept for young Glyde; she admonished, scolded, preached to him high doctrine of duty and honour; there was something benignant, a sort of pitying care shed from above. To him she may have been like Cynthia, stooping to the dreamer on Latmos. Whether she knew that, she must have known a good deal. She knew, for instance, that he kept vigil; for she had met him at night, as you have been told. She knew where to find him. Nothing had ever passed between them, of course, of her relations with the Master. I don't think that she was aware of his sentry-go under the windows —first under Ingram's, then under hers. I am sure she was not, or he would have heard of it in plain terms, have seen her eyes grow hard, and her mouth stretch to bleakness. She was capable of royal, cold rage when she was offended. But that he hated Ingram must have been plain to her.

And now, as she stood at gaze, lonely and pensive by the black pond, she saw that it was over, her busy life. She was at the end of her tether, must lose her power and the sense of it. She was to begin the world again, starting with her fifty pounds, and without that which had made it a pride before. With a little shiver of self-pity, a half-sigh and a tightening of the lips, she accepted her fate. That was her way.

She regretted nothing, asked neither for mercy nor allowance. What she had done, she had done; if it was to be done with, she could not help that; she must go her way. Never for an instant did it enter her head that she could marry Ingram. Nothing that he had urged, or Chevenix counselled, made the smallest difference to her. She did not love Nevile any more; he was horrible to her: enough of that. Whatever her fate was to be, she would accept it: she chose it so. Without reasoning it out, that was final for her. She had always had *sic volo* for her final cause. *Stet pro ratione voluntas.*

Marriage, even nominal marriage, with Nevile was the accursed thing: none of it. And why? Because she chose it so.

This was very sublime. I sing, or Mr. Senhouse sings, a Goddess in her own Right. That is to be observed, or we fail. Persons have existed, and do yet exist, who are law unto themselves, deliberate choosers of their fate, deliberate allies of Atropos with the shears, who go what seems to us, shivering on the brink of things, a bright and bloodstained way, and furrow deeply into life, because it must be so, because so they will have it. Great ones of time, a Caesar or so, a Catherine, a Buonaparte, come handily to mind, who, wreaking countless woes, wrought evenly their own. And since greatness is a relative term, and time an abstraction of the mind, in their company, says Mr. Senhouse, was Sanchia Percival, and in her blue-clouded eyes was to be discerned seated, like a captain, foreknowledge of her own fate, and will to choose it. But, as for Mr. Senhouse himself, at this time of envisaging of ways I don't believe that he entered her head. Small blame to her, either, seeing that the man, having renounced her, or failed of her, as you please, had taken up with his Mrs. Germain, and found her to be a Fact, as I have related.

But to do wrong or right, the prerogative of choice: she arrogated that. So, I think, if the sister of the Far-Darter had ever stepped aside from the path of her lonely delight—as some have

it she did on Latmos—she would have done it
without shame. It would have been her pleasure
and her choice; she would never change countenance or have to breast the flood of colour. It
must be hers to take up or discard an empire,
or a Nevile Ingram of Wanless Hall. So, in her
degree, did Sanchia Percival—of the stuff of goddesses.

IX

Mrs. Devereux having departed as impressively as might be expected of a lady with a sense of injury, there was little for Chevenix to do but to follow her; for whereas Mrs. Devereux considered herself badly treated by both parties in the house, the young man had to own that he had quarrelled with his host. "I laid for Nevile," he told Sanchia, "and he don't let me forget it, either. He don't like commentators on his text—never did. So he's making Wanless too hot to hold me."

Sanchia, with rueful eyes, feared that this was her fault. "I'm very sorry," she said. "On all accounts I'm very sorry. I shall miss you. It was nice to see you again."

"See me again," cried Chevenix, "as soon as you please; but not here—unless you feel you can make up your mind to settle down, as we call it."

She shook her head. "I don't think I can. I think it might be wicked—as things are."

Chevenix raised his eyebrows. "That's you all over, my dear. Other people's Right is your Wrong. Why question the decrees of the police? They tell you that you may do what you please when you're married, but not before. But you won't have that. Of course, if you can't swallow

Nevile, you can't—and there's an end of it. Only," he added, "there *must* be an end of it. You're in a false position—now."

"According to you I always was," said the candid young lady, and made him change countenance. She shirked nothing.

"I did think so once; we all did, you know. Even your bare-footed friend, What's-his-name——"

"Mr. Senhouse."

"Beg your pardon. Mr. Senhouse, of course. Well, he didn't take it sitting down, so to speak. Did he now?"

She considered. Her eyes grew gentle over the remembrances which this name always called up. "He knew that I was right. Oh, yes. I'm sure of that. But he was frightened. He lost his nerve because——"

"Because it was you, my dear," said Chevenix briskly. She owned soberly to that.

"I shall see your people when I get to town," he told her. "I shall make a point of seeing Vicky and your governor. And if I could drop in upon Senhouse, by George, I'd risk it. You don't know where he is just now, I suppose?"

"He was in the Black Forest when I last heard from him," she said, "and was going to the Caucasus—to collect plants. That was a long time ago. Three years, I should think. He doesn't write now. He's married, you know."

"Married?" he repeated, with open eyes. "I never knew that."

"He married a Mrs. Germain—a widow."

Chevenix stared, then slapped his leg. "Then that accounts for it! Didn't I tell you I met him when I went out to Brindisi to see Nevile off—met him on a steamer, with a pretty woman? That was Mrs. G.—*his* pretty woman. Good Lord, how rum!" He laughed, staring. Then, "What on earth did he do that for? She's not his sort. And I gave myself away—confoundedly—to each of 'em in turn. You'll never believe it, but I told *him* that she'd always been in love with Tristram Duplessis, and then I gave *her* to understand what had been the matter with old Senhouse." He exploded, then grew mighty serious. "That's rather a bore. I was counting on him, you know. I thought you might want him."

Sanchia made no reply. About the corners of her mouth there lurked the hint of a smile, which her wistful eyes belied. Chevenix watched her, but could make nothing of it.

"He was a rum 'un," he continued. "The first time I saw him after you came up here, was when I ran against him by chance in Norfolk somewhere. Spread abroad he was—in flannels—all his things strewn about. He had a little fire going, and a little pot on it. Doing a job of tinkering, he said, to oblige a lady. There was the lady, too, if you please, sitting on a bank, smoking a clay. She had a beard, and an old wide-awake on her head. Senhouse introduced me, I remember. He told me he was on his way North—Wastwater, I think.

A planting job up there—or something. Rum
chap that! Oh, one of the very rummest! He
asked me a lot about you. I didn't know how
much he knew, so I went very pussy. The chap
was as sharp as a needle. Spotted me. He said,
'My dear sir, I don't ask you what she is doing
or where she is. I ask you if she is well.' Then
I told him a lot—about you, and Nevile, and all
this business. I let out, I tell you. I was fairly
deep in the thing—you know that I felt pretty
badly, because it was my fault that you ever knew
Nevile at all. Don't you suppose I've ever forgiven myself that, Sancie; never you suppose it.
No, no."

He was much moved. She, by a sudden impulse,
put out her hand to him. He wrung it, and said,
"Thanks, Sancie; thanks, my dear."

After a wrestling bout, he went on: "Do you
know what that fellow said to me? I should like
you to know it. Mind you, he was yours, body
and soul, then—whatever he may be now. I think
he's yours still, for that matter—but *then!* He
never concealed it—so far as I know—from anybody. Now, listen to me. He heard me out,
never said anything till I'd done. Then he looked
out over the marshes into the weather, and he said,
"No harm ever came to a good woman. I shall
see her again, crowned." Now, what do you say
to that? Queer, isn't it?"

Sanchia blushed deeply and bent her head.
Chevenix marked her confusion, and varied his

tone to suit the case.   He became practical.   "Now, what'll he say about this new state of affairs, do you suppose?"

She lifted her head.   "He will think me in the right."

Chevenix shrugged.   "There's going to be trouble," he believed.   "There's bound to be, just on that account.   Nevile can be a brute when he's in the wrong, and knows it."

Sanchia squared her jaw for trouble.

"He wants you back, you know, awfully—because you won't come.   And the more he wants you the less he'll say so.   That's the pride of the cobbler's dog.   If he's uncomfortable, he'll scratch until he's comfortable again.   And he says, "If you can't get the best take the next best"; and runs about with Mrs. Wilmot at his heels, and is bored all the time.   That's Nevile all over."   His eyes grew rounder.   "You'll have to go, you know."

She admitted that.   "Yes, I must."   Then she sighed.   "I don't want to go.   There's such a lot to be done here."

"Yes, yes, my dear," said Chevenix with some irritation.   "No doubt there is.   But you can't afford it."

He stammered out his next.   "I should like to say, Sancie, that there's nobody on earth I respect—for whom I have more respect than for you.   I don't understand your point of view—don't pretend to.   But I know a fine thing when I see it.   I'm not much of a chap, I know—no brains, and all

that—simple, rotten chap, I know; but if we're not
going to be friends I shall be unhappy."

"We are, I hope," she said, smiling kindly at
him. She gave him her hand.

"Right, Sancie. Look here," he said sternly.
"I'll punch Nevile's head for you, if you like."

"I shouldn't like it at all," she assured him.

"We're old acquaintance, you know. He'd take
it from me better than from anyone else—like
Senhouse."

"Mr. Senhouse would never touch him," she
was sure. He dropped in Chevenix's estimation
immediately.

"Quaker, eh? I didn't know that."

Sanchia explained. "He can't be changed in
those sort of things. He would only use force
against wild beasts."

"Well," cried Chevenix, "what do you think
Nevile's going to be? My advice to you is to get
out as soon as you can. And when you're in town,
command me." They parted firm friends.

Mrs. Wilmot remained, against her inmost judgment, against her maid Purcell's clear advice, for
one more day. The night of Chevenix's departure
she was there, and on the morrow was to be conveyed to the Trenchards', across the county. Wanless had her steadily in its score pair of eyes for
twenty-four hours, as Purcell, her maid, had fore-
seen. "You are doing a strange thing, ma'am,
permit me to say." Purcell was an elderly spinster,

who only required her own permission to say what she pleased. "You will be watched and reported. I suppose I am not in the servants' hall for nothing." Mrs. Wilmot said feebly that she supposed she was there for meals. Purcell stiffened her wiry neck. "Meals, ma'am! In the best houses there's a second table. The butler may be there, and perhaps the valet. The lady's maid, of course. But where there's no lady, one may put up with the cook, though the cook in such houses is rarely a female. But the housekeeper here! A Miss Percival! Dines alone—or is said to—and the cook sits at the head of our table. This is no house for you, ma'am."

The lady gave a little cry and hoisted a white shoulder. "Oh, Purcell, you are hurting me dreadfully. Do be more gentle with me. You are tearing my hair out by handfuls. What can it matter to you where Miss—where the housekeeper dines?"

"Ho," said Purcell, "little or nothing—to me, ma'am. I cannot help my thoughts. But I keep them to myself. Not one word in this house—downstairs—of Miss Percival. Not one word. They keep their mouths shut, I promise you, and their eyes open. But what you will, you will. As for Mr. Ingram, the less I say the better."

"Much the better," said Mrs. Wilmot, fretfully wriggling under the comb.

That fine afternoon—April budding into May—this lady listened to Ingram in the garden. Of all sounds in the world the sweetest music for her ear

was made by a man's voice embroidering the theme
—"*You are lovely, you are cruel, I die.*" Ingram's
descant on the golden phrase was querulous, after
his manner. He took his lover's smarts, as one
must suppose them, hardly. As thus: "*You are
lovely*—but what's that to me, if I can't touch you?
You sting my eyes, you inflame, you wound—or I
think you do; here am I, tied by the leg to a dead
woman—for dead to me she is, the she-cat Sanchia
—looking at you because I can't help myself. You
are soft and lax, you purr when I stroke you; I
could make a pet of you. Was ever a man of
property and station in such a case?

"*You are cruel*—because, though I could put out
my hand and take you, yet you expect me to do
it. That's all over, for me. I've done that sort
of thing—Sanchia knows. Now I must trouble
you to advance. I'm sick of life on these terms:
you could make life worth living. I must really
trouble you: sorry to seem languid, but I *am* languid. You, with your fine sensibilities, ought to
be the first to feel that; but no: you wait, looking
exquisite, with eyes like blue-black water, and a
mouth, a mouth like a flower. You soft gossamer
beauty, I could crush you where you hover; but
you won't come and be crushed. Certainly, you
are cruel.

I die. He avoided that. It was absurd. She
thought for one moment that he hinted it when he
said, shrugging off his ranges of hot-house—"Good
of their kind, I fancy. But what good are they to

me—a solitary beggar? I never go into 'em, you
know. I thought I should take an interest when
I had 'em put up. It looked like it—But now!
who cares whether I go into 'em or not? Who
cares whether I live or die?" There had been a
pathetic ring there.

She had murmured a gentle rebuke; her eyes
had brimmed, reproaching him. It was then that
he had taken her hand, at the going-out from the
fig-house. "Ruth," he had said, "my kind, pretty
Ruth." Then he stooped his head and kissed her.
Through three pairs of doors Glyde, in the peach-
house, had seen the act, and paused in his spraying.
It was over in a minute. The pair strolled away
and passed out of the walled-garden. Glyde, who
had turned very white, compressed his lips and
went back to his work—like a machine. Presently
a light step made him start, look guardedly up,
watch and wait. Sanchia, bare-headed, fresh and
débonnaire, came in, like a stream of west wind.
Her eyes beamed her health and pleasure. "Oh,
Struan," she said, "do come and see the *Susianas*.
They are on the very point of opening. Do come.
There's nobody about. They've gone down to the
river."

He could not face her, knowing what he knew.
But he could not resist her either. "I'll come," he
said, and followed her.

She went gaily and eagerly. "You've never
done so well with them as this year. I counted
a dozen. Huge! I felt rather miserable this morn-

ing; I've been worried rather. I thought I would just see what they would do for me. They made me feel ashamed of myself. Their strength, their contentedness—just to grow, and be strong and well! Nothing more. What else ought we to want? Food — the sun — strength to grow! Isn't that enough?" She was echoing Senhouse here, and felt an added glow to remember it. He had been much in her thoughts since her last exchange with Chevenix.

Out of the warm brown soil, sheltered by the eaves, the iris clump made a brave show. Its leaves like grey scimitars, its great flower-stems like spears. Stiffly they reared, erect, smooth, well-rounded, and each was crowned with the swollen bud of promise. She displayed them proudly, she counted them, made him check her counting. She glowed over them, fascinated by their virile pride. Struan watched her more than her treasures. He was pale still, and bit his lip; had nothing to say.

She knelt and took one of the great stalks tenderly in her hand. A kind of rapture was upon her, a mystic's ecstasy. She passed her closed hand up and down, feeling the stiff smoothness; she clasped and pressed the bursting bud. "Feel it, Struan, feel it," she said. "It's alive." He turned, shaking, away.

"They say," she went on, caressing the bud, "that this is really the Lily of the Annunciation. It's a symbol, I've read. Gabriel held one in his

hand when he stood before Our Lady. Did you
know that?"

Glyde broke out. "Don't. Don't. Come away.
I must speak to you—quickly—if I dare. Come
away from here."

He spoke fiercely, meaning what he said. Grave,
sobered, she rose and followed him. He drew her
after him to the yew-tree walk, to the enclosure at
its end, where the leaden Faun capered and grinned.
There he faced her.

"You must leave this place," he said shortly.
She looked to the ground.

"I know," she replied in a low voice.

"Every moment you stop here insults you, puts
shame upon you. Shame! And on you! It's not
bearable. It's not to be suffered. I'll not suffer
it for one."

At this she lifted her head and reproved him by
a look. It was mild, queenly mild, but not weak.
Remote from him and his world, it said, "I can't
hear you."

He understood it so. "Who says I may not
speak to you? Who else is to speak to you if I
don't? How can you bear yourself and speak
nothing? Is it natural?" He seemed on the point
of angry tears; with a gesture infinitely kind she
bore with him. Her hand just touched his arm.

"Dear Struan," she said, "I know how nice you
mean to be to me; I am very grateful to you. Of
course I am going away. I have brought everything on myself, and must bear the consequences

by myself. But I have been happy here, lately, and shall be most unhappy to go. I have so many friends here." Then, after looking at him, reflecting, she added, "Of course I know that you care."

"Care!" he cried out, scornfully. "Do you think that I've watched you, in and out, for three years without caring? Do you think that I have schooled myself to put up with—with him—without caring? And when I thought that he was coming back here to—to prove himself an honourable man—I thanked the Lord. Yes, I did that. I was ready to go when I knew he was coming back for that. I told you I would go—and I meant it. I should have cut my heart out and left it here, and gone away—clean away, glorifying and praising God. But—oh, it's hideous, hideous! You are discarded—you! Cast off—you! Peerless as you are—you! Oh, my Saviour, what's this?" He broke away, and sobbed. He dashed his arm over his eyes in a rage with himself. She was very gentle with him now.

She put her hand on his shoulder, and though he shook it off, put it there again. "You hurt me, Struan, really. If you are my friend, you shouldn't doubt me. I don't feel about it as you do, you know."

He lifted his head at the challenge. "Then you should," he said. "Dog that he is. He's insulting you. He had better have died than do as he does. Damn him, he shall pay for it." She shook her head, smiling rather dismally.

"I can't talk to you any more if you don't understand why I can't talk to you," she said. "There are things which friends cannot do for each other—which we have to do alone."

The lad gasped and made a step towards her. He could not control himself—he shook.

"Not you—never you. I'll die for you—and you know it." She looked at him full, then left him.

X

Mrs. Wilmot stayed for the better part of a week longer than she had intended, and then, perceiving by subtle but unmistakeable signs that she would wiselier go, went. To Wanless that had been a week of strain; the air was charged with trouble. One could not have pointed to anything—it was beyond the range of weathercock or glass; but everybody felt it. Sanchia, graver than she was wont to be, pushed herself sharply from duty to duty, and avoided sympathy by a dry manner. Or she was obtuse, affecting a foolish interest in trivialities. She never went into the garden, and saw nothing of young Glyde. Mrs. Benson, glooming thunder from her brows, Minnie with scare in her russet eyes turned Purcell's feasts into fasts. The wiry tire-woman, to do her justice, was as uncomfortable as any of them; but loyalty spurred her to feats of endurance undreamed of by any but servants. They, in a world of their own, where speech is rare, and skins rarer, where everything must be done by glances and hints, are perhaps more aware of themselves than any other children of men. They are for ever judging their betters; how shall they escape from judgment of each other? Judge not, says the

Book; but if you pry for vice, what can you be yourself but a prying-ground? So Purcell agonised, and felt her very vitals under the hooks. The case was past praying for. She suffered and was dumb.

At last the delicate beauty, seeing Adonis faint in the chase—for Ingram, as a lover, was languid and gloomy—was helped into her lacy draperies, helped into the carriage, driven to the station; and Ingram, on horseback, rode by her side. He helped her into the train, stored her with magazines, kissed her mouth, revolted at her tears, and returned sulkily, with hard-rimmed eyes, at a foot's pace to his halls. Midway of the carriage-drive, instinctively, he tightened the rein; for Glyde stepped out of the undergrowth some ten paces ahead, and stood, waiting for him. He was dressed, not for the garden (in shirt-sleeves and baize), but in his blacks, and had a soft felt hat on his head, basin-shaped, with the brim over his eyes. "Now what the devil does that chap want, play-acting here?" was Ingram's enquiry of the Universe.

Glyde, as the horse drew level, came within touch of his flank, and told Ingram that he wished to speak with him.

"Eh?" said Ingram; and then, "oh, what a nuisance." He felt himself injured. "Well, what is it, Glyde?"

Glyde said, "I wish to give notice, if you please." The manner of address was curt and offensive.

"Oh, do you?" Ingram said. "Well, then, you had better do it in the proper way. See Miss

Percival about it, will you?" He pressed his knees in as if to continue his way.

Glyde, however, stood by the horse's head.

"I have seen Miss Percival about it, Mr. Ingram," he said. "I saw her—a week ago. And now I've got to see you about it."

Ingram looked at him sharply—a sudden stiffening of the spine; spine stiff and eyes sharp, acting together. What he saw made him the more alert.

"What on earth do you mean?" he asked.

"I'll tell you," said Glyde. "I'm free of your service from this minute, so I'll tell you. I say that you are a damned scoundrel, and that you know it." A concentration of many grudges, kept very still, as by white heat, characterised this remarkable speech.

Ingram blenched. "By George, my man," he said, "you'll have to make that good."

Glyde said, "And I will. You have behaved, you are behaving, like a dog in this house; and you're to take a dog's wages."

Ingram jumped in his saddle, rose in his stirrups. "By God," he said, "by God—" but he said no more.

Glyde sprang up at him where he stood above his saddle, unseated—sprang up at him, took him by the shoulders and then dropping, pulled him off his horse. The freed animal, startled, kicked out, shook his head, and cantered gaily homewards. Glyde, having Ingram on the ground, took him by the collar of his jacket and belaboured him with his open hand. He cuffed him like a schoolboy, boxed him about the ears and face, shook him well, and then cast him into the young bracken of his own avenue. "There's for you, seducer," he said; and that done, he walked steadily up the road towards the lodge gates.

Ingram, on his feet, in a rage which was the most manly he could have suffered, went after him at a run, and caught him up. "You blackguard," he said, and panted. "Turn and fight with me."

Glyde stopped. "I'll not fight with you, Ingram," was his measured reply, "because I've that in me which would kill you. No mercy for you there. You can go as you please; you can send me to gaol or not; but you shan't get me hanged. I've something to do with my life—as much of it as you leave me; and I want it." As Ingram glared at him, crimson now, with bulging eyes and teeth at lips, the other went on. "I'm going no farther to-day than my lodging. Your police will find me there when you send 'em. I shan't fight them, because I can't afford it; and I shan't fight you, dog that you are, for the same reason." Ingram cursed, and sprang at him, but Glyde stiffened his arm and held him off. Master was no match for man, and felt no better for the knowledge of that. It did serve, however, to bring him to his senses. He saw that he was making an ass of himself.

"You'll hear more of this," he said, and turned and walked rapidly back to the house.

Mortification inflamed his rage; his furious walking blew into it a sense of incurable injury. Injury, shocked pride, and animal heat altogether made a devil of him. He went directly to his own room, and rang the bell. "Send Miss Percival to me," he told Minnie, "at once."

Then he waited for her, with a face like a rat.

XI

SHE might have gathered warning from Minnie's panting summons, but had been busy over her accounts and had noticed nothing amiss.

"He wants you, Miss Percival! Don't go!" She had scarcely heard. She said, "Who wants me? Mr. Ingram? I'll come;" and though the maid stammered, "I wouldn't, oh, I wouldn't," had gone.

The face he showed her from his bureau, where he sat huddled over a litter of papers, prepared her instantly for crisis; snarling, white and wicked, yet it had tragedy in it—as if he knew that he had himself to reckon with beyond all.

For some time he seemed not to see her, though he looked at her. He sat glooming, like a man dumb in high fever, working his lower jaw, screwing and unscrewing his hands. Afterwards she believed that he had been groping for the cruellest thing he could say, and was goaded into what he did say by the sense that he could find nothing.

"So that was your work? Your choice way! To set one of my own servants to club me."

She looked at him blankly; but her face glowed with sudden fire. "I haven't the least notion what you mean. Who has clubbed vou?"

His eyes flickered. "Glyde. Your friend. You seek your champions all about, it seems. You make things snug for yourself. It's master or man with you—it's all one."

He spluttered his venom broadcast. She held up her head. "Are you insulting me?" He wheeled round full in his chair.

"Is it possible to insult you?"

At that she lowered her panoply of fire, and grew still. "I see that you are. I can't allow that."

He foamed. "Bullies in your hire. Now I see what Bill Chevenix was after. And Glyde—faugh! who else?"

She watched him steadily without fear or disgust. His words held no meaning for her. "I think you must be mad," she said. "It will be better if I go."

He scoffed at her. "Better! You are right." He rose in his place. "You'll go to-day."

Sanchia regarded him deeply, almost curiously, as if he had been a plant, interesting for its rarity.

"Naturally," she said, and left him in his staring fit.

The ordered little realm of Wanless went on its diurnal course. Luncheon was served at two by a trembling parlour-maid; the coffee was set in the hall, the cigar-box, the spirit-flame. Frodsham came for orders, Mr. Menzies reported Glyde absent without leave. These things were done by rote: yet the whole house knew the facts. Sanchia, dining in the middle of the day, plied her knife and fork with composure. It was her way to face facts once for all, tussle with them, gain or lose, and be done with them. She had been angry with Glyde, but now could think of him as "poor Struan," Punchinello in a rustic comedy. Of Ingram, deliberately, she thought nothing. It had been necessary to survey her feelings of eight years ago, to make a sour face of disgust over them, before she could shake them out of her head. Now they were gone, and he with them: the world, with May beginning, was too sweet a place for such vermin to fester in. She had swept and ridded herself, rinsed her mouth with pure water, and now could sit to her dinner and review her plans.

But the storm burst over Wanless, at half-past four. Minnie came into her room, breathless, Mrs. Benson stertorous in her traces.

Minnie wailed, "Oh, Miss, oh, Miss Sanchia, oh, dear Miss Percival, what's going to become of us? Struan's beaten the Master, and the Sergeant's here!"

"Apes and tigers"—Mrs. Benson tolled like a bell. "Apes and tigers. What says the Book?"

Sanchia let them run, so the distorted tale was pieced together. At a quarter to twelve—it must have been that, because Emma heard the stable-clock chime the half-hour—Struan was seen in his blacks. He came out of the wood-house, an ash-plant in his hand. "Apes and tigers, apes and tigers," from Mrs. Benson—his face was dreadful to see. Who said so? Who saw him? Not Minnie, for sure. It was Bella the laundrymaid—she saw him from the window, and had a turn. The window was open. "Why, Struan," she said—but he told her to shut mouth and eyes. "The less you see, and know," he said, "the better for you." Poor Struan, with his tragedy airs! Bella told that to Minnie, and that she would never forget it to her dying day. It turned the beer in her stomach, she said—and now she was lying down. As he went out of the yard, a cloud came over the sun, and Bella felt the chill. She had the goose-flesh all up her back. That, they say, betokens a person walking over your grave. Somewhere in England we all have our grave-ground lying green under turf. It awaits the spade and the hour. In the morning it is green and groweth up—this was Mrs. Benson's piece, but Minnie had the rest of the stage.

The saddle-horse came flinging into the yard at one o'clock—no later. That's certain, because Frodsham was at his after-dinner pipe—or should have been: instead of which he came running in after him. Just about that time, or maybe a little before, Mr. Menzies had been asking for Struan? Where was he? Did anyone ever see such a wastrel? No man's account, he called him. Mrs. Benson tolled her apes and tigers all.

It was Minnie had seen the Master when the bell pealed. She had gone with her heart in her mouth—and oh, his collar and tie! His red ear!

She had never seen anything like his face, and never must again on this side of the tomb. Wicked, oh, wicked! He showed his teeth. His face was as white as a clout. His voice was like a nutmeg-grater. "Miss Percival—here—at once." It was all he said. She did her bidding, for servants must —but her heart bled for Miss Percival, and she felt like fainting at any minute when she waited at lunch-eon. He drank brandy—jerked his head towards the sideboard when he wanted more. Never said a word. And how he ate, wrenching at his food! Fit to choke him. How she had lived through the luncheon she didn't know at all. But that Struan, that quiet in an ordinary way, should have dared—with a stick in his violent hand! And the Sergeant ready for his warrant—stiff in the hall.

"A villain has got his deserts," boomed Mrs. Benson. "My dear, you're going, it seems, and I with you. This is no place for a young lady—no, nor ever was, God be good! I know my place, to all parties; but I know that better—and now it's come upon us like a thief in the night. Well, well, well—my pretty young lady! Old women must put up with what they get, we all know—but not murderers in gentlemen's seats: no, nor beastly doings in and out of doors. I shall go, my dear, when you go—ah, me! When the wicked man . . . but he's got his deserts. What! a widower—with duty and pleasure before him, combined for once, and no thanks to him!—to dally with a French doll—movable eyes and separate teeth and all—

when he might have gone on his knees to a splendid
young lady! And I'd have kept him there to say
his prayers, which he's never done before, not since
his mother died, poor old gentlewoman, worn out by
the gnashings of a tiresome, God-Almighty, wicked
old man, and a slip of sin who nothing was too good
for. Not in this world, no! But it will be made up
to him in the next, by the unquenchable worm—as
he'll find out when he tries his 'down, dog' tricks;
his 'drop that, will you?' None of that down there
in the fire. What says the Book? My dear, my
dear," and she took the girl in her arms with a fine
look about her of Niobe amid arrows, "I've a bosom
for your head and a roof to shelter us both, and
we'll see what we shall see. There's castles and
towers for the great oneyers and their minions;
but mine is in the Fulham Road, my dear; my
own property out of a building society that does
business for the widow and the orphan—makes it
their special line, as I understand, and have treated
me squarely throughout—that I will say. Yes,
yes, and I'll tend you fairly, will Sarah Benson,
widowed mother of a graceless son, who can feel
for her poor dead mistress, mother of a worse.
My lamb, you shall want for nothing."

Fast in a good pair of arms, Sanchia snuggled
and smiled. She patted Mrs. Benson's cheek, and
put up her lips to her. Minnie, like a thawing ice-
pack, ran rivers of water.

"You *are* good to me," she said; "you *are* sweet
to me. I don't mind anything when I can be sure

of such friends. But you mustn't leave, you know. Really, you ought not. I shan't forget you, be sure of that, whether you stay or go."

Mrs. Benson crooned over her, "Oh, you're not one that forgets, my precious, with your golden heart. And there's more than me will find it out." She wiped her spectacles, breathing on the glasses, and Sanchia shook out her plumage, escaped from the nest. Ingram, without knocking, came into the room.

His rage was now cold and keen. He took in conspiracy with one glance at the three.

He spoke to Minnie. "I have been ringing for twenty minutes. The brandy in my room, and some soda-water. At once." Scared Minnie fled. Then he turned half to Sanchia, but didn't look at her.

"I understood you were leaving this afternoon. You had better order a fly. There's the telephone." He held out an envelope. "I think that you will find this correct."

Sanchia was at her bureau. "Put it on the table, please," she said, without turning; and while Ingram hovered, Mrs. Benson heaving like the sea, gathered into a combing wave and, breaking, swallowed him up.

"Money—ah! You come with money to a lady of the land! Offer me money, Mr. Ingram, if you dare. Your bread I've eaten, having baked it, and your father's bread, and not choked yet, though each mouthful might be my last. By every word out of the mouth of God, says the Book; and what shall He say of you? I've watched for this, I've seen it coming. You keep long accounts, but there's One keeps longer—and in His head, as we read. To breaking mother's heart so much, to scandal of matrimony so much—and to perjury and dirty devices, wicked dalliance, so much. When she came here—this fine young lady, so fresh and sweet— I waited. I shook my fist at you, Mr. Ingram; 'I know what this means,' I said, 'a false tongue and a young heart.' And I waited, I tell you—for I could do nothing else. She could have come to me at any hour of any day and welcome; and I'd have told her, 'He's bad—he's rotten at the heart. He'll tire of you—neglect you—trick you—and cast you out.' But she was too proud for that; she bore it all, and not a word. And she did your work as never before, not in your time, nor your father's time; and made friends of the poor, and kept her place— sweetly and smoothly it was done. And you on your travels with foreign women——"

Ingram now emerged from the flood. "Are you mad?" he said. A dreadful calm came over Mrs. Benson, succeeding the tempest.

"'I am not mad, most noble Festus,'" she said; "but I am mother of a graceless son, and will not be cook to another. I leave your service from this hour. Your dinner is a-making, and Emma is a steady worker." She turned to Sanchia. "The best vegetable-hand I ever had under me, Miss Percival, and I've had a score." One further cut at Ingram she allowed herself. "I would not take a penny piece of your money now, not to save my darling from the lions."

"You won't get it, you know," said Ingram. "But you've had lots of 'em." She braved that truth.

"And earned them, Mr. Ingram, as you know, better than I do."

Ingram, ignoring her, observed quietly to Sanchia, "The sooner the better, I think."

That was the manner of his farewell.

It was not the way she would have chosen to leave; but she reasoned with herself, as she packed her belongings, that it was probably the best way. It gave no time and little inclination for sentiment. Now, it was almost certain that had a term been ahead of her, whose end could be felt nearing, there would have been good-byes, last interviews, and last interviews but one, which are apt to be more poignant than those of the last moment of all. Even as it was there were threatenings of emotion. Wanless was stirred deeply. Mr. Menzies brought in a nosegay, and grasped her hand. "You will be sorely missed here, Miss Percival, sorely missed. Less said's the sooner mended, but you're a true young lady, greatly to be deplored."

"Good-bye, Mr. Menzies," she had said, "and thank you a thousand times for——"

"They are from my own plot of ground," said the grizzled gardener, and looked away. She had his tulips in her hand, and now buried her face in them.

"Then I love them all the better," she told him; and put in a word for Struan. "Be kind to him when you see him again—please do."

Mr. Menzies became far-sighted. He had very blue eyes. "Ahem!" he said, in his Scotch fashion. "He'll not be here again, I doubt. He'll be away, the headstrong young man." But he warmed to it. "Ay," he said, "ay, Miss Percival. For your sake I'll listen to what he has to tell me." She felt that she must be content with that. Each servant in degree must be dealt with, and Minnie comforted in her place. She was all for going that night; but had a mother and four sisters in Doncaster—all at home. Would Miss Sanchia forgive her, and accept of this Prayer-book? Miss Sanchia would; kissed her, and did.

In the carriage drive she told Mrs. Benson of her immediate intention. "I must say good-bye to Struan. We will stop at his cottage on the way. There's plenty of time."

Mrs. Benson was strongly against it, but rather showed her mind than declared it. Mischief enough had been done through that youth—and in him, she doubted. Better let him alone. Are you to countenance violent hands? Raised against them in authority? Then where's authority? Where are Principalities and Powers? Much as she contemned Ingram, she was on his side against Struan any day.

On the other hand, Sanchia was, in a manner, her guest, and could not be spoken to plainly about it. She could only shake her head.

"He's better alone, Miss Percival, alone with his devil. While the fit's on him, let 'em fight it out. And what can he be—to the likes of you?"

"He's always been a friend of mine," she said. "He's been very foolish, very wicked; he had no business whatever to do as he did—to put me in the wrong. I'm angry with him, and he will see that I am. But—" Mrs. Benson knew the force of that "but." It had brought the young lady to Wanless.

Yet Mrs. Benson might have triumphed if she would. Sanchia, at the cottage door, was met by the anxious tenant of it with whom Struan lodged. "He's not here, Miss," she was told, and then, "oh, Miss, they've took him away. The Sergeant's come for him and took him. And we hear—" There had been no stopping her, but by Sanchia's way.

She walked into the cottage and put up her veil. She showed a pale, sad face. "How dreadful! I must write a note. Will you let me write here, and leave it with you—to give him when he comes?"

She wrote in pencil, "My dear Struan, I am very sorry. You made me angry, but I'm sorry now. I came to say Good-bye, as I am going away. Mrs. Benson is with me. See Mr. Menzies when you can. He has promised to help you, and,

of course, I will too, if I can.—Yours always, S. J.
P." With the fold of the envelope to her tongue
she paused, reflective. Then she took the note out
again, read it over, and ran her pencil through the
last two letters of her signature. And taking two
Parma violets from the knot at her breast—a recent
gift from Wanless—she put them within the paper.
Thus she did deliberately—as the Fates would have
her. Addressing "Mr. S. Glyde, by Mrs. Broughton," she gave her letter in charge. "Be sure to
give it him when he comes back," she said. Then
she and her protector were driven to the station.

XII

As Chevenix, once his friend, had said often, Nevile, when his back was up, shrank from nothing. Even while the Hall was in tempest, the Sergeant had visited Glyde as he sat at his tea. They nodded to each other, while the officer stood powerfully in the doorway.

Glyde's strong teeth bit through a crust. "I know your errand," he said.

Sergeant Weeks replied, "I can't doubt it." Impassivity became him; he figured the Law as the everlasting hills.

Glyde too, in his way, was impressive. Between long draughts from his tea-cup, he asked, "Where's your warrant?"

The Sergeant produced his folded paper, opened and scanned it, to see that all was in order, before he passed it into the room. "Here 'tis for you, made out by Sir Trevor Gell. Why, man!" he broke out, humanely indignant, "what in thunder were you about?" A flaxen-haired child, nursing a doll, edged herself through a door ajar, and gazed blue-eyed upon the pair. Glyde saw her.

"That's my business," he said. "Run away, Flo. I'll tell, or I'll not tell, in my time and place —which aren't here, saving your presence." He got up and put his hand on the child's poll. "Well, I'm your man," he added.

The Sergeant blinked. "Nay, nay, you can finish your tea. I'll just step in amd smoke my pipe with you. 'Tisn't often I get the chance, in the daylight."

"Right," said Glyde, and poured off the rest of his brew. Flo's finger went into her mouth.

The Sergeant lit, the Sergeant puffed. A remark seemed proper. "Seemingly," he said, "there's a storm about. 'Tis like to be the end of our spell of fair."

Glyde laughed; but there had been no sidethrust. A police officer is not gnomic. Safety, for him, lies in smooth running. Thus, every man is a potential criminal; but every criminal, once taken, is a fellow-man. Nobody could have been more tactful than he while Glyde made his preparations to depart. Mrs. Broughton was in tears, Flo sobbed in her mother's apron; but Glyde spoke plain words of comfort.

"Don't take on, Mrs. Broughton; this is a small matter to what's been done. You'll see to my things I know. The papers here may be valuable—who knows? A deal of candle has gone up in smoke over them—rivers of ink! I'll ask them of you when I come back." He took with him his *Virgil* and Sanchia's *Dante*—nothing else. At the lodge gates he mounted the cart, the Sergeant after him, and by six of the evening was lodged in Felsboro' gaol. There he lay for a week, awaiting Petty Sessions.

There was a full bench, a crowded court when
the accused was brought in. The hush that pre-
ceded him and the buzz when he stood up made Ingram set his teeth. The reporters, with racing pen,
cleared the ground. Thus the world might read of
"The Squire of Wanless, every inch a soldier," in
one journal, and of "Nevile Ingram, Esquire, of
Wanless Hall," in another. There are no politics
in police reports, but broadcloth is respectable. The
prisoner was described as "Struan Glyde, 23, a
sickly-looking young man, who exhibited symptoms
of nervousness." It was allowed that he spoke
"firmly but respectfully to the Bench," but, on the
other hand, "to the complainant he showed considerable animosity, and more than once had to
be reproved by the Chairman." The proceedings
were short. "At the close there was a demon-
stration, which was immediately checked by the
police."

Glyde, in fact, was revealed as a narrow-faced
young man, slim and olive-complexioned, having
light, intent eyes, and very long eyelashes. Nervous
he undoubtedly was; he twitched, he blinked, he
swallowed. He looked effeminate to one judge.
Another said of him to his neighbour, "As hardy
as a hawk." A newspaper called him "puny," a
rival "as tough as whip-cord." It depended upon
your reading of him—whether by externals or not.
He had a quiet, fierce way with him, a glare, the look
of a bird of prey. He was very self-possessed. All
the papers observed it.

Ingram, playing his privilege to the last ounce, told his tale to his brother-magistrates, shortly, but with considerable effect. He had had occasion to dismiss a servant, and the prisoner had taken upon himself to resent it. Yes—in answer to a question—a female servant. Prisoner had attacked him in his own carriage-drive, had pulled him out of the saddle before he knew what he was about, and had beaten him while on the ground. He had no witnesses. There had been none. His voice, as he chopped out his phrases, was dry, his tone impartial. He took no sides, stated the facts. He spoke to the Chairman—even when he replied to the question which made him, for a moment, take breath; and he never once looked at the accused.

The Bench consulted together. Old Mr. Bazalguet, the Chairman, leaned far back in his chair and gazed at the ceiling, while two younger justices whispered to each other across his portly person, peering sideways at Ingram, who showed them his smooth head and folded arms. Colonel Vero, the fourth of the tribunal, was drawing angels on his blotting paper. Then they settled themselves, one of them with a shrug, and Sergeant Weeks told of the arrest. Accused had declined to make a statement, but had spoken certain words to his landlady, one Mrs. Broughton, to the effect that what was to come was "nothing" to what had been done. He had left in her charge papers, which the Sergeant had afterwards examined, and now had in his care. This had led to a brief interlude.

Mr. Bazalguet had caught the words. "Papers? What papers?" he asked. "Newspapers?"

"No, sir," said Sergeant Weeks. "They were writings. Poetry and the like—and foreign tongues." The bench sat up, and now Glyde had the hawk-look in his light eyes. Ingram stifled a yawn, and impressed the Bench.

Mr. Bazalguet, inclining his head to either side, enquired only with his eyebrows. Did we want these papers? Should we, perhaps, for form's sake examine them? Mr. Max Fortnaby was of opinion that we should. As they were handed up, the prisoner, who had been wetting his lips, said plainly, "There's nothing in them about this business," and was reproved by Sergeant Weeks.

A formidable pile of MS. was passed up by the Clerk, whose deprecating glances were not lost upon the Chairman. But Mr. Max Fortnaby cut open the budget in the midst, and peered in.

"*Janua vel domina penitus crudelior ipsa*"—he read. It was a footnote. He lifted his eyebrows—then his eyes upon the accused.

"Propertius? You know Latin?"

"I know some, sir."

He returned to the MS., then again to Glyde.

"You are a bit of a poet, I see."

"Yes, sir. I hope so."

"If it leads you to battery, my young friend—" was his private comment. To Mr. Bazalguet he whispered, "The fellow's got scholarship. We might give these back, I think." Mr. Bazalguet

was only too happy, and Glyde saw his offspring
returned. Sergeant Weeks, safe in Mr. Fortnaby's
good opinion, scrupulously wrapped and tied them.
Mr. Fortnaby said, "Let them go back to his landlady," and caught the prisoner's eye.

It was now time to ask him whether he had anything to say. Glyde, perfectly master of himself,
said that he pleaded Guilty, but would like to put
a few questions. The Chairman, biting the tips
of his fingers, nodded; and Mr. Fortnaby watched
him.

Facing Ingram, who looked always to the Chairman, Glyde asked—"Did you dismiss your servant,
as you put it, before I met you, or afterwards?"
All eyes flew from Glyde to Ingram.

"Actually, afterwards," it was explained. "But
the thing was understood before."

"By whom?"

"By me," said Ingram, "and—" He stopped
there. A very interesting struggle, momentary, and
done in silence, took place. Glyde was daring Ingram to bring in Sanchia's name, and Ingram could
not do it.

"And—?" said Glyde. "And by whom?"

Ingram paused, biting his lips. He was pale.
He took a long breath, and then said, "And by
you, I have no doubt."

"Thank you," Glyde said. Then he began again.
"Did you ask me to fight with you?"

"I believe I did."

"And I refused?"

"Yes," said Ingram, "you did."

"Did I say that I didn't fight with dogs?"

Ingram smiled at the Chairman. "You did not."

"I say so now," said Glyde, and stirred the Court. Mr. Bazalguet interfered. "You mustn't talk like that, Glyde. We can't have it, you know." Colonel Vero added, "Certainly not," and stretched his long legs out.

Glyde recovered himself, and begged pardon. He was told that he might go on, in reason, but declined. "Thank you, sir. I think I'll leave it so. I own to what I did."

He was told that he could be dealt with summarily, or sent for trial. "I'll take it from you, gentlemen," he said, and settled himself reposefully. The Bench drew together, with the Clerk intervening.

Mr. Bazalguet, double-chinned and comfortable squire, was disturbed by this case. What troubled him was that Ingram had not been straightforward. What was this dismissal of a servant? He knew, and therefore he asked the question. Fortnaby knew also, but didn't intend to say. Everybody, indeed, knew. Romance appeals to us all in diverse ways; and it was actually romance which settled Glyde's romantic affair.

Fortnaby, Maximilian Fortnaby, had been a schoolmaster, had succeeded to an estate at forty, and retired. He, with his keen face and trim whiskers, leaning his head on his hand, thus spoke in undertones, and carried the day. "The case is clear. The young man's taught himself tongues, and has poetry. He's been taught other things, too, and has got some of them wrongly. One thing he ought to learn is that to relieve your feelings is not the way to help the oppressed. He's set himself up for a champion, and tongues have got to work. I should give him three months." Mr. Bazalguet looked at the Clerk, who said it was a bad case. Mr. Ingram was a magistrate and—the maximum was two years. The third magistrate saw his way to impressing himself,— "Make it six months," he said. The Chairman agreed with him, until Colonel Vero said, "I should give him a year." That shocked him. "It'll take a long time for it to blow over, you know," he whispered to Fortnaby, who smiled and shrugged. "I don't suppose six will hurt him. He'll be able to write after a bit." "Ingram will go abroad, you know," said Mr. Bazalguet. "Did you happen to know the—party?" Fortnaby looked up quickly. "I? Oh, dear no. But I gather that the less we say the better. It was not an ordinary servant." Mr. Weir, the third magistrate, said, "A lady, I hear;" but his colleagues ignored him. Then they all sat up, and the Clerk sank into the well.

"Glyde," said Mr. Bazalguet, "you will have to go to prison for three months, with hard labour. I hope this will be a warning to you. I do indeed."

The prisoner was removed amid murmurs. There was some cheering outside the court—at which Ingram grimly smiled. But he was very pale, and did

not leave the Sessions house until late in the afternoon. Old Mr. Bazalguet was very cool with him
after court. He grunted when they met in the hall.
"You go abroad?" he asked him. Ingram said, it
was probable.

BOOK III

INTERLUDE OF THE RECLUSE PHILOSOPHER

I

A NOTABLE difference between the sexes is this: that a man will thrive for years—that is, his better part—upon love denied, and woman upon love fulfilled. So Senhouse, in his hopeless plight, starved and did well; dreams nourished him in what passes in England for solitude. From the grey of the mornings to the violet-lidded dusk his silence was rarely broken; and yet the music in his heart was continuous; his routine marched to a rhythm. The real presence of Sanchia was always with him, to intensify, accentuate, and make reasonable the perceptions of his quickened senses. Sense blended with sense—as when the sharp fragrance of the thyme which his feet crushed gave him the vision of her immortal beauty, or when, in the rustle of the wind-swept grasses, he had a consciousness of her thrilled heart beating near by. All nature, in fact, was vocal of Sanchia by day; and at night, presently, she stole white-footed down the slant rays of the moon and fed his soul upon exhalations of her own. Idle as he might have appeared to one who did not know the man—for beyond the routine of his handiwork he did nothing visible—he was really intensely busy. Out of the stores reaped

and garnered in those meditative years was to come
the substance of his after-life.

But no man in England may live three years in
a grass valley unreported; his fame will spread
abroad, scattered as birds sow seeds. Discreetly
as he lived and little as he fared, he was at first a
thing of doubt and suspicion, and won respect by
slow degrees. Was he a coiner, stirring alloys
over his night fires? Was he Antichrist, blas-
pheming the Trinity at daybreak? He was talked
of by gaitered farmers at sheep-fairs, by teamsters
at cross-roads, by maidens and their sweethearts on
Sundays. The shepherds, it was thought, might have
told more than they did. It was understood that
they had caught him at his secrets times and again.
But the shepherds had little to say of him but that
he was a mellow man, knowing sheep and weather,
and not imparting all that he knew. Similarly the
gypsies, who alone travel the Race-plain in these
days, and mostly by night, were believed to know
him well; but they, too, kept their lore within the
limits of their own shifty realm.

Rarely, indeed, he was seen. Sunday lovers,
strolling hand in hand up the valley, came to a point
where they went tiptoe and peered about for him.
He might be described motionless, folded in his
white robe, midway between ridge and hollow;
or a gleam of him flashed between the trees of the
brake would perhaps be all that they would get for
an hour of watching. The hill brows would, on
such days, be lined with patient onlookers; all eyes

Ploughman in the vales would sometimes see his gaunt figure
on the sky-line.

would be up the narrow valley to its head under Hirlebury, where, below the little wood, his grey hut could be seen, deep-eaved, mysterious, blankly holding its secrets behind empty windows. None ever ventured to explore at close quarters; and if the tenant had appeared, a thousand to one they would all have looked the other way. The Wiltshire peasant is a gentleman from the heart outwards. So, too, carters, ploughmen, reapers in the vales would sometimes see his gaunt figure monstrous on the sky-line, cowled and with uplifted arms, adoring (it was supposed) the sun, or leaning on his staff, motionless and rapt, meditating death and mutability. He lost nothing by such chance apparitions; on the contrary, he gained the name of a wise man who had powers of divination and healing. In the cottage whither he went once a week for bread, a child had been sick of a burning fever. His hands, averred the mother, had cured it. Groping and making passes over its stomach, rubbing in oils, relief had come, then quiet sleep and a cool forehead. After this, an old man, crippled with rheumatics, had hobbled up to the very edge of his dominion, and had waited shaking there upon his staff until he could get speech with the white stranger. He, too, had had the reward of his relief. If he was not made sound again, he was relieved and heartened. He had said that, if he was spared, he was hopeful to stretch to his height again, which had been six feet all but an inch. The stranger, said he, had put him in the way of

new life, and whatever he might mean—whether
that he were a Salvationist or a quack doctor—he
would say no more. After that, a young woman
went to him to get him to name the father of her
child, and returned, and was modest for a month,
and a good mother when the time came. And true
it was that her chap came forward and saw the vicar
about it, and that they were asked in church. Out
of such things as these his fame grew.

The hunt struck upon him now and again, when
the hounds in full cry streamed down his steep es-
carpments and threatened panic to his browsing
goats. At such times he would rise up, white-
robed and calm, and stay with a quiet gesture the
scattering beasts. The whips would cap him, and
the Master with his field find themselves in company
of an equal. For his ease of manner never left him,
nor that persuasive smile which made you think that
the sun was come out. He had none of the airs of
a mystagogue, but talked to men, as he did to beasts,
in the speech which was habitual to them. The
lagging fox understood him when, grinning his fear
and fatigue, he drew himself painfully through the
furze. So did the hounds, athirst for his blood.
Buck-skinned gentlemen, no less, found him affable
and full of information—about anything and everything in the world except the line of the hunted
fox. "Oh, come," he said once, "don't ask me
to give him away. You're fifty to one, to start
with; and the fact is I passed him my word that I
wouldn't. I'll tell you what, though. You shall

offer me a cigarette. I haven't smoked for six days." Which was done.

His powers with children, his charm for them, his influence and fascination, which in course of time made him famous beyond these shores, arose out of a chance encounter not far from his hut. Three boys, breaking school in the nesting season, came suddenly upon him, and paled, and stood rooted. "Come on," he said, "I'll show you a thing or two that you've never seen before." He led them to places of marvel, which his speech made to glimmer with the hues of romance: the fresh grubbed earth where a badger had been routing, the quiet glade where, that morning, a polecat had washed her face. He brought them up to a vixen and her cubs, and got them all playing together. He let them hold leverets in their arms, milk his goats, as the kids milk them for their need; and showed them so much of the ways of birds that they forgot, while they were under the spell of him, to take any of their eggs. Crowning wonder of all —when a peewit, waiting on the down, dipped and circled about his head for a while and finally perched on his shoulder while he stood looking down upon her eggs in the bents! Such deeds as these fly broadcast over the villages, and on Saturdays he would be attended by a score of urchins, boys and girls. To a gamekeeper who came out after his lad, sapling ash in hand, he had that to say which convinced the man of his authority.

"'A says to me, 'There's a covey of ten in thicky

holler,' where you could see neither land nor bird. 'I allow 'tis ten,' he says, 'but we won't be particular to a chick.' There was nine, if you credit me, that rose out of a kind of a dimple in the down, that you couldn't see, and no man could see. 'Lord love you,' I said, 'Mr. John, how ever did you see 'em?' He looks at me, and he says, very quiet, 'I never saw the birds, nor knew they was there. I saw the air. There's waves in this air,' he says, 'wrinkled waves; and they birds stirred 'em, like stones flung into a pond. Tom,' he says, to my Tom, 'if you look as close as I do,' he says, 'you'll see what I see.' And young Tom looks up at him, as a dog might, kind of faithful, and he says, 'I 'low I will, sir, please, sir.' I says to him, 'Can a man be taught the like o' that?' 'No,' says he, 'but a boy can.' 'What more could thicky boy learn?' I says, and he says, 'To understand his betters, and get great words, and do without a sight of things—for the more you do without,' he says, 'the more you have to deal with.' 'Such things as what, now, would he do without?' I wants to know. He looks at me. 'Food,' he says, kind of sharp; 'food when he's hungry, and clothing, and a bed; and money, and the respect of them that don't know anything, and other men's learning, and things he don't make for himself.' Heard any man ever the like o' that? But just you bide till I've done. 'Can a boy learn to do without drink?' I wants to know—for beer's been my downfall. 'He can,' says thicky man. 'And love?' I says; and 'No,' says he straight, 'he

cannot. But he can learn the way of it; and that
'ull teach him to do wi'out lust.' 'Tis a wise thought,
the like of that, I allow."

The gamekeeper paused for the murmurs of
his auditory to circle about the tap-room, swell
and subside, and then brought out his conclusion.
There was book-learning to be faced. "How
about scholarship? 'I'd give him none,' says the
man. 'Swallerin' comes by nature, and through
more than the mouth. I'd open him his eyes and
ears, his fingers and toes, and the very hairs on the
backs of his hands; and they'll all swaller in time,
like the parts of the beastës do.' Now, that's
a learned man, I allow. My boy must go to the
Council School it does appear; but thicky man
will give him more teaching in a week than schoolmaster in a year—and there he goes o' Saturdays
—and wants no driving, moreover." He returned
to his beer, thoughtful-eyed.

The gamekeeper's son was twelve years old,
and was the nucleus round which grew the Sen-
husian school of a later day, where neither reading nor writing could be had until the pupil was
fifteen years old. But this is anticipatory, for the
school was a matter of long gestation and tentative
birth.

II

ONE September midnight, as he stirred a late
supper over a small wood-fire, he was hailed by a
cry from above. "Ho, you! I ask shelter," he
was adjured. The quarter moon showed him a
slim figure dark against the sky.

"Come down, and you shall have it," he answered, and continued to skim his broth.

The descent was painfully made, and it was
long before the traveller stood blinking by his fire
—a gaunt and hollow-eyed lad. Senhouse took
him in at a glance, stained, out-at-elbows with the
world, nursing a grudge, footsore and heartsore.
He had a gypsy look, and yet had not a gypsy
serenity. That is a race that is never angry at
random; and never bitter at large. A gypsy will
want a man's life; but if the man is not before
him, will be content to wait until he is. But this
wanderer seemed to have a quarrel with time and
place, that they held not his enemy by the gullet.

"You travel late, my friend," said Senhouse
briskly.

"I travel by night," said the stranger, "lest I
should be seen by men or the sun."

Senhouse laughed. "'*In girum imus noctu, non
ut consumimur igni*.' They used to say that of

the devils once upon a time. Devilish bad Latin;
but it reads backwards as well as forwards, like the
devil himself."

"My devil rides on my back," said the stranger,
"and carries with him the fire that roasts me."

He was at once bitter and sententious. Senhouse
put down his hurts to bruises of the self-esteem.

"I hope that you dropped him up above," he
said cheerfully, "or that you will let me exorcise
him. I've tried my hand with most kinds of devil.
Are you a Roman?"

"Half," he was told, and, guessing which half,
asked no more questions.

"You are pretty well done, I can see," he said.
"You want more food. You want warm water,
and a bed, and a dressing for your feet. You've
been on the road too long."

The stranger was huddled by the fire, probing
his wounded feet. "I'm cut to pieces," he said.
"I've been over stubbles and flint. This is a cruel
country."

"It's the sweetest in the world," Senhouse told
him, "when you know your way about it. When
you have the hang of it you need not touch the
roads. You smell out the hedgerows, and every
borstal leads you out on to the grass. But I'll
own that there are thistles. I wear sandals myself.
Now," he continued, ladling out of his pot with
a wooden spoon, "here's your porridge, and there
are bread and salt; and here water, and here goat's
milk. Afterwards you shall have a pipe of tobacco,

and some tea. Best begin while all's hot—and
while you eat I'll look to your wounds. Finally,
you shall be washed and clothed."

He went away, returning presently with water
and a napkin. Kneeling, he bathed his guest's
feet, wiped them, anointed, then wrapped them
up in the napkin. The disconsolate one, meantime, was supping like a wolf. He gulped at his
porridge with quick snaps, tore his bread with his
teeth. Senhouse gave him time, quietly eating
his own supper, watching the red gleam die down
in the poor wretch's eyes. Being himself a spare
feeder, he was soon done, and at further business
of hospitality. He set a great pipkin of water to
heat, brought out a clean robe of white wool, a
jelab like his own, and made some tea.

The stranger, then, being filled, cleansed and
in warm raiment, stretched himself before the fire,
and broke silence. He was still surly, but the
grudge was not audible in his voice. "I took your
fire for a gypsy camp, and was glad enough of it.
I've come by the hills from Winterslow since dusk.
You were right, though: I was done. I couldn't
have dragged another furlong."

Senhouse nodded. "I thought not. Been long
on the road?"

"Two months."

"From the North, I think? From Yorkshire?"

The stranger grunted his replies. His host judged
that he had reasons for his reticence. There was a
pause.

"You sup late," was then observed.

Senhouse replied, "I generally do. I take two meals a day—the first at noon, the second at midnight; but I believe that I could do without one of them. I never was much of an eater—and I need very little sleep. Somehow, although I am out at sunrise most mornings, I rarely sleep till two or thereabouts. Four hours are enough for me—and in the summer much less. Sometimes, when the fit is on me, I roam all night long, and come back and do my routine—and then sleep where I am, or may be. Precisians would grow mad at such a life—and yet I'm awfully healthy."

The stranger watched him. "You live here, then—and so?"

"I have lived here," said Senhouse, "for three years or more, but I've lived so for over twenty. I've wandered for most of that time, and know England from end to end; but now I seem to have got into a backwater, and I find that I travel farther, and see more, than I did when I was hardly for a week together in the same place. But that's reasonable enough, if you think of it. If you can do without time, space goes with it. If it don't matter *when* you are, it don't matter *where*."

The stranger lent this reasoning his gloomy meditation, which turned it inwards to himself and his rueful history. "I don't follow you, I believe," he said, "for very good reason. I hope you will never learn as I have that it does matter where you are." He stopped, then added, as if the admission was wrung out of him, "I've been in prison."

"So have I," said Senhouse, "and in Siberia at that. I was there for more than a year, though not all that time within walls. They let me loose when they found that I could be trusted, and I learned botany, and caught a marsh fever which nearly finished me. They wouldn't have me in after that, being quite content that I should rot in the open. I was succoured by a woman, one of those noble creatures who are made to give themselves. She gave me what blood she had left. God bless her: she blessed me."

"It was a woman," said the stranger, "that sent me to prison."

Senhouse, after looking him over, calmly replied, "I don't believe you. You mean, I think, that there was a woman, and you went to prison. You confuse her and your feelings about her. It is natural, but not very fine-mannered. No woman would have put the thing as you have put it to me."

The stranger shifted two or three times under his host's quiet regard: presently he said, "This is the tale in a nutshell. She was beautiful and kind to me; she was in a hateful place, and I loved her—and she knew it. There was a man with claims—rights he had none—preposterous claims, made infamous by his acts. The position was impossible, intolerable. She knew it, but did nothing. Women are like that—endlessly enduring; but men are not. I dragged him off a horse and thrashed him. He had me to gaol, and she went her ways, leaving a note for me, hoping I should do well. Do well! Much she cares what I do. Much care I." He ended with a sob which was like the cough of a wolf at night, and then turned his face away.

"Why should she care," asked Senhouse, "what becomes of you? By your act you dropped yourself out of her sphere. If she was to be degraded, as you call it, by whom was she degraded? But you talk there a language which I don't understand. You say that she was beautiful, and I suppose you know what you mean by the word. How then is a beautiful person to be degraded by anything the likes of you, or your fellow-dog, do to her? The thing's absurd. You can't claw her soul or blacken the edges of that. You can't sell that into prostitution or worse. That is her own, and it's that which makes her beautiful,—in spite of the precious pair of you, bickering and mauling each other to possess her. Possess her, poor fool! Can you possess moonlight? If you have degraded anything, you have degraded yourself. She remains where she is, entirely out of your reach."

The young man now turned his trapped and wretched face to the speaker. "You little know—" he began, then for weakness stopped. "I can't quarrel with you; wait till I've had a night's rest."

"You shall have it, and welcome," said Senhouse. "But you'll never quarrel with me. I believe I've got beyond that way of enforcing arguments which I fear may be unsound. I doubt if I have quarrelled with anybody for twenty years."

"There are some things which no man can stand," said the other, "and that was one. Your talk of the soul is very fine; but do you say that you don't love a woman's body as well as her soul?"

Senhouse was silent for a while; then he said, "No,—I can't say that. You have me there. I ought to, but I can't. And I think I owe you an apology for my heat, for the fact is that I've been in much of your position myself. There was a man once upon a time that I felt like thrashing— for much of your reason. But I didn't do it— for what seemed to me unanswerable reason. I did precisely the opposite—I did everything I could to ensure a miserable marriage for the being I loved best in all the world. I loathed the man, I loathed the bondage; but that's what I did. Now mark what follows. I didn't—I couldn't— degrade her; but I saw myself dragging like a worm in the mud while she soared out of my reach. And there I've been—of the slime slimy ever since. Where she is now I don't know, but I think in heaven. Heaven lay in her eyes—and whenever I look at the sky at night I see her there."

"You are talking above my head," said the stranger, "or above your own. Either I am a fool, or you a madman. You love a woman, and give her to another man? You love her, and secure her in slavery? You love her, and don't want her?"

"It is I that am the fool, not you," said Senhouse. "I do want her. I want nothing else in earth or heaven. And yet I know that I have her for ever. Our souls have touched each other. She is mine and I am hers. And yet I want her."

"Won't you get her? Don't you believe that you will?"

"God knows! God knows!"

"She was beautiful?"

"The dawn," said Senhouse, "was not more purely lovely than she. The dawn was in her face—the awfulness of it as well as its breathless beauty."

"My mistress," said the young man, "had the gait of a goddess in the corn. One thought of Demeter in the wheat. She was like ivory under the moon. She laughed rarely, but her voice was low and thrilled."

"Her breath," Senhouse continued, "was like the scent of bean-flowers. She sweetened the earth. It is true that she laughed seldom, but when she did the sun shone from behind a cloud. When she was silent you could hear her heart beat. She was deliberate, measured in all that she did—yet her spirit was as swift as the south-west wind. She did nothing that was not lovely, and never faltered in what she purposed. When first I came to know her and see the workings of her noble mind, I was so happy in the mere thought of her that I sang all day as I worked or walked.

It never entered me for one minute that I could desire anything but the knowledge of her."

"I wanted my mistress altogether," the other broke in, "from the first moment to the last—fool, and wicked fool, as you may think me. I could see her bosom stir her gown—I could see the lines of her as she walked. She was kind to me, I tell you, and there were times when—alone with her —in her melting mood—in the wildness of my passion—but no! something held me: I never dared touch her. . . . And then he—the other— came back; he, with his 'claims' and 'rights'; and the thought of him, and what he could do— and did do—made me blind. You tell me that I sinned against her——"

"I don't," said Senhouse. "I tell you that you sinned against love. You don't know what love is."

"You say so. Maybe you know nothing about it. If you have reduced yourself to be contented with the soul of a woman, I have not. What have I to do with the soul?"

"Evidently nothing," said Senhouse. "How, pray, do you undertake to apprehend body's beauty unless you discern the soul in it—on which it shapes its beauty?"

"I know," the other replied, "that she has a lovely body, and gracious, free-moving ways; and I could have inferred her soul from them. I'll engage that you did the same thing. How are you to judge of the soul but by the hints which the body affords you?"

Senhouse made no answer, but remained musing. When he spoke it was as if he was resuming a tale half-told. . . .

"She was in white—white as a cloud—and in a wood. Her hair reflected gold of the sun. She pinned her skirts about her waist, and put her bare foot into a pool of black water. She sank in it to the knee. She did not falter: her eyes were steady upon what she did."

The stranger took him up where he stopped, and continued the tale. "She could never falter in her purpose. She bared herself to the thighs. She went into the pool thigh-deep. Whiter than the lilies which she went to save, she raked the weed from them—you helping her."

"She did," said Senhouse, his eyes searching the fire. "And when, afterwards, she did what her heart bade her, she never faltered either, though she steeped her pure soul in foulness compared to which the black water was sweet. But do you suppose that any evil handling would stain her? You fool! You are incapable of seeing a good woman. In the same breath with which I spurned myself for having a moment's fear for her, I thanked God for having let me witness her action."

The rebuke was accepted, not because it was felt to be justified; but rather, it passed unheeded. The stranger had questions to ply.

"Knowing her, loving her—loveworthy as she was—how could you leave her?"

"I beg your pardon," said Senhouse, "I have

never left her." But in the next breath he had to qualify his paradox.

He spoke vehemently. "I had of her all that I dared have. That has never left me. I had all that she could give me—she that was self-sufficing, not to be imparted. She did not love me, as you could understand love: I don't think she could love anybody. But I only could read her thoughts and grasp her troubles for her. She was at ease with me, let me write to her, was glad to see me when I came, but perfectly able to do without me. She was, of course, not human; she inhabited elsewhere. Her 'soul was like a star and dwelt apart.' She remembered things as they had been, yet not as affecting her to pleasure or pain; she remembered them as a tale that is told, as things witnessed. So she remembered me—and so she still does. If I was there, with her, she was glad; if I was not there, she wasn't sorry. I was nothing to her but a momentary solace—and I knew it and taught myself to be contented. I believe that she was the spirit of immortal youth fleeting over the world. I called her Hymnia. What Beatrice was to Dante, the visible incarnation of his dream of holiness, such was she to me. I picture her and Beatrice together in heaven.

> 'In the clear spaces of heaven,
>   As sisters and lovers, sit
>   Beatrice and Thou embraced—
>   Hand and hand, waist and waist,

> And smile at the worship given
> By Earth, and the men in it
> To whom you were manifest.'

I quote my own poetry, because, oddly enough, nobody else has remarked upon the fact."

He continued: "When she did what it pleased her to do, it was said by fools that I had inspired her. Fool among fools, I thought so myself at the time, and moved Earth and Heaven, and Hell and Ingram, to save her from an act of magnanimity the like of which I have never heard of. Bless you! if I had never lived, she would have acted as she did, because she was incapable of seeing evil, incapable of acting against her heart. Well! and the thing was done—and I had to face it. I had it all out with myself, and decided that no harm could come to her. From that hour I have never seen her with my waking eyes. Yet she is here. She is always here. . . .

"My answer to you is simple. I have all of her of which I am capable. I have never left her because she has never left me. . . .

"I wrote out my heart in my first years of knowing her; but since then I have gone under the harrow of this world, where there can be no singing. Now that I am at peace my voice has come back. I listen to what she tells me, and note it. Like Dante, *vo significando :* I am a drain-pipe for her spirit. She was Hymnia to me once, and I sang of Open Country; now she is Despoina, Mistress of the Night. Words come thronging to me, phrases, rhythms; but not Form. I shall get out a poem one of these days—when the harrow rests. And that will be its name: Rest Harrow."

He broke out after a pause—"Her beauty! What is it to the purpose to put its semblance into words? Its significance is the heart of the matter. We see the earth as hill and valley, pasture and cloud, sky and sea. Really it is nothing of the kind, but infinitely more. It is tireless energy, yearning, force, profusion, terror, immutability in variety. What are words to such a power? It is to *that* I stretch out my arms. I must lie folded in that immensity, drown and sink in it, till it and I are one. I must be resumed into the divine energy whose appearance is but a broken hint of it. So it is with Her: not what she appears, but what she stands for is the miracle. Her beauty is not in dimple and curve, though her breasts are softer than the snowy hills, and the liquor of her mouth sweeter than honey of limes. If I lay on the floor of the Ægean and looked up to the sun I should not see such blue as glimmers in her eyes. But these are figures, halting symbols. Her form, her glow, her eager, lovely breath are her soul put into speech for us to read. You might say that her nobility was that of the Jungfrau on a night of stars. So her body's beauty is but a poem written by God about her soul."

Glyde sat up and looked at him across the fire. "I know you. There is but one man who has loved her as you do. You are her poet. You are Senhouse."

Senhouse nodded. "That is my name. You know her, then?" His face glowed darkly. "You have known her—you!"

"I saw her four months ago. I was in servitude in a house where she too was made a servant. For her sake, I tell you again, I downed Ingram."

Senhouse said sharply, "It was for your own. You aren't fit to talk to her. You have unclean lips. You don't hurt her, for you cannot. You hurt yourself infinitely. Why, a dog would do as you did, and possibly be right; but you, not being a dog, have broken your own rules. You have trodden on your own honour, and, like the dull fool that you are, come out wrapped in your silly self-esteem as if it was a flag. I wish that you could see yourself as I see you—or rather I hope you never may; for if you did you would see no reason to live." The words, frozen with scorn, cut like hailstones. The guest cowered, with the whip about his face. Senhouse rose.

"Follow me," he said.

Glyde also rose to his feet, and, as if he was giddy, looked blankly about him. "O God, what have I done? O God, what am I?" He dashed his hand over his eyes. "I can't see. I suppose I never could." He turned upon Senhouse. "You! Why do you harbour such a rat as I?"

Senhouse gave him pitiful eyes. "If you think yourself a rat, you are in the way to be more. Come, we will be friends yet. You're near the end of your tether, I think. Let me tuck you into a blanket."

III

In the morning Glyde, in a humble mood, drank quantities of small beer. In other words, he told his story of Sanchia, of Ingram, and of Mrs. Wilmot. He was so steered by questions from Senhouse that he came, towards the end, to see that if any one had driven his mistress into a life of bondage to Ingram it was himself and his presumptuous arm.

"You must have offended her beyond expression," he was told. "First, her fine esteem in her own spotless robe, which you have smeared with beastly blood and heat; next, her sense of reason clear as day; next, and worst, her logical faculty by which she sees it to be a law of the earth that nothing can be bought without a price. Oh, you precious young donkey! And who the mischief are you, pray, to meddle in the affairs of high ladies—you who can't manage your own better than to do with your foolish muscles what is the work of a man's heart? Love! You don't know how to spell the word. But I am getting angry again, and I don't want to do that. I'll tell you what I shall do with you. You shall stay with me here till you are well, and then you shall go to London and find Despoina——"

"Do you mean Sanchia?" Glyde was still unregenerate at heart.

"I mean whom I say, your mistress and mine. You are not fit to name her by any other name."

"No, no—I know it," said the youth; "but her name is so beautiful."

"Everything about her is beautiful," said Senhouse, "therefore see that you go to her cleansed and sweetened. Now, when you have found her you shall beg her pardon on your knees——"

"Never!" said Glyde, grittily in his teeth.

"On your heart's knees, you fool," cried Senhouse, with a roar which rolled about the hills. "On the knees of your rat's heart. You shall beg her pardon on your knees for your beastly interference, presumption, mulishness, and graceless manhood; and then you shall leave her immediately, and thank God for the breath of her forgiveness. This also is important. You are not to name me who have sent you." His eyes shone with the gleam of tears. "Never name me to her, young Glyde, for I'll tell you now that for every stripe I've dusted your jacket with you owe me forty—and you can lay on when you please."

"For I," he continued, after a pause for breath, while Glyde stared fearfully upon him, "for I, too, have betrayed her."

They said no more at that time, but all day Glyde followed Senhouse about like a dog.

In the evening of what to the undrilled youth was a hard-spent day, Senhouse unfolded his heart and talked long and eloquently of love and other mysteries of our immortal life.

"The attainment of our desires," he said, "appears to every one of us to be a Law of Nature, and so, no doubt, it is. But that is equally valid which says, 'To every man that which he is fit to enjoy.' The task of men is to reconcile the two. That once done you are whole—nay, you are holy."

"I believe that I am in the way of that salvation, look you, for I know now that there is hardly a thing upon the earth which I cannot do without. That being so, and all things of equal value, or of no value, *I have them all*. They are at the disposal of that part of myself which enters no markets and cannot be chaffered away. Wind, rain, and sun have bleached me; dinners of herbs have reduced my flesh to obedience; incessant toil, with meditation under the stars, have driven my thoughts along channels graved deep by patient plodding of the field. I am become one with Nature. I have watched the wheeling of the seasons until, to escape vertigo, I picture myself as a fixed point, and see the spheres in their courses revolve about me."

Mystic sayings, aphorisms oozed from him like resin from a pine.

"It is error to suppose that discomfort is holy. Holiness is harmony. Men have lost sight of the sanctity of the body. Rightly considered, indigestion is a great sin."

"Passion, which is a state of becoming, is not holy, for holiness is a state of being. But it is noble, because it is a straining after appeasement, which is a harmony.

"Man is an ape, or a god, but certainly a god in this, that he can make himself either. It is by no means certain, however, that this potentiality is not also possessed by the ape.

"Appeasement of passion is fulfilment of our being, which out of ferment makes wine, though riot seeks rest."

He was not always so transcendental. Here we have him closer to the matter.

"A woman when she loves is a seraph winged. When she does not she is a chrysalis, a husk, or a shell. In love she follows the man, but appears to fly him, as a shepherd goes before the sheep he is really driving. Out of it she is an empty vase, to be revered by us for the sacred wine which she may hold, as a priest handles fearfully the chalice.

"She has but one law, the law of her love, which says to her, 'Give, give, give.' See here how she differs from the man, to whom love is but one of many healthy appetites—not a divine mission. Love, hunger, hunting, or a taste for picture-dealing, say to him, 'Take, take.'

"Yet it is no wonder that the sexes go in fear of each other, each a mystery to each. For my part, I have never been close to a woman without a desire to cover my eyes."

And here he got level with her, and showed her radiant beside him.

"A young woman with shining eyes, blown-back

hair and face on fire, holding out her heart from the threshold, stretching it out at arms' length, crying, 'Who will take this? To whom may I give it?' A vision here of Heaven's core of light. I have seen it. I, Senhouse, have seen the Holy Grail.

"She stood with me upon the threshold of the world, just so, with blown-back hair and shining eyes. Blessed one, blessed prodigal! She poured out her heart like water—for a dog to lap. He was dog-headed, full in the eye, a rich feeder. She decked him with the fair garlands of her thoughts, she made him glisten with her holy oils. She crowned him with starry beams from her eyes, she sweetened him with the breath of her pure prayers. She robed him in white and scarlet, for he was wrapped in her soul and sprinkled with her passion. And she said, 'I love a divine person. I am ready to die for him. Make haste. Pile the fire, sharpen the knife; bind me with cords, and drive deep. I die that he may live.' O Gods, and Sanchia gave herself for Nevile Ingram!"

He was never alone, it appeared, for she was with him constantly, a vivifying principle. He had ensphered her in light; she was unassailable— his fly in amber. Ingram, Chevenix, all Wanless, might have daily converse with her, and one might grudge her her self-sufficiency, and another see her a pretty girl in a mess. To him she was a fairy in harness, "a lovely lady garmented in light," to whom the rubs of the world could do no harm. She wore crystal armour. They did not know her, could not see her, those who used her for their elemental needs. "Her soul was like a star and dwelt apart."

He told young Glyde that he had reached this transcendental eyrie of his by painful degrees. No person of Sanchia's acquaintance had suffered more than he by her desperate affair. He had been her first lover, and her only confidant, for she had been what one calls a "difficult" girl, who gave out nothing and had no friends. Her sisters knew very little about her, her mother nothing. It had been Senhouse who had called up the spirit that was in her—that extraordinary candour of vision which shrank from the judgment of nothing in heaven or earth "upon the merits." He had himself been at first amazed by her quality; but before he had discovered it he had adored her; so it had seemed all of a piece with her exquisite perfection. That first sight he had had of her, in the sun-dappled woodland glade, with her gown above her knees, setting her foot in the unknown depths of a black pool—that she might rescue lilies from suffocation —was surely typical of that which followed—when, barely twenty-one, she trod deliberately, in her world's shocked face, a road which leads without return to a point at which the world says, "I cannot see you, you are dead." But she had never faltered, had seen no shame, and felt none. Nevile was unhappy, and needed her. If there was no other way of serving him, she must take that way. So she told him, Senhouse, her only friend; and he cried aloud in his agony, "God save her," while his soul was saying, "Beatrice never shrank from hell, nor ever looked back. No more, God be thanked, does Sanchia." When the thing was done, and she had gone with unbowed head into the deeps, he had known his hours of desolation; but from that hour she had stood for him "a thing enskied and sainted." He felt that he was set apart for her worship, and only regretted that Beatrice had had a better poet for the business than Sanchia could ever hope for.

For a year after her flight he continued a correspondence with her which had begun with their first acquaintance; and then he had stopped it, not she. His reason shall be admitted, to his credit or not. It appeared that she read his letters, as they came, to Nevile Ingram—she told him so —and, further, that Ingram was bored. Sanchia did not tell him that, but he gathered it; and whether he felt that the intimacy was fatally invaded, or whether he was piqued—he stopped. Within two years or so from that he wrote once more to tell her that he was about to "join fortunes" with Mary Germain, a young widow.

She knew what he meant by that; he was too much of a poet to be anything but shocked at the marriage-bond. She hoped the best for him, but his letter did not encourage her.

He wrote, "She is good, sweet and wholesome.

I have taught her what she knows—I mean by
that that I have helped her to pick up a clue here
and there to take her by some means to the heart
of our mystery. She has had a dreadful mauling
by the world; but her brain is sound. I intend
to make her happy, but not here. We go to Baden
a-painting. She vows she will keep the door of
my tent like a Bedouin's wife. It's a great test.
If she comes through it—with her upbringing—
she will show mettle. Farewell, Queen Mab. One
does what one must, being man. Pray for us both."

She answered him frankly and kindly. Ingram
was away on one of his long absences, and she felt
acold. "I shall always wish for your happiness.
How could I ever forget what you did to give me
mine?" He read that as meaning that she had
found and had it still, so wrote no more—not even
when his venture, not too hopefully begun, had
ended. His head was low in the dust, his zest
was gone. It needed his austerities and solitude
to restore his tone.

But now, in his hidden valley, she never left
him, though she was always veiled. He could not
call up her blue eyes' magic, nor her slow smile,
nor the touch of her thin fingers. She had no
bodily semblance; she was a principle. In his
exalted mood, being tiptoe for Mystery, he identified
her with the Spirit of all Life. For life to him was
a straining at the leash, a reaching for the unattain-
able, a preparation to soar. He saw all things
flowing towards heaven, which to him was Harmony,

Rest, what he called Appeasement. And all this straining and yearning in infinite variety was figured to him in Sanchia, as he discerned, but could not perceive, her presence. He made her out in elemental images, into the contours of the hills read her bountiful shape, into the onslaught of the wind her dauntless ardour. In fire leaped her pride, in the mantling snow her chastity was proclaimed. The rain was her largess, her treasure poured to enrich mankind. All flowers were sacred to her—frail beauty salient from the earth. He never looked on one but he blessed her name.

On a later day he read a poem to his guest— which he called the Song of Mab. By this name, it seems, he also figured Sanchia, whose synonyms, threatened to be as many as those of Artemis or the Virgin Mary. From poring for signs of her in the face of earth he was come to see little else. If the west wind was her breath and the hills were her breasts, it needed a mystic to see them so; and he was become a mystic. A glorified and non-natural Sanchia pervaded the poem, which, for the form, was a barbaric, rough-hewn chant, stuffed with words and great phrases which had the effect rather of making music in the hearer than of containing it in themselves. It was poetry by hints, perpetually moving, initiating, lyrical phrases, then breaking off and leaving you with a melody in your ears which your brain could not render. Either the poet was inchoate or the subtlest musician of our day. He said of himself that he was a drain-pipe for the spirit—a dark saying to Glyde, who was himself, we have heard, something of a poet, of the Byronic tradition. The youth was extremely interested, though seldom moved by this chaotic piece. He was for ever on the point to drink, and had the cup snatched away. Senhouse tormented you with possibilities of bliss—where sight merges in sound and both lift together into a triumphant sweep of motion—whirled you, as it were, to the gates of dawn, showed you the amber glories of preparation, thrilled you with the throb of suspense; then, behold! coursing vapours and gathering clouds blot out the miracle—and you end in the clash of thunderstorms and dissonances. Something of this the listener had to urge. Senhouse admitted it, but he said, "You know that the splendour is enacting behind. You guess the opening of the rose. One stalks this earth agog for miracles. It is full of hints—you catch a moment—for flashed instants you are God. Then the mist wraps you, and you blunder forward, two-legged man swaying for a balance. Translate the oracle as you will—with your paint-pans, with your words—we get broken lights, half-phrases. But we guess the rest, and so we strain and grow. Who are you or I, that we should know her!"

He stuffed the pages into the breast of his jelab, and sat brooding over the paling fire for a while; then, by an abrupt transition, he said—"A fatal inclination for instructing the young was, perhaps, my undoing. I believe that I am a prig to the very fibres of me. If I had kept my didactics for my own sex, all might have gone well: I have never doubted but that I had things to teach my generation which it would be the happier of knowing. But it's a dangerous power to put into a man's hands that he shall instruct his betters. I was tempted by that deadliest flattery of all, and I fell. Despoina heard me, smiled at me, and went her way regardlessly; but my poor Mary was a victim. She heard me, and took it seriously. She thought me a man of God. I failed absolutely, and so badly that by rights I ought never to have held up my head again. But she is happy, dear little soul, after her own peculiar fashion,—which she never could have been with me. She writes to me now and then. The man, her husband, is her master, but not a bad one. She knows it, and glories in him. Isn't that extraordinary?"

"Not at all," Glyde said, who knew nothing of Mary. "It's a law of Nature. The woman follows the man. I suppose you treated her as an equal?"

"No, as a superior, which she plainly was," said Senhouse.

"Then," Glyde said, looking at him, "then you made her so. If you fly against Nature, you must get the worst of it." He waited, then asked, "It's against your principles to marry a woman, no doubt."

"Quite," Senhouse said. "It seems to me an insult to propose it to her."

"Your Mary didn't think so."

"She did at first; but she couldn't get used to it."

"She felt naked without the ring? And ashamed?"

"God help me," said Senhouse, "that's true. The moment I realised what had happened, I gave in."

"And then she refused?"

"She neither accepted nor refused. She lived apart. We were in Germany at the time. I was naturalising plants for the Grand Duke of Baden —filling the rocks and glades in the Black Forest. She went into an hotel in Donaueschingen, and I went to see her every day. We were friends. Then we went to England, to London. She held to that way of life, and I did the best I could for myself. At any moment I would have taken her. I considered myself bound in every way. I could have been happy with her. She had great charm for me—great physical charm, I mean—and sweet, affectionate ways. I could have made her a wife and a mother.

"I intended her the highest honour I could show to a woman. To make her your property by legal process and the sanction of custom seems to me like sacrilege. But, however—One day she told me that a former lover of hers wanted to marry her, and left it for me to judge. She wouldn't say whether she wished it herself or not; but I knew that she did, for when I advised her to accept him she got up and put her arms round my neck and kissed both my cheeks. I was her elder brother,

I perceived, and said so. She laughed, and owned to it. And yet she had loved me, you know. She had refused that same man for me. She was afraid of him, and gave me her hand before his face."

"That to me," Glyde said, "is proof positive that she loved him. Of course she feared him. It is obvious. My poor master!"

Senhouse serenely replied, "She's happy, and I've done her no harm at all. But it's impossible for me to treat any living creature otherwise than as my better."

"I believe you," said Glyde, "and so it may be in a rarer world than this. In this world, however, a man is the most cunning animal, and in that both are flesh he is the stronger of the sexes. In this world the law is that the woman follows the man." He thought before he spoke, then added, "That applies all this world over. You will marry Sanchia."

Senhouse would not look up. He sat, nursing one leg. He bent his brows, and a hot flush made his skin shine in the firelight.

IV

THE poet and his disciple continued their partnership through the sogging rains of Christmas, well into the chill opening of the new year. Then came the snow to fill up the valley in which stood the hut, and blur the outlines of the folded hills. Poetry and Sanchia drew together a pair who could have little in common.

But Glyde became the slave of the strange man who blended austerity with charitable judgment, and appeased his passion by blood from his heart. He was not himself a mystic, but a sensitive youth whom the world's rubs had taught the uses of a thick hide. Either you have that by nature, or you earn it by practice. Glyde had found out that the less you say to your maltreaters the less, in time, you have to say about it to yourself. He was conscious of his parts and all too ready to be arrogant. Senhouse's goddess had been kind to him, and he had presumed upon that. Senhouse's own method was to alternate extreme friendliness with torrential contempt. He knocked Glyde down and picked him up again with the same hand. He treated him as his equal whenever he was not considering him a worm. There is no better way of gaining the confidence of a youth of his sort. At the end of a fortnight there was nothing Glyde would not have told him; at the end of six months he would have crossed Europe barefoot to serve him.

He was nothing of a mystic, and therefore had his own ideas of what seemed to afford his master so much satisfaction; he was enough of a poet to be sure that Senhouse's romantic raptures were only a makeshift at best. To his mind here was a man aching for a woman. He thought that the poet sang to ease his bleeding heart. He came to picture the mating of these two—Sanchia the salient, beautiful woman, and his master of the clear, long-enduring, searching eyes, and that strange look of second-sight upon him which those only have who live apart from men, under the sky. It is a look you can never mistake. Sailors have it, and shepherds, and dwellers in the desert. The eye sees through you—into you, and beyond you. It is almost impossible for any person to be either so arresting in himself or possessed of such utterance as will cause the weathered eye to check its scanning of distance and concentrate upon an immediate presence. To such an eye, communing with infinite and eternal things, no creature of time and space can interpose solidly. Each must be vain and clear as bubbles of air. Behind it float spirits invisible to other men—essential forms, of whose company the seer into distance really is. He will neither heed you nor hear you; his conversation is otherwhere. And what then would Senhouse do confronted with Sanchia? Would he look beyond her, towards some horizon where she could never stand? Or would he not see in her blue eyes the goal of all his searching—the content of his own? What would he say but "You!" and take her? What she but sigh her content to be taken? Appeasement is holiness, says Senhouse. And what of their holy life thereafter, breast to breast, fronting the dawn? Glyde's heart, purged of his dishonesty, beat at the thought. He turned all his erotic over to the more generous emotion, and faced with glowing blood the picture of the woman he had coveted in the arms of the master he avowed.

When February began to show a hint of spring, in pairing plovers and breaking eglantine, Senhouse, in a temporary dejection, ceased work upon his poem, and Glyde said that he must know the news. All through the winter they had had little communication with the world beyond their gates. A shepherd homing from the folds, a sodden tinker and his drab, whom he touchingly cherished, a party of rabbit-shooters beating the furze bushes, had been all their hold upon a life where men meet and hoodwink each other. Once in a week one of them ploughed through the drifts to the cottage at the foot of the third valley, and got as he needed flour and candles, soap or matches. It had not yet occurred to either of them—to Senhouse it never did occur— to beg the sight of a newspaper. But Saint Valentine's call stirred the deeps of Glyde, who now said

that he must have news. He departed for Sarum,
and stayed away until March was in.

He returned with certain information, absorbed
by Senhouse with far-sighted patient eyes and in
silence. The only indication he afforded was in-
scrutable. His cheek-bones twitched flickeringly,
like summer lightning about the hills.

Sanchia, Glyde said, was well and in London.
She was living in a street off Berkeley Square, with
an old lady who wore side-curls and shawls, and
drove out every afternoon in a barouche with two
stout horses and two lean men-servants. Sanchia
sometimes accompanied her, stiff and pliant at
once, bright-eyed and faintly coloured. She was
taken about to parties also, and to the opera—and
very often there were parties at the old lady's house
—carriage-company, and gentleman in furred coats,
who came in hansom cabs. He thought that she
had suitors. There was a tall, thin man who came
very often in the afternoons. He was sallow and
melancholy, and wore a silk muffler day and night.
Glyde thought that he was a foreigner, perhaps a
Hungarian or Pole.

He had seen Sanchia often, but she could not
have caught a glimpse of him. He admitted that
he had haunted the house, had seen her come out
and go in, knew when she dressed for dinner and
when she went to bed. Long practice had ac-
quainted him with the significance of light and
darkness seen through chinks in shutters. "I know
her room," he said, "and the times of her lights.

She looks out over the streets towards the Park twice every night—once when she is dressed, and once before she goes to bed. It is as if she is saying her prayers. She looks long to the west, very seriously. I think her lips move. I believe that she always does it." Senhouse, who may have been listening, bowed his head to his knees, below his clasped hands.

"Twice she looked full at me without knowing me. Why should she know me now? Her pale and serious face, master, was as beautiful as the winter moon, as remote from us and our little affairs. No words of mine can express to you the outward splendour of her neck and bosom. She was uncovered for a party at the house. In the morning she came out to walk. You know her way, how she glides rather than seems to move her feet—the soaring, even motion of a sea-bird. She walked across the Park, and I followed, praising God, whose image she is. On the further side the Pole met her in his furs, and she walked with him for an hour in the sun. She had no wrappage to hide her blissful shape. Close-fitted, erect, free-moving, gracious as a young birch-tree. Master, she is the Holy One."

"You played Peeping Tom, my ingenuous young friend," said Senhouse, who was fastidious in such matters.

But Glyde cried out, "God forbid! Are you prying when you look at the sun! Master, you need not grudge the Pole. He is nothing."

"I grudge no man anything he can get of her," said Senhouse. "He will get precisely what lies within his scope."

"He has the eyes of a rat," Glyde said.

Senhouse answered, "Rats and men alike seek their meat of the earth. And the rats get rat-food, and the men man's food. Despoina's breasts are very large." He turned to his poem, folded his jelab about his middle, and went out over the downs. Glyde saw him no more that day, nor, indeed, till the next morning, when he found him squatted over a pipkin simmering on the fire.

The year went on its course, and windy March broke into a wet, warm April. Glyde sat at the knees of his master, and imbibed learning and fundamental morality. But now and then he absented himself for a day at a time, and was understood to get news from Salisbury market. He came back one day with a newspaper. Senhouse read without falter or comment:

"A marriage is arranged, and will take place in July, between Nevile Ingram of Wanless Hall, Felsboro', Yorks, and Sanchia-Josepha, youngest daughter of Thomas Welbore Percival of — Great Cumberland Place, W., and The Poultry, E.C."

In that night, or very early in the morning, Glyde disappeared without word or sign left behind him.

BOOK IV

SANCHIA IN LONDON

I

Lᴏɴᴅᴏɴ in mid-May, slogging at its pleasures under the pale sun, might read one morning of an affray in Yorkshire, of a magistrate assaulted, or undergardener in arms, and forget it in half-an-hour; but to Sanchia, unaccustomed to cower, some such chance paragraph seemed one spot the more upon her vesture, which contact with the Fulham Road had smirched already. She had never taken cover before—and how could one be in such a place but to hide in it? With contracted brows and bosom oppressed, she watched the drifting millions go by, and her heart sank. Was she become as one of these? Is not to be ashamed to be shameful? And had she not been put to shame? If she was to hold up the head and feel the mouth of the winged steed that she rode, she must stable him elsewhere.

She wished to forget Wanless. Let it be as if it was not, and had never been. But she found that Glyde and his outrageous act made that not possible. They brought her down to London's level—her in her white robe out of stainless air; here she was still, as Glyde had made her there, just a woman for men to quarrel over, or a bone for dogs. Her heart surged hot against Wanless; she could not, if she would, forget it—least of all in the Fulham Road.

She felt spotted in Mrs. Benson's spotless dwelling
—largely because it was Mrs. Benson's, partly because a smell of fried herrings drifted in daily from
the street.   She felt herself the chosen of a servant,
one for whom a clown had held battle; and then she
found herself resenting the phrases, growing hot
over them.   A servant—Mrs. Benson, that staunch
protectress! A clown—Struan—his thin frame throbbing with fire, and his eyes of a hawk in a cage, far-
set, communing with invisible things! Why, when
he was rapt in his work he never saw her at all.
She was a speck at his feet! He had sent her away
once.   "I'm busy," he had said, without looking at
her; and she had gone away on tiptoe.   These things
vexed her to remember, and she felt that Mrs. Benson's dwelling could not be hers.

Mrs. Benson, too, it must be owned, had an in-
cumbrance, which she kept as far as might be in the
lower regions of her house, but which was now and
again encountered on the stair—a shambling son,
one Joe, mostly in shirt-sleeves, distilling familiarity
and beer from every pore.   He was a ne'er-do-well,
whom it was his mother's cross and crown to keep in
complete idleness.   He cast dreadful looks, as of an
equal in snugness, a fellow-minion, at the chiselled profile of our goddess, and was not long before he tried
for a full-faced effect.   Sanchia's eyes of clear amaze
should have cut him down, but they did not.   His
"Morning, Miss," was daily reminder of a shared
clay.   Sanchia made herself inaccessible, and Mrs.
Benson agonised.

To apologise for her son had been as futile as to make excuses for death; but she tried it. "You'll overlook the partiality of a mother, Miss Percival? What am I to do? It's not that I want him to lap syrup from a spoon—far from that. Idleness leads to impiety, and impiety anywhere, from Tattersall's to the public, we all know. But think of what stings me. I can't abide the thought that here am I, large Mrs. Benson, with money to spare, turning my back upon my fatherless child. Yet nothing short of that will do it." Sanchia readily excused her; and then she turned her own back upon the Fulham Road. Pimlico found her a lodging, at the gates of whose dingy mysteries were parks, Westminster, the sky and the river, eternal things, making for tranquillity.

It had been her first impulse, the moment she reached London, to go to her father, with whom alone she had corresponded during her years of exile. There was Vicky Sinclair, to be sure, her sister next in age; but Vicky was married to a man she knew nothing of, and she found herself shy. Fought for! Blared across London in a paragraph—championed by a clown! How was she to meet a Captain Sinclair? Her father, surely, was different. She never doubted his love, nor that he would take her to his heart if she asked to go there. But could she? It would have to be done by stealth; she must go to the city, to his office—for her mother ruled in Great Cumberland Place, and she could not go there. She hated secrets, and couldn't pose as a culprit; so she delayed and delayed. It was a comfort to her to know that he was at hand: meantime, she sought about for scope to spread her wings.

For a fortnight she drank of the gales of liberty, filled her bosom with beauty, and let art smooth out her brows. She listened to music, looked at pictures, renewed her reader's ticket, and spent whole days browsing under the Bloomsbury dome. Climbing the heights, she planned out schemes of work, felt her critical faculties renewed, studied men and women, and found her old pleasure in quiet chuckling over their shifts. But she had to chuckle alone, for she never spoke to a soul. For a fortnight or so all went well—and then, quite suddenly, without any warning, going, as it were, to the fountain for water, she found there was no bottom to her cruse. She went to bed sanguine, she awoke morose. She saw the day with jaundiced eyes, scorned herself, cried "Liver!" and took medicine. She was glued to her books all day, returned late to her lodging, and found herself in tears. She discovered a tenderness, a yearning; she lay awake dreaming of her childhood, of her girlhood, of Vicky, of her father's knee, of Senhouse, her dear, preposterous friend, whose grey eyes quizzed while they loved her. Golden days with him—golden nights when she dreamed over his eager, profuse, interminable letters! All these sweet, seemly things were dead! Ah, no, not that, else must she die. She cried softly, and stretched out her arms in the dark to the gentle ghosts that peopled it. Then, being practical in grain, she jumped up, lit candles, and wrote deliberately to each of her sis-

ters—finally, after much biting of the pen, to her
father. Before her mood could cool she dressed
hastily, slipped out, and posted her letters. Coming
back to bed, she paused in the act to enter it—one
knee upon it. Wide-eyed she wondered why she
had not written to Senhouse. To him, of all people
in the world, first of all! And his answer—a certainty. Hot came the reply to her question, and
smote her in the face. Never to him again—never.
There are certain things no woman can bring herself
to do. The more she has need of a man the less possible is it to tell him so. She sighed as she got into
her bed, and her eyes were very kind.

Of the five fair daughters of Thomas Welbore
Percival, East India Merchant in The Poultry, Philippa, the eldest, the trenchant and clear-sighted,
lived in Bryanston Square, mother of three children.
Her husband, Mr. Tompsett-King, was a solicitor,
but he was much more than that, An elderly, quiet
gentleman, who talked in a whisper, and seemed to
walk in one too, he presided over more than one
learned Society, and spoke at Congresses on non-con-
troversial topics. A sound churchman, he deplored
Romish advance on the one hand and easy divorce
on the other. The salvation of human society lay,
he held, within these limits. Distrust the emotions;
submit all things to reason—love of God and love
of women. On these terms he prospered like his
father before him. It all seemed very simple to him.
The handsome Philippa respected him, obeyed him

particularly, and never differed from him in opinion. But she coloured every compliance with his decrees with an idiosyncrasy so marked as to make them seem her own. Where he held that Rome pandered to the emotions, she laughed it to scorn as a forcing-house of spiritual foppery; where he saw in divorce a treason to the law of contract, she said that it tempted women to fall. Is it not easy enough to sin? Must we legalise it? Why put a tax upon marriage? Mr. Tompsett-King deprecated all dottings of iotas; when Philippa stormed at society he hummed a sad little tune. Before he left for Bedford Row he patted her shoulder and said, "Gently does it." Some such scene must ensue upon the prodigal's letter.

Hawise, Lady Pinwell, next in age to Philippa, lived in the country. Her husband was a baronet, and a handsome blond. A pretty, apple-cheeked, round-eyed girl, very much of a kitten, she was now grown plump, sleek, rather slow to move, and many times a mother. She deferred to her husband in all things, and by his wish received her parents on a formal visit once a year. She saw very little of her sisters, and as for Sanchia—the thing was not to be heard of, not even mentioned to Sir George. As, in fact, she burned the child's letter before she left her bedroom, she does not come into the tale at all.

But the pensive Melusine, three years younger than Philippa, seven older than Sanchia, may be reckoned with. She was also married, to a Mr. Gerald Scales, the son of a baronet. He was not,

however, to inherit the title, for he had a brother,
Sir Matthew, and frequent nephews. But his means
were ample for his rank and discreet amusements,
and went further and did more for him than prolific
Sir Matthew's; for Melusine gave him no sons. His
circle of being, in and through which trailed with
charming languor his wife, was of more dappled
sheen and of ampler circumference than that of
Bryanston Square. Having its centre in Kensington Gore, it reached to Ranelagh on one side, to
Maidenhead on the other. There was a riverside
villa down there, where Mrs. Scales gave parties in
the summertime and was printed about by flushed
gentlemen in pink shirts. She was the tallest of the
five sisters, and the most graceful; near-sighted
enough for lorgnettes, an elegant young woman.
She had an instinct for attitudes, turns of the head,
which were useful in *tête-à-tête* conversations. Mentally, she was not strong, and perhaps her manner
was too elaborate: she draped herself when she sat
down as if her skirts were window-curtains. Toy
Pomeranians were a hobby of hers, and the early
Florentine masters. She could read off the names of
the saints in a sacred conversation as easily as you
or I a row of actresses in a photograph shop. Mrs.
Jameson's books were at her fingers' ends. Her
mother favoured her more than any of her children,
and was often at her house on visits. Gerald Scales
called her the Dowager, and pleased her vastly. He
himself was Tubby to his friends.

Vicky, a year older than Sanchia, had married a

Captain Sinlcair, who was stationed at Aldershot.
She had been the romp of former days and, when
the storm had burst, hotly on the culprit's side.
But Vicky had been flighty, and marriage changes
one. Sanchia's eyes grew wistful as she sat, her
letters on the wing, and thought of Vicky.

Her first response was from Melusine, in a telegram from Taplow which read, "Darling, alas!"
and no more. Her comment was shrewd: "Mamma is there"—and she was right. Then came her
father's letter, to pluck at her heart-strings. He
invited her to the Poultry at "any hour of the day—
and the sooner the better;" but was clear that she
could not visit Great Cumberland Place without
writing to Mamma. "Doing the civil" was his
jocular way of putting it—one of Papa's little ways
when he meant more. She knew that he was right,
and postponed the fond man and his injunction.
His love might be taken for granted by a favourite
child. Just now it was her sisters' judgment she
craved.

Philippa wrote with her accustomed steel. It
might have been a bayonet: yet she meant to be
kind.

BRYANSTON SQUARE,
Thursday.

My Dear Sanchia,—I may as well say at once that I am not
surprised to hear from you; in fact, I have been expecting
some such letter as yours ever since I read in the *Times* of
Claire Ingram's death. Poor unhappy woman, it was time!
Some of the Pierpoints (the Godfrey P's) are intimate friends

of ours: we dined there last week; no party—just ourselves— and heard all about it. I learned that Mr. Ingram had gone abroad, but imagine that he will be in London before the end of the season. Have you written to Mamma? If not, *pray do so*. I assure you that it will be taken as it is meant. Nothing but good can come of it. Of that I am sure.

Now, as to your proposals. I think I will ask you to come to me *here*. I am very busy, with calls a thousand ways. I really have no afternoons free for as far forward as I can see— except Sundays, which I devote entirely to Tertius and re- ligion. No woman ought to separate the two—love of God, love of husband in God. Sooner or later, all women learn it. Then the mornings are naturally occupied with the house and the children. They have Miss Meadows; but she is young and absurdly inconsequent. I don't see how you can expect a girl in her teens to work miracles. In fact, I don't want her to, and am at hand to see that she doesn't.

I have spoken to Tertius, and you must forgive me for saying that we both think, under the circumstances, it would look, and be, better in every way if you came here, in the first instance. Without discussing what is done, and (I pray) done with, you will see, I think, that for me *to seek you out* would be, to say the least of it, unusual. You left our father's house for reasons of your own; I had left it to be married to Tertius. Forgiveness, if you wish it from me, is yours: countenance of the step you took—never. You will not ask it. So come here any morning that suits you, and I shall be pleased. You will find ¦me ready to do everything I can, to put you on your proper footing in the sphere to which you were born.—Believe me, my dear Sanchia, your affectionate sister,   PHILIPPA TOMPSETT-KING.

P. S.—The Church's arms are very wide. One cannot be too thankful, as things have turned out, that Claire Ingram never sued for divorce. God is most merciful.

There was some knitting of brows over this, and some chuckling. Comedy is the Art of the Chuckle;

but it is very seldom that one of the persons in the play can practise that which delights us. Sanchia was such a person. She could detach herself from herself, see her own floutings and thwackings, and be amused. At the same time her reply to Philippa was curt.

"You," she wrote, "are busy, and I am not. I will come to you one of these fine mornings, and must trust to Miss Meadows' sense of fitness not to work miracles that day."

A day or two later came a telegram from Vicky Sinclair. "Just got your letter. Coming at twelve. Vicky." Sanchia glowed. "Just like her, the darling." Philippa's astringent proposal was put aside.

At twelve thirty-five there lit from a hansom an eager and pretty little lady, all in gauzy tissues and lace scarf, who knocked at the door like a postman and flew up the stair into Sanchia's arms. "Oh, Sancie, Sancie, how sweet of you to write! Now we are all going to be happy again forever after. Oh, and here's Cuthbert—I forgot." In the doorway stood the erect form, and smiled the bronzed face of Captain Sinclair of the Greys. His "How d'ye do, Miss Sanchia!" was accompanied by a look of such curious enquiry that Sanchia gave him two fingers, said, "Quite well, thank you," and no more. Much more had been expected, and the Captain was somewhat taken aback. He had been ready to welcome the prodigal and admire her too. What's more, he had already very much admired her. To have one's generous motions damped by a coolness of that sort is sickening. But there it was: what could one say? what could one do? He went to the window and stood there, whistling in a whisper until his wife dismissed him. To the Cavalry Club stalked he, working himself into virtuous heat. There, at luncheon with a friend, he expatiated, which was unwise and unmannerly at once. But his own wrongs swallowed up his wife's rights.

"I'll be damned, Jack," he took up his parable, "I'll be damned if ever I do a woman a good turn any more. Never, never again. Gel I know— relative of mine she is, by marriage—goes a purler with a chap. Knew something of the chap too— so did you, I expect. Not a bad chap, by any means, barring this sort of thing. Well, now she's in town—all over—settled down, y'know. Writes to my wife. Well, I thought it was no good bein' stiff in these things. Against the spirit of the age— what? So I said we'd do the handsome thing and go up. We both wanted a spell of easy—so it was handy. Besides, I wanted to see the gel. I own to that. And there's no doubt she's a clinker; quiet, you know, and steady; looks right at you, far in; sees the lot at a glance. Palish gel, not too big; but well set up. Square shoulders—deep-chested gel. That sort." He stared at the table-cloth hard.

"I was taken by her, mightily taken. So when she and my wife had done kissin', I put in my little oar. 'How d'ye do, Miss—' I won't mention names, though upon my dick I don't know why I should be squeamish. But there it was; and I'd have kissed her, as you do kiss your wife's—well, cousin, let's say—if you want to. Bless you, not a bit of it. Proud as pepper. Gives me a finger. 'Quite well,' says she. 'Quite well, thank you—' and drops me. Drops *me!* Good Lord!"

He drank deeply of beer. "Well now, I tell you, that's the last time, absolutely the last time I do the civil thing to—well, to that sort, if she's my wife's grandmother." He stared out of window, mist over his blue eyes. "They're all for marrying her now. It seems it can be done. Chap's to be screwed up. Then she'll be patronising me, you'll see. Because I was decently civil—that was as far as I was prepared to go; bare civility—and two fingers for it—'Quite well, thank you!' Oh, damn it. Waiter—more beer."

II

VICKY was enchanting; for half-an-hour Sanchia was at the top of bliss. To be petted and diminutived by a butterfly—it was like that; for though the child was a year older than she, six years of marriage had made a baby of her. Her audacities of old had become artless prattle, her sallies were skips in the air. Yet to be purred over by a kitten was pure joy. "You darling! You darling little Sancie! You beautiful, pale, Madame-de-Watteville kind of person! Oh, my treasure—and I thought I should never see you again!" So she cooed while she cuddled, Sanchia, for her part, saying little, but kissing much. Her lips were famished; but Vicky's must be free for moments if her words were to be intelligible. During such times she stroked or patted the prodigal, and let her browse on her cheeks.

By-and-by, raptures subsiding, the pair settled down for talk, and the discrepancies which eight years had made began to show up, like rocks and boulders in a strand left bare by the ebb. Grotesque the shapes of some of them, comical others; but wrecks and dead things come to light at low water— spectral matter, squalid, rueful matter. And there are chasms set yawning, too, which you cannot bridge. Sanchia was to be lacerated.

No doubt it was laughable at first, as *naïveté* is. "Cuthbert was very funny about it"—for instance. "He was awfully anxious to see you, you know— you had never met, I think?—and yet not quite liking it. He said it was a great risk; he seemed to think I ought not to be there. He takes great care of me, the darling. And there was little Dickie, you see. Sancie! he can just walk—a kind of totter from my knees to Cuthbert's—and then so proud of himself! Cuthbert said that my duty was to Dickie; but I told him that I meant to come."

Yes, it was comical. "Did Captain Sinclair think I should give him a complaint?" Sanchia was smiling, with eyes and mouth; but the smile was fixed.

Vicky hugged her. "You dear one! prettiness is your complaint. I should like him to have some of that." She held her at arms' length, looked and glowed, and kissed. She took a serious tone, for the matter was serious. "You know, Sancie, you're the only beauty in our family, the only real beauty. Philippa's awfully handsome, I know, and greatly admired—and I've always said that Melot was *lovely*. There are those three sorts of women, you know. Philippa's handsome, Melot's lovely, and you're beautiful. Then there's prettiness. I know I'm rather pretty: everybody says so. Besides, there's Cuthbert. Oh, you can always tell! For one thing —he's so fussy about my clothes—you've no idea." She preened herself, like a pigeon in the sun, before she returned to her praises. "But you! You're quite different. You're like a goddess." She touched her curiously. "Yes, I thought so. Exactly like a goddess." She sighed. "I can't think how you do it. Swedish exercises? I know it's wonderful what they do for you—*in no time*. But you have to think about them all the while, and I think of Cuthbert— and Dickie—and the horses—and, oh, all sorts of things! Those sort, I mean,—nice things." She pondered Sanchia's godhead, shaking her pretty draperies out, then recalled herself. "Oh, yes, about coming here. Of course I knew that Mamma would make a fuss—but I had determined long ago, before I dreamed that it would ever happen, not to tell *her* a word. It was only Cuthbert who made me feel— well, *serious*. He is so wise, such a man of the world! But I told him that I meant to come whatever he could say—and afterwards it turned out that he wanted to come too. He was really quite keen. Wasn't that sweet of him? You would adore Cuthbert if you knew him as well as I do. But, of course, that's absurd." She suddenly became intense. "Sancie!" she said, then stopped and peered.

"Yes?" It was a sobered goddess who waited for close quarters. Vicky put her question, but peered no more.

"I wish you would tell me one thing, which— has always puzzled me. But don't, if you would rather not. How did you—I simply can't under- stand it—how did you ever—? I suppose you loved him very much?"

Sanchia was in a hard stare. "Yes," she said slowly, "I suppose I did." Vicky's head darted back.

"Ah! But now you don't a bit. I knew you didn't! Sancie, that's what I can't understand. Because, you know, when you're married you do. You always love the same person. You must— you can't help it. He's so natural; he knows things that you know. He knows—everything. Oh, Sancie, I can't talk about it, but you understand, don't you?"

Poor Sancie nodded, not able to look up. Alas for her secrets, offered, taken, and forgotten! But Vicky's vivacious fingers groped in her empty cupboard. "And then, as well as that, you *ought* to love him. You see, you've promised; it's all been made so sacred. You never forget it—the clergyman, and the altar, and the hymns. You're all in white— veiled. And you kneel there—before the altar— and he holds your hand. And the ring, oh, Sancie, the feeling of the ring!" She opened her little hand and looked down at the smoothed gold, coiled below the diamonds and pearls. "You never forget the first feel of that. It means—everything!" She blushed, and said, in a hushed sort of way, "It meant —Dickie, to me."

Sanchia drooped and bled. Vicky, deep in her holy joys, was remorseless. Even when she turned once more to her sister's affairs her consolation made wounds.

"Cuthbert said that it would come all right now —now that Mrs. Ingram—the wife—was— That's

rather horrible. Even you must feel that. Instead
of being sorry that his wife is dead, one has to be
awfully glad. I suppose you felt that at once; and
of course *he* did. Poor woman! I wonder if she
was buried in her ring." She eyed her own. "No
one would dare take it off. I made Cuthbert promise me this morning. But—of course people do marry
again, and it will be practically the same as that."
She reflected. "Yes, practically, it will, but—oh,
it's very extraordinary! You've had all your fun of
engagement and all that, long ago." She looked
down deeply at her hand; and then she gazed at her
sister. "And, oh, Sancie, you've had your honeymoon!" Before the deadly simplicity of that last
stroke Sanchia fell, and lay quivering. She could
not ask for mercy, she could explain, extenuate,
nothing. Huddled she lay. At this aching moment the one thing that the world held worth her
having seemed to be the approbation of this butterfly child. For Vicky's happiness was specific.
Nuptial bliss lay, as it were, crystallised within it.
There are moments in one's life when love itself
seems lust, and safety the only holy thing. Vicky,
tearing at her heart, had turned her head.

Vicky once gone, with promise of frequent intercourse by letter and otherwise, it was to Philippa's
fine house and respectable man-servant she next
surrendered herself. The meeting was cool, but not
intolerable to a goddess sore from Vicky's whip.
Philippa could ply a longer lash, but not by the same

right, nor with the same passion to drive it home.
Sanchia's eyes met hers upon the level; and if the
elder had a firmly modelled chin, so had the younger
sister. Her strength, too, lay, as it always had, in
saying little, whereas Philippa's *forte* was dialogue.
But it needs two for that. After the first greeting
there came a pause, in which the embarrassment,
upon the whole, was Mrs. Tompsett-King's.

The trenchant lady had had her sailing orders,
and was going to follow them. Mr. Tompsett-
King had told her that Sanchia must be led, not
driven, into Ingram's arms. "Assume the best of
her, my dear friend," he had said, "if you wish to
get the best out of her. Take right intentions for
granted. It is very seldom that a woman can resist
that kind of flattery. So far as I can read your
sister's mind, she has suffered from your mother's
abrupt methods. I beg of you not to repeat them.
Nothing but mischief could come of it." When Mr.
Tompsett-King called her his dear friend, she knew
that he was serious.

But Sanchia's mood had not been reckoned with:
Philippa was not Vicky. In the old days, in a wonderfully harmonious household, there had been a
latent rivalry between her and all her juniors. The
greatest trouble had been with Sanchia, the deliberate.
And so it was now that when the elder warmed to
her task of making bad best, she was suddenly chilled
by that old pondering and weighing which had
always offended her. Sanchia replied to her assump-
tions and suppositions by saying simply that she

didn't know where Mr. Ingram was, and that he was
no better informed of her than she of him. But
surely—Philippa raised her brows—but surely she
knew when he was coming to London? Sanchia's
head-shake shocked her. There was but one con-
culsion to be drawn from it.

"There's been a quarrel," then said she.

"No," Sanchia answered—as if thinking it out—
"no, I shouldn't say that. I should say, a difference of opinion."

"My dear," said Philippa—and the phrase with
her was one of reproof—"on essentials there can
have been none. He will wait a year, of course.
Under the circumstances, a full year. But——"

Sanchia had replied, "I don't know what he
means to do. I have left Wanless."

"Oh, of course, of course. But—I was going to
say—I fully expect that he has written to Mamma."
Sanchia's eyebrows and her, "I should think that
unlikely. Why should he write to Mamma?"
frightened Philippa, while to Mr. Tompsett-King's
mind they were clear gain. It was necessary, after it,
to get on to surer ground. The interview terminated
by an understanding that Sanchia should write to her
mother.

Philippa took her husband to dine in Great Cumberland Place that night; and there, he with Mr.
Percival, she with the lady, obtained the terms of a
settlement. Sanchia was to be allowed a hundred
a year—for the present. (Mr. Percival intended

privately to make it two.)   Everything was to be
assumed in her favour; but she was not to be asked
to meet company.   Neither Mrs. Percival nor Philippa could be brought to that, and Mr. Percival, so
far as he was concerned, had no desire for any sort
of company but hers.   He was one of those men
made rosy-gilled for happiness.   Good fellowship,
the domestic affections—if they were not there, they
must appear to be.   His friends of the city were
always on his lips—Old Tom Peters—Old Jack
Summers—Old Bob—Old Dick.   Good fellows every
one.   All the pet names in the family had been his.
To him belonged Pippa and Sancie, Melot and
Vicky.   "My girls," or "My rascals," he used to
call them to Tom Peters or Jack Summers, and
bring them home jerky little tin pedestrians from
the city, or emus pulling little carts; or (later on)
bowls of goldfish or violet nosegays from Covent
Garden.   If he had a nearer passion, it was to stand
well with all the world.   That's two passions, however, to his score; and the struggle between them,
in Sanchia's case, had taken him as near tragedy as
the easy man could go.   Heaven be praised, the
good times were come again.   Now he was all for the
return of the prodigal, without conditions—"and no
questions asked," as he put it.

But in this he could not get his dear desire.   Philippa's sense of justice was inflamed, as well as her
moral sense.   What! you eat a cake, and then,
instead of sitting down to your plain bread and
butter—away you flounce, and get ready to eat

another cake! That's dead against the proverb, that's monstrous, that's offensive. "Mamma, mamma," Philippa had protested, "you can never have her back to flourish her sin in all our faces."

"Thank you, Philippa, for reminding me, however gratuitously, of my duties to society," had been Mrs. Percival's acknowledgment. She liked sin as little as Philippa, but she liked being lectured a great deal less. Poor Mr. Percival had pulled his whiskers throughout the debate, and now sighed as he bit them. His girl was to be denied him—but he could give her two hundred a year, and go to see her often. That was comfort.

And then the meeting took place. First with Mamma, who had never liked her, and was now a little afraid of what she might do. For Philippa had made it quite plain that if Sanchia was not humoured, she would have nothing to say to Ingram. "She's exhausted her criminal passion—that's what it comes to," was Philippa's judgment. "Now she will have to be cajoled." So Mrs. Percival was cowed into civility.

The pair conversed, rather painfully, for perhaps an hour. They had tea. All the effort to talk was made by Sanchia, who broached the children—Philippa's three, Vicky's one—and got nothing but perfunctory enthusiasm in reply. Mrs. Percival was far too sincerely interested in herself to care for children. The sons-in-law proved a better subject. Here she could point a moral inwards. She extolled

them highly—never was woman so blessed in her
daughters' husbands. Mr. Tompsett-King—"Tertius, the soul of honour: the most delicate-minded
man I have ever known. And sensitive to a fault! I
assure you—" Captain Sinclair was "our gallant
Cuthbert," or "my soldier son." "Sweet little
Vicky's knight! chivalry lives again in him. It has
been the greatest blessing in my days of trouble to be
sure of the ideal happiness of those two young lives.
Ah! one does have one's consolations."

Such eulogium seemed to leave little to be said
for Melusine and her prize; and yet it was certain
that Mrs. Percival favoured Gerald Scales above
the others. A lift of the voice was observable—
"Gerald, who, naturally, is quite at home at Marlborough House . . ." "Gerald, with that charming old-world courtesy of his . . ." "Dear Lady
Scales told me that of her two sons, Gerald should
have been the baronet. Poor Sir Matthew suffers
from hay-fever to that extent. . . . But Gerald is a
splendid young man. Darling Melot is, I need not
tell you, fully appreciated at Winkley." This was
the seat of Sir Matthew, in Essex.

Sanchia, for her part, having regained the throne
of her serenity—from which Vicky had toppled her
of late—by means of Philippa, was able to contem-
plate this singular parent of hers with the interest
due to a curious object, and some internal amusement. She was too far removed from her to be
moved, too much estranged to be hurt. She wondered at herself for feeling so little of what, in the

days of babyhood, she had firmly held to be the devout opinion. She found that, from a child, she had always judged her mother, and was sure now that her mother knew it. She remembered how hopeless she had always known it to be, to explain any attitude of mind she may have exhibited and been blamed for. So now, though it was abundantly clear to her what was hoped of her, and though she could see perfectly well that the chance of her doing it was so risky that she must be handled like a heavy fish on a light line, she made no effort whatever to show why what was to be hoped for was absurdly impossible. She watched her mother sail about it and about in ever narrowing circles, heard herself commended for her promptitude in leaving Wanless, answered enquiries as to Ingram's behaviour under what Mrs. Percival otiosely called "his bereavement," echoed speculations at to his whereabouts—played, in short, vacantly an empty part, and kept her mother upon tenterhooks. She gained civil entreaty that way.

But her father's bustling entry changed all this. She had not known of herself how susceptible she still was. Vicky had made her cower; but her father made her cry.

He affected a bluff ease in his manner of greeting her. "Well, Sancie, well, my dear, well, well"— and then he cleared his throat; but he did not dare to look at her. Sancie answered him by jumping into his arms, and upset him altogether. "Oh, my girl, my girl—my little Sancie—" and then the pair of them mingled tears, while Mrs. Percival, who thought this exhibition out of place "under the circumstances," and not in the best possible taste, tapped her foot on the carpet, and wished that Philippa had been here.

But, once they were beyond a certain flood mark, as she know by long acquaintance, Mr. Percival's emotions must be given play. She retired, therefore, and left the clinging pair. Directly she was gone, the good gentleman's embrace of his child grew straighter, and his kisses of her brows and hair more ardent. He humbled himself before her, thanked her for coming back to him. "My darling, it was fine of you to come! 'Pon my soul, it was fine!"

"No, darling, no," she protested, smiling sadly at his fondness.

"I always loved you, my child! My Sancie—you know that of your old father, hey?" He pinched her cheek before he kissed it again. "'Pon my life, it cut me down like a frost to do—what was done."

"I know, I know," Sanchia murmured, and then begged him not to speak of it.

"Ah, but I must, you know," he vowed. "What! A damned unnatural father! . . . " And then he held her closely, while he whispered his anxiety. "Sancie—tell me, my lamb—put my mind at rest. He—that fellow—that Ingram—he was good to you, hey? He didn't—hey?"

She vowed in her turn. "Oh, yes, dearest, yes. Of course he was. I was very happy, except for—what couldn't be helped, you know."

"Yes, yes—it couldn't be helped. I know that you felt that. I was bound—for the others, don't you see?—sake of example. That sort of thing, don't you see?" He shook his head. "We can't have that, you know. It don't do—in the long run. Very irregular, hey? And your mother, you know —she takes these things to heart. Goes too far, *I* say. Sometimes goes a little to extremes, you know." He grew quite scared as he recalled the scene. "I shall never forget"—shuddering, he clasped her close. "My darling girl, let's be happy again! It shall be right as—well, as rain, you know —now. We'll have you with a child on your knee in no time,—hey?" He seemed to think that marriage alone could work this boon. Again—as before with Vicky—Sanchia had not the heart to gainsay him. She allowed him to speculate as he would; and her mother, returning, found the pair, one on the other's knee, with the future cut and dried.

But Sanchia rose at her entry.

"Dearest, I must go now," she told him, "but I'll see you again very soon."

He urged her to stay and dine. "We're quite alone, you know! No ceremony with our child, hey!"

But she smilingly refused. "No, darling, I won't stop now. I'll come again—" her mother's stretched lips, stomaching what she could not sanction, stood, as it were, before the home doors.

He looked wistfully at her—aware, he too, of the sentries at the gate. "You might—we are pretty

lonely here, we old people—I should have said you
might come back—there's your old room, you know
—eating its head off, hey?"

Sanchia kissed him. "Darling—we'll see. We'll
talk about it soon. But I must go now—to my
books. I'm working very hard, at my Italian. I've
forgotten—lots."

He had to let her go—but, manlike, he must relieve himself in a man's way. He drew her into
his study, bade her "see what she should see."
He went to his desk and sat to his cheque-book. He
returned with the slip wet in his hand. "There,
my child, there. That will keep the wolf from the
door, I hope. For a day or two, you know." She
read, "Miss Sanchia Percival—two hundred pounds
sterling." It brought the tears to her eyes again.
It was so exactly like him.

"You darling—how ridiculous of you—but how
sweet!"

He glowed under her praises. "Plenty more
where that came from, Sancie,"—then piously added,
"Thank God, of course."

Sanchia, in the hall, turned to her mother. "Good-
bye, mother," she said, and held her hand out. Her
mother took it, drew her in, and kissed her forehead.
"Good-bye, my child"; she could not, for her life,
be more cordial than that. The offence itself seemed
a pinprick beside the rankle of the wound to her pride.
This child had set up for herself, and was now returned—without extenuation, without plea for mercy.
Mrs. Percival was one of those people who cannot

be happy unless their right to rule be unquestioned. Had the girl humbled herself to the dust, grovelled at her feet, she would have taken her to her breast. But Sanchia stood upright, and Mrs. Percival felt the frost gripe at her heart. It must be so.

Her father went with her to the door—his arm about her waist. "Come soon," he pleaded, and when she promised, whispered in her ear— "Come to The Poultry, if you'd rather: I'm always there —as you know. Come, and we'll lunch together. You'll be like a nosegay in the dusty old place."

"Yes, yes, I shall come—often," she told him, and nestled to his side. Then she put up her cheek for his kiss. "Good-night, Papa dear," He wept over her, and let her go. Then he returned to his hearth and his wife. In his now exalted mood he was really master of both, and Mrs. Percival knew it. "You gave her the money, I suppose?" she said; and he, "Yes, my dear, I gave her two hundred pounds." He had doubled the sum agreed, but Mrs. Percival let it pass.

III

Upon this footing her affairs now stood; she was to be one of the family, with two hundred pounds a year to her credit, the run of her teeth in the house, and (by a secret arrangement) as often in her father's company as she could find time to be. Meantime, by her own deliberate choice, she maintained her lodging in Pimlico, and read at the Museum most days of the week. She prepared herself to be happy, and under a buoyant impulse, due to the softening of her affections, wrote to her friend Mr. Chevenix, and asked him to come to see her. That he briskly did.

She received him cordially. It was good to see the cheerful youth again, and to be able to rejoice in the man of the world he affected to be. A man of the world—throned, at it were, upon the brows of a suckling.

Wisdom was justified of her child. "So you cut it? Thought you would. Wanless Hall is all very well in its little way—when the rainbows are jumping, what? D'you remember that fish? And old Devereux—*Salmo deverox?* My certy, what a lady! But Nevile—" he shook his head. "No, no. Some devil had entered into him: he was a gloomy kind of tyrant. I don't know, by the way, what's happened to him. Travelling, or something, I fancy. He was always a rolling stone, as you know. But he'll come round, you'll see. Oh, Lord, yes. He'll sulk out his devil—and be the first to apologise. Well—never mind old Nevile. You'll see, one of these days. Now, I say, what are you doing with yourself up here? Any good?"

She named her Italian studies, and made him open his eyes.

"Italian? *Tante grazie*, and all that! But that don't take you very far, you know. Your teeth will crack a tougher nut. Now, I'll tell you what you do. You come and see my old Aunt Wenman——"

She was highly amused. "Why should I see your old Aunt Wenman? Does she know Italian?"

"Italian! God bless you, if she knows English, it's as much as she does. Learnt the Catechism once, I s'pose. She's a good old sort—Lady Maria Wenman, widow of my old Uncle Charles, and my mother's sister at that. She'll take to you—she'll take to you."

"I don't see——" said Sanchia, puzzled. The youth explained.

"Well, you see—you'll forgive me, I know—it's *tone* you want just now. She'll give you that. She's something to pull against. You get your back up against her, and hang on. That's the ticket. She's a good soul, is Aunt Maria—lots of tone—gives parties to all and sundry. You meet some rare fish in those waters—Jews, Turks, infidels, and heretics. They'll amuse you—give you bones to pick. I don't get on

with 'em myself—too simple, I am, you know. They
talk their politics, or domestic afflictions, and I feel so
delicate I don't know what to do. There was one
chap I remember—Golowicz his name was—big,
red-whiskered, conspiracy chap . . . told me all
about his mother—tears running down his cheeks.
I didn't know her from Adam, you know, but still—
Oh, you'll like Aunt Wenman. She'll want you to
live with her, and you might do much worse."
Sanchia listened, smiled, and pondered. It was not
her way to be disposed of so simply.

What was impressive to her about this conversation was the real reticence underlying the chatter
of her friend. She could feel his conviction of her
want of tone; she was convinced of it herself. Her
purpose in life seemed gone. Once it had been
love, next it had been the ordering of affairs. The
second had been so absorbing that she had not
missed the first; indeed, she had believed it there
until the very end, when she had called it up, and had
no answer. But now—what aim had she, in this
lonely, empty life she was leading, whose hours were
so many that she had to fill them up with Italian got
out of books? Without knowing it, it was life she
wanted, not books. She with her brains, vitality,
beauty, and charm had been growing in these graces
unawares, flowering in secret at Wanless under her
aprons, behind her account-books and garden gloves.
Now that all these swaddling bands were stripped
off her, behold her, armed at all points for the lists.

So Chevenix had beheld her, it seems. Let her see the world, approve her mettle, run her career. Chevenix, watching her, judged in those pondering eyes, in that half-smile which had charmed him before, a kind of quivering expectancy new to her. He judged her tempted, and renewed his suggestions on a later day.

"What you want," he then told her, "is to try a fall or two with the world. You've been too snug, you know—too long under glass. You left the schoolroom to go to Wanless—and where were you there? Under cover. You want the sun, the wind, and the rain; you want to know what these things feel like— and how the rest of us take 'em. And you want to be seen, if you let me say that. We all like being looked at, I believe. I know that I do, when I'm quite sure about my hat. Now you won't get much of that in a Warwick Street two-pair front, let me tell you—no, nor in your B 17, or whatever your seat is, at the Museum. You're a star—you're to shine. Well, give 'em a turn in Charles Street. I'll fix it up for you. I wish you'd think it over."

She gave him grateful looks, but said little. Nevertheless, he went away encouraged. A week or so later she found a card upon her table: that of a Mrs. John Chevenix.

"That's my sister-in-law," the friendly youth presently told her. "That's Mrs. John. You go and see her. She's a good sort of woman. You'll meet Aunt Wenman there. I thought it all out, and that's the way to get at it. She'll jump at you, in my

opinion. She loves orphans. Collects 'em. You
go!"

She was due in the city on a visit to her father,
was, in fact, dressed for it in her best white frock,
roses in her hat. She promised to think of it—
and of course would return Mrs. John's call. The
amiable Chevenix accompanied her as far eastward
as it was possible for him to go. He went, indeed,
farther, and in full view of Saint Paul's decided upon
a visit to that sanctuary. You never know your
luck, he said. He might meet Senhouse there. He
had been hunting the recessed philosopher high and
low.

"Great sport if we met him now—you, who look
like lunching at the Savoy or somewhere, and he
like a fakir! What should you do? Fall in his
arms?" Sanchia had mist over the eyes.

"I believe I should," she admitted. "I should
love to see him again."

"He'll turn up at Aunt Wenman's, I'll bet you,"
Chevenix felt sure. "She rakes 'em in—all sorts.
Do you think about her, now, there's a dear. You
won't be able to stick it at home, you know."

"I am sure that I shan't go home," Sanchia said.
"And I *am* thinking abou your aunt."

"Right," cried Chevenix, and briskly mounted the
steps of the cathedral.

Mr. Percival had provided a tea for her which had
the appearance of a banquet. The table seemed
sunk in flowers; a great urn held the tea. There

were buns in pyramids, snow-mantled cakes, apricot jam, strawberries, clotted cream. Nothing was too good for his beloved, as he cried aloud when he saw her, fresh and glowing in her lace frock and flower-wreathed hat.

"My girl—and upon my soul, a picture!"

She blushed at his praises, and came within kissing distance. "You make a school-treat of me, dearest. You mustn't be wicked with your money, or I shan't come any more to see you. I won't be spoiled."

"No, my dear, no—and you can't be," he assured her. "Good Lord, my child, you're the only one I've got left. All my birds flown but you! And I had five of the sweetest, sauciest, happiest girls in England once upon a time. . . . Now, come you and pour out a cup of tea for your foolish old father. We're snug here—hey? Better than Great Cumberland—hey? You monkey!" He pinched her ear —and felt that they shared a secret.

She caught his happiness, and bathed in his praises, feeling as it were the sun upon her cheeks. How she loved to be loved! How she loved to be praised for her good looks! The world had grown suddenly kind again; the world was good. There, ahead of her, stood Mrs. John Chevenix and a friendly Lady Maria, beckoning her to London delights, a friendly world of admiring eyes. She was to be looked at—she was to listen—and be heard. Her heart beat, eyes shone starry. Life, which had seemed behind her, now danced before, a gay procession. She told her father what seemed to be in the wind. He listened and stared.

"Lady Maria, hey! We *are* going up in the world. The peerage! Charles Street, Berkeley Square! I remember young Chevenix: he had swell connections—yes, yes. How things come about. This will please your mother, my dear. She sets a store by such things." Their eyes met, and she nodded.

"Yes, I thought of that. But what do *you* feel about it, Papa? You see—I couldn't very well come back to Great Cumberland Place."

He did see that, poor man. "No, chick, no. That wouldn't work out—that sum. You and your mother never did add up very well—No, no. Much as I should have liked it. But Charles Street? Hʋm. I'm a plain man, you see, a plain, old comfortable merchant—and the older I grow, the more comfortable I get, I believe. Now, I don't see myself in Berkeley Square, making a bow to Lady Maria. My poor old back's too stiff for that. But if you're contented—if you're to have your deserts—for you're a little beauty, my love, and there's no mistake about it—why, what can I say? And I know you won't forget Papa in The Poultry—hey?"

She held him her hand across the tea-cups, smiling with her eyes. "Do you really think I shall?"

He caught fast to the little hand. "No, child, no! Though, mind you, I deserve it. When I think that I let you be packed out of my house—neck and crop —to the devil, for aught I knew—I grow cold. My dear, it's taken me suddenly at night—when I've been wakeful—and I've groaned in my agony. It don't do to think of—hideous! Women make fools of us men, and knaves as well. But there! You know your mother's way. I mustn't speak against her, of course. No, no. She's a good woman." He looked as if he tried hard to believe it.

Sanchia, her hand still held, had grown serious. "Papa," she said, "I want you to understand me altogether. I should do it again, I believe, if I really loved somebody."

He looked at her anxiously, then away from her, while he patted her caught hand. "Yes, my dear, yes. I understand that you feel like that. It's queer—to me, you know. I don't pretend to see it as you do. But I trust you. I know you're a good girl. Only—it's not the old-fashioned way; and your mother——"

"Mamma,'" she said, "is different. She thinks I'm wicked; you think I'm good. I don't know what I am—I don't understand myself at all; but I'm quite sure that I should do it again, if it had to be done." Her eyes grew large with the certainty of her argument. She had a divine seriousness, a rapt look, as of one inspired from within. "I don't see how you can help it, if you see quite clearly that the person needs you. It seems disloyalty. It seems making too much of yourself—as if what happened to that part of you mattered! And it seems making too little of yourself, too—as if you shrank, as if you were afraid of vile people. One can't afford to be afraid—for the sake of such a small thing."

Mr. Percival, nodding, patting her hand, put in a gentle remonstrance. "I shouldn't say that, Sancie, I shouldn't indeed. It used to be considered everything in the world, to a woman."

She mused, then decided. "No. I can't understand that. It's not everything in the world. It's almost nothing compared to other things—like freedom. To me the only thing that seems to matter is one's mind. Freedom for that! You can give up anything else. But that you must have—if you are to live at all."

He made a loyal effort to follow her thought, but it led him into dismal regions where he found himself unnerved. "I don't know, upon my soul, where you get these notions of yours, my dear. I don't indeed. Not from me, I believe."

She smiled gently at him, but with a wistful tinge, as if she felt her isolation. "I don't know, either—but there they are. I always know what I've got to do. I see it, or feel it, ahead of me. There's a path that way, a path the other. I see the fork, and have to follow one of them. I always know which."

That was equally beyond him. He left it, and returned to a more practical puzzlement. "But when—when you make up your mind about—*him*, you know? I wish you would tell me."

"I'll tell you everything I can, dearest, of course."

"Well, now, your freedom, you know. Your freedom of mind. Now, you gave him your freedom, didn't you! And your mind too? Didn't you, now?"

She had to consider that, and he watched her with anxiety. But she looked him fairly in the face with her answer, so that he read the truth in her eyes. "No," she told him. "No. He never had that, luckily for me. I always knew what I had to do before he did. I could always see where he was right and I was wrong—or the other way about. I don't think I could ever give up my judgment. At least—" She had to think again; and again she answered him, but with heightened colour. "If I did—it would be a different sort of person altogether. Quite a different person."

His face fell. This didn't sound like marriage-bells. "Oh, my dear!" he said ruefully. "You don't mean to tell me——"

She jumped up and hugged him. "You darling old thing, of course not." But she kept her face buried in his whiskers. "If I ever did that—give up my mind, I mean—I believe I should be happier."

Mr. Percival had no doubt about that. He had old-fashioned opinions.

IV

MRS. JOHN CHEVENIX, a young and lively woman with ash-coloured hair, audacious nose, and a clear complexion, was devoted to her husband's family, and especially tender to our young friend and Sanchia's, with whom she had a strong alliance. Her husband had a sense of humour, which he indulged for the most part in silence. He spoke rarely, swallowed his laughter, and yet was good company. You felt his sympathy, found yourself depending on it. You gauged his relish by a twinkle, by a deeper shade of purple in his cheeks, by a twitching ear. The Stock Exchange gave him a sufficiency, and his wife, with her taste for dinner-parties, saw to it that it gave him no more. "Let's bleed old John," was Bill Chevenix's pleasant way of suggesting an escapade which might run into hundreds. "It will do him good," Mrs. John used to agree; and John Chevenix would chuckle internally, and say, "Go it, you two." On these terms they were all very happy.

Bill Chevenix had told his sister-in-law as much about Sanchia as he thought fitting. To begin with, he took all responsibility upon himself for the opening scene of her wild adventure. He had introduced "the chap" into the Percival household, and it was he, too, who had *not* introduced the fact of his unhappy marriage. "Took it all for granted —thought they knew it—forgot they didn't belong to that gang—your gang, my gang, Nevile's gang. Rotten of me, my dear, but there you are." Mrs. John understood him to feel more contrite than he appeared. And next he lauded Sanchia, after his own manner. As thus: "A queer young fish. You can't judge her by the rules of the game. She shows her strength by breaking 'em. She'd break anything and anybody. Oh, she's as deep as the Dogger. But mighty pleasant with it, you know, Fine, quiet style of her own. And a beauty. My word, but she's like a rose." Then his eyes met hers confidentially. A wink passed. "No. We're great friends. That's all there is to it, on my honour. But you can't leave a girl like that stranded, can you now? Especially when you've run her aground yourself—in a way. So I thought of old Aunt Wenman in a minute. In fact, I've seen her about it, and, by George, she hit on a phrase in a trice. 'Unfortunate attachment.' She's perfectly happy with that, and rather keen. Now all you have to do is to give a party, and I'll ask Sancie."

Mrs. John thought that was too casual. "You mustn't treat her like a dancing man," she told him. "I shall call on her, and you can tell her I'm coming. We'll do the thing in form."

All this had been done, and the call returned. Sanchia's still serenity, seen through the rosy mist

of her momentary confusion, pleased Mrs. John.
The invitation was made and accepted in parting.

"Do come. We shan't have many people, you
know; but I won't let you be dull. And Bill will
be there, of course—and you rather like Bill—and
a queer old Aunt of ours who knows everybody.
So I hope you won't mind."

"I'm sure I shan't," Sanchia said, and then they
shook hands.

Bill Chevenix, who had been present, waved himself away from the doorstep. "By-by, my dear,"
he said. "You've done bravely by me. Isn't she
splendid?"

"I like her," said Mrs. John. "But she's rather
unapproachable."

Bill chuckled. "That's her little way. She don't
kiss easily."

Mrs. John said that he ought to know.

The party was anything but dull. Lady Maria
dined with seven other people, the best that could
be mustered on short notice—and Sanchia came in
at ten o'clock, when the drawing-room was full.
She came with an elderly friend, a Mrs. Quantock,
whose acquaintance she had made in an omnibus,
and renewed at the British Museum. Mrs. Quantock was an authoress by profession, a poetess by
temperament. Her emotions, not always under
control, consorted oddly with her broad and placid
face. She knew Lady Maria Wenman, and it was
she who actually performed the introduction, Mrs.
John being fast at her stair-head.

"I particularly want you to know my dear friend —Miss Sanchia Percival—Lady Maria Wenman. A great heart, Lady Maria, in a frame of steel."

"Oh, indeed," said Lady Maria. Then, "Come and sit with me, my dear; I've heard about you. But I hope you've left your steels at home."

"If I had a trumpet," said good Mrs. Quantock, "instead of a penny whistle, all the world should hear what I think of Sanchia."

"Then it's a very good thing you haven't," said Lady Maria. "The less young ladies are trumpeted in public the better!"

Sanchia, during this interchange, had stood smiling and self-possessed; but she was a little fluttered, and looked none the worse for that. Without a word she obeyed the twinkling and puckered old lady, sat by her on the sofa and awaited, her hands folded in her lap, what might be in store for her. She liked the looks of Lady Maria, and had no disrelish for her sharp tongue, nor fear of what might fall to her share when Mrs. Quantock took herself off. She liked the little, deep-set, dark grey eyes, the beaked nose, like the prow of a trireme, and the drawn-in mouth, which seemed to be victim of the astringencies it was driven to utter. And then she liked the signs of race, the disregard of opinion, the keen look which lit on a man or woman and saw him negligible and left him in the road. She had herself an artist's eye for style, and saw in Lady Maria the grand manner. The praise or blame of such as she would be worth having; awaiting either, she felt herself braced. She could envisage the past, collect it, display it in her lap without fear. "Here's my life's work, so far as it has gone. Now beat me, if you will; I'm not afraid of honest blows." She knew there would be no sham outcries from this high-looking old dame.

Lady Maria Wenman was rich, imperious, whimsical, and afraid only of boredom. By birth a daughter of Lord Starcross, by fate the widow of a judge, she was strongly of opinion that she could do as she pleased. It was not so clear to her that other people could also; but the reason of that was that other people, not immediately about her, were not themselves clear. She once said of a prime minister, "My dear, he seemed to me a very good sort of man"; and that was her attitude all the world over towards those not connected with her by blood or the affections. Marks of race she had, but not pride of it. She was her own fountain of honour, and were you omnibus-tout or commander-in-chief, if she liked you you were in being, if not, you didn't exist. One consequence of this was that she hated nobody, and was offended at nothing. The vices or crimes of a non-existent world were mere shadows, naturally; those of her circle of cognizance she had a way, very much her own, of accounting for. A trick of hers, which had become inveterate, was to explain states of being by phrases. These not only explained, they seemed to condone; and to her there's no doubt, they accounted for everything. Mr. William Chevenix, aware of her foible, did not scruple to turn it to his ends when putting before her Sanchia's case. "You see, Aunt, one rather admires her loyalty to the chap. He was precious miserable, and she pitied him. Well, we know what comes of that, don't we? It turns to liking, and gratitude, and all those swimmy feelings; and then they swim together, all in a flux, eh? And there you are." To which, when Lady Maria had nodded her head of kindly vulture sagely, and mused aloud, "I see; an unfortunate attachment. Very common, I believe, and quite sad," he knew that he had scored a point. When she had added, "We must do what we can, of course; I'll see her; I've nobody with me just now," he presumed that he had won the rubber.

Apart from the comfortable *cliché* in which she was seen enfolded, Sanchia pleased the eye. Her father, in league with her throughout, had "stood" her a frock, the cunningest that Madame Fréluche could supply, and would have added pearls for her hair and neck if she had not tenderly refused them. She took his counsels in the general—that she was to show them what was what, "for the honour of the Percival girls"—and her own for the particular; would have no ornaments at all. By an entirely right instinct she chose to wear black. It set her off as dazzlingly fair, as more delicate than she was. Her eyes, from her pale brows and faintly tinted cheeks, gleamed intensely, burningly blue. Her strength appeared in her shut lips and firm chin— subtle, and, as Mrs. Quantock said, like that of steel wire.

She did not talk much, but what she said was simple and direct. She seemed to be reticent about herself, not by any means from shame, but because her acts and intentions appeared too obvious to be worth rehearsing. Once or twice her laugh, low and musical, showed that she relished a joke. Lady Maria occasionally made jokes. Here was a girl who understood them.

To the old gentlewoman, who never beat about bushes, but mostly walked through them, Sanchia's bluntness made immediate appeal. Her reply, for instance, to the enquiry, What had induced her to go on with the affair, was a counter-question. "What else could I do?" she had asked, with pencilled brows arched. "I thought it made no difference. I wanted to, you see. What you do is nothing compared with what you want to do."

"Then why do it, my dear?" said Lady Maria. Sanchia did not blink the answer, "Nevile wanted me. He was very unhappy."

"Well," said the old woman, "what is he now?" This time Sanchia did not reply.

Lady Maria drew her lips in until her mouth looked like a dimple in her face. "Oho! That's it, is it? He's neglected you, and now you don't care?"

"I care for some things very much," said Sanchia. "I want to please Papa, and Vicky, my sister, you know—and I think I want to put myself right with the world. But——"

"But you don't care two pins about him?"

"I think," her ladyship resumed, "I think I like to think of him best in prison;" and then washed him out of her memory as she faced more serious topics.

"It will be much better for you to come to me," she told Sanchia. "I'm an old woman, and an old tyrant, I daresay, but I'm somebody, you know. And I'm pretty lonely, and happen to want company just now. It will be good that you have a foothold to your name when your Nevile Ingram comes after you. I shall bring him to reason quicker than most people, I don't doubt. Your quarrel is absurd; you can't afford to quarrel with your bread and cheese. You've your father, you'll say; but my answer is that it's not very decent to live upon your father when you've got yourself kicked out of his house. I quite see your point of view, mind you. These things will happen, and in theory you're perfectly in the right. It's your practice that won't do. All for love and the world well lost—very fine indeed. But so long as we're in the world, you see, we *can't* lose it. There it is. Now you've had your kisses, and can afford to settle down; but you must do it in the world's way if you want peace and quietness; and I'm very ready to help you. Really, I don't see anything better for you—short of your own home."

"I shall never go there again," Sanchia told her, directly.

"Very right, my dear," said the old lady. "Then you had better come to me."

Sanchia said, "I should like that," and Lady Maria, taking her by the chin, patted her cheek.

"And so should I, my dear," she said—and the thing was as good as settled.

Mrs. John, released from her stair-head, came up presently; Bill Chevenix was with her. "Dear Aunt Wenman," she said, "I haven't had a word with you since you came; but I'm sure you've been happy."

"Miss Sanchia and I have been swearing eternal friendship," said Lady Maria.

"Exchanging drops of blood, eh, Aunt?" chirped the cheerful youth. "Nothing like it."

"I have no blood to spare, William," she replied, "and if I had, Miss Sanchia has too much. Now you can take her away while I talk to Helen. Good-by, my dear," she bade Sanchia.

"Good-by, Lady Maria," the girl replied, with deeply sincere eyes. "You've been very kind to me."

"Fiddlesticks," said Lady Maria. "I like you. Now run away, the pair of you."

"Right, Aunt," said Chevenix, and crooked his arm.

After a decent interval, in which we may suppose formal visits exchanged between Charles Street and Great Cumberland Place, Sanchia set up her rest in the former mansion. The time was full June.

V

THE string of episodes which discovered before the autumn was over the heart of Mr. Cyrus Worthington at her feet hardly deserves record in her history but for the fillip which it gave to her spirits. Tribute is tribute, and Mr. Worthington was a warrantable gentleman. The tarnish she had discerned upon her armour, the foxmarks upon her fair page, dispersed under his ardent breath; she realised herself desirable and loveworthy; she arose from the thicket in which she cowered with the light of triumph prophetic in her eyes, the flush of victory after victory prophetic in her cheeks. Therefore Mr. Worthington's career in the Charles Street lists shall be chronicled.

He was a portly widower, a banker, a father, who made his bow to Lady Maria some three times a year when he dined in Charles Street. In return, he received her ladyship once during a summer at his mansion of Fallowlea, Walton-on-Thames. On such occasions the Misses Worthington and their cousins, the Pascoe girls, who lived at Esher, would enact a pastoral play in the shrubberies with various entangled curates, with young Sam Worthington from Oxford and friends of his. Mr. Worthington himself, master of the difficult art of declining verse

as if it were bad prose, rehearsed the Prologue and
Epilogue in a master's gown and mortarboard, which
he would retain for the rest of the afternoon. It
was in that guise that, his caution deserting him,
he allowed himself to dwell upon Sanchia's beauty.

Lady Maria had taken her down to Walton in mid-
July; she had chanced to meet Melusine there, and
the two had embraced as sisters should. It is to be
owned that her adoption by Charles Street had restored her credit with her family more certainly
than any white sheet and taper which she could
have supported would have done. Her mother was
highly gratified, though she affected a shrug when
good Mr. Percival, in the simplicity of his heart,
overflowed with the joy of it. "Sancie in Berkeley
Square—where Lord Rosebery lives: think of that,
my dear!" And Mrs. Percival, who knew where
Lord Rosebery lived as well as anybody, would reply,
"These things will be balanced hereafter. Neither
you nor I, Welbore, are assessing angels, I believe.
I pray to God that she has made her peace with our
Church." "Chapel Royal," said Mr. Percival, "will
be her ladyship's ticket—or St. James's, Piccadilly.
They tell me that the great world go there now in the
evenings, dressed for dinner." Privately he vowed
that, should his Sancie be one of those immaculate
worshippers, she should not fail in toilet. And he
had not missed the point so far as you might think.
Philippa Tompsett-King, who had been present
when these things were discussing, had lifted an inflamed face over the dinner-table. "I only know,"

she had said, "that I would rather live in Bloomsbury than have her conscience. Cynicism has
always seemed to me the sin against the Holy
Ghost." But Melusine Scales, the gentle creature,
had written meekly of her joy; and Vicky Sinclair
said to her husband, the captain—"Sancie always
tumbles on her feet. She always did—like a sweet
cat." Shrewd and affectionate at once, she alone
had discerned the god's prerogative immanent in the
youngest daughter of Thomas Welbore Percival.

But the picture of Sanchia and Melusine, two
fair girls, standing together embraced under the
cedarn shade had smitten deep into the well-cased
heart of Cyrus Worthington. He had come upon
them at a pretty moment, when Melusine, the wil-
lowy and tall, having opened her arms to the dear
truant, one arm still about her, with her free hand
touched her cheek that lips might meet lips. "Darling, I'm so glad—so very glad," she was whispering,
and Sanchia, with the same light laughing in her
eyes, "Dear old Melot—how sweet you are to me."
Mr. Worthington pushed back his mortarboard and
revealed the crimson chevron which it had bitten into
his bald brow. "A charming scene—two charming
young ladies! Mrs. Gerald Scales and her sister,
I think. Lady Maria's adoption—charming, charming!" A right instinct sent him tiptoe over his lawn,
another made him doff his mortarboard.

"Mrs. Scales, we begin. The hunt is up. Poesy
calls, 'Follow, follow, follow!' Your sister, I think?"

Sanchia played the rogue. "Oh, Mr. Worthington, have you forgotten already? Lady Maria explained me half-an-hour-ago. Must Melusine introduce me again?"

"Not for the world, Miss Percival, not for the world!" the banker protested. "I was in a sense explaining myself. Pray, do not suppose that I forget either you or my manners so completely. No, no. But I am a little near-sighted, I fear; there is a little difficulty of focussing; nothing organic, no loss of function." He cleared his throat, and to give himself assurance, jingled half-crowns with his plunged hand. "No loss of function whatever." He took the thing a little more seriously than he need, was in danger of labouring it. Melusine turned the talk. He invited them to the play, as "master of the revels," and walked between them, looking a very decent figure of a don on a college lawn, substantial, serene, and with an air of displaying his possessions: *"Parva sed apta mihi; Deus nobis haec otia fecit!"* He still possessed the rags of his Latin. "This little bay-tree will interest you, Miss Percival. It was planted many years ago by the late Lord Meeke—the uncle of the present peer. We had had some business relations; they were happily cemented into something more intimate by this little fellow." He touched it tenderly. "A sturdy growth! Like my affection for my noble but departed friend. Dear me! *Labuntur anni*, indeed!" His fig tree, which some one else had planted, his laburnum—a slip from one at Rick-

mansworth, the seat of the late Lord Mayor Burgess
—a catalpa seedling from Panshanger, which the late
Lady Cowper did him the honour to present with her
own hands: as Sanchia said afterwards to Melot, his
garden was rather like a cemetery of dead friend-
ships. . . .

Then they sat to witness the revels. Sanchia's
fancy, uplifted by her contentment, played with the
play, and suggested flights undreamed of for many a
year. She sat by Melusine and her husband, and Mr.
Worthington watched her in the long intervals of
his duty. Charming indeed, and most high-bred:
now where did old Welbore Percival, whom he met
daily in Throgmorton Street, fetch up such a strain
of blood? His wife, too, Kitty Blount, as she had
been—what had Kitty Blount been but a high-
coloured, bouncing romp of a girl when they had
all been paddling together at Broadstairs? Extraordinary! And now here was one of his girls sister-
in-law of a county baronet—none of your city
knights, mind you—and the other, with the lift of a
princess and the clear sight which is hers by title.
Extraordinary!

And there was another thing: where had old
Welbore and Kitty Blount kept her all this time?
And why wasn't she married, a girl like that? She
came next to Mrs. Scales, he supposed. Well, but
there was another, younger still, married only the
other day—to an army man. He remembered
Welbore chirping about it at a Board meeting. What
was that in the Bible—what was it? Ha!—"But

thou hast kept the good wine until now." By George, he must remember that for old Welbore. And now he came to think of it, old Jack Etherington had come in one morning full of Percival's daughter—"A lovely gal"—he had said, that old Jack—"colour of a Mildred Grant—quiet as the truth."

Such were the ruminations of Cyrus Worthington at his own garden-party, and he pursued them at favoured moments—with his glass of port at dessert, with his last cigar, with his whisky night-cap. In the city next day he rallied Thomas Welbore, who betrayed unlimited relish for the diversion; and within a few days more he left a card in Charles Street and took a late train to Walton-on-Thames. Asked in due course to dinner, he handed Sanchia to the table, and spent the evening by her side. He begged her better acquaintance with his daughters, made the most of that which he had with Melusine Scales, and ended a successful adventure by winning Lady Maria's acceptance "for herself and her young friend," of a banquet at the Cooper's Company of which he was warden. The occasion was a great one—a foreign potentate, the Prime Minister, Lord Mayor, and Sheriffs. The Coopers were to distinguish themselves, or be extinguished. He could promise them of the best. Sanchia, new to courtship, was quietly elated, and her amusement did nothing to diminish her elation. She had never been wooed before: there had been nothing of the kind in those shuddering days when she and Ingram, trembling in each other's sight, had mutely cried across the waste of London for balm upon their wounds. The flattery of attentions had never been hers, nor the high credit of admiration so respectful as the good merchant's. He esteemed her the fairest and holiest of women, was as timid as a boy in her company, gasped like a fish and grew unmannerly hot; but I defy a young woman to be anything but gratified. Miranda shunned Caliban; but had she not rather he had been there to be shunned?

Thus, under Lady Maria's watchful eye, the thing proceeded, and Mr. Worthington, within an ace of committing himself, scared his family. The climax was reached at Kissingen, whither the infatuated gentleman had followed his charmer.

She was very kind to him, but perfectly clear that she could not, and would not, make him the happiest of men. She said that she was flattered, which I believe to have been true, though he deprecated the phrase. "My dear young lady—ha! I must really be allowed—I assure you that you overwhelm me. Flattered—oh, Lord!" He limped the conclusion, and left for England that night.

She felt the thing to have been rather ridiculous, and yet she was pleased. She was gently elated, and had a kindly eye for herself as she dressed before her glass. Power lay with her; she could choose and weigh, accept or refuse. She was loveworthy yet. In spite of her disaster, a man had sought her. Others would do that same, moved by what had moved him. Shining eyes, body's form, softness, roundness—she had hardly thought of these things before, nor looked at them with an eye to their value. Mr. Worthington's ardent glances had illuminated her own, and by-and-by she found, oddly enough, that they threw a backward beam, and illuminated others. She found herself smiling tenderly as she thought of Jack Senhouse, and repeating some of that poetry which he had literally poured into her lap. It was so long ago! But when she remembered how much it had puzzled her, she now found that she was not puzzled by it at all.

Your eyes are twin mountain lakes, and the lashes of them
Like the swishing sedge
That hideth the water's edge. . . .

Were her eyes, then, so fair! Mr. Worthington had found them so. Others would—others had.

"Thy face drinketh the light,"—he had written that of her—and now she knew that he had believed it. Had Nevile felt these things? Could Nevile—as she knew him? Her lip curved back. If she could not think of herself without thinking of Nevile —who wanted to mangle her—better take the veil.

But she felt the strange reality behind that wild and adoring passion of Jack Senhouse's, which had made him so incalculable a mixture. He advised her, and adored, he received her confidences, and emptied verses out of his heart into her lap. And she had had nothing to give him, who had given her all! All indeed; for now she saw that he had loved her beyond measure, reason, or stint.

There had been that last of his letters—a despairing cry from Chanctonbury, written when she was Nevile's shadow, and he hers. She felt stabbed to the heart to remember how perfunctorily she had read that. How did it go? What had he said? She could not recall the words, but their sense beat upon her. Oh, he had set her too high! He had called her Artemis—the chaste, the bright. Artemis the Bright had been one of his names for her—and Queen Mab another. He had set her too high! And how far had she fallen? She bowed her burning head, and even as she did so, remembered another phrase of his, sent with flowers—a line from the Anthology, begging her to grant his rose "the grace of a fair breast." No longer fair, no longer fair—except to Nevile, who craved it—and to a Mr. Worthington.

The bravest gentleman, a poet, a thinker, a man like a beacon-fire, had loved her and cried her aloud as a goddess out of his reach. "Farewell, Sanchia, too dear for my possessing!" She had the words. And she had passed him by for Nevile, who made her a housekeeper, and loved her when he wanted solace. What more had Jack said? What, indeed, had he not said? That her life was like the scent of bean-flowers over a hedgerow—a fragrance caught in passing by wayfarers, whereby men and women might thank God for a fair sight who had chanced upon her in the street. Praise indeed! But he had loved her, and saw her so—and all that was gone for ever. He had left her because he dared

not do otherwise, and now he was happy without her.
Her new-found elation was like to die in self-pity.
It required more than the complacency inspired by
Mr. Worthington to clear her eyes.

Thus were the flowers laid up for her by an honest
merchant changed for a wreath of rue as he was
reminded of his better—his better and (she thought)
hers, alas! A wave of desire to catch back at far-off
things played her a trick. She found herself yearning for her childhood, found herself crying for her innocence, for the sweet scent of opening life. Even
as she longed and strained, she knew herself vain.
But the temptation for the semblance of what was
gone was strong and took a subtle form. If she
could not have the thing, she would have the thing's
name; if she could not be innocent again, she would
ape innocency. Prodigal of Pity as she has been, she
could say to Senhouse's ghost, I am no more worthy
of thee; and from that to being worthy was but a
short step. The rest of her sojourn abroad was preparation for what was to be done on her return
home.

Her treasure lay hidden there, in a desk in her
room: three portly packets of letters, tied with ribbon,
and labelled "Jack to Me." Stained and yellow,
she now turned over the pages, and inhaled the faint,
sweet scent of them—a scent as of lavender and tears.
Her eyes filled, her heart beat; but she read on and
on. Impossible praises! Love beyond reason, with-

out bounds—immeasurable homage! Did any man ever—save Dante—love a woman so greatly, set her so high? So presently she was caught up into a kind of heaven of wonder, and spent a night with the past. . . . From that she arose clear-eyed to meet the future. If she had been so loved, so served by man so generous and so fine, the rest of her life might well be spent in testimony. Her single aim now should be to recover herself, to be what he had once seen her. And for all this high remembrance and high hope—thanks to Mr. Cyrus Worthington!

Lady Maria, as the weeks went by, watched her carefully, and marked the change. Sanchia was very subdued, and now went to church. This to the old lady, who did not, was remarkable. She was not aware, naturally, of a passage in a letter which pictured her in church—with her "dear obsequious head, bowed in a fair place to a fair emblem." She could not have understood, if she had had it explained, that the girl, conscious of her stiff neck, was teaching herself obsequiousness for the sake of him who had seen her so and found her dear. None of these things were for Lady Maria's comprehension; but she reflected aloud upon church-going, and got her young friend to explanations.

"Yes," Sanchia said, "I do go to church. For a long time, you see, I couldn't—but now I feel that I can. We were all brought up to go to church."

"So was I," said Lady Maria, "and that, I take

it, is why I don't go now. I was taught to take it as physic."

Sanchia's explanation, which she yielded on pressure, of why she had stopped, was very artless. "I wanted to do something that they thought wicked, but which I thought quite good. If I went to confession, I should have been told that I was wicked. So I couldn't go. It was a difference of opinion, you see."

"Beg pardon," said Lady Maria, "but I don't see. What you mean is that, if you'd told your priest you were going off with Ingram, he'd have said, Don't, and put you under the necessity of disobeying him." She owned to it. And then she owned to something more. If the difficult choice came before her again, she would think twice. "I can't see, even now, that I was wrong in what I did. I am sure it must be right, somehow, to follow your own conscience. But I do see that it's a pity to break rules. Yes, I see that."

"I didn't suppose myself religious," Lady Maria had replied, "but if that is what your religion tells you, I agree with it. It's common sense. What's a heart or two compared with peace and quietness? And how, pray, is a child of eighteen to know what her conscience is worth?"

"It is all she has to go upon," said Sanchia; but the old lady retorted, "Nothing of the kind. She's got the experience of all Nature behind her, from the poultry-yard to the House of Lords. You'll find that the Ten Commandments are rigidly en-

forced among the cocks and hens. If a member
of the zenana breaks bounds there, she rues it.
How else do you suppose this world is to be peopled?
Read the history of marriage, my dear. You'll find
that the more primitive your man the more com-
plicated his marriage laws. Why, bless my soul,
I don't need the Church to tell me that I mustn't run
away with a married man. I can learn that from the
pigeons in the piazza at Venice. But I suppose
I'm an old pagan. Now, you run away to your
priest and make a clean breast of it."

Perhaps Lady Maria was fanciful, but she put
down this return to the Church's knees to the fact
that Mr. Worthington had gone upon his. "The
child finds that she's a valuable article," she said to
herself; "so she locks herself up in the cupboard,
like the best china." Sanchia's resolution persisted,
and enthusiasm followed its growth. She frequented
the churches early in the mornings, and one fine day
presented herself in the vestry of one of them. Upon
her knees, but with unbent head and eyes fixed
steadily to the grille, she rehearsed her tale from the
beginning, neither faltering nor losing countenance.
What followed upon that was not communicated to
her protectress, nor do I care to pry. I imagine
that she had always said her prayers, but that now
she was answering them.

That is, when one thinks upon it, the first office of
prayer.

VI

LADY MARIA WENMAN grew to be extremely fond of Sanchia, really as fond of her as she was capable of becoming of anybody. She had been good to travel with, and was good to live with. She found her so reasonable, she said. One could discuss anything without shocking her, or without fear of being made uncomfortable by seeing her discomfort. Lady Maria, in fact, being entirely without prejudice, experienced the little luxury of being able to express herself without trampling.

On her side also, Sanchia sincerely liked her old protectress, and found Charles Street agree with her. There was a primordial air about it, which made habits seem like laws of Nature; an absence of fuss which soothed her nerves, and did much better than slay her monsters for her, when it exposed them for no monsters at all, but simple, everyday, rather tiresome concomitants of our makeshift existence.

"You will, of course, marry Nevile Ingram,"— thus Lady Maria disposed of the most dread of all monsters—"because it is, on the whole, more agreeable to avoid scandal, and because it is certainly more decent to pay one's bills. Long credit is a mistake; but you found it a convenience, I suppose; and now you are in funds, you will, of course, get out

of debt. If only that you may run into it again at
need, you will draw a cheque. Now, you had eight
years of it at Wanless, you tell me? Very well, my
dear, that must be written off Society's books. Meanwhile, the more you see of amusing, emancipated
people like Alexis Morosine the better."

This man was understood to be a Pole in exile,
though his title to that distinction could only have
been on the side of the distaff, since his father's
descent from a ducal family of Venice was not denied; but neither nationality nor expatriation was
very obvious upon him. At first sight you would
have supposed him a sallow Englishman, spare of
flesh and too narrow in the chest; you might have
put down his dead complexion and his leanness to
India or Jamaica, and been inclined to attribute his
dry cynicism to the same superfervent experience.
But presently you would be alive to his hungry mind,
to his hungry, raging air, his restless habit and large
way of looking at circumstance—as if by no possibility could it be any concern of his. And then the
trick he had of considering our people as Europeans,
of dividing the races of the world by continents rather
than kingdoms; and that other of judging all cases,
including yours and his own, upon their merits—
such traits, to an experienced mind, would have
established him for a foreigner, one of a people who
had had too much elbowing for breath to have time
or space for prejudice or minute classification. Su-
perficially, to be sure, he was English enough—
from his speech to his tailoring; and his phlegm (of

which we boast) was unassailable. Nobody knew much of his history; Bill Chevenix used to say that he was born whole, and thirty, out of an egg dropped upon our coasts by a migratory roc; that he stepped out, exquisitely dressed, and ordered a whisky and Apollinaris at the nearest buffet. This, said Chevenix, was his ordinary breakfast. When Sanchia objected that he might have stepped out in the afternoon, he replied that it also formed his usual tea, and, so far as he knew, was the staple of all his meals. "And cigarettes," he added. "But he would have had those with him. I bet you what you like he came out smoking."

It was certain that he had been to Eton and to Oxford, and was member of two good clubs. He was extremely rich, and he was by profession, said Chevenix, a prince. He had no territory, and was not apparently scheming to get any, either of his own or other people's. Nobody at the Foreign Office believed that he corresponded with any intransigent; he used to go there often and exchange urbane gossip with under-secretaries. He lodged in Duke Street, gave dinner-parties at the Bachelors, had a large visiting-list, and was, as they say, always "about." One saw him everywhere—in the city, in Mayfair drawing-rooms, at Kensington tea-parties, and at Lambeth Palace. Chevenix swore that he had met him at a Church Congress —and the only answer to that was that if Chevenix had truly been there to see, Morosine might well have been there to be seen. But this catholicity

of experience was characteristic of the man; his
attraction to the nice observer lay precisely in that,
that he was a nomad, unappeased and unappeasable, ranging hungrily. There was a probability, too,
that below a surface exquisitely calm there lurked
corrosive tooth and claw. Here are sufficient elements of danger to draw any woman; so Sanchia
found herself presently drawn.

He came to Charles Street one evening late in
November, to what Lady Maria called a little party.
There was an autumn session that year, and London full. To her little party, then, came a solid
wedge of three hundred people into rooms capable
of holding with comfort fifty.

Chevenix was by Sanchia's side at the top of the
stair, chatting pleasantly about every new-comer,
when he suddenly stopped. "Hulloa," he said,
"here's Morosine, as smooth as a glass stiletto.
He'll amuse you. I'll introduce him."

Sanchia followed the leading of his eyes. She
saw a tall and slim young man, inordinately thin,
slightly bald, with a moustache like a rake, and
heavy-browed, mournful eyes, pushing his way
slowly upstairs. Without effort, his hands behind
his back, working from the shoulders, he made room
for himself, but so quietly that nobody seemed to
observe how aggressively he was at it. Occasionally
some ousted dowager turned redly upon him, or it
might be some pushing gentleman smothered an oath
as he faced the attack. But Morosine's mournful

eyes gazed calmly their fill, seemed to be communing beyond the surging guests, beyond the wall, with the eternal stars, and, without faltering, the narrow frame glided forward into the space which indignation had cleared. Sanchia, above him, and out of the game, was highly amused.

"He's very selfish, your friend. He takes care of himself; but no one seems to know it."

Chevenix chuckled. "That's the beauty of Alexis. But, as he asks, whom else should he take care of? It's not queer if the Poles have learned that lesson."

"Oh," said Sanchia. "Is he a Pole?" Jack Senhouse had been in Poland.

"Half of him is hungry Pole. The other part is bad Italian—pampered Italian, fed for generations on oil and polenta. He's always dining out, but he eats nothing because the Pole is feeding on the Venetian all day." Then he told her about the miraculous birth, the whisky and Apollinaris, and concluded, "Oh, he'll amuse you vastly. Stay where you are. I'll net him at the top."

Presently after she saw the process. It consisted in violent effort on Chevenix's part, languid attention from the other. Morosine dreamed over the speaker as if he were a lost soul. Then, his consideration being caught, he looked about him, and presently fixed upon her his melancholy eyes. She felt a little shiver, the sensation of goose-flesh in the spine—not unpleasantly. It was as if a light wind had ruffled her blood. Shortly afterwards Morosine was bowing before her. In this, perhaps, he betrayed himself; his hat covered his heart, he inclined from the hips, and his head bent with his body. An Englishman bows with the head only, and does not nowadays carry his hat upstairs.

He began to talk quietly and at once, and maintained a perfectly even flow of comment, reflection, anecdote, reminiscence, and sudden, flashing turns of inference. He seemed always to be searching after general principles, cosmic laws, and to be always jumping at them, testing them, finding them not comprehensive enough, and letting them drift behind him as he pursued his search. She remarked on this afterwards to Lady Maria, who said that principles were the last thing to interest Morosine. He had none at all, said Lady Maria, unless his own immediate gratification was a principle; and perhaps with men you might almost say that it was.

Chevenix remained, chuckling and interjecting here and there an exclamation, just (as he told her later) to "start the chap on his meander," and presently betook himself elsewhere. It was then to be observed that Morosine allowed himself to drift into the discussion of matters not usually subjects of ordinary conversation; but he did so without consciousness, and therefore without offence. Sanchia neither disapproved nor felt uncomfortable. They were, moreover, interesting, and rather material.

It began with Poland, a country which, the less it existed politically, he said, was the better to live in, and be of. We live by our emotions, the beasts

by their appetites—a material distinction. Now,
the condition of the Poles was perfectly adapted to
the quickening of the emotional parts. Shorten
time, you make love a precious ecstasy; restrict
liberty, freedom is a lust—none the worse for being
lawful. No Pole knows how long he may have to
live: Russia or phthisis will have him late or soon.
What he pursues, then, must be fleeting—imagine
with what rapture he takes it to his breast! with what
frenzy he guards it, never knowing when it will be
required of him again. Feverish? (This was upon
a remark from her.) Yes, and why not? Are not
dreams more vivid than waking life? Can you gal-
lop your material horse as your courser of the mind?
Better to burn than to rust. That's the secret of life
—which all the laws of bureaucrats are directed
to destroy. The establishments want to see us as
fixed as themselves. They are tentacled, stationary
creatures, feeding at ease. They would have us
handy of access, falsely secure, so that they can
fasten on us one by one and suck our juices. But
the world is changing, thrones and churches are
slackening in their hold. Men are discovering how
short a time they have to live, and that eternity is
more than questionable. A mild Epicureanism is
gaining ground. Instincts founded on the patriarchal
system must give way to that. "Have you ever considered," he asked abruptly, "that the flocks and
herds of the Semitic patriarch are the sole cause of
the moral code which we still profess? Thou shalt
not steal. Why not? Because you injure the pa-

triarch. Not murder? You might attack one of his
family. You have the habit in England of tracing
prejudices to the Feudal System: believe me, there
is hardly anything in Europe so modern. I should
date at 4000 B.C. nearly all our present conventions,
from the British Sunday to the law of conspiracy.
So long as you say that property is sacred, you uplift
the Patriarch and lose sight of the man."

Sanchia, reminded of Senhouse—a Senhouse with
his tongue dipped in vinegar—objected that society
may have demanded some of these laws in defiance
of the engrossing patriarch; but Morosine shook
his head. "Society is the patriarch's weapon.
Society is a syndicate of patriarchs who cannot live
unless all men are enslaved. Man is not by nature
gregarious; he's solitary, like all the nobler beasts.
Wolves and dogs hunt in herds, but not the great cats;
oxen and buffaloes, but not elephants; rooks, but
not eagles; bream, never salmon. And the time is
not so very far when man will discover why it is that
he is herded and marshalled hither and thither by
police, legislatures, and monstrous assemblies called
armies or fleets. He has but to know it to abolish
these things; they fade like dreams in the morning.
But hitherto everything has been banded to make
his sleep secure—his religion, his cupidity, his timidity, his affections. Religion tells him it is wrong
to love without the Church; patriotism, that it is
glorious to bleed in making other men bleed; timidity, that property keeps the wolf from the door; appetite, that under cover of the law you may devour

your neighbour and fear no indigestion. Finally, there are the affections of a man which have been so guided that they see the aged more venerable than the young, the old thing more sacred than the new 'Woodman, spare that tree,' they cry: 'it dates from at least 2000 B.C.' Because old wine is good, they argue, old laws must needs be. As well might a man say, Because I relish old wine, I will love only old women. And so we go on!" He shrugged and broke off—to talk shrewdly of books. They got to Leopardi, from him to Dante; he heard of her studies at the British Museum, and hoped he might meet her there. She reads there often? Mostly in the after-noons? The light was bad: he usually devoted his mornings to what work he had there. He was study-ing Persian, he said, but fitfully, as the mood took him.

So far he had scarcely looked at her, but had talked out his monologue as if he had been alone, clasping one thin ankle, staring wide-eyed over the heads of guests, occasionally, when he was vehement, throwing his head up, shooting his words at the ceil-ing as if they had been Greek fire. Now, as he got up to leave her, his eyes dwelt earnestly on her. "It will be a pleasure, to which I shall aspire—that of meeting you again. There or elsewhere."

She thanked him as she gave him her hand. Ex-citement made her eyes bright, mantled her cheeks. She felt that she was communing with Senhouse at third hand.

"Then—it is understood—we meet again," he concluded. He bowed over her hand, on a second thought kissed her fingers, then left her immediately and went downstairs. He paid no farewell to Lady Maria; was ascertained to have left the house at once.

VII

Morosine had been called emancipated by Lady Maria, who after a week or so found it proper to explain that he was by no means so free from chains as he appeared. Sanchia, she thought, was seeing a good deal of him. "He's the victim, like the rest of us, of his constitution. His, as you may see, is deplorable. Weak heart, they say—but it may be lungs. I never heard of a Pole who could live in any climate, least of any his own. As for his mind, that follows his wasted body; it's hectic. He affects a detachment which he will never have. It's a pose. He is exceedingly sentimental, has an imagination which—if you could follow it—might alarm you. I have no doubt at all but that, in imagination, he has you safe in some island of Cythera or another, and has slain every other male inhabitant of it lest some one of them should happen to look at your footprints in the sand. Jealous! He would sicken at the word—not because he would be ashamed, but because it would conjure up the vision of some satyr-shape, and haunt him day and night. He has no need to study Persian poetry, I assure you. He has rose-gardens enough and to spare; for, if you are inclined to be flattered at my suggestion of Cythera, I hasten to assure you that yours is not the only island of his dominion. Bless you, he'll have an archipelago. But I have no fear for you; you can afford a sentimental education."

Sanchia did not tell her old friend how far that education was proceeding—not because she was afraid, still less because she was ashamed, but in obedience to her nature, which was extremely reserved. She spoke of herself and her affairs with difficulty—never unless she was forced. But it had become a custom just now—in the dull days on either side of Christmas—to look for Morosine in the reading-room about noon, to stroll the galleries for half-an-hour, to receive and to agree to a lightly-offered proposition that they should lunch together, and (it might well be) to accept his escort homewards. This, I say, had become the rule of three days in the week, more or less. And it's not to be supposed that so clear-sighted a young lady could see so much of so keen-sighted a man without a good deal of self-communing.

Her capacity for silent meditation, during which she would sit before her fire, gazing far, smiling at her thoughts, into the glowing coals, had never left her. But there was a slight difference to be noted. She could not think of Ingram—the past, the present, or any future Ingram—without contraction of the brows. Smooth-browed she thought of Morosine.

He interested her greatly; she was conscious of anxiety to learn his opinion, of a wave of warm feeling when she awaited it. She credited him with in-

sight, had a notion, for instance, that she could discuss her own affairs without any preliminary apology.
He took so much for granted—surely he would take
her youth into full account. She had never said to
him a word of herself as yet; but there had been
times when she had felt near it—had seen herself row-
ing a boat, as it were, within range of a weir, been
conscious of effort to keep a straight course, and of the
fruitlessness of effort. There had been moments when
she had been tempted to throw down her oars with
a sigh—by no means of despair. Morosine seemed
to her so extraordinarily reasonable, so ready, with
well-known laws, to account for unheard of vagaries,
that it would have been real luxury to her to find herself and her escapade the mere creatures of some such
law. To be discovered normal: what a relief from
strain!

Lady Maria, it seems, charged him with Oriental
aptitudes. Sanchia gave that judgment careful attention, studied her friend in the light of it, weighed
every word of his to her, watched him closely in
company when he could not be aware of it. She
decided against the opinion. His manners with
women were his manners with men, those of urbane
indifference to sex. To sex! To much more than
that. He was, in fact, outwardly polite to the point
of formality; but his attitude of mind towards the
person he happened to be with seemed to her—when
she examined it closely—to be sublimely insulting.
No created thing, with the passions and affections
common to his kind, ought to take up such a posi-

tion with his fellow-creature—that which says, "I infer your existence from my sensations: apart from them, I cannot bring myself to believe in it." She was aware that he must needs regard her from this stand-point, and the knowledge piqued her. If she did not exist for him, why did he seek her out? If she did, why did he pretend she did not? Or was Lady Maria right? Were his sensations awake, and had they fired his imagination, to carry her to Cythera, and keep her hidden there? These questions amused her, and she made no attempt to answer them. Amusement might cease that way: she indulged herself and left her questions open. One thing may be added. Morosine no longer reminded her of Senhouse. Quite otherwise—for of Senhouse just now she dared not think.

Her friend Bill Chevenix gave her no warnings. Even when she sounded for them, he gave none. "I like Alexis," he said once. "He's not so original as he makes out, but there's enough to give him a relish. A handy chap, too, in a dozen ways—he'll model you in wax, or draw you in pastels, or sing about you on the guitar, or whistle you off on the piano; but he's not strong, isn't Alexis. The one thing he can do—no, there are two. He can ride anything, and he can use a revolver. I saw him empty the ten of hearts once: very pretty. I dare say, if he was put to it, he could use an iron to some purpose; but we don't stick each other here, so he'd be out of practice. I rather wish we did, you know. It's far more gentlemanly than laying for a chap outside his club with a hunting-crop, and getting summoned for assault at Vine Street. Not a bit more vicious, barring the Ten Commandments."

"Prince Morosine doesn't believe in them," Sanchia said. "He's vowed to abolish them."

"So he may tell you, my dear. Don't you believe it. So long as they are good form they will be Alexis' form. He'd sooner die than covet his neighbour's wife." She reserved this for consideration. Meantime, she saw more of Morosine than of any other man, and got through January very well by his help.

She particularly liked his company in galleries, because, though he never allowed himself raptures —of which she, too, was incapable—he was always seeking the roots of rapture. Sanchia had a fund of enthusiasm for art all the richer, perhaps, for being denied expression. It was comfortable to have that securely based.

"Do you ever consider," he asked her once, when they stood before the great group of the Pediment, "why it is that these things are so beautiful; why, although they are bare of colour and all that stands for life to us in art, they are more than life? It's because they point to a state of being exquisitely conform to the laws of being. Such a perfect conformity soothes us into believing that while we witness it we are of it—ourselves conforming. These splendid creatures here, so superbly static—idle, you might say (only they wouldn't understand you), indulging their strength—are strong and able precisely because they have submitted themselves——"

"Unlike the Poles?" She reminded him of their first conversation, and saw that he remembered it. He bowed to her.

"Let me finish. These existences, emanations, essences, what you will, are submiss, not to man, but to Nature. They are as passive as Earth herself, and as immune. They derive their strength from her. That's our only reasonable service." Whether he intended it or not, the effect of this kind of talk was to make her view submission to the world's voice as a reasonable service.

It was not so odd as it may seem that her intimates had always been men. That reticence of hers which repelled her own sex was precisely that in her which attracted, by provoking, the other. After her dumb childhood, to which she never looked back, came her opening girlhood, and on the threshold of that stood Jack Senhouse, the loyal servitor, the one man who had loved her without an ounce of self-seeking. Then came Nevile Ingram, and swallowed her up for a while, and when he had tired of her she was once more without a friend. To Chevenix afterwards, rather than to Mrs. Devereux, she had struggled to utter herself. That cry of distress, "he wants me, to ravage me," would never have been made by her to a woman. She would have died of it sooner. And now came the Pole, Morosine, and by taking for granted (as even Lady Maria could not have done) much that could not have been explained,

put her at her ease. She found him a Jack without
the spirit—without the divine spark. She could
never have loved him, though she liked him well,
and she had no idea that he thought of nothing but
the greatness of his reward when, after patient toil-
ing, she might fall into his arms. Every nerve in
her body was now strung up to obedience to Jack's
idea of her. She saw, as clearly as if it was printed,
her fate before her. She was to put herself under the
law. Jack should not have loved in vain her "dear
obsequious head." Nevile would come back and
require her. For Jack's sake, who had seen her too
noble to be touched by sin, she would dip herself deep
in sin.

Morosine, who frankly desired her to be the wife
of a man she did not love in order that she might the
more easily find consolation in himself afterwards,
had the wit to see that she needed some of his sophis-
try, though not enough to know exactly why. It was
perfectly true. Her churchgoing was an ointment.
It could soothe but not heal her. Sanchia had a
mind. To do wrong by the world because it had
seemed right to her was not to be remedied by doing
a right by it now, which to her reasoning would glare
before her as a monstrous sin. She forgot that Senhouse had also taught her that the great sin of all was
insincerity. She could not have afforded to remember that. All her present desire was to be, as nearly
as she might, what she had been when Jack had seen
her first, what he had found excellent in her and loveworthy—pious, bowing her head in a fair place, ob-

sequious, obedient to the law.   He had loved her, of course, whatever she did—outraging the law as well as keeping it, loving Nevile, letting himself go away. She could not remember that.   He had loved her meek; she would be meek.   That was what her heart told her; and Morosine, to serve his own ends, lulled her head with his sophisticated anodynes, and sent her brain to sleep.

That he should know her story, as he obviously did, was not so disconcerting to her as it would have been to most young women.   Taciturn as she was, it was not by reason of timidity, but rather that her own motives seemed too clear to her to be worth stating.   She was, perhaps, rather given to assume her prerogative right to be different.   Her first thought, therefore, was that she was saved the trouble of explaining herself, and her second that it was satisfactory to have a friend who understood her without explanations.

As for Morosine, he may or may not have felt that he had broken the ice; he pushed forward, at any rate, as if he had clear water in front of him. Sanchia felt, when she next met him, that their acquaintance had entered on a new phase.

Then suddenly, before she knew where she was, her fate was upon her.

It was in the Park on a fine Sunday forenoon in February.   She was with Lady Maria, and had met with Melusine and Gerald Scales.   Morosine also, seeing her and meeting her eyes, instantly left his companion and came to greet her, hat in hand. He addressed himself to her exclusively, having saluted Lady Maria; but she named her sister, and he saluted her too. Gerald Scales, bronzed, plump, and very full in the eye, having looked the new-comer over, decided against him, and gave him a shoulder. "Foreign beggar," was the conclusion he came to, which does credit to his perspicacity, because the Pole had a very English appearance, and Scales himself the look of a Jew.

When they turned to walk, Morosine took the side next Sanchia, and though he talked to both ladies, so contrived that she should read more in what he said than her sister. He did it deftly, but continuously. Sanchia was entertained, slightly excited, and ended by taking part in the game of skill. It is impossible to say by how much this sort of thing increased the intimacy already established between the pair. It was by so much, at least, that when Melusine joined her husband, by dropping behind and waiting for him to come up with the old lady, it came as no sort of shock to Sanchia that he took up the talk where he had ended it in the gallery.

"You have been to church, I see. But you are not a Christian?" He did not look at her.

Nor did she turn her head to reply. "I don't know. Nominally, at least; fitfully, at the most."

"That must be the outside of it," he continued. "The thing is the antithesis of the Hellenic ideal—which is yours. Your seemingly passive martyr is really in an ecstasy. He aims at outraging Nature; begins by despising and ends by dreading it. Nature, however, has ways of revenging herself."

"Yes, indeed," said Sanchia soberly.

They walked on together, she by this time very much absorbed. She was not conscious of the shifting crowd, the lifting of hats, the chatter, the yapping dogs that ran in and out of women's skirts.

Presently he spoke again. "You believe that you failed?"

Her voice came low. "I know that I failed."

Then he looked at her, and spoke with vehemence. "And what is that to you? What is, failure in such a cause, to such as you?" But she could not meet his face, kept hers rigidly to the front.

"The cause," Morosine told her, "is everything, the aim, the loyalty, the great surrender. Beside this failure is nothing at all. Do you say that the sapling fails that springs out of a cleft rock and towers—seeking, as we all seek, the sun, the light in heaven? A gale gathers it up and tears it out: over it goes, and lies shattered. Is that failure? How can it be when nothing dies?"

Sanchia, very pale, turned her face to his at last. Her mouth was drawn down at the corners, to the tragic droop. She almost whispered the words, "Something did die."

His intuition worked like a woman's, in flashes. He knew immediately what she meant.

"I know, I know," he said. "You were mistaken. But you never faltered. You followed a call."

"You tell me," she said, "that there was none."

"I do."

"But," she argued, "that with which I began

failed me. I was entirely certain, at the time; I could not possibly have hesitated. And then—it died." Her eyes loomed large. "It is quite dead now, and I feel that I have betrayed myself—broken faith with myself."

He shook his head. "You could not break faith; you are the soul of truth."

This praise she accepted. "I don't tell lies, I hope—and I don't shirk things. But you see that I can stultify my own acts. I believed, and acted on my belief; and then I ceased to believe, and acted on that. I cannot trust myself—I ought to be ashamed to say so, and I hope I am."

Morosine met her eyes again, and held them. "I can never believe that you would fail. I tell you that you have not failed. It is that you have been failed. You cannot give if what you give is not taken. Failed—you! Ah, no, you have succeeded, I think."

She bent her brows as she faced resolutely forward. "I must take the consequences of what I have done. I see that."

"Ah," said Morosine, "that is a question of courage. Courage you have."

"I need it," she said in a hush, and stopped dead. Ingram stood before her, and took off his hat.

"Well, Sanchia," he said, "here I am."

"Well, Sanchia," he said. "Here I am."

"Well, Sanchia," he said.   "Here I am."

VIII

THE scattered party was suddenly strung to tensity; Morosine drew himself up, stiff as steel, but stood his ground. Here was the man he had waited for, who was necessary to him. Lady Maria, blinking her little black eyes, Melusine, with hers in a blur of mist, Gerald Scales, level and impassive, joined the other three.

Ingram, with a stretched smile, was volubly explaining. "I've been in London a week—to-day's the first glimpse of the sun I've had. I do think they might make better arrangements for a man home from Africa. I met your mother last night at a play. She told me that I might see you here." He turned, without effrontery, to greet Melusine. "Ages since we have met. Ah, Scales, how are you?"

The tall Melusine stooped her head; Scales nodded, then, by an afterthought, shook hands. "I'm very fit, thanks," he said. "Been travelling?"

Sanchia sought the side of Lady Maria, to whom she named Ingram. His exaggerated bow was accepted. "So you've arrived, I see," said Lady Maria.

"One does, you know." Ingram shrugged at the inevitable. "All roads lead to Rome."

"Most roads lead to Lady Maria," Morosine said to Sanchia, who replied from her heart, "I'm very glad that mine did." Moved either by loyalty to his friendship, or touched by his recent words, she then brought him bodily into play. "Mr. Nevile Ingram; Prince Morosine."

The two men inclined; Morosine lifted his hat, Ingram touched his brim.

Ingram, whom Morosine judged as a hard worker just now, supported his part with great gallantry. If he was naked to all these people who knew him, he appeared quite unashamed. Morosine, watching him carefully, believed that he had devoted a night's vigil to getting word perfect. He described Khartoum with vivacity—the English drill sergeant reigning over mudheaps, flies, and prowling dogs; getting up cricket-matches for the edification of contemptuous blacks. "They judge us, those fellows, you know. They are measuring us with their glazed eyes. The cud they chew has gall in it. I don't suppose anything offends them more deeply than our idiotic games. Is there a more frivolous race in the world than ours?"

Lady Maria suggested that the Boers might ask that question; Morosine that the Germans might answer it. Sanchia standing between these two, faced by Ingram, kept silent. She was conscious of being closely under observation. Morosine did not once lose sight of her. Whatever he said was addressed to her. Once, when she looked at him, she saw the gleam of knowledge in his eyes. He and

Ingram never spoke to each other directly; indirectly Morosine capped whatever Ingram said. It was these two who maintained the talk through her sensitive frame.

Melusine and her husband exchanged glances—she in obedience to his fidgety heels. He had dug a hole in the gravel deep enough to bury a kitten. Her curtsey—it was almost that—to Lady Maria was very pretty. She drew in her suffering sister, almost embraced her. "Dearest, dearest!" she whispered. Sanchia, who was very pale, made no answer, and hardly returned the salute.

"Insufferable beggar," was Gerald Scales' outburst. "I could have shot him at sight. But you women will go through with it, I suppose."

"Oh, Gerald," faltered Melusine, "it's dreadful —but what can she do?"

"'Pon my soul, I'd take Morosov—the Polish party—what's-his-name—first. I would indeed—on the whole."

There was nothing to say. Melusine knew that could not be.

Lady Maria, however, who never made a fuss over spilt milk, lost no time in ladling up what might be possible. She asked Ingram to luncheon, and was accepted with a cheerful, "Thanks, most happy." It may have been malice which turned her to Morosine with the question. "And you? Will you join us?"

Morosine promptly excused himself. He had

guests, and must consider them. He took ceremonious leave. "You remember, I hope, that I am to see you on Thursday, Lady Maria. And Miss Percival?" He looked to Sanchia, who did not turn him her eyes.

"Perfectly," said her ladyship. "What's your hour?"

"We will dine at half-past eight." He named the restaurant. He turned to pay his farewells to Sanchia. She looked him No, being unable to speak to him. Her eyes, deep lakes of woe, were crying to him. His answered.

He held out his hand and received hers. "Thursday," he repeated, and left her with her fate.

Lady Maria, at luncheon, made what she called the best of a bad business. She treated Ingram to a brisk curiosity. "So you're a wanderer, I hear—like the Gay Cavalier of my childhood. Your mother may have heard the song. Mine sang it. I believe that that kind of thing was considered heroic in her day; in ours, heroism is more difficult, and much more dull. You might try heroism, Mr. Ingram."

"I might, no doubt," Ingram said. "Hitherto, I've preferred to travel. But I'm home for good now, so far as I can see."

"We all hope so," said Lady Maria. "But that remains to be seen."

"Of course it does," said Ingram blandly, and turned to Sanchia. "I thought your mother looking very well. Your father wasn't there. I saw Philippa, by the way; but I suppose she didn't remember me. That was her husband with her, I take it. Stiff old boy." So he went on, letting bygones be bygones. It was after luncheon that her ordeal came.

Lady Maria having departed for her siesta, he came instantly to Sanchia with his hand out for her. "Sancie, I couldn't talk before all those people. You must forgive me, my dear. You are too good a sort—you must forgive me."

He had to wait; but slowly she lifted her hand and let him take it. "I have forgiven you," she said. He stroked her arm.

"That's nice of you—that's like you. I know that I behaved like a brute. I was awfully cut up about it afterwards—but, as you know, I had great provocation."

"Not from me, I think." Her eyes were upon him now.

"No, no," he admitted; "certainly not from you; but—well, perhaps I may say that I had some ground for thinking that you—possibly— No, I don't think I ought to say that. At any rate, I thought then that I had. As for that young friend of yours—but he's nothing. It's you I want to make my peace with."

"It's not difficult," she said. "I tell you that I don't bear any malice. I bore none at the time. I wanted to go."

He let her hand slide from his, and plunged his own into his pockets. "I know you did; I felt that at the time. That hurt me a good bit. I had come

to rely upon you so much—oh, for every mortal thing.
I expect the whole place has gone to the devil now.
You had your hand on the tiller, by Jove! You
kept a straight course, You see, I'd got into the way
of thinking we were—married, don't you know, and
all that——"

"I think you had, indeed," she said. He saw her
wry smile.

"I know what you mean by that. You mean,
if that's marriage—many thanks! Well, my dear,
all I can say is, you were absolutely wrong. It was
not marriage—it never had been, and you know
it couldn't have been. But if it had been, Sancie,
you'd have been as right as rain. You know you
would. Your own place—everything to your hand
—Society—all that kind of thing. Why, you'd never
have thought it amiss in me to go off tiger-shooting
for a bit. You'd have had your whack of travelling,
playing the grass widow; you'd have entertained,
had all sorts of little games—and both of us been all
the better. No! But it was just because our rela-
tionship was so infernally irregular that you felt those
separations—took them, if I may say it, so hard.
Depend upon it, that was it."

Her lip curled back, though she said nothing.
She wondered if he had always been quite so fatuous
as this, quite so sublimely unhumorous. If he had,
what under heaven had she been about? That she
could have believed this smug cockscomb to have
loved her—to have been capable of anything but
hunger and thirst for her—incredible! It made her

out precisely as fatuous as he. And yet she said nothing. With the likes of him nothing seemed worth doing except to forget him.

And she was to marry him, to live in his house, to see him daily—ah, and more than that; and yet she said nothing of what her curled back lip expressed. She was in the presence of her fate, and, as ever, was dumb before it. To make him shrivel under scorn, to wind her tongue about him like a whip till he writhed; to play the honest woman and tell him quietly that she did not love and had nothing more to say to him; or to ask him urgently for release— she did none of these things: none of them entered her head. She had never shirked the apportioning of the Weaving Women. Destiny was unquestionable. She felt that she abhorred Ingram. What she was to suffer from him she knew but too well. And yet she knew also that she was going to marry him, to be neglected by him, put to scorn, betrayed. All these things she would undergo, because they could not be avoided. She was bound as well as gagged. Her destiny was before her, as her character was within. The one had begotten the other. She had sowed, and now she was to reap. Her stony mind contemplated the harvest, and saw that it was just.

Therefore she said nothing, but stood with her foot on the fender, shading her face from the fire with her thin hand. In this attitude, though able to see sideways what was coming upon her, she stood nerveless to his approach. "Sancie, my own

Sancie," he said, and put his arm about her, and drew her bodily to his side. She stiffened, but allowed it.

"Dearest girl, tell me that you forgive me—tell me that. I am wretched without you—I can't go on like this. It's not good for me; my health suffers. Darling Sancie, forgive poor old Nevile. He was once your boy—you loved him so much. For the sake of old times, Sancie, my dear."

She could only say, "I have forgiven you—you know that. I have told you so." He pressed her closely to him, feeling his urgent need to make the most of what she had to give him. Her apathy struck him mortally chill; he wooed her the more desperately.

Holding her to his heart—an inanimate burden —he kissed her cold lips, her eyelids, her hair; called her by names whose use she had long forgotten, whose revival caused her pain like nausea. If he could have known it, this was the last way to win her. It was like pressing upon a queasy invalid the sweets which had made him sick. But he, remembering their ancient potency, seeing himself the triumphant wielder of charms, felt secure in them still; therefore she was his darling, his hardy little lover, his Queen of Love, his saucy Sancie, his lass. On fire himself by his own blowing, at last he fell upon his knees and clasped hers: "Dearest, most beautiful, my own, I love you more than ever. Comfort me, be my salvation—I pray that I may be worth your while. Marry me, Sancie, and save my soul alive."

Honestly, for the moment, he believed himself irresistible, and so far succeeded with her that her disgust hid itself in a cloud of pity. She felt pity for a man abject at her feet, and could speak more kindly to him.

But she could not bring herself to touch him. Looking down at him there, her eyes were softer and her lips took a gentler curve. "You mustn't be down there," she said. "I don't like to see you there—and can't talk to you till you get up. Let's sit down and talk—if you will." He rose obediently and stood with heaving chest, while she drew a chair to the fire and seated herself. Then he took to the hearthrug, and possessed himself of her hand.

"What a cold hand, my dear! Oh, Sancie, how I could have warmed you once! Is that ne' r to be again? Don't tell me so, for God's sake."

"Oh, how can I tell!" cried she. "Surely you can understand me better than that? Do you ask me to forget everything that has has happened in eight years?"

"I asked you to forgive me, my dear."

"And I have forgiven."

"But do you store these things up against me? That's not too generous, is it?"

"I don't store anything," she assured him; "but it wouldn't be honest of me to pretend I am what I was—once. I was a child then, and now I'm a woman. You have made me that. I am what you made me."

He stared into the fire, dropped her hand, which she instantly hid under the other.

"You mean to tell me, then," he said, "that I have made you cease to care?"

She tried to soften the verdict. "You seemed to me not to care very much yourself. You left me for a year together——"

"Once, my dear. I left you for one year."

"One whole year, you know," she replied, "and for other times too."

"I never ceased to love you," he vowed. "You must be aware how much I depended upon you. You were always with me."

She could have laughed at him. "I don't pretend to the same state of mind. During those absences of yours I learned to be happy alone—and I was happy, too."

This seemed horrible to him. "I could not have believed it of you," he said, aghast. "You must have changed indeed."

"I have changed," she owned. He started to his knees and clasped her.

"Beloved, I can change you again—I am the man who had your heart. I must do it—it's my right as well as my duty. Trust me again, my own; give me your dear hand again—and you shall see. If you are changed for the worse, I am changed for the better. You have redeemed me. What is it they say in the Bible? By your stripes I am healed. Yes, yes—that's precisely it. Kiss me, my own girl; kiss me." His eyes implored: she stooped her sad head that he might kiss her. He strained upwards and held her until she broke away with a sob. "Oh, leave me, leave me for a little while," she prayed him brokenly. "I can't talk any more now; I assure you I can't."

He begged her pardon for his vehemence. "I'm pretty bad myself, you know. This kind of thing plays the deuce with a man's heart."

She could thank him with a woman's for this naïve assurance. "I don't doubt you for a moment," she said. "You have been rather eloquent."

"Eloquent, my dear!" He raised his eyebrows. "You might spare me congratulations upon my eloquence. I don't deserve very much, perhaps—though God knows I tried to make you comfortable; but perhaps I deserve credit for sincerity."

She was not to be drawn that way. "I don't doubt your sincerity in the least," she said. "But I wish you to allow for mine. I am changed, and have told you so."

"I can see that you are. Heaven knows that. Perhaps I deserve it: I don't know. It's hardly for me to talk about my own points, is it? Criticism, from whichever side it comes, does seem to me out of place in a love-scene. And you found me eloquent in spite of it! Surely I may congratulate myself upon that."

She looked at him standing before her, his arms folded; she showed him a face too dreary to be moved by sarcasm. "You may congratulate yourself on lots of things, I'm sure."

Annoyance began to prick him; he showed spirit. "You are tired—and I may have tired you. I won't do that any longer. I think I'll go, if you'll excuse me to your Lady Maria. Sensible lady, that. She goes to sleep. . . ." He took a turn over the room, then came back and stood over her. "I have not had my answer yet. I'll come for it in a few days' time. May I hope you'll have it for me—say, to-day week?"

"What is the question I have to answer?" She looked up for it, though she knew what it was to be quite well.

"Do you wish it repeated?" He was perfectly cool by now. "I'll put it categorically. I have wronged you, and wish to repair my fault: will you allow it? I love you more than before: will you permit me to prove it? I believe that I can make you happy: may I try?"

She had scarcely listened, and when she answered him, did not lift her head. "I can't answer you now, Nevile. Don't ask me."

"I have not asked you. I have simply put my questions fairly. I will come for my answer next Sunday afternoon. Good-bye, Sanchia."

He held out his hand and received hers, which he kissed. Then he turned and left her alone.

.   .   .   .   .   .

"I should swallow him, if I were you," was Lady Maria's spoken reflection upon what her young friend was able to tell her. "I should swallow him like a pill. You won't taste him much, and he'll do you worlds of good. The world? I'm not talking of the world. I never do. He'll put you right with yourself. That's much more to the point. He's in love with you, I believe. From what you tell me, that's new. You suppose that he was in love with you before. I do not. He was in love with himself, as you presented him. Most men are. Now you are to occupy that exceedingly comfortable position of a woman out of love with her husband, extravagantly beloved by him. Next to being a man's mistress there's no surer ground for you than that, with respectability added, mind you. No mean addition. Take my advice, my dear, and you won't regret it."

But Sanchia knew at the bottom of her heart that Ingram was not in love with her. He wanted her restored to his collection.

IX

On the Monday morning, after a night of broken sleep, she received a letter from her mother.

"My dear Child," Mrs. Percival wrote, "I met Nevile Ingram, *quite unexpectedly*, on Saturday evening. Yesterday he called here, after he had seen you in the house where you choose to remain. Our interview was naturally distressing, and I should be glad to feel sure that you could spare me a *third*. I need not remind you of the first.

"But I feel bound to own, from what I could learn from him of his *discussion* (as I must call it) with you, that I am most uneasy. If I were to say *unhappy*, tho' it would be less than the truth, you might accuse me of exaggeration. That I could not bear. Therefore, let 'uneasy' be the word. Is it possible, I ask myself, that my youngest child—my latest-born—can find it in her heart to *torture* the already agonised heart of her mother? I put the question to you, Sanchia, for I am incapable myself of finding the answer. I blush to write it—but such is the terrible fact. I can only beg you to put me out of suspense as gently as may be. I am growing old. There are limits to what a grey-haired mother's heart can bear.

"Mr. Ingram's proposals towards a settlement of the untold *ruin* he has wrought in a once smiling and contented household were (I must say) liberal. That they were all that they should be, I must not declare—for how could that ever be? He put himself, however, and his extremely handsome fortune unreservedly in my hands and those of your father, who was not present at our interview. He was *resting*, I believe—his

332

own phrase. Philippa came in to tea, with her trusty, honourable Tertius, and was more than gracious to N. You know her way. She *stoops* more charmingly than any woman I have ever met. Her manners, certainly, are to be copied.

"His position in the county—I return to Nevile—I need not dwell upon. It may be *brilliant*. A Justice of the Peace at thirty-two! I leave you to imagine what he might become, building upon that, if he were blessed with the loving companionship of a *tender, chaste and Xtian wife*. Such an one could guide him into Green Pastures—and such an one only. Secure in the gratitude of his inferiors, the respect of his peers, reconciled to the Altar, and his God, one sees before Nevile the upright, prosperous, honoured career of an English Gentleman. There is no higher, I believe. But it is clear to all of those who truly love you, my child, that you only can ensure him these advantages. He is sincerely penitent now—of that I am sure. Who can tell, however, what relapse there may be unless he is taken in hand?

"You have been his curse, but may be his Blessing. You have my prayers.

"I beg my compliments to Lady Maria Wenman if she condescends to recognise the existence of—Your affect^e Mother,
                              "CATHERINE WELBORE PERCIVAL.

"*P. S.*—Nevile assures me that his cousin, the Bishop, would perform the rite. This would be a *great thing*. One must think of N's position in the county."

"Venus, wounded in the side . . ." is the opening line of an old poem of Senhouse's, one of those "Greek Idylls" with which he made his bow to the world—old placid stories illuminated by modern romantic fancy; nursery-rhyme versions, we may call them, of the myths. "Venus, wounded in the side," recounts how the Dame, struck by a shaft of her son's, ran moaning from one ally to another

seeking Pity, the only balm that could assuage her
wound. To the new lover, to the old, to the fresh-
wedded, to the long-mated: from one to the other
she ran—hand clapt to throbbing heart. None
could help her. "Pity! What's that?" cried the
first. "I triumph: rejoice with me. Is she not like
the sun in a valley?" The second cursed her for a
procuress. The bride stirred in her sleep, and whispered, "Kiss me again, Beloved." As for the
fourth, he said, "All my Pity was for myself. It is
gone; now I am frost-bound." Venus wept: Adonis
healed the wound.

Sanchia, reading long afterwards, saw in it a par-
allel to her case, when she, stricken deep, ran about
London ways for a soothing lotion. She saw herself trapped; felt the steel bite to the bone. Tears
might have helped her, but she had none: pray she
could not, nor crave mercy. It was not Ingram
who held her caged, but Destiny; and there's no
war with him.

She thought of Vicky, of Melusine. Their kisses
would have been sweet, but she knew what they
would say. Melusine's sideways head, her sighed,
"Dearest, how sad! But life is so serious, isn't it?"
She saw the gleam in Vicky's eyes, and heard her
"Dear old Sancie, how slendid! Now you'll be all
right." Then she would clasp her round the neck
and whisper in her ear, "Do make me an aunt—I
shall adore your baby. Quick, darling!" She turned
her back on Kensington and Camberley, and went
into the City, to The Poultry, with her griefs.

Poor Mr. Percival's rosy gills and white whiskers, his invariable, "Well, Sancie—well, my dear, well, well—" called her home. She ran forward, clung to him, and lay a while in his arms, short-breathing, breathless for the advent of peace. To his, "What is it, my love? Tell your old father all about it," she could only murmur, "Oh, dearest, what shall I do?" He urged her again to tell him what the matter was— "What has hurt you? Who has dared to hurt my darling? Show me that scoundrel—" but she was luxuriating in new comfort and would say nothing. Into her false peace she snuggled and lay still; and the honest man, loving her to be there, let her be.

Presently she opened her weary eyes, looked up, and smiled, then snuggled again. He led her to his office chair, and took her on his knee. "Lie here, my bird, make your pillow of my shoulder. That's more comfortable, I hope. Why, Sancie, you've not been here, in my arms, since you hurt your foot at Sidmouth deuce knows how long ago—and I kissed it well! Do you remember that? Ah, but I do. I'm a foolish old chap, with nothing else to think about but my girls. And you're the only one left— the only one, Sancie. And I always loved you best —and behaved as if you were the worst—God forgive me!" She put her hand up and touched his cheek. "Hush, dearest. We don't talk about that."

"No, no, my darling—that's over, thank God. You have forgiven me, I know—my great-hearted

Sancie. Now, if you feel stronger, tell me all your troubles." She murmured what follows.

"He came to see me. Nevile came."

"I know, my love. Your mother told me."

"She wrote to me. Rather a dreadful letter. She's on his side—she talks about his position in the county."

"I daresay, I daresay. But you know, your mother thinks a great deal of that kind of thing. She says we owe a deal to our station, you know. There's something in it, my dear. I'm bound to say that."

"Papa, he—wants me again. He thinks he does."

"Oh, my dear, there's no doubt about that— none at all. He proposes—well, it's *carte blanche;* there's no other word for it. A blank cheque, you know. We must do Master Nevile justice. It is the least he can do; but he does it."

"What am I to do, Papa?" The poor gentleman looked rather blank.

"Do, my dear? Do?" He puzzled; then, as the light broke on him, could not help showing his dismay. "Why, you don't mean to say— Oh, my child, is that what you mean?"

She clung to him convulsively, buried her face.

"God help us all!" His thought, his pity, his love whirled him hither and thither. He shivered in the blast. "'Pon my soul, I don't know how we shall break it to your mother. I don't, indeed." He stared miserably, then caught her to him. "It breaks my heart to see you like this—my child; it cuts me to the heart. Sancie, what are we to do?"

She sat up and brushed her dry eyes with her handkerchief. "I know. There's nothing to do. It's my fate."

This was rather shocking to old Mr. Percival, who shared the common opinion of matrimony, that it should be marked by champagne at luncheons. It was a signal for rejoicing—therefore you must rejoice. White stood for a wedding all the world over, black for a funeral. To go scowling to church, or tearless to the cemetery, was to fail in duty.

"We mustn't look at it like that, my darling. I don't think we ought, indeed. Fate, you know! That's a gloomy view of an affair of the sort. I don't pretend to understand you, quite, my love. You see, a year or two ago, you would have asked nothing better—and now you call it fate. Oh, my dear——"

She could not have hoped that he would understand, and yet she felt more like crying than at any time yet. "My heart is cold," she said. "It's dead, I think."

He echoed her, whispering, "Not dead, Sancie, not dead, my child. Numbed. He'll warm it asleep, he'll kiss it awake. He loves you."

She moaned as she shook her head. "No, no. He wants me—that's all."

"Well, my dear," pleaded good Mr. Percival, "and so he may. We do want what we love, don't we now? He's come to his senses by this time,

found out the need of you. And I don't wonder at
it. You're a beautiful girl, my dear—you're the pick
of my bevy. But I must bring back the roses to
those cheeks—Mildred Grant, eh? Jack Etherington used to call you that: he was a great rose-fancier
—old Jack. Do you remember our tea-party last
summer? And how happy we were? Let's be
happy again, my lamb! Come, my child, can't you
squeeze me out one little smile? You'll make the
sun shine in this foggy old den of mine." He pinched
her cheek, peered for the dimple which a smile must
bring; then he drew her closer to him and whispered
his darling thought: "Shall I tell you something,
Sancie? What your old dad prays for when he's
by himself? I want another grandchild, my dear
—one I can spoil. I ought to be a happy man with
what I've got—I know that. But you were always
the pet, my love; you know you were—until, until—
ah, Sancie! And one of yours! Aren't you going to
indulge your old father? He's only got a few years
left, mind you. Don't want any more. To see his
darling happy, smiling down on her baby—bless me,
I'm getting foolish." He blinked his bravest, but had
to wipe his glasses. She rewarded him with a kiss,
and did not leave till she could leave him at ease.

X

SANCHIA, after many nights' stony vigil, decided that she must fight her beasts by herself. She was going to make her parents and sisters happy; she was going through with her bargain; but there was no need to tell them any more about it. In her hard mood she told herself that that was the only wear. If she should be wept over, she might well recant. When the fatal word was once spoken, she would write to her mother—that was all that she could do. For the same reason—that she dreaded a tender moment—she did not go to church with her griefs. The Gods there were too human—the Man of Sorrows, the Mother with the swords in her bosom. It was Destiny that had her by the heel. As ye sow, ye shall reap. Vaster gods, heartless, blind, immortal shapes, figuring the everlasting hills, were her need. She was going to her fate, because the Fates called her. There's no war with them.

There had been one who would have had it all out of her in a trice. But he was remote, a part of her childhood. She hardly called him to mind at this hour. It was dangerous work to think of him, she knew—and her old fortitude stood by her, which said, Turn your mind resolutely away from that which may influence your judgment. Senhouse was not a stoic; he was an epicurean, she now considered. She wanted something flintier than Senhouse. He might have tried to dissuade her; but her mind was now made up. She intended to marry Nevile.

She breakfasted alone, and immediately afterwards went upstairs to write her agreement. The thing was to be gone through with, and the sooner the better.

"MY DEAR NEVILE," she wrote, "if it can ever be right to marry without love, it must be in my case. I don't blame you in the least for what happened. It was as much my doing as yours—and I still think that I was right. And now I think that it is right to fulfil one's bargain—as it would have been if I had married you. If I had been married to you, I should not have left you unless you told me to go, and I don't think that I ought to now. If you really wish it, you shall marry me when you please, and I will do my duty by you always. Whatever arrangements you make will suit me quite well; but the less fuss we make the better. I am sure that you will think so too. Don't come to see me for a few days if you don't mind. I want to think.—Yours affectionately, SANCHIA.

It was not a very gracious letter, it must be owned. So young and so untender! One would have said that the man must be a courageous lover who would take marriage on such terms; but either Ingram was very much in love, or honestly hoped to be loved again. I incline to the opinion of Bill Chevenix, to whom he showed it. "Nevile, old chap," he said, "you take her on any terms. You've no idea how set up you'll feel by everybody saying you've done the square thing. I tell you frankly that she's too good for you. Look how she's shaped in Charles Street! As if she'd been born to it. And never once—never once—allowed to anybody that she's been in the wrong. Not to a soul. And neither you nor I believe that she has—nor did old Doss-house, or whatever his name was." Ingram knew quite well to whom he so airily referred.

"I shall have landed that chap once for all, any-how," he said.

"Landed him!" cried the other. "Why, bless you, didn't you know? He landed himself two years after you did. He's married."

"Married, is he?" Ingram asked, not thinking of Senhouse in particular. "Who did he marry?"

"He married a rather pretty woman, a widow, a Mrs. Germain."

Ingram looked sharply up. "I'll take my oath he didn't. I met her the other day. She's Mrs. Duplessis."

Chevenix stared at him. "Why, I know the chap. Where did you meet her? Where do they live?" he asked his friend.

But Ingram had other things to think of, and returned to his letter. "I shall take this as she means it, Bill. She wants me to go slow—I can take a hint. She shall have her head. When I get her down to Wanless we shall be all right. The place isn't fit to live in now, you know. I was up there last week—and found everything going to pot. Not a horse fit to ride—not a sound one amongst 'em. Plantations all to pieces—gardens—tenants in arrears

—oh, beastly! She'll have it all to rights in no time, and she'll simply revel in it. She'll come round— you leave that to me. If *I* can't get a girl round I ought to."

Chevenix listened, and judged. He knew his Ingram pretty well, and took his confidence, like his confidences, for what they were worth. "Where did you say that the Duplessis lived?"

"I think she's in a hotel. It might be Brown's. I believe it *is* Brown's. What d'you want her for?"

"Think she knows some of my people," said Chevenix, and presently took himself out of the Coffee Tree Club.

But Sanchia, her day's work done, went—not to church, but to Bloomsbury. Entering the portals of the Museum, she swam to the portico, full of her cares. But smoothly, swiftly, she went, with that even, gliding gait peculiar to her kind, which has precisely the effect of a swan breasting the stream. Past the door, she turned to the left, not glancing at the aligned Cæsars, scarcely bowing to Demeter of the remote gaze. In that long gallery, where the Caryatid thrusts her bosom that her neck may be the prouder to the weight, she saw the objects of her present pilgrimage—beaten, blind, and dumb, immovable as the eternal hills, the Attic Fates; and before them at gaze, his arms folded over his narrow chest, Morosine the Pole.

Whether she had sought him here or not, she did not falter in her advance. Smoothly, swiftly, and silently she came to him and stood by his side. He turned his head, looked sharply at her pale face and sad eyes, then resumed his meditation before the Three. Neither of them had a care to speak.

Presently Morosine said, "I knew that you would be here." He kept his face towards the mystery, and so did she when she echoed him. "Did you know that? You know me, I think."

"I believe that I do. You have come here for strength. You will get it."

Ruefully enough she answered, "I wish I could believe that."

"You have it in you already. These great ladies will call it out. I wish you had been here, say, the day before yesterday. They might have helped you."

"But they did help me," she said. "They were with me. I remembered what we had talked about before them."

He nodded his head. "I had intended that you should. I was rightly inspired."

"Without them," she went on, "I don't know what I should have done. It seems absurd to say so, but——"

He interrupted. "It's not absurd at all—to you and me. If it's absurd, then Art is pastry-cook-stuff: sugar and white-of-egg. The man who fashioned these things had walked with God. Here are his secrets, revealed to you and me."

She followed her own thoughts, not his. "I came to-day because I have made up my mind. I

wanted them to confirm me—to say that I was right.
If you weren't here, I should go up to them and
whisper to them, as I've seen women do to the Ma-
donna abroad. I should tell them everything."

He looked at her keenly. "Do it now. I'll
leave you."

She smiled faintly. "No, don't leave me. I
couldn't do it now. But I meant to when I came
in."

"You didn't think that I might be here?" He
watched her.

"No. I remember that you said we were to meet
on Thursday. And I have a great deal to think of;
I'm in great trouble."

"I know you are," he said. "I fear to be im-
pertinent; but if I can help you——"

She gave him a grateful look. Her trouble was
very real, and made almost a child of her. "I should
value your advice. It would help me to have it—
even if it couldn't change my intentions."

"You shall have it, assuredly," he said. "Shall
we find a seat?"

"No, no. I would rather stop where we are.
Perhaps they'll hear us." They looked at each
other and smiled at a shared sentiment.

"Tell me, then," he said.

"He wants me to marry him," she said hurriedly,
"and I think that I must. All my people wish it,
and my friends—I mean those who have known
me for a long time. I don't mind very much about
most of them; but one of my sisters—Vicky—who

was always my closest friend, expects it—and it
would break my father's heart if I did not do it.
The others don't count; but those two do. And
there are other things—one other person who would
think I am doing right."

"Would you"—Morosine spoke slowly, addressing the statues—"would you consider the possibility
of marrying any one else?"

She spoke as one in a trance. "No—I couldn't
—I shouldn't dare. Besides, there is no possibility
—there would be Papa and Vicky again. That
would never satisfy them. And then I feel that it's
my punishment—if I deserve punishment, as they
all imply that I do. At any rate, it's part of my
bargain. I began this thing, and I must go on with
it, at all costs to myself. I mustn't think of myself
in it at all. I'm only part of the world's plan; but I
happen to know that I am; and so I must go where I
am called to go. I must follow my Destiny, just as I
did at first. That time I followed it against everybody's opinion; this time I must follow against my
own will. Don't you agree with me?"

Morosine reflected in silence. Then he said,
"Yes, I agree with you. I recommend you to follow
your determination."

Her eyes looked blankly at him; for the first moment he thought her disappointed, but he corrected
his impression in the second.

"I'm glad you agree with me," she said. "I
should have been disappointed if you hadn't."

He smiled. "You are stronger than you think.

You can suffice to yourself. But I hope that I shall never disappoint you."

"I have no fear of that," she said, young again and confident. She thanked the Immortal Three with her eyes, and turning to Morosine, asked him, "Shall we go?" They went together. Passing the Demeter of Cnidos, her swinging hand touched his. He held his breath. Her face, sharply in profile, was as pure and pale as a silver coin. Her breast held her secret. To her own heart she voiced the cry, "Have I done well, dear one? Have I done well? Do you approve of me? Do you?" It may be that Senhouse heard her in his Wiltshire hills.

XI

NEVILE INGRAM was capable of fine ideas, we have seen, and could sometimes carry them out. He had had a moment of generosity, with Sanchia's letter in his hand, and held in the main to his expressed intentions. When he went to see her, at the end of three rigorous days, he behaved like a gentleman. She entered the room where he awaited her, pale for his embrace: he came to meet her, put his hand upon her shoulder, and, stooping, kissed her lightly. "My dear," he said, "I'll deserve you yet;" and he really meant it. She was touched, and quite kind to him. He exhibited his version of her surrender.

"We're friends, eh? We know each other of old, have no surprises, and can take raptures for granted. That's your notion, I fancy? It's not mine, but I'll be thankful for what you give me, and it shall be my fault if you find me backward when you're ready. Bygones are bygones, then? We make a new start?"

She sat staidly under his gaze, not aware at the moment that his steel-blue eyes searched her avidly for a hint of more than he stated. "So far as I am concerned—certainly," she said. "I shall never unlock any cupboards."

"Better to burn the contents, perhaps," he laughed. "I tell you fairly, I had rather they were cleared out. Now, I'll confess to anything you please to ask me. That's a firm offer." He would probably have done it, but she told him that she had no questions to put. "Very well, my dear," he said. "Have it as you will. It's sublime of you—but it's not love. If you don't want to know it's because you don't care."

"No, indeed," she sighed, with such conviction that he was stung.

"Hang it all, Sancie," he cried, "you can't have known me for eight years without feeling something." She looked up at him, and he saw that her eyes were full.

"Oh, Nevile," she said, with a quivering lip, "don't let us look back. Indeed, I can't do it now." He put his arm round her and, drawing her closer, kissed her forehead. "My pretty one, we won't. I had much rather look forward. The future is to be my affair—if the past was yours." Then he went away, and she saw nothing of him for two days. On the second of them he dined with Lady Maria, and met some of the Percivals—the father and mother, the Sinclairs, and Mr. Tompsett-King. (Philippa had declined to come.) He behaved with great discretion, and so continued. After a week or ten days of courtship, she could hardly believe that their relations had ever been interrupted. His reliance upon her was absolute, his confidence no less so. He babbled of himself and his concerns in the old vein of mocking soliloquy, careless whether she heard him

or not. Now that he had her promise, he seemed in
no hurry for possession. His kisses were fraternal,
his embraces confined to a hand on her shoulder, an
arm lightly about her waist. She was inordinately
thankful to him, and by a queer freak of the mind,
poured all her gratitude into Senhouse. She told
herself that but for him she would never have brought
herself to her duty; but for him, therefore, would
never have discovered how little she had to fear.
Here was a crown for her "dear obsequious head":
shutting her eyes tightly, she thought that she could
feel his fingers putting it on, smoothing out her hair
so that the circlet should fit closely. Night after
night she knelt to receive it. It came as a result of
prayer.

The marriage-announcement, got into the paper by
Mrs. Percival, was accepted for what it was worth.
It was partly the price of her crown. A few letters
from old friends were formally answered. Sanchia
had never been a free writer; nobody but Senhouse
had found her letters eloquent—he only had been
able to feel the throb beneath the stiff lines. Her
handwriting, round and firm, had for him a provo-
cative quality; it stung his imagination. He used
to sing her "divine frugality of utterance," and protest that it was all of a piece with the rest of her life.
No one, he had told her once, but a sculptor could
embody her in Art—her chill perfection, her severity
and definite outline. A poet might not dare, for he
would have to be greater than love itself, greater
than the love which inspired him, able to put it

down below him, and stand remote from it, and regard it as a speck in the landscape.

> Your sober thought, and your pride
> To nurse the passion you hold and hide

he had written of her in his day. That austere concealment of her heart, which so impassioned him, chilled enthusiasm in all others of her acquaintance. So her letters were few, and now she was thankful enough. She herself wrote to nobody, and never spoke of her future unless she was compelled to answer questions.

Once a day, however, she took out a writing-block and traced upon it the words "~~ ~~ ~~~, I think I ought to tell ~~~ ~~~ ~~ ~~~~~, ~~~~, I ~~ ~~ a similar exordium. She ~~~ ~~~~~~. How could she tell him that ~~~ ~~t telling him more? And how tell him more ~ hen, of her own accord, she had sent him about his business, and set her approval upon his marriage, or what must be considered his marriage? An instinct forbade her. She didn't reason with it: her reason was paralysed. "It's part of the price. It's what he would have praised me for"—and she flew to her text.

"*A great power is in your thin sweet hands, my sweet; you are in the way of being a great artist.*" She looked at her hands, and loved them for his sake who had loved them so well. Her "thin sweet hands!" Could one write so of her hands and not love them well?

But the power, the power that she had! Hear her

rhapsodist. *"If you can so work upon your delicate surface as to mould it close to your noble soul; if in the gallery of the world you can unveil yourself for a thousand pair of eyes to see, and praise God for the right to see—why, what an artist you are, and what an audience you have! . . . Like a whiff of thyme on a grassy down, like the breath of violets from a bank, or of beanflower blown across a dusty hedge, some gentle exhalation of your soul sighed through your body will hint to the passion-driven wretch things innocent and quiet. The blue beam of your steadfast eyes may turn his own to heaven; a chance-caught, low, sweet tone of your voice may check clamour; an answer may turn his wrath. . . . You can be picture, form, poem, symphony in one. . . . Think of it, Sanchia, before you turn away. Think well whether upon that exquisite medium you cannot express your best."*

She found herself trembling—in these days she easily trembled—as she re-read these words. That such a power should indeed be hers—and how could she fail to believe it?—was inspiration enough to send her to the fire. She read no more, but used to sit shivering, thrilling through every fibre of her body, with the strength of such splendid praise. For whatever might be her fate, splendid it was to have been so loved, so seen, and so praised. It was well for Ingram that she read her old love-letters—and extremely unfortunate for the writer of them, who anguished for her now in his desert place. Odd situation! that the love-letters of one man should reconcile her to the arms of another.

From Torquay, where she spent the Easter holidays with her father, the two alone and happily together, she wrote two or three times to Nevile. He was at Wanless, professedly getting some order into things there, and protesting to her by every word he sent her upon the need there was of her hand upon affairs. There was not a word of love used between the pair. All the love-making, indeed, was done by Senhouse, whose master-stroke was called for by and by.

Towards the end of April she was alone in Charles Street, preparing the house for Lady Maria's return from Rome. Ingram was still at Wanless, grumbling through his duties of magistrate, landlord, and county gentleman. "They seem to think up here that a fellow has nothing to do but 'take the chair,'" he wrote. "I can tell you I'm pretty sick of it, and fancy that they will be before long. I'm an awkward customer when I'm bored—as I am now, damnably." She sent him matter-of-fact replies, and wrote principally of the weather.

The Pole continued his discreet and temperate wooing after the plan he had formulated. He strove to interest her perpetually, never left her without having, as he taught himself to believe, impressed himself anew upon her imagination. Watching her as a cat a mouse, he learned to read her by signs so slight that no one who had not the intuition of a woman could have seen them at all. Unfortunately for him, he misinterpreted what he read. The slap-dash Ingram thought all was well; Chevenix, the

more observant, thought there was a bare chance;
Morosine alone could see how her quivering soul
was being bruised, and if he thought that she looked
to him for balm, he may be excused. She was
drowning, she held out her hands. To whom, but to
him upon the bank? How should he know what
shadow stood behind him, with praise in his dim eyes
for a "dear obsequious head"?

Playing deputy to Senhouse, little as he guessed
it, he devoted himself to bracing her for the match,
having made up his mind that there was no other
way of making her happiness his own. His mistress she might be, his wife never. As he read her,
she would keep the letter of the law—since the law
required it of her. The rest, he flattered himself,
might be left to time and him. His present aim was
to interest and stimulate her, without alarming.

He counted greatly upon some sudden emotional
stimulus, which would cause her to fall to him; and
one came, though it had no such effect.

The opera of *Tristan and Isolde*, to which she was
taken by Lady Maria—where she sat in his box, by
his side, absorbed in the most sensuous expression
of the love-malady that has ever tormented its way
out of a poet's heart—had been a real test of his
restraint. He had not once met her eyes—though
hers, craving sympathy at any hand, had sought his
often; he had not once permitted himself to gaze
upon her beauty, though it was her beauty, so carven,
so purely Greek, which had drawn him to her from
the first. While the great music went sobbing and

chiding through her frame, like wounded nightingales, he had sat in the dark, with his arms folded, never looking at her fully, nor seeking to win a glance from her soul to his own. That it stirred her to the deeps he knew. He could watch sideways, listen sideways, both hear and see that she was rapt. Her quick-heaving breast, the whistle of her short breath, the strained line of her head and shoulder—all this he marked and stored without a sign. Even when, on going out, he had been conscious of her overcharged heart, of her breast full of emotion; even when she had told him under her breath that she was happier, though he shivered, he drew away. He had nodded quickly, smiled, blinked his eyes. "I was sure of that," was all he allowed himself in the way of intimacy.

Swift, fire-consumed, intensely sensitive, subtle-minded, this was a man who relished suggestions more than things. He had far rather deal mentally with the lovely image of Sanchia, as he saw it, than actually with the breathing, palpitating flesh. To picture her longing, straining, trembling—to keep her always so, always holding out her arms, never obtaining what she sought: his bliss lay in that. He knew himself, after much experience of the sort; he had missed so often by blundering in, that now he dared not risk a wreck. Here at last, he told himself, was perfection: let him look to it that he kept it at its perfect poise. He must poise himself to do that, balance himself upon a knife-edge. Little of an ascetic as he was by temper, he could

The great music went sobbing and chiding through
her frame, like wounded nightingales.

train himself to the last ounce if the prize were worth
it. And it was. Never had musician had instru-
ment more sensitive to play upon. It seemed to him
worthy of a lifetime of preparation to have her for
one moment of time throbbing in his arms.

So Morosine went into the palæstrum, and fasted
with prayer. His *sangfroid* through *Tristan*, and
the going out with all its cry ringing in him, and in
her, surprised even himself, who knew himself well.
"My friend," he thought, as he stalked to his club,
"you have done well."

But he had not reckoned with the flinty core
which lay beneath her fair and delicate seeming.
Her frugality of utterance, which charmed and
chained him, really implied no reserve. She did not
speak, because she had nothing to say, did not reveal
herself, because she knew of no mystery. She was
at once very simple and very practical; she had
healthy tastes which she desired to gratify, and a
deliberate mind which instructed her how far she
might do so. Once in her life those had played her
false, when they told her that the pity she had for
Ingram was love, and the need he had for possession
of her was her own need to give it him. She had
been bitterly mistaken, and was now so weary with
herself that she seemed to have no desire in the
world but that of sleep. Tristan and Isolde, drowning soul and body in music which made love, and
love which was the heart of music, were not to be
thought of on this side of the grave. The Fates had a
sterner way for her. She was never to empty herself

in a kiss or to watch out the stars with Jack Senhouse. Homing in the carriage with Lady Maria,
she denied him, like Peter his Lord. "I know not
the man." Vaguely dreaming at her open window,
under the fire-fretted roof of that May night, she
suddenly thought of him again—nay, knew him
bodily there, alone with her under the sky—and for
the first time in her life felt his eyes upon her, seeking
of her what he had never dared to seek, and then his
arms about her, touching her as assuredly he had
never dreamed to do. She had denied him once too
often, it seems. Here was a sudden attack, a trick
of the sprites. She held her breath, she trembled,
her breast heaved, she shut her eyes, and her lips relaxed their hold of each other. "Not yet, my
blessed one, not yet!" and "Come, Rose of the
World!" Thus they murmured to each other and
strove. An expectancy, the shiver and thrill of it,
possessed her; she seemed to feel the touch of a beloved hand, which drew her, trembling and panting,
closer and closer to some high experience of which
she had never dreamed before, to the expression of
inexpressible things, to a giving of the utmost, to a
wild strife of emulation which of them two should
give the most. The dark was all about them like a
bed—and closer he drew her, and closer yet. For
one wild moment that endured—O heaven, they
two in love under the stars! He was of the Open
Country—as free as the wind. Thus he would love
her, if he ever loved. Tristan's crying would be
his—and Isolde's whimper of hurt would be her

answer. Thus, if ever, she might be loved. And then, if ever in this world, peace!

Shivering still, with the sense of an arm still about her, of wild breath beating on her cheek, she looked wonderfully out at the stars which had seen her possessing. They burned steadily in their violet hold—a million kindly eyes welcoming her to the Open Country. The great town lay so still below that but for the glare behind the houses, which told her that it lived, she might have thought herself enfolded in the hills. So sure she was that she had been wedded, she glanced swiftly up and down the street, lest one chance passenger should have seen her naked soul. So a young girl, kissed by her lover, will search the emptiness in fear. Not a soul could be seen; Charles Street under its lamplight showed like a broad white ribbon curving towards the Square, towards the Park. To her heart she whispered, "Dearest, you may love me—we are alone under the stars"—and then shut her eyes fast, and with parted lips breathed quick and short.

Out of the night, out of an empty street, a voice came up, "He loves you—none so well. He lies out on the down in a white robe. He watches for you and waits. I have seen him, talked with him of you. Can you refuse such love as his? Goddess though you are, you will get no higher love."

The voice was very real. She knew it well. From the close arms that held her, she answered it. "Oh, Struan, I know! I knew before you told me. It's wonderful. Love is a wonderful thing."

"It's all we have in the world. I am here to tell you that he waits for you. Good-night."

"Good-night, Struan," she said. "I'm quite happy now."

She remembered afterwards, with a shock of dismay at her selfishness, that she had never asked Struan of his welfare.

.   .   .   .   .   .

She came to herself with a shudder and envisaged her circumstance. She had had "a rare vision," like Bottom the weaver—and that was all. Jack Senhouse had never loved her so. To him she had been Artemis, the cold goddess, or Queen Mab, whom no man might take. He had said so often—and had looked it whenever she was near him. Meantime, she was to be married—and *Tristan* was unprofitable provender. It had given her an indigestion of the mind. She would go to bed.

That she deliberately did—with one ceremony, characteristic of her frugality. She opened a locked drawer, and looked at its contents. There lay three goodly piles of letters, tied with blue ribbon. Each packet was labelled "Jack to Me," and dated with beginning and ending. She contented herself with looking at them, smiling wisely and thoughtfully as she did so. Then, like a child, not trusting to her eyes alone, she looked at them with her fingers; touched them delicately in turn, with a caress. Immediately afterwards she locked them up; and turned to her disrobing. She slept quietly, and went about her affairs of the morrow with a calmness that surprised her.

At a later day, in a conversation which Morosine had with her, he permitted himself a reference to the Museum. "You go no more? They've done their work—the Three?"

She smiled upon him, looking up from a little blue-covered book which lay half-cut upon her lap. It had arrived by the post that morning without message, or even inscription. But it was dedicated, she observed, "To the Fairest," and had smiled wisely to herself, observing it. A finger in the book, she answered Morosine. "Yes, they've done their work. I'm much happier now. I've thrown up my arms, you see. I'm drowning." She suddenly blushed, to remember her dream; and he perceived it.

"Drowning?" he asked.

"Drifting with the tide," she explained. "And I like it."

It was on his tongue to refer to *Tristan*, but—such was her hardihood—she saved him the trouble. "I was fearfully excited with the opera. During the performance, and after it."

His heart beat high. "You were not more so than I was," he said, looking at her. "I thought of things possible and impossible. I had a vision."

So had she had a vision, whose force was such that she could not continue to talk of such things. She had flashed her eyes upon him vividly for a moment, but was compelled to turn them away. He read in them a wild surmise; he thought that she understood him and was perturbed—perturbed, but not displeased. The bustling entry of Chevenix, unannounced, prevented him from pursuing his campaign.

Chevenix was gay. "Hulloa, Sancie—this is ripping. I say, I have something frightfully interesting to tell you." Then he saw Morosine. "Hulloa, Alexis, is that you? Now we'll sit each other out, and Sancie won't have her news."

"But I hope I shall," she cried. "I haven't got a secret in the world. Don't go, Prince, please. Mr. Chevenix shall tell you the news too. I haven't the faintest idea."

"It's something you want to know very badly. At least, I should think you did. It's not Nevile's address." She took him gaily.

"I don't want to know that at all, if it's a new one. I have three already."

"Perhaps," said Morosine, with a friendly look, "it's to cancel some of them."

She held up a book. "Is that what you mean? Do look. *Songs*, by S. Glyde. Did you mean to tell me of that?"

Chevenix stared. "The poet Glyde? No. By Jove, though, not a bad shot. I referred, my dear, to the poet Senhouse."

She received that full in the face. She paled, then coloured. Her heart leaped, then stood still. She spelt with her blue eyes, "Tell me."

Chevenix peered at her. "Thought I should fetch you, my dear. The poet Senhouse is run to ground, and I'm going to see him. That's all."

It was plain to Morosine that she was very much concerned with this intelligence. She simply sat there, staring at Chevenix, shaking, moving her white lips. She was as white as chalk and her eyes burned black in her face. What on earth—who on earth—? He couldn't for the life of him make it out. He had never heard of the man. It was a shock to him to discover—so soon we flatter ourselves—that Sanchia had any reserve of confidence. He had felt so sure of her!

"Another new poet?" he asked her. She recovered herself, shook her head.

"He's not new—to me. He's the greatest friend I ever had." That was all she could say. She turned to Chevenix, her desire fainting in her eyes. "You're going to see him? Oh, take me with you!"

"Right," said Chevenix.

BOOK V

OF THE NATURE OF AN EPILOGUE, DEALING
WITH DESPOINA

I

Her spirits on the rebound, her courage waving
in her face, like the flag on a citadel, she hesitated
at nothing. On Chevenix's suggestion that they
must "play the game with Nevile," she told her
betrothed what she proposed to do. He had raised
his eyebrows, but said, "Why not?"

"I thought you didn't love each other," had been
her answer, and he had responded:

"Well, I have no reason to dislike him. In fact,
he gave you to me, if you remember." He chuckled
over the memory. "When the thing between us was
at its reddest heat, your man came pelting up to me.
He had seen you, it appears, and nothing would stop
him. I never told you this tale, but you may as
well have it now. The man's a lunatic, you know.
What do you think he wanted? How do you think
he put it? As thus: 'I loathe you, my dear man'
—I'm giving you the substance—'You stand for
everything I'm vowed to destroy; but I hope you'll
marry her, and tie her to you for life.' That was
his little plan. As you know, I couldn't oblige him.
He thought I could!"

She had been staring out of the window while he
harangued from the hearthrug, his favourite post in
a room. At this time she had no eyes but for the

that he had never kissed her. Love such as that, rendered in kisses, was unthinkable. She knew that she must not think of it, though she could not help her dreams. But there was no fear. The man who had not dared to kiss her when he might should find that she was worthy of such high honour.

Through the strings blew the wind from the south-west. "I love him—I shall see him to-morrow—I shall never tell him so—but he will read it in my eyes. He never kissed me when he might —he will not do it now when he must not. I am a fool, a fool, a fool! Thank God, I am a fool again!"

II.

"I FANCY," said Chevenix, as they breasted the down, "that to the candid observer we present a very pretty sight. He's not here, but I wish he were. A free-moving young lady—this is my idea—a Diana of the Uplands—wasn't there a picture of the name?— going to see an emancipated party of the Open Road, with a chain round her heart, in the custody of a gentleman-friend."

She took him on his own terms. "Explain your idea. What, for instance, is in the gentleman-friend's custody? The chain or the heart? Because, I assure you——"

"A truce," said Chevenix, "to your assurances. What I mean is this. It's jolly decent of Nevile to let you off. I don't know how he can bear you out of his sight after the way he's behaved."

She was in high spirits. She laughed at the vision of Nevile, deeply contrite and afraid that she would find him out. "I don't think Nevile cares much, whatever I may do." But Chevenix shook his head.

"You never know where to have Nevile. What says the Primer? *Timeo Danaos*—don't you know?"

She pleaded, Might they not forget Nevile out

here in the open? "Do you know," she asked him, "that I haven't been out like this——"

"On the loose, eh?" he interposed. She nodded.

"Yes, like this—free to do as I like—the world before me—" She fronted the blue valley for a moment, and then turned to the wind—"and the wind in my face, ever since I left Wanless?" Then she reflected with wide and wondering eyes. "And before that—long before. I haven't been free, you know, ever since I knew Nevile. Oh!'—and she inhaled the spirit of the hour— "Oh, I could fall down and hug the earth. Don't you love the thymy smell? I don't know why, but it always makes me think of poetry—and *that*." She lifted her rapt face to where, like a fountain of sound, a lark flooded the blue. "To lift up, and up, and up, to be so lovely because one was so glad! Nobody could do that!—except Jack," she added half in a whisper.

"That old chap's not a man," said Chevenix, "he's a spirit."

"They used to call him the Faun, at Bill Hill, where I first met him," she said. "I fancy now that I never knew him at all. But he knew all about me. That's why I'm so happy. Nobody has ever known me since—and it's such a bore to have to explain yourself. Other people seem to think I am extraordinary. I'm not at all—I'm the most ordinary person in the world. But he liked me like that."

Chevenix, watching her, said, "He'll like you like this, I expect. May I tell you that you're a heady compound? Do be quiet. Remember that I'm holding the chain. I won't swear to every link." She laughed, and pressed forward, the wind kissing her eyes.

They reached the racecourse, and had, behind them and before, two valleys. Their road lay now due west, keeping the ridge—a broad grass track belted rarely by woods on the north, but open on the south to hill and vale in diversity of sun and shade, a billowy sea of grass where no sign of man was to be seen. Sanchia's heart was so light she scarcely touched the ground. She swam the air, not flew. Chevenix pounded in her wake.

"You know," he told her by and by, "he's alone here? A solitary figure? Doing the hermit? Crying in the Wilderness?"

She had guessed, but not known that. Caution set a guard upon her eyes and tongue. "Do you mean—that he's always alone?"

"Bless you, yes. His lady couldn't stick it. She fled. But she's quite fond of him—in her way. I found out his address from her. She was quite glad I was going to see him. But she never goes herself, I believe. She's married. Other views altogether, she has. Or *he* has—her husband, you know. It was a rum business altogether, her taking up with old Senhouse. I could have told her what would come of that, if she'd asked me. No malice, you know—now. They're good friends. Write to each other. As a fact, she's married. She was a widow. She married a man I know, a chap in the

House, name of Duplessis. Sulky chap, but able. Keeps her in order. Old Senhouse will speak about it—you see if he don't."

She was full of thought over these sayings. What had he been about when he mated with a woman of this sort? "A man don't live like that," had been Nevile's explanation of part of his own history. Was this the meaning of her friend's vagary? Would he tell her? She would never ask him, but would give worlds to know.

Presently, and quite suddenly, as they pushed their way, now in silence broken only by Chevenix's cheerful whistling, upon that backbone of a broad hill-country—quite suddenly her heart leaped, and then stood fast. "Look, look!" she said softly. "There's Jack, close to us!" In a sheltered hollow some hundred feet below the level at which they were, a hooded figure in pure white was startlingly splashed upon the grey-brown of the dry hills. The peak of a cowl shot straight above his head, and the curtains of it covered his face. He sat, squatting upon the turf, with a lifted hand admonishing. About him, with cocked ears, and quick side-glances, were some six or seven hares, some reared upon their haunches, some, with sleek heads, intent upon the herbage, one lopping here and there in quest, but none out of range of a quick hand. Above his head, high in the blue, birds were wheeling, now up, now down. Peewits tumbling heavily, pigeons with beating wings, sailing jackdaws—higher yet, serene in rarity, a brown kestrel oared the sky.

Sanchia's soft eyes gleamed with wet. "Saint Francis and the hares! Oh, dearest, have I never known you?"

"What a chance for a rifleman!" said Chevenix. "That beats the cocks."

They stood intent for a while, not daring to disturb the mystery enacting. Chevenix whispered, "He's giving 'em church, to-day being Sunday," while Sanchia, breathless, said, "Hush! hush!" and felt the tears fret a way down her cheeks. Presently she put both hands to her breast and fell upon her knees. Chevenix, not insensible to her emotion, lit a pipe. Thus he broke the spell.

"Go to him, please. Tell him that I'm here," she bade him, and then turned away and sat waiting upon a clump of heather. She sat, as not daring to look up, until she heard his soft tread on the turf. Then she lifted to him her wet and rueful eyes.

His long strides brought him close in a second. He was changed. Leaner, browner, older than she had known him. And he wore a strange Eastern garment, a hooded white robe, short-sleeved and buttonless, made of coarse woollen cloth. He had thrown the hood back, and it sat upon his shoulders like a huge rolling collar. Yes, he was changed; there was mystery upon him, which sat broodingly on his brows. But his eyes were the same—bright as a bird's, frosty-kind as a spring morning which stings while it kisses you. "Queen Mab!" he said. "You!" and held out both his hands. It was evident that neither of them could speak. She rose; but there was no touching of the hands.

"And Peachblossom, attendant sprite," cried the resourceful Chevenix, following him up. "Don't forget him."

"Puck, I think," said Senhouse. "Robin Good-fellow." He had recovered himself in that breathing-space. "How splendid of you both. Come and see my ship. I'm in moorings now, you know. I've cut piracy."

"And preach to the hares," said Chevenix. "We saw you at it. What does his lordship say?"

"His lordship, who, in spite of that, is an excellent man, likes it. His lordship was pleased to catch me, as you did, at it, and to suggest that he should bring out a party of her ladyship's friend to see me perform. I told him that I was his hireling, no doubt, but that my friends here were amateurs who didn't care to say their prayers in public. His lordship begged pardon, and I bet you he's a gentleman. Nearly everybody is, when you come to know him."

Chevenix revelled in him. "Still the complete moralist, old Jack!" he cheered. "I'll back you for a bushel of nuts to have it out with Charon as you ferry across. And here, for want of *us*, you turn to the hares! Sancie, you and I must get season tickets to Sarum, or he'll forget his tongue."

Sanchia, overcome by shyness, had nothing to do with this brisk interchange. She walked between the contestants like a child out with her betters. Senhouse led them down the scarped side of a hill into his own valley; rounding a bluff, they suddenly

came upon his terraces and creeper-covered hut.
The place was a blaze of field flowers; each terrace a
thick carpet of colour. In front of them the valley
wound softly to the south, and melted into the folds
of the hills; to the right, upon a wooded slope, in
glades between the trees, goats were at pasture.

"Goats! Robinson Crusoe!" Chevenix pointed
them out. "*Dic mihi, Damœta, cuium pecus? an
Melibœi?* Are they yours, Senhouse?"

"I drink them, and make cheese. I learned how
to do it at Udine ages ago. You shall have some."

Sanchia saw them. The sun gleamed upon fawn
and white, and made black shine like jet. Deep in
the thickets they heard the bell of one, cropping
musically.

Senhouse led them to his verandah, which was
shadowed from the heat, made them sit on mats, and
served them with milk and bread in wooden bowls
and trenchers. He was barefooted, which Sanchia,
must by all means be—for the day: divining her, as
he only could, he knelt without invitation and untied
her shoes. "Stockings too, I'll bet you!" was what
Chevenix thought; but he was wrong. Senhouse
went into his cabin, and returned with sandals.
Sanchia had taken off her own stockings. They
were sandals to fit her. "I made them for Mary," he
explained; "but she preferred boots." "Most of
'em do," Chevenix said, "in their hearts," and Senhouse quietly rejoined, "So I've found out."

Chevenix, the tactful, withdrew himself after a
civil interval. He said that he should go goat-

stalking, and, instead, went for a ramble, well out of sight. Then he found a place after his mind, smoked his pipe, and had a nap.

The pair, left to themselves, resumed with hardly an effort their ancient footing.

He said, after looking long upon her, "You are changed, Queen Mab; you are graver and quieter —but you are yourself, I see."

"I am not changed really," she said. "I love all the things I did. But sometimes one doesn't know it."

He did not appear to heed her, occupied in his gentle scanning of her. "You are, I suppose, more beautiful than you were—I was prepared for that. You have been very much with me of late."

Her excitement grew suddenly quick. "Have I? It's very odd, but——"

"It's not at all odd," he said. "Nothing is. I will tell you what happens. After I go to bed— which is always lateish—I feel you come down the slope. I am not surprised—I wasn't the first time. You come in a blue gown, with bare feet. I can't see anything of you as you come but gleaming ivory— an oval, which is your face—two bars for your arms —two shafts,—and your feet. Your hair is loose all about your shoulders, and close about your face. It makes the oval longer and narrower than I see it now; your face is fuller by day than by night. You come to me out here, where I wait for you, and hold out your hand. I rise, and take it—and off we go. I realise now that I am in the conduct of a fairy. I was inspired when I hailed you—how long ago?—as Queen Mab. You show me wonderful things. Do you know that you come?"

"No, but—" She stopped, and bent her head. Her experience had not been so simple. "I have thought sometimes—" She could not finish—broke off abruptly. There was a beating pause, during which neither of them dared look at the other. She broke it. She asked him what he did out here alone.

"I live," he said, "very much as I did. I read— in three tongues; I paint rarely; I do a great deal of work. At night I write my book. And then—you come."

"And what is your book?"

"It began as Memoirs—in three volumes, but those have stopped. There was plenty to say, but after certain experiences which came to me here— singular enough experiences—nothing in it seemed worth while. Now I call it Despoina, after the principal character. Despoina, or the Lore of Proserpine."

"Who is Despoina?" She showed him that she had the answer already.

He looked at her, smiling with his eyes. "You are Despoina."

"Oh," said she, "I thought I was Queen Mab."

"It is the same thing. Despoina means the Lady —the Lady of the Country. She is a great fairy. The greatest."

It was now for her to smile at him, which she did a little wistfully. "Your Despoina is either too much fairy, or not enough. She does very humdrum things. She has done mischief; now she is going to repair it. She is going to be married."

He was watching her quietly, and took her news quietly.

"Yes, so I learned. There was a youth here who told me."

She stopped him, flushing wildly. "A youth! Struan was here? Then it's true—it's true?"

He was quite calm under this outcry. "Yes, your champion Glyde was here. A good fellow in the main, but, Lord! what a donkey! I think I did him good. He left me a week ago. He had told me about you—found out where you lived, and what was happening." She sat with her face between her hands, dared not let him see it.

Senhouse resumed the question of her marriage. "It doesn't matter what you do. You are you. So Ingram has forgiven Master Glyde, and now——"

She lifted her pale face at this name of duty.

"His wife died a year ago; rather more. He wants me to marry him, and I think I must."

"You don't want to?" She shook her head, watching her fingers tear the grass.

"No," she said, "not in the least. But I shall do it. Don't you think that I should?"

He thought, then threw his arms out. "God knows what I am to say! If the world held only you and me and him—here—fast in this valley— I tell you fairly, I should stop it." She looked up quickly, and their eyes met. Hers were haunted with longing. He had to turn his head. "But it doesn't. To me what you intend to do seems quite horrible because I am flesh, and cannot see that you are spirit. That is a perfectly reasonable reading of the Laws, which says, What I did as a child I must abide as a woman. It's a law of Nature, after all's said; and yet it can be contradicted in a breath. It's one of those everlasting propositions which are true both ways, positively and negatively; for Nature says, That is my rule, and immediately after, Break it if you're strong enough. Now, you are, but I am not."

Once more they looked at each other, these two who had but one desire between them—and who knew it each of each. And again it was he who broke away.

"I'm a coward, I'm false to my own belief. It's love that makes me so. Oh, Heaven, I see so well what it would be! And it would be right, mind you. These laws of Society are nothing, absolutely nothing. But you are pleased, for reasons, to submit. You are deliberate, you are strong. It's the old thing over again. Hideous, vile, abominable servitude! But you are pleased to do it. You say it is Destiny, and you may be right. I tell you once more, I dare not say a word against it."

"No, no," she said hastily; "don't say anything to stop me. I must go on with it. I have promised. He knows I don't love him, and he doesn't care."

Senhouse pricked up his head. "Does he love you, do you suppose? Do you believe it?"

She shrugged half-heartedly. "He says so. He seemed to when I told him that I was going away.

"When was that?" he asked her. She told him the whole story as the reader knows it. Senhouse heard her, his head between his hands.

At the end of it, he looked out over the valley.

"Would to God," he said, "you and I had never met, Sanchia."

Tears filled her eyes. "Oh, why do you say that?"

He took her hands. "You know why." There was no faltering in the look that passed between them now. They were face to face indeed. He got up, and stood apart from her. She waited miserably where she was.

"We may be friends now, I believe," he said. You'll let me write to you? You'll trust me?"

"I shall live in your letters," she said. "I read nothing else but those I have. They are all the help I have." Then with a cry she broke out, "Oh, Jack, what a mess you've made of our affairs!"

He laughed bitterly. "Do you know my tale?"

"I guess it," she said.

"I played the rogue," he told her, "to a good girl, who was as far from my understanding as I was from hers. I thought that I had got over—it, you know, and that she and I could be happy together. Absurd, absurd! God bless her, she's happy now. I swear to you that I meant to do her honour—and directly I found out what she really wanted, I would have given it her. You'll not believe that I was such a fool as to suppose she could feel happy with my ideas of wedded life—but I did. Oh, Heavens! Poor dear, affectionate, simple soul, she felt naked! She shivered at her own plight, and wondered why I'd been so unkind to her, seeing I was by ordinary so kind. I shudder to think what she must have gone through."

"But," she said, anxious to save him, "but she knew what your beliefs were—and accepted them. You told me so."

"Queen Mab," he said gravely, "she was a woman, not a fairy. And please to observe the difference. She, poor dear, felt as if she was stripped until she married. You will feel stripped when you do. Yet you both do it for the same reason. She obeys the law because she dare not break it; you because you choose to keep it. Despoina! Despoina!"

She laughed, a little awry. "You used to call me Artemis. I'm not she any more."

"You are all the goddesses. You do what you please. Your mind is of Artemis; you have the form of Demeter, the grave-eyed spirit of the corn—and your gown, I observe, is blue, as hers was. I see Hera in you, too, the peering, proud lady of intolerant eyelids; and Kore, the pale, sad wife—which makes you your own daughter, my dear; and Gaia, by whom the Athenians swore when they were serious,—Gaia, the Heart of the Earth. All these you are in turns; but to me Despoina, the Lady of the Country, whose secrets no man knows but me."

She was now by his side, very pale and pure in her distress. She put her hand on his shoulder as she leaned to him. "Dearest, there is one of my secrets you have not learned. May I tell it you?"

He listened sideways, not able to look at her. She felt him tremble. "I think not—I think not. You will tell Ingram first—then do as you please. Don't ask me to listen. Haven't I told you that I see you every night?"

"And I tell you nothing of my secret?"

"I never ask you."

"But do I not tell you? Can I keep it?"

"You don't speak to me. You never speak. You look. Fairies don't speak with the tongue. They have better ways. "

"What do you do with me?"

"I follow you, over the hills."

"And then?"

"At dawn you leave me."

"I am a ghost?"

"I don't know. You are Despoina. You go at dawn."

A power was upon her, and within her. She put both hands on his shoulders. "One night I shall come —and not leave you. And after that you will not follow me any more. I shall follow you." Perfectly master of himself, his eyes met hers and held them.

"It shall be as you will."

She smiled confidently. 'I shall come. I know that. But I shan't speak."

"What need of speech between you and me?"

She saw Chevenix upon the high ground above. He stood on the grass dykes of Hirlebury, and waved his hat.

"I must go now," she said. "Good-bye, my dear one."

"Good-bye, Despoina. In seven hours you will be here again. . . ."

"It is to be observed," says a gifted author, "that the laws of human conduct are precisely made for the conduct of this world of Men in which we live and breed and pay rent. They do not affect the Kingdom of the Dogs, nor that of the Fishes; by a parity of reasoning they should not be supposed to obtain in the Kingdom of Heaven, in which the Schoolmen discovered the citizens dwelling in nine spheres, apart from the blessed Immigrants, whose privileges did not extend so near to the Heart of the Presence. How many realms there may be between mankind's and that ultimate object of Pure Desire cannot at present be known, but it may be affirmed with confidence that any denizen of any one of them, brought into relation with human beings, would act, and lawfully act, in ways which to men would seem harsh, unconscionable, without sanction or convenience. Such a being might murder one of the ratepayers of London, compound a felony, or enter into conspiracy to depose the King himself, and, being detected, very properly be put under restraint, or visited with chastisement either deterrent or vindictive, or both. But the true in-

ference from the premises would be that, although
duress or banishment from the kingdom might be
essential, yet punishment, so called, ought not to be
visited upon the offender. For he or she could not
be *nostri juris*, and that which was abominable to us
might well be reasonable to him or her, and, indeed, a
fulfilment of the law of his being. Punishment, therefore, could not be exemplary, since the person pun-
ished exemplified nothing to Mankind; and if vindictive, then would be shocking, since that which it
vindicated, in the mind of the victim either did not
exist, or ought not. The ancient Greek who withheld from the sacrifices to Showery Zeus because a
thunderbolt destroyed his hayrick, or the Egyptian
who manumitted his slaves because a god took the
life of his eldest son, was neither a pious nor a reasonable person.

"Beyond question," he continues, "there are such
beings upon the earth, visitors or sojourners by
chance, whose true commerce is elsewhere, in a
state not visible to us, nor to be apprehended by most
of us; whose relation with mankind is temporary.
The spheres which govern us, govern not them, and
their conduct is dictated by their good pleasure, where
ours goes after the good pleasure of our betters.
Thus a man may, if he can, take a goddess or nymph
to wife, but should not be disconcerted with what she
may elect to do."

Sanchia returned silently to London by the 6.50
from Salisbury, and arrived at Charles Street by

half-past eight, which was Lady Maria's usual hour. She changed her dress hurriedly and came into the drawing-room. Ingram was waiting there, his hands behind his back. He looked at her as she entered, but did not greet her. Perhaps he saw his doom in her eyes.

"Had a good day, Sancie?" he asked, after a while of gazing.

"Very good," she said.

"Saw your man?"

"Yes, I saw him."

"Mad as ever?"

"Ah," she said, "who is mad?"

"Well, my dear, if he is not, we are. That's certain. What have you done with Bill Chevenix?"

"He's gone home to dress. He will be here directly."

"I hope," said Ingram, "he played the perfect squire." She stood by the window looking out towards the west. Luminous orange mist flared up behind the chimney-stacks in streamers. Above that, in a sky faintly blue, crimson clouds, like plumes of feather, floated without motion.

Ingram called her to him. "Sancie, come here a minute. I want you." She turned her head and looked at him, then slowly crossed the room. She kept her eyes upon him, but did not seem to see him. They were haunted eyes. She came in front of him, and stood, questing his face, as if she was trying to see him within it.

He continued to smile jauntily, but his lips twitched

with the strain. He put his arm round her shoulder and drew her towards him. "This day month, my girl," he said, and kissed her. She stiffened at his touch. Her lips were cold, and made him shiver. His arm fell back. "Pooh! what do you care?" She stood in her place before him without speaking. If she had looked at him she might have stricken him blind. When Lady Maria came in, she moved away, and returned to the window. The glow had almost gone; nothing remained but wan blue, white towards the horizon. It was the colour of death; but a single star shone out in it.

Chevenix came in briskly, fastening his sleeve-links. "Here is the Perfect Chaperon, here is he!" he said, and bowed to Lady Maria. "My dear Aunt Wenman, you've no notion how hungry I am. We saw Senhouse teaching the hares their catechism. Afterwards we lunched on conversation and water. Ah, and salad. Excellent salad. Then I went goat-stalking, and had a nap. Sancie and the Seer conversed. A great day."

Lady Maria took Ingram's arm, Sanchia that of Chevenix, and they went downstairs. Half-way down she stopped. Chevenix looked at her. She was white; she could hardly breathe. "Good God, Sancie, what's the matter?"

She stared, gasped, moved her head about. "I can't go on—I can't—I can't. It's horrible—it's awful—I'm afraid. Hush—don't make a fuss. I'm going away. This isn't possible."

The other couple were in the dining-room by now. Chevenix didn't know what to do.

"There's dinner, you know, Sancie," he said. "That's an institution, eh? You'll feel better, I expect. Keep your pecker up. I'll have a go at Nevile for you. I swear I will. Now, where's your pluck, my dear?"

She shook her head, struggling all the time to get her breath. "It's gone—clean gone."

"You want food, Sancie; that's what you want. Come. Don't let's have a commotion. You leave all this to me."

She leaned against the wall, and brushed her hand across her face. Chevenix was in depsair. Nevile, from below, called up, "What are you two conspiring about?" Sanchia shivered, and stood up.

"Go down alone," she said. "I can't."

III

She dragged herself upstairs, and locked herself in her room, stumbled to the window, caught at it by the sill and leaned out. Her skin burned, her blood beat at her temples, and her breath came panting from her. Her white breasts ached with the burden of her strife. "I was born to live, not die. Air! or I shall fall."

It was mellow dusk by now, the lamps below her lighted, and above the chimneys and broken roof-line, above the trembling glare which meant London, there were stars in a violet sky. The stars which looked on London, looked also on the dim grass wolds, on hills rolling like waves, on muffled woods, rivers swift under their banks, on cornlands stiff and silent in the calm, on pastures and drowsy sheep. But the hills stretched out on either side of a valley, fold upon fold, everlastingly the same. There Despoina walked, at the deepest hour of the night. Even now she was looked for by one who sat in the valley and watched the East—intent, hooded, white, his chin upon his knees. A knock sounded at her door. She turned and ran to open. "Her ladyship have sent to know if you would have something sent up, miss." "Nothing, nothing." She sped back to the window.

At midnight, Despoina should be there. At midnight! In three hours! It was time to get ready; there wasn't a moment to lose. She watched the night as if she were listening to it, counting its pulse. Then, kneeling where she was, she began to unfasten her hair, running her hands through it as each clinging coil loosened and grew light. So presently she was curtained in her hair.

It drooped about her burning cheeks and veiled her bosom. She looked like the Magdalen in the desert, facing, wide-eyed, the preacher. There she knelt on, in a trance, waiting for the hour.

It struck ten—eleven.

She changed her dress and put on again the blue cotton gown of the day's wearing—but she left her hair loose about her face and shoulders, and her feet were bare. She looked at herself in the glass. Her face was white, her eyes were wide and strange. She did not know herself, smiling so sharply—like a goddess wild with a rapture not known by men and women. Fiercer delights than theirs she knew, the joy of power mated with its equal, coping fellow to fellow. Consciousness of immortal bliss dawned upon her wise lips, and flickered in their curve.

"Despoina is here," she said, and blew out the light.

IV

It was intensely dark in the cup of the hills, but by the difference of a tone it was just possible to make out where the sky began. Looking closer yet, you could guess at a film of light, as if the rim of down absorbed and reflected a caught radiance from the stars.

On a quiet night the stars seem to burn more fiercely, and on this night you might have believed they gave you heat. There was no moon; but the sky was illuminated by stars. Jupiter had rays like a sun, and Sirius lay low down and glowed, now fiery, now green. A winged creature, crossing up the valley, would pass unnoticed; but if it struck suddenly upwards for a higher flight, above the hills into the upper air, you would see the light upon its pinions, and even the glitter of its watchful eye.

There was no wind; the silence could be felt, throbbing about you. It was past the hour when the creatures go hunting; the time when every breathing thing submits to the same power. Men and women forgot each other and their loves; foxes lay coiled in their earths. The shriek of the field-mouse startled you no more, nor the swift dry rustle of the grass-snake. Presently, very far away across the hills, in some valley not to be known, a dog barked; but the sound just marked the silence, and died down.

The hooded figure down there sat like a Buddha on his rock, motionless, unwinking, breathing deep and slow. His hands clasped his shins, his chin was on his knees; he pored into the dark. He sat facing the ridgeway where it came from the East, and watched the courses of the stars.

Through the window of the hidden hut a faint light glimmered, and within the open door there was to be discerned a pale diffusion of light. In the beam of this he sat, cowled in white, but his face was shadowed. He was like the shell of a man who had died in his thought, and stiffened in the act of meditation. No relation between him and the rest of the world could be discerned. He was as far from the sleepers as the dead are.

Yet within him was the patience which comes of wild expectancy. His mind was as couched as his body for the moment. He had not fasted for years in the wilderness, and communed with the spirits of the hidden creatures without learning the secret of their immobility. To him who could speak with plants and beasts, with hills and trees, the Night itself could converse. So surely as the crystal fluid which is the air streams in circles of waves about our sphere, so surely ranged his sense.

At a certain moment of time, without stirring, he changed. Intensity of search gathered in his eyes, and filled them with power. He remained for a little time longer in a state of tension so extreme, so

strung to an act that there might have streamed a
music from him, as from the Memnon in the sands
when light and heat thrill the fibres of the stone.
His look was concentrated upon a point above him
where, look as one might, one could have seen nothing to break the translucent veil of dark.

Yet, after a time, looking just there, one might feel
rather than know a something coming. The watcher
certainly did. Deep within the shadow of the cowl
his eyes dilated and narrowed, his lips parted, his
breath came quick and sharp. But he did not move.

The sense of a presence heightened; one knew it
much nearer. By and by, one could have seen pale
forms wavering in the fluid violet of the night, like
marsh-fires going and coming—and could guess
them one and the same. Bodily substance could
only be inferred. But he who waited, tense for the
hour, knew that the hour had come.

Her white face, made narrow by the streaming
curtain of her hair, her white arms and feet were
luminous in that dark place, and revealed the semblance of her body. His cowl was thrown back;
he had bowed his head to his knees. She stood over
him, looking down upon him, not moving. Her eyes
were clear and wide, and her parted lips smiled.
The rise and fall of her breasts could be heard as
they stirred her gown.

She put out her hand and laid it on his head; she
stooped to him as he looked fearfully up, and, meeting his face, kissed him. No words passed between

them, but he rose and stood by her, and she took his hand.

Together, hand in hand, they went deep into the valley, and the night hid them under the stars, and the silence swallowed up the sounds of their bare footfalls.

V

THE philosopher sat barefoot in the hollow of his valley, and wrote diligently in a book. He paused, pen in hand, and looked over the folds of the hills where the haze of heat hung blue, and brown at the edges. It lay upon the hill-tops like a mist. The sky was grey, and the land was pale, burned to the bone. Heavy masses of trees in the hanging wood showed lifeless and black. No bird sang, but there were crickets in the bents, shrilling inconceivably. The swoon of midsummer was over all, and Sanchia was coming.

He knew that she was coming before he saw her. She came along the edge of the plain above him. springing barefoot. He saw her legs gleam under her swirling skirts. He strained his eyes to her, but could not see her face for the mist over them. He waited for her, watching, feeling her approach. She began the descent of the scarp timidly, as if she was playing with the thought of his bliss, which she held daintily in her hands. "Dangerously beautiful, my Beautiful One, art thou. Heedless always of thyself. Now a wind blows from thee to me. Thy herald, O Thou that shrillest on the wind!"

He heard her gay and confident voice. "Jack! Jack! Where are you?" He rose and went to meet her; she saw him, and suddenly faltered in her stoop. She stopped, poised as if for flight; he saw her wings fold behind her, and lie quivering where they touched each other.

Her heart urged her. "Go to him."

She looked at him. "I can't see him perfectly, and can't trust myself."

Her heart cried, "I have brought you so far. I daren't stop." Still she stood and flickered.

Senhouse mounted to meet her. Blushful and bashful she stood; but her eyes, deeply watchful, never left him.

He, too, had lost his tongue. "Queen Mab! I knew that you were coming."

Her eyes were timid and her tongue tied. She was like a rueful child.

"How did you come, my dear?"

"I don't know."

"You came last night?"

"Ah, you knew me?"

"Well, Queen Mab?"

She had nothing to say.

"Oh, my dear, my dear," he asked her, "why are you come?"

"I can't tell you if you don't know." She looked at him, and he knew.

"You came to me—not because I love you?"

"No, no! Not for that!"

"You are beautiful beyond belief, Queen Mab. And you are the soul of truth. My dear one, do you love me?"

She hung her head, and looked up from under her long lashes. He saw, not heard, her answer.

He encircled her with his arm, and felt her trembling at his side. "My dear," he said, "I was writing my Memoirs. Now we'll burn the book, for I see that I am now going to be born."

She looked up at him laughing. She was the colour of a flushed rose. "My bride," he said, and kissed her lips. She turned in his arm and clung to him. The storm swept surging over her; passion long pent made her shiver like a blown fire. They took their wild joy. . . .

He led her by her hand to the shade of the valley, where the deep turf is hardly ever dry. She was barefoot, as he was, and bareheaded. In her bosom was a spray of dog-rose.

"You are blue-gowned, like Despoina," he told her, "and, indeed, that is your name. I am to have a fairy wife."

"Artemis no more," she laughed.

"You fulfil all the goddesses. Artemis was your childhood. But let's be practical. What is to be done?" She faltered her answer.

"I have found out by myself what to do," she said. And then she kissed him. "It's done now."

They picked up their lives where they had dropped them. They were content to wait for the fulness of their joy. He busied himself with food for her; he cooked, and she helped him; they talked of his affairs as if they had always been hers.

Something stirred the practical side of him. She was to see him as near a man of the world as it was possible for him to be. It might have been a shock to her, but its simplicity was all his own.

"I must see one person, and you must see one. I'll go to your father, and you shall tell Ingram what's going to happen. We don't owe him much, but there's that, I think. I've a great idea of treating the world with civility. The one thing it has worth having is its sense of manners. Let us have manners, then. Don't you think so?" He held her close as he spoke, and with a strange discrepancy between sight and sound, looked at her with dim eyes of love, before which she had to close down her own. To his, "Don't you think so?" she could only murmur without breath, "You mustn't love me so much—not yet, not yet!" but he pressed her the nearer and laughed his joy of her. "What! After eight years! And if I don't hold her very close, Mab, the tricksy sprite, may slip me."

Then he returned to his moralisings. "You'll see Ingram, my blessed one, don't you think?"

She said gravely, with hard outlook upon the distant wold, "Yes, I must see him—" and then, with a sudden turn to him and a wondrous veil of tenderness upon her eyes, "You know that I think what you think from now onwards." Their lips sealed the pact.

He broke away at last. "Practice! Practice! Do let's be practical. Think of this. My house is yours until we marry; that can't be for a week." A week! This was Senhouse practical. She blushed her answer.

"What will you do? I mustn't turn you out." He opened his arms wide to the airs of the down.

"I sleep in the open. The stars for me. They shall see you wedded. Meanwhile, I shall wait upon you. But do let us be practical. We wait a week; we marry; but then what shall we do? Shall we reform the world? I think we shall do that in spite of ourselves; for if two people dare to be simple, there's no reason why two million shouldn't." She lay at peace considering; her blue eyes, searching wonderfully into his, saw peace like a crown of stars.

"I'll tell you what I should like to do," she said. "I've thought about it this minute. It never occurred to me before, but I should like to teach better than anything in the world."

He looked far out to the white rim of horizon. He took her very seriously. "It's the highest profession of all, of course. Let's think. I've begun on it already, oddly enough. And yet, you know, it's not odd. Nothing is after our experiences. . . . We will teach. Woodcraft, weathercraft, husbandry, beast-craft, sky-craft. I can do that much for them. Lit., hum., Greek, Latin, English, Dante. History, shadowy; geography, practical. Tinkering, carpentering, planting. No mathematics; I can't add two to two."

"But I can," she told him. "I'll teach the babies, for we must have babies."

His eyes flashed upon hers for one beating second of full interchange. Then he turned them away, and scanned again the hazy hills. But hers remained on their watch, charged with their wistful dream.

"Our school," he presently resumed, "I see it. We teach first of all Nature's face and the love of it. We lead their hungry mouths to Nature's breast. No books! No books for them to glue their eyes upon. They shall learn by ear; their eyes have a better book to read in. Classics by ear and by heart, eh?"

She glowed at a memory. "You wrote to me about that. You said that, before the Printing Press, people used to get poetry by heart."

He looked down at her where she lay at ease. "'As I have got you,' I said." She dreamed beneath her flickering eyelids.

"You had me then. I didn't know it; but you had. And you have me still. That's wonderful. But now I have got you!" She lay awhile under the spell of him and the thought, and glowed and blossomed under them until at last, flowering like a rose, she turned and hid her face in his arm. Senhouse, grave and strong, let her lie where she was; but he felt the pulsing of her bosom, and was moved to utterance. Nothing in the eyes he bent down to her beauty, and nothing in his words betrayed the passion of his heart.

"The loveliest thing in all the world to me," he

Senhouse came back to her bedside and put a little flower
into her hand.

said, "is a beautiful thing bent in humility, stooping to serve. I shall see you teaching your children. They will be at your knees, on your knees; you will kiss them, and I shall go mad with joy. Flowers and you! Yes, we'll have our school. We'll teach people the beauty of their own business by means of the most beautiful things. Flowers and you!"

They talked long and late, walking down the valley to the farmstead for bread. On this, with milk and fruit, they supped after Sanchia had bathed, and clad herself in one of his Moorish robes. Hooded and folded in this she sat at meat, and Senhouse, filled with the Holy Ghost, discoursed at large. The past they took for granted; the present was but a golden frame for the throbbing blue of the days to come.

.   .   .   .   .   .

Very early on the morning after the night when, as has been foretold, she was made a wife under the stars, Senhouse came back to her bedside and put a little flower into her hand. It woke her out of her dreams; glozed and dewy from them she looked at it, and smiled at him through it. In grey-green leafage, dewy and downy, lay a little blossom of delicate pink, chalice-shaped, with a lip of flushed white. Watching him, she laid it to her lips. "My flower, our flower," she said, and watching him still put it deep within her bosom. "My dear one, we have earned it."

"'Rest-Harrow,'" said Senhouse, in a sententious mood, "'grows in any soil. . . . The seed may be sown as soon as ripe, in warm, sheltered spots out of doors. . . . It is a British plant.' So says Weathers, the learned botanist. I praise Weathers. And I like his name." Then he kissed her.

"Why not?" asked the lady with her lifted brows. "Why shouldn't I?"

"Influence! The likes of him!—Gypsy blood at midnight—soft-voiced, murderous——"

She gave no coherent answer, but smiled always, then leaned forward and stroked Mrs. Benson upon her personable cheek. "Dear old thing, let me do as I like. It's much better for everybody," she presently said.

II

IT had clouded over after sunset: there was no moon visible, but an irradiance was omnipresent, and showed the muffled yew-tree walks, and the greater trees colossal, mountains overshadowing the land. Here and there, as you went, glimmered daffodils, like the Pleiades half-veiled, and long files of crocuses burned like waning fires.

Miss Percival, at about nine o'clock, came gently down one of these alleys, with a scarf over her head and shoulders. She looked like a nymph in Tanagra. And as if she knew where she was going, exactly, she walked gently but unfalteringly between the linked crocus-beacons to where the alley broadened into a bay of cut yews, to where ghostly white seats and a dim sun-dial seemed disposed as for a scene in a comedy. The leaden statue of a skipping faun would have been made out in a recess if you had known it was there. And as she entered the place a figure seated there, with elbows on knees and chin between his palms, looked up, listening, watching intently, then rose and waited.

"Struan," said Miss Percival comfortably, "are you there?"

"I'm here," she was answered.